The Gothica

Patrick C. DiCarlo

THE GOTHICA

iUniverse books may be ordered through booksellers or by contacting:

iUniverse
1663 Liberty Drive
Bloomington, IN 47403
www.iuniverse.com
844-349-9409

Because of the dynamic nature of the internet, any web addresses or links contained in this book may have changed since publication and may no longer be valid. The views expressed in this work are solely those of the author and do not necessarily reflect the views of the publisher, and the publisher hereby disclaims any responsibility for them.

Any people depicted in stock imagery provided by Getty Images are models, and such images are being used for illustrative purposes only.
Certain stock imagery © Getty Images.

ISBN: 978-1-6632-2385-2 (sc)
ISBN: 978-1-6632-2386-9 (e)

Library of Congress Control Number: 2021912951

Print information available on the last page.

iUniverse rev. date: 07/21/2021

Acknowledgments

Maps and illustrations by Jack Ryan DiCarlo

Contents

Chapter 1

The Hun Storm

Theoric's horse shifted nervously behind rows of infantrymen and archers. Goth lines had formed before dawn, and the soldiers grew weary in the midday heat. The warm spring day did nothing to slake the terror hanging over the rolling grasslands. Even the breath of the horses turned sour.

Scouts had reported large numbers of Huns approaching. Ermenaric, king of the Ostrogoths, had gathered his full strength. Theoric was stationed near the end of a long line stretching far to the north, with heavy cavalry behind them. They were the last line of defense before the mighty Dniester River, which separated the Ostrogoth and Visigoth worlds.

As the enemy drew close, Theoric saw a spearman puke on the man in front of him. He wondered whether he'd be puking too if it was his job to stand and fight. Theoric tried to distract himself. He had heard the anticipation of battle could be worse than the battle itself. He hoped that was true. *If I can just live out this day, I'll be on the journey home in the morning*, he thought. It struck him as strange that he now even missed his little brother and sister. He longed to hear their voices, to be again with his parents and friends at home. But that seemed a world away as he awaited the thundering horde that approached.

They could feel it before they heard it. A low, deep, rumbling vibration like the sound of a distant thunderstorm. It grew steadily louder and became almost deafening before they saw a single Hun. Even the insects fled. Theoric's horse bucked as the rows of spearmen packed closer into a tight phalanx formation.

The first group of Hun cavalry appeared over the eastern horizon near the southern end of the line. Their horses walked slowly at first but began galloping. Just before they crashed into the phalanx, the leading edge of Hun riders swerved sharply north, galloping parallel with the Goth line. The Huns twisted in their saddles, firing longbows powerful enough to pierce armor. Their ranks appeared endless. The man who had puked rose to throw his spear and was shot in the neck. He clutched his throat as blood squirted through his fingers with each heartbeat. Another man next to him turned to help, but the captain cried out, "Hold the line!" Compassion was a luxury they didn't have.

Goth archers returned fire, but rarely did their arrows find Huns riding at such breakneck speed. After the Huns fired, they swerved back out of range of the Goths to reload and approach again but only when ready to fire. Theoric began to see the Goth line was weakening. Many screamed. Few died quickly.

As the situation deteriorated, Theoric looked nervously to the north. At last, he saw a lone rider galloping south toward him, clad in the blue garments of his people. The rider was a middle-aged man with a black beard and intense blue eyes.

"Father, the battle goes ill," Theoric cried as the rider pulled next to him.

Guntheric scanned the battlefield and saw the danger. "The cavalry yet may turn the tide," he said without conviction.

The Goth riders behind the lines soon began their charge, swinging around the southern flank and driving headlong into the coming Huns. As the cavalry charge developed, Theoric noticed that the Goths rarely got close enough to bring their swords and spears to bear. The Huns kept a distance from the Goths sufficient to avoid their weapons but close enough for accuracy with their arrows. Few Goth horsemen had bows, and even fewer were accurate enough to hit a galloping target. Often the Huns simply shot the Goths' horses from under them. Horses pierced with arrows bucked their riders and bleated horrible sounds. Blood soaked the battlefield. It took time to wear down the Goth formations, but the Huns were persistent. Only when the cavalry was decimated and the line fractured did the Huns make a direct charge. By that point, the Goths were too disorganized to mount an effective defense, and the end of the line began to crumble.

"The line will not hold," Guntheric cried, keeping his eyes on the field. "Reinforce the end!" he screamed. "The Huns cannot be allowed behind the line!" It wasn't his place to command the Ostrogoths, but someone had to. Some of the captains responded by shouting orders to protect the end. Guntheric swung his horse around and raced north, with Theoric struggling to keep up. In places, it became difficult to stay ahead of the line, which collapsed like a rolling wave.

They reached a tent on a hill, where the Ostrogoth general Saphrax and his captains commanded the southern end of the line. Guntheric swung down from his horse before it had stopped moving and quickly strode inside. While Theoric tended the horses, he could hear loud voices within.

"You cannot defeat them on an open plain," he heard his father shout. "You must fall back to the river!"

He also heard Saphrax urging an orderly retreat before the battle turned into a rout. The others he didn't recognize, but they must have been Ermenaric's emissaries, and they insisted the king wouldn't retreat.

Theoric jumped when his father shouted, "I shall tell him myself!" as he burst from the tent. Saphrax followed and began giving orders for the reserves to deploy to the end and prevent the Huns from outflanking them. Theoric followed his father as they raced toward Ermenaric's headquarters.

By the time they arrived, the sun hung low in the western sky. Ermenaric and his entourage stood under an open tent on a high hill, surveying the field. The Huns charged up and down the Goth lines as far as the eye could see. Theoric had always been terrified of Ermenaric—a most warlike and fierce monarch. But now Ermenaric appeared pensive and withdrawn. He looked out at the field as his advisers quarreled.

Guntheric strode toward the king while the generals were urging a retreat. Ermenaric, ignoring the chaos, mounted his horse. His advisers vied for his attention, but the king spurred his horse to a trot toward the front.

The collapse of the line began to accelerate and Ermenaric's horse progressed into a gallop down the hill and into the collapsing line. As he became surrounded by Hunnic warriors, Ermenaric spread his arms wide and lifted his gaze toward the heavens, sacrificing himself to the Huns' onslaught. His body was pierced by many arrows, and his horse shot out from under him. One Hun rider swung his sword as he galloped past, cleanly decapitating Ermenaric in one fluid stroke. The Huns rejoiced in the death of the Ostrogoth king, displaying the head and hacking his body as it lay dead.

The rest of the leaders watched in stunned silence. Once Ermenaric fell, panic ensued. Some of the generals called for Vithimer, the king's son, to be made king.

General Saphrax wasn't waiting. He grabbed Guntheric by the shoulder. "You must ride for the river. You must raise the alarm!"

Guntheric nodded curtly and grabbed Theoric by the arm as they hurried to the horses. "We ride now."

Guntheric gathered his retainers, and the group rode hard west toward the quickly fading sun. It wasn't until the screams of battle faded that Theoric realized he was breathing too fast. The night was well lit by a full moon, and Guntheric kept looking over his shoulder toward his young son with a worried expression. Only after midnight did they feel safe enough to rest their exhausted horses. They had come to a small village, which looked mostly deserted.

"No doubt the folk have fled west," Theoric said as their horses walked toward the town's wooden gates.

"As word spreads, most will seek refuge across the river," his father responded.

"And the river will protect us too?"

"It will slow them down, perhaps long enough to prepare another defense."

As they neared the wooden gate, an old man with a torch confronted them. "Who goes there?"

Guntheric explained who they were, but the man wanted to know of tidings from the front. Guntheric gave the grim news, and the man agreed to let them sleep in abandoned dwellings. Some of Guntheric's men feared a Hun raiding party, but he explained they'd be worse off if their horses started falling from exhaustion. They posted a guard, and Guntheric and Theoric walked into a small hut.

Theoric was shaking. He'd been a bit wobbly getting off his horse. Guntheric turned and put his hand on Theoric's shoulder. Theoric avoided his father's gaze.

"Look at me, son."

Theoric lifted his head. He was a man but just barely so. His scant, dark beard adorned a boyish face with the handsome look of his father.

"I know it's hard to see what you've seen—the blood, the screams. Especially the first time. It's all right to be scared. I'd be worried if you weren't. But you mustn't let the fear drive you. Do not think of what you have seen so often that you lose focus on what happens now. You hear me?" Theoric nodded curtly and looked back down as his father continued. "We're going to make it through this. We're going to make it home."

Theoric looked back up at his father, forcing a fragile smile.

They got a fire going and made pallets of straw. As they both lay on their backs, Theoric tried again to distract himself. He asked, "Father, why did Ermenaric sacrifice himself like that?"

"He was a pagan. Many of his people believe the Huns are a scourge brought by the gods displeased with his rule. He thought the only way to appease the gods was to sacrifice himself."

"Do you think it will work?"

"I think we need to defeat the Huns ourselves."

"Do Christians believe in sacrifice in battle?"

"I don't think so."

"Do you?"

"No."

"Father Ulff told us that we're Arian Christians, like Emperor Valens. Do you know what that means?"

"There are two kinds of Christians—Arian and Nicene. I can't really say I understand the difference."

"Both are still Christians, right?"

"Yes."

"Well, then ..." Theoric's voice trailed off.

"You wonder if it matters?"

"Yes."

"It matters not to me. If the emperor will help Arian Christians against the Huns, so much the better."

"You don't think it's real, do you?"

"I don't know, my son. I hope it is. Get some sleep. We'll have plenty of time to talk during the journey home."

The two slept soundly for a few hours but were awoken before dawn. A group of retreating soldiers had entered the village, and the horrifying screams of the wounded pierced the night sky. Guntheric rendered what aid he could, but most were beyond his help. At daybreak, Guntheric led his company southwest, and more retreating soldiers began to arrive.

By the end of the second day, they were exhausted, dehydrated, and lost. As the sun faded, they looked for a good place to sleep but then saw firelight on the horizon. They rode toward an isolated campfire on the rolling prairie and could hear men speaking loudly. As the watchman observed their approach, the group became silent.

The guards nodded at Guntheric, recognizing his garb, and he dismounted and walked his horse into the firelight. The captain stood and announced, "I am called Dagno, captain of the guard of Osteria. How are you called?"

"I am called Guntheric of the Visigoths. I come from the front."

"Aye, you're not the first. Come, join us."

Theoric collapsed in exhaustion as he attempted to dismount. The men helped him to the fire and gave him water. Once the color started to return to his face, the captain turned his attention to Guntheric.

"You're one of Fritigern's people?"

"Yes. We ride to bring news of the battle."

"And what news is that?"

"The lines are broken. The king has fallen. What's left of Ermenaric's army will fall back to the river." Guntheric recounted the battle, and the men were fascinated to hear the details of Ermenaric's dramatic death.

"Who now rules the East? Vithimer?" Dagno asked.

"I believe so," Guntheric responded. "We didn't stay for the coronation."

The men chuckled lightly.

"And Athanaric's not your king?" Dagno asked somewhat suspiciously.

"The West has no kings."

"Ah, right, only judges?"

"Yes. And in times of war, generals."

"Aye, it's definitely times of war, eh, boys?" The men murmured agreement, and Dagno continued, "You can stay the night here. We're only a day's ride to Osteria. There'll be quite a lot of folk wanting to cross now, I suspect."

"And what of Alavivus? Are his men near?"

"No, haven't heard nothin' 'bout any westerners near."

They talked late into the night about the battle and the prospects for the remainder of the Ostrogoth army to make it across the Dniester. At dawn they rode for Osteria and made the city before nightfall.

Osteria was a large town on the eastern bank of the Dniester. A bridge nearby offered passage over the mighty river. The road became overcrowded with civilians and soldiers seeking the safety of the western shore. The city itself had no walls, but the garrison at the end of the bridge was surrounded by a wall of sharp wooden poles.

Only at the river did Theoric begin to feel his body start to relax. He and his father were given accommodations in a tall building, and he collapsed on his bed. When he rose the next morning, his father was meeting with the town's leaders. From his window Theoric could see huge numbers of civilians and soldiers massing near the bridge, waiting to cross.

His father walked into the room with a loaf of bread. "Good morning." He gave Theoric half, and they ate like hungry wolves.

"Have you slept?" Theoric asked between bites.

"Yes. I rose before dawn. The leaders were anxious to hear tidings. They say Vithimer is pulling the rest of the Eastern Army back to the river. They will guard the people's retreat, then cross and try to hold the river from the other side."

"You don't think they can?"

"It's hard for any army to cross such a wide river with an enemy waiting on the other side. But we should not just hope the Huns will be stopped at the river. Take some rest while you can. We'll remain here a few days to see what's left of the Eastern Army and how goes the defense of the river."

As the days passed, Guntheric became convinced that he had learned all he could on the eastern bank and led his band of scouts across the river. They spread out to observe the defenses. When the group reconvened near the bridge, all bore news of Hun raiding parties crossing the river at many places. The groups weren't large but too numerous and spread out to stop, and the growing number of Huns west of the river was becoming a threat to the rear. Guntheric came to believe the river wouldn't be held, and the Ostrogoths would fall back to form a new line in the realm of the Visigoths.

Uldin the Hun rode with his warriors out of camp before first light. The morning air was cool, and a nearly full moon lit the way. They bore no armor and dressed in thick animal hides. Each man carried a bow and quiver, and most had pillaged swords. Hundreds streamed out of camp behind the Hun chieftain.

Scouts told of a prosperous Goth town less than a half day's ride west. He knew the Goths wouldn't know they were coming. They never did. So confident was Uldin that he had already ordered the camp to move west by midday. They would slumber near the conquered town and feast over tales of their conquest.

Uldin rode with his vanguard, eager to catch the scouts before the alarm could be raised. As they drew near, he slowed the march until the sun began to peek above the horizon. By the time they reached the place where Uldin expected scouts, the sun blazed bright behind them, blinding the Goths to their approach. When the first scout began to feel the thunderous charge approaching, Uldin could see the boy's eyes turn from puzzlement to terror.

The Goth mounted his horse in a panic and furiously galloped west. Uldin and his riders closed the gap quickly. Just before they reached the town, Uldin overtook the scout, grasped the back of his collar, and pulled the boy off his horse, dragging him to the outskirts of the town. Uldin threw him to the ground just before the town's entrance. The boy sprang to his feet and rushed through the open wooden gate just ahead of scores of Hun riders, who were flooding in.

Uldin dismounted and walked his horse into the village, taking pride in the panic overtaking the Goths. Women screamed, children cried, and the men scurried to arm themselves. Some tried to run. Hun horsemen quickly chased down those who fled and ensnared them with lassos, dragging them brutally back to the village. Resistance inside the town was meager. So heavily outnumbered, many quickly laid down their swords. Those who didn't faced four or more foes and were butchered.

The boy's father charged Uldin with a sword upraised. Uldin deftly deflected the blow and stabbed the man through the eye. A woman screamed and rushed to the limp body as it fell. The boy gasped, and Uldin looked him in the eye, knowing he had just killed the boy's father. Two Huns grabbed the woman under her arms and dragged her into a thatched cottage. The boy moved to protect his mother, and two more soldiers grabbed him from behind, forced him to his knees, and brought a cruelly curved knife under his chin. Uldin barked a loud command, and the knife was sheathed.

Uldin strode forth, staring intently into the boy's eyes as his warriors continued to rape and pillage. He grasped the boy under the chin and turned his head from side to side. The boy maintained eye contact throughout. Uldin released his grasp, straightened, and tugged lightly on his long, thin beard—never breaking his stare.

"This one has courage," he announced. "He shall be spared and become my slave."

The boy said something in a strange tongue and looked toward the cottage. Uldin didn't understand the words but knew what the boy wanted.

"Uh," he grunted, "the mother too."

Uldin made judgments of who was to live in slavery or die. Most of the men of fighting age, the elderly, the wounded, and the children too young to work were slaughtered like animals. The boy's hands were bound, and he was tied to many others who would be taken. The sounds of execution and rape as well as the iron smell of blood hung heavy in the air.

The boy's heart pounded, and his throat was so dry he thought he'd die of thirst before getting wherever the Huns would take them. The Huns set the village ablaze, and the heat was so intense the boy could feel his face begin to burn. His whole body shook with fear, and he was able to calm his nerves only when the monotony of the march focused his attention on putting one foot in front of the other. Those who stumbled along the way were savagely whipped. A few died. The march over the rolling grassland ended only after nightfall, when the Huns found their camp.

The boy was put to work immediately. The Huns knew he didn't understand their gruff orders but barked them anyway. He was shown how to move gear, fetch water, and hobble the horses. His mother was made to butcher and cook. When finally he was allowed to sleep, bound to other prisoners, he could hear the warriors around the campfire laughing and speaking in a foreign tongue. What did they say? Was the man who had killed his father boasting of the deed? Hatred filled his heart, and he thought their guttural speech as ugly and deformed as their faces.

Despite his exhaustion, he was too terrified to sleep. As he lay on his side in the dirt, he realized another boy was also awake and staring at him. When they made eye contact, the other boy whispered, "I am called Hamil of the river country."

"I am called Thoris son of—" The image of his father's death choked off the utterance of his name.

"It's OK," Hamil replied. "You can cry, at least at night, if you're quiet."

"How long have you been here?" Thoris asked once his composure had returned.

"Seven days. They did the same thing to my village."

"What have they made you do?"

"Butcher animals, mostly. Pull down and put up tents when they move. Try to always look useful. I'm not sure what they'd do to those they have no use for. They're just as cruel as they are ugly."

"I've never seen such deformed-looking men, if that's what they are," Thoris agreed.

Thoris heard a guard who must have noticed their whispering. As the guard inspected the prisoners, Thoris shut his eyes tightly and tried to imagine that none of this was real. When he was awoken before dawn, just for a fleeting moment he didn't remember that the world he had known was gone forever.

Guntheric led his company out of Osteria on a warm, cloudless morning. They rode on a dirt road winding southwest through a sea of grass and across gently rolling hills. Along the road, they met many refugees fleeing the fighting. They heard tales of Hun savagery. Those able to flee took what possessions they could carry but were often reduced to pleading for food from strangers. As word spread, more and more villages began to empty before the Huns arrived.

After many days of hard riding over the prairie hills, they came to the line of the Visigoth army. For the first time in months, Theoric began to feel safe and relax just a little as they entered the large encampment. The camp was covered with hundreds of tents, campfires, wagons, horses, donkeys, and livestock, all surrounded by guards who kept a constant vigil. Guntheric was provided tents for his men. As they began to make their camp, Fritigern came striding up with a broad grin for his old friend.

Fritigern was stout but shorter than most and not particularly handsome. He had a gregarious, jovial personality that made him seem larger than his stature. His bald head bore the scars of many battles, as did his face.

Fritigern enthusiastically embraced Guntheric, and the two appeared to be good friends, reunited after a long separation. Fritigern noticed Theoric. Turning to him, he said boisterously, "This must be your son. He's handsome. Must take after his mother!" The two old friends laughed, and Fritigern put his hand on Guntheric's shoulder, leading him toward a large tent at the center of the camp, in which the Visigoth general held council.

In the days that followed, Guntheric spent long hours in Fritigern's council, and messengers from the East arrived daily. Theoric was assigned shifts on the Visigoths' line and took his turn among the camp guards. Theoric shared stories of the Huns with the other young men in camp and enjoyed the company of those closer to his age. At the line, Theoric was primarily employed as a scout, surveying the land just east of the line on horseback.

One evening, word reached Theoric's ear that the Ostrogoths had been forced to abandon the river. They had fled mostly northwest and formed a huge circle of wagons on the rocky plains near the foothills of the Carpathian Mountains. From there, they had stretched out a line southward toward the Black Sea. Although the Visigoths provided reinforcements for the Eastern Army, the Ostrogoths' line wasn't long enough to stretch all the way to the sea, and the Huns were left with a lightly defended path to move southwest.

One day, as spring gave way to summer, Theoric was finishing his watch on the line when a group of riders arrived from the East. They rode under the banner of Saphrax, and as they drew closer, Theoric hailed Saphrax himself. After introductions, Saphrax sought an audience with Fritigern. Theoric rode with them back to camp and escorted Saphrax and his personal guard to Fritigern's large tent. He then led the other men to food and water. Saphrax's men told tales from the front.

The news wasn't encouraging. Vithimer had fallen in battle. The Ostrogoths were now leaderless and sought counsel on the path forward. Saphrax wanted to convene a meeting of leaders. In the morning, Fritigern dispatched messengers, inviting all the Goth generals to his camp for a war council.

Many were skeptical Athanaric would come. An imposing and fierce man, Athanaric had previously fought with Fritigern over control of the West. Athanaric considered himself the leader of all Visigoths. Fritigern embraced the West's tradition of independence, pledging fealty to no king. The two set aside their feud only of necessity.

On a bright summer day, Theoric served as his father's guard inside Fritigern's great pavilion. He stood with a spear near the entrance and watched the leaders seated in a great circle, endlessly debating strategy.

But Athanaric did arrive, with a large retinue, on a bright summer day. He made it a point to be the last to arrive, believing this enhanced his importance. He didn't pause for rest or greeting as he entered the camp, but rather he strode confidently into Fritigern's tent, where the other leaders were already debating strategy. Theoric stood with the guards, watching from the shadows. Despite his arrogance, Athanaric was welcomed warmly and took one of the chairs arranged in a circle in the center. The tent was dark but lit by many torches, which shone dimly off the faces of the assembled as if they were sitting around a campfire.

Saphrax spoke first. "Our people cling to the edge of the mountains for protection." The Ostrogothic general was calm, and his pale blue eyes slowly moved around the group as he spoke. "We cannot make our line all the way to the Black Sea. The more Huns come through the south, the more we have to pull back our line to keep them from our rear, and the wider the doorway west becomes."

"The attacks on our line are getting more frequent and more intense," Fritigern added. "We must choose. The mountains or the Danube Valley."

"It cannot be the valley," Athanaric interjected. "Too close to the Romans. We'd be caught between a hammer and an anvil."

"Hiding in the mountains may be no better," Saphrax responded.

"He's right," said Fritigern. "More come from the east every day. They tell of the Huns coming in ever-greater numbers. What makes you think they'll stop at the Danube? This is the Romans' fight as well. We must involve them to withstand this Hun storm."

"Of course, *Fritigernicus* wants an alliance with the Romans," Athanaric sneered. "You scheme to bring your Roman friends for your own ambitions."

Fritigern sprang to his feet. "Do not question my honor!" His guards put their hands to their swords. "These Huns will be the death of us all. How many more battles must we lose before you realize we cannot defeat them ourselves?"

General disorder ensued, and Athanaric struggled to regain control. Once the room again quieted, Athanaric turned his large, portly frame toward Fritigern. "What if the Romans aren't so interested in helping you this time? What if they decide you'd make a better buffer against the Huns?"

"They don't have a choice," Fritigern replied calmly, returning to his seat. "Valens and the Eastern Roman Army are fighting the Persians. The river is lightly guarded. We can cross without a deal if we must."

"Then we'd be fighting the Romans also," Saphrax replied.

"Better than fighting the Huns on an open plain," Fritigern insisted. "The valley offers cover. And we should not be so quick to think we cannot make a deal. The Romans will see the threat they face. They will see the benefit of working together—for a time."

Saphrax added, "Getting pushed into the mountains risks starvation. And we have no chance of an alliance there. In the valley, perhaps we can gain an alliance with the Romans, and we'd be better off come winter."

"You'd still be putting us at the mercy of the Romans," Athanaric replied impatiently. "We should not abandon the work to build a fortified line."

"We lack time," Fritigern protested.

"You lack courage!" Athanaric roared, springing to his feet.

The debate again devolved into contentious chaos, with some favoring Athanaric's view and some favoring Fritigern's.

Athanaric's voice rose again above the din. "We've said all there is to say. I'm not going to trust my fate to the Romans. I will stay and defend my country with all who remain. Each of us must now say their choice." Athanaric's loyalists and some of the Ostrogoths were willing to follow him into the Carpathian Mountains. Saphrax led his people with Fritigern, and the Visigoth General Alavivus did the same.

Winter had nearly begun, and Theoric's horse walked slowly across the frozen road to his village. It was a mid-sized town of over one thousand residents, mostly protected by a wooden wall. The houses were packed close together, with barns and stables outside the gates. Theoric was relieved to be home after a year away, but his face was ashen and his mood somber as he moved slowly toward the village late in the day.

Not long after the town came into view, a boy with long blond hair and blue eyes raced toward Theoric. Even before he could see his face clearly, Theoric recognized the excited child as his brother. He'd grown quite a bit but was still a few years from manhood. He'd lost none of his enthusiasm.

"Theoric! Theoric!" Alaric shouted. "I knew you would soon return. Where are the others? Is Father with you?"

Theoric didn't answer but slowly dismounted and began to walk his horse. He ruffled the boy's hair and put his arm around his shoulder. "You've gotten taller," Theoric observed.

"And you look older. Is everything all right?" Alaric asked.

Theoric didn't answer.

As they approached their home, a middle-aged woman came racing outside. Alenia wore her blonde hair in an elaborate weave and an apron over her woolen dress.

"My son, my son!" she cried, showering him with kisses and long hugs. Theoric smiled but only a little. Even the excitement of his little sister could barely brighten his mood.

Theoric picked up the little girl. "Daria, you've gotten so big!"

She smiled and wrapped her arms around her oldest brother's neck as they walked inside.

The house was among the largest in town. Several servants performed household chores, and all greeted Theoric warmly. The family gathered in a dining room with a large wooden table and two benches. The room was well lit by a window and several candles. Theoric sat down with his sister on his lap, and his mother and brother sat opposite.

"Has Father stayed at the front? Why is he not with you?" Alaric asked.

Theoric struggled for words, and tears began to roll down his face. Finally, he was able to say it. "Father is dead."

The family sat in stunned silence for a few moments. They all wept quietly until Alaric demanded, "What happened?"

Theoric struggled to compose himself, and his voice wavered as he told the tale.

"We were scouting beyond the line. Father rode alone to the top of a hill in the east. As soon as he reached the top, he immediately turned his horse and started galloping back toward us. He gave the sign to flee west. Then the horizon was filled with Huns. We had enough of a start to make it back to the line before the Huns overtook us, but they were close enough to shoot Father's horse out from under him."

"If they just shot his horse, maybe he was taken captive," the boy observed.

"No, Alaric. I saw it. I saw them cut him down. I saw ..." Theoric placed his hands over his face but couldn't hold back an anguished sob. Alenia reached across the table and clutched her son's hands.

"Why did you ride off?"

"Alaric! Bite your tongue, young man," Alenia scolded.

"Why did you not stand and fight with Father?" he persisted defiantly.

"There is nothing I could have done, little brother. The Huns were too many."

"You don't know that!" Alaric shouted. "I wouldn't have left Father. I would have fought—"

"I know you're upset, son," Alenia interjected as she put her arm around his shoulder, "but—" He jerked away and dashed out of the room.

After a few moments, Alenia said, "He'll come around. No one really believes—"

"I know, Mother," Theoric said with a heavy sigh. After a moment of reflection, his mind turned to other matters. "The army retreats westward, seeking the protection of the woodlands near the river, and there are already Huns behind the line. I must speak with the elders. We must leave by dawn two days hence."

"We're just going to live outside? Wouldn't we be safer here?" Alenia pleaded.

"Not when the Huns arrive. They will burn the village. Slaughter the men. Rape the women. Any who survive will be taken as slaves."

"Surely we need more time to prepare," Alenia responded, her eyes drifting off in thought. "I shall have a crate built to pack the plates."

"No!" Theoric shouted, pounding on the table. "Mother, you do not understand! Once Fritigern passes this place, we will be at the mercy of the Huns. We can take only what we truly need. And we don't have room for damn plates!"

Alenia looked at her son sadly and took a deep breath. "OK, son."

Theoric took a deep breath and used his hands for emphasis. "Now that Father is gone, you must listen to me. At least about such matters. I've seen the Huns. I know what we face. If we're to survive the coming winter, we must take as much food as we can carry. No plates, no furniture, no silverware. We take only what we truly need."

Theoric was without time for grief. He took his leave to speak with the town's elders.

Word spread quickly that Fritigern would fall back to the Danube. Villagers spent the next day packing horse-drawn wagons with tools, clothes, weapons, and food. Alenia commanded the servants to pack their wagons, while Theoric organized a group of riders to defend the people's march. Theoric was anxious to leave soon, and it showed. Although among the youngest of the men, he was the only combat veteran, and the older men were willing to follow his lead. He feared a Hun raid and firmly denied many requests to delay the departure just one more day. As dawn broke on the second day, Theoric led a train of wagons, horses, livestock, and peasants toward the great Danube and the edge of the Roman Empire.

Chapter 2

Seeking Refuge

The road to the river was long and crowded. Whole towns emptied. Many wounded soldiers sought their families. Some from the East desperately looked for loved ones in the stream of refugees that moved across the prairie like a great river. A male servant drove the wagon in which Theoric's family rode, while Theoric led a scouting party, patrolling the rear and sides of the column. As he rode, Theoric often looked back at the eastern horizon. Rumors had spread of Hun raiders sacking nearby villages.

The wagon was covered and comfortable. Alenia sat atop a crate filled with her plates and silverware. Alaric sat next to her, with Daria and Brechta, one of her friends, sitting on the opposite side. Alenia struggled to conceal her grief. She willed herself to keep a brave face for the children, but in the silence, her thoughts turned to the husband she had lost, and her gaze was distant. The children pretended not to notice the tears silently streaming down her face.

Daria and Brechta took turns combing each other's hair as Alaric watched with a look of disinterest bordering on mild contempt.

Alenia smiled gently and caressed the back of her son's head. She struggled still to contain her emotions. She knew what her husband would have said. "You are a leader of the house of Balt. You must be strong!" She desperately wanted to but felt overcome by grief. Her thoughts turned to the last night she had shared with Guntheric. She so wished she could do it over. She wished she could take back those words. She had only been frustrated and angry at the unfairness—and such a long distance.

She could still clearly see the scene in her mind.

"Why must you be the one to go?" she had asked.

His brow had furrowed, his tone somber. "I must go because Fritigern asked it of me. I swore an oath. I owe him my allegiance."

"And what of me? What of our children? Do you not also owe us your allegiance?"

His eyes were so stony. So cold. "What have I ever done to make you question my commitment to my family?" he demanded.

"Leaving us!" she screeched. "What about Cniva? He's claimed higher rank. Why can't he go?"

Guntheric was exasperated and placed his hands on his hips. "Fritigern can't send Cniva because he's a well-known coward. It's an honor to be—"

"Oh, yes, such an honor. It's always about honor and glory. You'd be *so* happy for your name to live forever while I'm a widow raising our children alone!" She had cried, and he had pulled her close.

Now she remembered those words so clearly, but why had she not understood? If she could just do the moment over, she would have loved him that last night.

She would have told him … "Ahhhhhhh." The emotion boiled over, and she broke out in anguish, tears quickly bursting from her reddened face. The children sat in uncomfortable silence.

"Are you all right?" Alaric asked.

She forced a smile and wiped away her tears. "Yes, son," she said, nodding. She gently stroked his long hair.

Daria stared at her brother with disdain and rose. "Move," she demanded as she sought to sit next to her mother.

Alaric scooted over only slightly. Daria forced her way in and put her arm around her mother. Alenia scooped her daughter into her lap and held her close.

Daria asked Alaric, "What's that?"

"What?"

"The thing you're sitting on."

Alaric rose slightly and pulled forth a long dagger.

"Ah!" His mother gasped. "That is not a toy! Give me that."

"I will not," he said, jerking away. "Theoric gave me this. You'll be glad I have it if the Huns come."

Alenia shook her head and frowned. Daria began to lecture Alaric again about thinking he was an adult, but their conversation was cut short by the sound of horses cantering down the column. They could hear the alarm in Theoric's voice before they could discern his words. He shouted warnings that Hun scouts had been seen close by. He called on the men to arm themselves. Gathering as many riders as he could, Theoric turned back and led the horsemen back east. From that point until dusk, Alaric stared out the back of the wagon, never taking his eyes off the eastern horizon.

As the sun set, many demanded that they take rest, but the leaders insisted on pushing forward. The night was dark, and the lead horsemen struggled to keep the path. A woman's shriek pierced the night air—and then again, a few moments later.

"That's Bellsa," Alenia exclaimed with alarm. "Her baby comes." Alenia demanded that the column halt, and she climbed into a nearby wagon, where Bellsa lay in labor. She was a healer and had midwifed many women.

Some men began to clamor that the woman's screams would give away their location. Others insisted there was nothing that could be done, and if the Huns were within earshot, they were doomed anyway. Finally, it was decided that the wagon with the laboring woman would keep moving ahead out of earshot while the rest made camp for the night. Alaric was highly agitated by this plan, realizing his mother would be unprotected. But she convinced him his duty was to protect his sister and their belongings.

Theoric's company rejoined the group in the middle of the night. He was relieved to report no signs of Huns and was eager for rest, but he became furious when he learned his mother had been sent away with a laboring woman. He called the men cowards and angrily cursed their stupidity. He took only a small group of riders to find her. It didn't take long. They heard the cries of a newborn baby only a short distance down the road. By the time they rejoined the group, there was time only for a couple of hours of sleep. Theoric felt he had closed his eyes for only a moment before he was awoken to prepare for another day's ride.

The column pressed farther westward, and the road became ever more crowded. The going was slow, but Theoric was reassured by the growing strength in numbers. He had no authority to command allegiance, but he most valued his service and heeded his instructions. They traveled all day for many days before the prairie began to give way to patches of trees.

When they finally reached the edge of the forest, Theoric breathed a sigh of relief. Many soldiers remained at the edge, guarding the road into the woodlands. Their numbers and the dense trees offered protection from Hun cavalry. Theoric sent his family along and stayed to aid the defense.

Lupicinus stood atop a high wall on the Roman fortress of Durostorum. The fortress was a huge stone structure with heavy iron gates. Its walls provided a wide view of the river valley to the horizon in either direction. Lupicinus, a thin man with sharp eyes and a hooked nose, squinted as he peered across the river.

"How many are they?" he asked, still staring at distant Goths, who were washing clothes and bathing across the river.

"Don't know for certain. Thousands come each day," his first lieutenant, Maximus, responded. "They stretch up and down the river for miles, and more are living off the banks, deep in the woods. Could be as many as thirty thousand and growing."

"Why have they come?" Lupicinus asked gruffly, turning his gaze to Maximus.

"Scouts tell of heavy fighting on the plains. They're hard-pressed by invaders from the east."

Lupicinus paced for a minute with his head down and his arms behind his back under a crimson cloak. "They won't just stay there," he finally concluded.

"Maybe they'll seek our aid," Maximus replied.

"Or maybe they'll just cross once they realize we don't have the men to stop them," the commander shot back. "Find some Goth mercenaries to send across. I want to know what happened and what they're planning. And I need a messenger to carry word to the emperor."

Fritigern set up his command off the main road just inside the forest. The army he and Alavivus commanded had retreated as slowly as they could to give the civilians more time to flee. The Ostrogoths under Saphrax had also engaged in a fighting retreat and were now joining the Visigoths. Even after the combined army entered the woods, civilians continued to stream in. Most were survivors of Hun attacks. The army could do no better than set up a safe zone near the forest for those who could make it that far.

Fritigern held frequent war councils. Day after day he and the other generals weighed the risks. There were no good options. As Fritigern became weary of the endless debates, he announced that the time had come to decide. Fritigern's position was well known—he advocated sending an emissary across the river to seek the Romans' permission to enter.

Cniva was leery of the Romans. "We are safe here in the forest. The Hun cavalry can no longer reach us."

"We cannot stay here forever," Alavivus responded. "If crops are not sown in the spring, famine will soon be upon us. We are too many to just hunt in the woods for long. Dare we wait for the Huns? How many will come? Will we fare better here than we did on the plains? Do we want to find out with our backs to the river and no way out?"

"What of Athanaric's people?" Saphrax asked. "If the Huns attack us here, would they not expose their rear to his army?"

"We don't know how many the Huns number," Fritigern said grimly. "They may have enough fighters to divide their force and defeat both armies. We've done nothing but lose battle after battle on the plains. I fear we will not be able to look to Athanaric's people for aid. They will struggle to plant in the stony hills and are more exposed to Hun attacks. That leaves just one choice—seek an alliance with the Romans. The Huns will be a threat to them too. Why should the attempt not be made?"

"I fear we wouldn't just be seeking an alliance; we'd be refugees—at their mercy," said Saphrax. "I was educated in Constantinople—I know their ways. We will not receive kindness. They look down their hooked noses at all who are not Roman. To them, we are uncivilized barbarians."

"I know what the Romans are," Fritigern replied. "Many are cruel and most arrogant, but they can be reasoned with … if it suits their interests."

Saphrax lifted his chin as he responded, "The Romans will not let in such a large group of armed foreigners. That's not how they do things. If they let us in at all, they will strip us of our weapons and divide us up into small groups dispersed throughout the empire. That's how they 'subdue' refugees."

"If that's what they say, then we don't have to agree, but we should at least send the embassy. And besides, Valens is occupied with the Persians. They do not have the numbers to hold the river. Valens will see the benefit of having more soldiers on his side with the Huns approaching."

Thus, Fritigern convinced the others to send an embassy. Within days the Gothic ambassadors rowed across the river, and Lupicinus waited with his lieutenants to receive them at the dock. He had interpreters on hand, but the Gothic embassy was led by a priest who spoke Latin. Lupicinus greeted them warmly but feigned ignorance as to why they had come. His spies had already learned of the Hunnic invasion and the Goths' plan to seek asylum, but he made them say it anyway. After many skeptical questions, Lupicinus agreed to let them journey to Antioch to present their case directly to the emperor.

Life as refugees on the river was chaotic. More came each day, and the banks of the river became overcrowded. Disputes over space and resources were common. Some arrived with nothing other than the clothes they wore. They had no food and had eaten very little during the journey. Many had no choice but to find what space they could and simply sleep on the ground with no cover.

Alenia struggled to fill her thoughts with constant attention to domestic concerns. After the long journey, she relished the task of arranging the campsite. They had brought four wagons; she had arranged them in a semicircle and placed a well-built stone firepit in the center. She commissioned the servants to cut logs to size to use for seats around the fire. When the campsite was completed to her satisfaction, being one of the few with proper plates and regular access to food, she hosted groups of other prominent women and began to advocate for civic organizations to regulate certain aspects of camp life. She obtained Fritigern's consent and performed good works, including distributing food to the needy and planning sanitation. She was widely admired.

Also, among her ambitions was some type of education for the children. Father Ulff, the youngest of the Goth priests and a native of their village, volunteered to tutor children in Latin and religion. Alavivus attended on occasion and shared his knowledge of Roman culture and history. The groups were small, and most children of the lower classes weren't offered education. The camp was too large and sprawling to teach even the children of the nobility. Nevertheless, Alenia worked hard to create an outdoor school of sorts for her children and other prominent Christian families nearby. She also insisted that Ungmar, the child of a common man from their village and a friend of Alaric's, be included in the lessons.

Despite her achievements, Alenia's thoughts remained troubled. She took long walks alone, sobbing in the wilderness where none could hear. Her grief was displaced only by fear for her son. Theoric now served as a junior officer in Fritigern's army, and he returned only a few days each month. She struggled to banish visions of her oldest son meeting the same brutal death as his father. At times, she struggled to breathe but allowed none to know of her distress.

One day, after the morning's lessons, Alaric walked home with Ungmar when they were confronted by two boys, who demanded an apple Ungmar held. They claimed entitlement to it due to their family's status. Alaric stepped in front of his friend and refused their demand. One boy yelled at Alaric, getting very close to his face, while the other silently drifted to his left. Alaric anticipated the coming strike and deftly stepped back to avoid it. He then swung hard with his left fist, landing his blow solidly on the chin and bringing his attacker to his knees. The first kid pushed Alaric, trying to force him to the ground, as the other regained his footing and rejoined the attack. Ungmar ran as soon as the fight began, mindful of the consequences of a commoner's child fighting with the highborn, and he sought the aid of another boy he had seen at school. That boy ran to Alaric's defense, turning the tide in Alaric's favor. The attackers were beaten and forced to flee.

After the fight, Alaric panted for breath for a few moments, then looked at his new ally. "Thank you," he managed to say between breaths. "I am called Alaric. Here is my friend called Ungmar."

"I am called Athaulf," the boy responded. He looked to be about Alaric's age, and his accent was that of the West.

"Why did you help me?" Alaric asked.

Athaulf replied with a mischievous smile, "I saw two set upon one."

Alaric returned the smile. "I like you already."

The three walked back to the banks of the river and spoke of their home villages. Athaulf's father had also been killed in battle with the Huns, and his family was prominent in their village. When they returned to Alaric's camp, no one was there except a young woman he had never seen.

"How are you called?" he asked.

Her hands trembled, and her voice wavered. "I am called Luca. I am a friend of Theoric's."

"He's not here," Alaric said brusquely. "He keeps watch at the edge of the valley until the moon is new next." She stared at him in silence. "I will tell him you've come," he finally said.

"No! No! It's not important, really. Just, you needn't mention it at all."

Alaric became suspicious of how nervous she seemed. Perhaps she had come to steal?

"Just don't say anything at all," she pleaded. "Please. I must go now."

Alaric was still suspicious as she scampered off, but his mind turned quickly to showing his new friend the wooden swords he had carved. The boys spent hours play fighting near the camp before the others returned.

Alenia and Daria walked into the camp with a basket of fresh mushrooms, and Alaric told them about the strange woman who had come to see Theoric.

"What did she want?" Daria asked.

"She wouldn't say. Only that they were friends."

"How old was she?" Alenia asked.

"About his age. Maybe a couple of years younger."

"Oh. How is she called?"

"Luca, I think she said."

The day after the new moon, Theoric returned to the family campsite. His mother prepared him food, and while he ate hungrily, she told him a nice girl had come to visit while he was away.

"I've asked about her, and she's from a good family," Alenia assured her son. "They are camped not far from the creek." Theoric didn't respond. "You should pay her a visit."

"You should mind your own business," he said without looking up from his meal.

"Perhaps you should be nicer to your mother," she observed indignantly. "I look only to your welfare."

"My welfare?" He smirked. "You think that girl's going to improve my welfare?"

"She might," Alenia murmured, sitting near Theoric with her hands in her lap.

"I can't believe with all *this* going on," he said, waving a pheasant thigh, "you're thinking about me getting married."

"Well, even with all *this* going on, we must continue to live our lives. And besides, I'm not asking you to marry her—I'm asking you to pay her a visit." She gently elbowed her son in the ribs.

Later that afternoon, Theoric made his way to visit Luca, and her father welcomed him to stay for dinner. After dinner, Theoric asked whether Luca wanted to join him for a walk on a path he knew alongside the river. Luca hadn't yet had occasion to see the great river and was eager to join. Her father was happy to consent.

When they reached the river, Luca was awestruck by its size. "My God. I can't believe how huge it is! I knew it was big, but …" She covered her mouth. "Do you think a person could swim across?"

"A strong man could," he replied, "but you'd end up way downstream. It would be better to do it near a bend where the current would carry you to the other side. Let's hope we never have to try!"

She giggled.

The day had been partly cloudy, and a beautiful sunset began to reflect off the wide river. Theoric didn't know what to say.

"The path is a bit uneven," she said. "Do you mind if I hold your arm?"

"Not at all," he said with a smile, extending his elbow. She held his arm with both hands, smiling as they walked slowly along the bank. They enjoyed the sunset until it was almost gone and made their way back after nightfall.

Word reached Emperor Valens before the Goths arrived. Messengers from Lupicinus conveyed news of the Goths' defeats and the threat of the Huns. As the Gothic embassy awaited an audience, Valens sat on an ornate wooden chair at the head of a grand marble table within his headquarters at Antioch. The emperor wore his formal purple robes, and his hair and beard were pure white. His advisers sat in more modest chairs on the sides of the table laden with wine and fruit.

"What now shall I do about one hundred thousand Gothic refugees on our border?" Valens asked calmly. "Should we grant the protection they seek? And what if the horsemen who drove them into exile do not stop at the Danube? How shall we defend our borders?"

"Augustus, leaving the Goths where they are would provide a buffer against the Huns," said Saturnius, chief civil servant. "And they are not willing to be subdued but wish to remain together as a group."

"The Goths have already been defeated," said General Stilicho. "They will cross the river without permission to escape the Huns, if need be. They know we do not have the men in place to stop them. And if we would use them to fight the Huns, better to bring them over and incorporate them into our army. They would be useful allies in denying the Huns' passage across the river."

"If we let thirty thousand Goth fighters cross, *they* will be in charge of our frontier," Saturnius retorted.

Valens pondered for a few moments while stroking his beard, then slowly looked around the room and asked, "If we cannot stop thirty thousand warriors from crossing, what about fifteen thousand?"

"Augustus?" Saturnius asked with a puzzled expression.

Valens rose and began to pace the room behind the chairs. "I hear that only half are Visigoths under Fritigern. The rest are Ostrogoths who survived Ermenaric's defeat. Fritigern has been a reasonably reliable partner in the past. And he offers to convert his followers to the true faith. Why should I not grant him and his people asylum but deny entry to Ostrogoths unknown to me? Would that not divide their force into two more manageable pieces? We would have a buffer across the river *and* new recruits in our own land."

"A most wise plan," Saturnius said in a flattering tone, a wry smile spreading over his gaunt face.

"It is wise to divide their force," Stilicho said, "but even fifteen thousand soldiers are more than we now have guarding the river. Plus, another thirty-five thousand civilians. Containing and feeding a group that large will not be easy."

"Which is why we must conclude our business with the Persians as soon as possible and quickly reinforce the Danube frontier," the emperor said authoritatively. "If we do not allow them to bring weapons, Lupicinus should be able to manage the situation until help arrives. If we provide food, I think these refugees will be grateful. And we will have more men for the wars to come."

"Yes, Augustus," said Saturnius optimistically, "this should not be thought of as a decision forced upon us but as a great opportunity to fill the ranks of our legions—and at a low cost."

"Yes, my old friend," the emperor said with a smile, "you're always mindful of the perception of the people." Valens paused in thought a few moments, then declared, "So be it. Let us explain the terms to our new Goth friends."

The Goths were led into a great marble throne room. Valens sat on a high throne, which was adorned with gold and precious gems. Rows of the emperor's guards lined the path between the huge columns leading from the entryway to the throne. They wore dress uniforms, and the sun streaming in from large windows shone brightly off their immaculately polished armor. Trumpeters announced their arrival as they walked down a crimson carpet. It was an intimidating scene for Goths unaccustomed to such royal displays.

The Gothic ambassadors expressed much praise for Valens and gratitude for being granted an audience. They knew Valens was aware of their proposal but graciously described the offer, emphasizing the many benefits to the Romans.

When they had finished, Valens spoke solemnly. "In light of Fritigern's prior allegiance and devotion to the true faith, the Visigoths will be granted asylum and sufficient food subsidies until suitable lands can be found for them to farm. However, they are to bring no weapons. Men of conscription age will join the Eastern Army, and all Visigoth men will serve when needed to protect the empire. The Ostrogoths shall not be admitted and must not cross the Danube. Word of my decision will be sent to Lupicinus, and you will carry a copy to Fritigern."

The ambassadors weren't expecting this split decision but weren't about to express disappointment in front of the emperor. Instead, they thanked him profusely and praised his wisdom until the emperor rose, and they realized their audience had ended. With many bows and continued expressions of gratitude, they made their way back out of the great hall.

While the ambassadors were gone, the mood among the Goths had been grim. Most expected the emperor to refuse the request. Fear of the Huns was ever present. Fritigern and the other leaders spent most of their time planning a crossing without leave. When the ambassadors arrived, the camp came alive with great excitement, and they were led straight to a large wooden hall, in which Fritigern now held council. All the leaders gathered, and gasps were heard when the ambassadors explained that leave to cross had been granted only to the Visigoths.

"I see it as a gift," Fritigern said optimistically as the murmurs subsided. "Better only half should need fight their way across with the others already there."

"We will have no weapons," Alavivus protested.

"We will get weapons in," Fritigern replied with a broad grin. "It won't happen immediately but once the women and children are safe. Once we've had a chance to arm ourselves, we can move as an army. The Romans are too few to guard the river and face an army behind them."

"What if the Huns attack us once you're across?" Saphrax asked.

"It's a risk, but it would be easier to lead soldiers back across while you guard the river than to cross with the Romans waiting. What's more, the Huns haven't shown interest in the deep woods. They know their advantage is lessened. They've conquered much territory quickly, and their supply lines must grow thin. They still have Athanaric to deal with in the North. This is our best option."

Fritigern sent word to Lupicinus that he had accepted the emperor's terms, and the crossing would begin. Word spread like wildfire through the camps. Most Visigoths were overjoyed. The Ostrogoths were apprehensive. Preparations began immediately.

Theoric and his mother packed quickly. They hoped to get their wagons across on Roman ferries. As they started to leave, Theoric noticed Alaric just standing there, staring at him.

"I'm not leaving," the young boy declared defiantly.

"What? Of course, you are. You can't just stay here."

"I'm going to stay with the others and fight the Huns."

Theoric burst out laughing, and Alenia said firmly, "No, you're not!"

She jumped from the wagon and seized the boy by the arm. As she tried to force him in the wagon, a horseman walked up slowly.

Fritigern heard the exchange as he approached and addressed the boy. "You must listen to your mother." He then turned to Theoric. "I have a task for you. Can you swim?"

"Umm. Yes."

"I need you to stay behind. In five days, our people will be across the river. When the moon is again new and the night dark, you must stack weapons on rafts and push them across. The current will carry you far downstream. You must look to Roman scouts like debris floating down the river. Pick two dozen men to help you with this task."

Fritigern turned to the boy. "How are you called?"

He had been staring at the ground but now locked eyes with the great general. "I am called Alaric."

"Alaric, your father was like a brother to me. He understood that when great armies are moving, men must put their wishes aside and follow orders. If every man here did whatever he wanted, we'd have chaos, and the Huns would come slit our throats at will. You understand me, boy?"

Alaric now felt ashamed and sheepishly replied, "Yes."

"Yes, sir," his mother corrected.

"Get your mother and sister safely across. The river swells with rain, and the journey will be dangerous. Show me you can follow orders, protect your mother and sister, and you will honor your father."

Fritigern turned his horse to leave but paused and spoke over his shoulder to Alaric once more. "We do not leave our brothers to their fate. They will join us when the time is right." The general spurred his horse and trotted away.

It rained hard the day the crossing began. The banks were slick with mud, and boarding the ferries was treacherous, especially with horses. Some crossed in hollowed-out tree trunks. Many fell overboard. Few could swim. Some Visigoths paid bribes to Roman soldiers to ignore the weapons they carried or allow them to bring additional possessions. It was a chaotic, ugly crossing, but even Fritigern was impressed with the efficiency of the Romans in moving so many people in only a few days.

Once across, the Romans made it clear they were in charge. The Visigoths were led into fields far away from the river, where they could make camps in the mud while the Romans stood guard. As cramped and chaotic as it had been before the crossing, the new situation was far worse. The Romans divided the Visigoths into several separate camps and strictly limited their movements.

True to his word, Alaric worked hard to help his mother as they transitioned to a new camp. They now had only three wagons (still more than most). They used the wagons to make an L shape and pitched tents around a firepit. Alenia again labored to organize designated places for worship, school, and sanitation. No longer were they allowed to range in the woods to hunt or fish in the river. They had to eat only what they had brought with them. Alenia was thankful that at least the stream of wounded warriors had ceased.

Life under New Masters

As the sun set on a dark, cloudy night, Fritigern convened a council and spoke solemnly in the torch-lit tent. The Goths had been pushed into areas far from the river and had few weapons. Roman patrols were constant. The great general spoke solemnly. "Tonight Theoric's company will cross, pushing rafts laden with weapons we left behind. They will land miles downstream. They will not know how to find us. Any men we send to find them will be caught by Roman patrols, and our plans ..."

The room grew silent as the guards outside caused a commotion. "What's this? A spy?" a guard shouted.

The guard entered the tent, grasping a struggling boy, whom he hurled on the ground at Fritigern's feet. "He's been hiding between the tents, listening the whole time!"

Fritigern commanded the child to rise and grasped him by the chin. "I know this boy. You're Guntheric's son, aren't you?"

"Yes, sir," Alaric replied.

"And why do you spy upon my council?"

"Please, sir. I wasn't spying. I want to know about Theoric. You can't just leave him to be found by the Romans."

"I'm afraid that's a problem a child cannot help us with," Fritigern said sternly as he released his grasp.

"But I can, sir."

"How?"

"I watch the guards every day. I know when they move. The Romans grow suspicious when men watch, but they don't care about me. I can go unnoticed. I've been listening to your councils ..." He thought better of completing the thought.

Fritigern hooked an eyebrow and looked intently at the boy. "What if you're caught?"

"I'll say I'm a lost child. I was playing in the woods and lost the path home. You said it yourself. If men are caught, the Romans will know your plans. But if a child is caught ..."

"They'll sell you to slavery," Fritigern said gravely.

"At least I'd be alive. And—and I'll escape. What other choice is there? Will you just sit here? Will you do nothing?"

"Be careful, boy," Fritigern said menacingly. "It's not your place to question the courage of any here. We think only of your safety. I see your mother. I see the grief in her eyes. Would I now deprive her of a son? Perhaps two?"

"If no one finds Theoric, the Romans will kill him. I won't get caught. I'll wait as long as it takes until the Romans aren't looking. And I can lead Theoric's company back along the same path."

Fritigern raised his hand and said loudly, "I admire your courage, boy, but I will not tell your mother she lost two sons tonight. Guards! Take him back to his mother and tell her he is not to leave their camp until first light."

When the guards left their camp, Alenia flew into a rage. Her face was twisted tight, and for the first time in his life, Alaric feared his mother. She attempted to beat him with a stick, but the boy was too quick, and she landed few blows. Daria wailed in protest, and exhaustion finally quenched Alenia's rage. Her anger dissipated into sorrow, and she sobbed deeply as Alaric sought to reassure her. He pledged not to leave and waited for sleep to overcome his exhausted mother.

It was easy to get past the Romans who guarded the camp—Alaric knew where they were and when they moved. He encountered other Roman guards along the way but was so stealthy, and the night so dark, that his light steps went unnoticed. He was able to proceed in this manner throughout the night.

Just before dawn, he finally reached the river a few miles south of the Goth encampment. He walked downstream near the river for a while, then heard steps. He froze, unable to see far in the darkness. After a minute, he again started to creep away from the river. Making his way slowly, he grew confident the noise was just in his head, or perhaps it had been an animal.

His body became more relaxed but stiffened instantly when he felt a firm hand grab his shoulder and spin him around. He'd been caught.

Alaric expected to see the face of a Roman soldier, but there was just enough light to see it was Theoric. It had been long since either experienced joy, and they hugged and smiled until the danger they were still in crept back to mind. Theoric quietly gathered his men. They had brought more weapons than they could carry and so hid most in the dense brush and took what they could. The thick fog just before daybreak allowed them to go unnoticed about halfway to the camp. At Alaric's suggestion, they hid all day in a densely wooded area, daring to complete the rest of their journey only under cover of darkness the following night.

Although Alaric had saved his brother, his mother was a different story. He expected a beating, but she seemed somehow defeated, and that was even worse, as if the fear that she had lost both of her sons was more than she could bear. She clung to Theoric for so long that he had to pull her away when summoned to Fritigern's council. The sorrow on her face was so evident that it brought Alaric to gentle tears. The pride he had felt now gave way to guilt, and he spent the rest of the day trying to bring his mother cheer.

Lupicinus convened his subordinates to discuss handling the Visigoth refugees a few weeks after the crossing. They sat at a rough-hewn oak table in the middle of a dark stone hall lit by torches and candles. Maximus took his place at the head of the table opposite Lupicinus. It was a presumptuous gesture, not unexpected from such an ambitious climber. Lupicinus was aware that the Visigoths were running low on food and asked for an update.

Maximus was quick to speak. "We've started to receive some of the food subsidies. Not all that left Adrianople has arrived, and some of what did has already been sold to those who can pay. We still have the bulk to do with as we wish."

After a short pause for thought, Lupicinus asked, "Why have you not already distributed the rest?"

"I do not think it wise to just give away food to whoever stretches out their hand," Maximus replied with great confidence. "I fear being overly generous might make the Goths lazy and unappreciative."

Lupicinus suppressed his irritation at the insubordinate tone. "Many of the Goths crossed with no food at all. Those who did have little or nothing left. If they start to get desperate—"

Maximus interrupted his commanding officer. "They might rebel. I understand that. But it's also true that if they're well fed, they might become more ambitious. We remain outnumbered. And I hear some Goths now suddenly have weapons. Our situation grows more precarious."

Lupicinus had no love for the Goths and saw the logic in using starvation as a tool of submission but feared Maximus would spur a rebellion.

"Feed them enough to keep them alive but no more," he finally declared.

A more junior officer protested, "Sir, starvation is already beginning to take the weak and elderly."

"Weeding out the weak? I'm not sure that's a disservice to our guests," Maximus replied with a sneer. "Hunger will be a powerful tool and motivator."

The junior officer protested with a glance toward Maximus. "And what of the profiteering among the—"

"I see nothing wrong with a little free enterprise," Lupicinus interjected, shifting his gaze to Maximus. "Let the men earn a little extra. Just don't let it get out of hand."

It had been Fritigern's custom to walk frequently among the people, asking after their welfare. Now he had no need. Hunger was everywhere. Starvation started to take the sick and elderly. The people grew gaunt, agitated, and angry.

Only late at night, alone in his tent, did Fritigern allow himself to weep bitterly. The decision to cross lay at his feet. What if Athanaric had been right the whole time? He had brought his people to this cruel fate. He rose and walked to a wooden chest. From inside he pulled a rolled piece of parchment. Unrolling it with great care, he began to weep again at the image of his two sons as children. They had grown to be strong men, only to be trampled beneath Hun riders. His wife had been an artist and created the image from fine charcoal. He'd always been amazed by the likeness she created. If only she were here now. If only they could all be together again as a family. He took the time to feel his pain only a little each night before sleep took him.

When the food began to run out, the numbers of rats infesting their camps dwindled quickly—an obvious and foreboding omen. The few rats that remained became hunted. Not much meat, of course, but even a mouthful was a precious commodity. When even that sustenance was no longer available, people grew desperate, and theft became common. Alaric's family had coin to buy food from the Romans, but the prices were exorbitant, and Alenia was generous with those who were starving. They couldn't persevere much longer.

Early one morning, Fritigern and the other Visigoth leaders strode through camp, surveying the plight of the people. Only the wealthy had eaten recently, and signs of starvation were everywhere. Warriors looked gaunt and unenergetic. The ribs of children could be seen through their skin. Funerals were too common.

Fritigern noticed Maximus and a group of Roman soldiers negotiating with a Visigoth man over dog meat. He also saw Alaric watching this scene intently from afar. Fritigern was particularly distrustful of Maximus. Many times he had seen this scoundrel take advantage of starving people to enrich himself while wearing a sinister and self-satisfied expression.

As Fritigern approached, it became clear the Romans were trying to convince the Goth to sell his oldest son into slavery in Rome.

Maximus proclaimed confidently, "In Rome, your son will be safe and well fed. Better to work diligently in some trade than to starve to death in the woods." The mother wailed uncontrollably as the father sought assurances about the boy's well-being. Alaric dashed from the scene as soon as he realized the mother's protestations would go unheeded.

"So, this is what it's come to," said Fritigern grimly to no one in particular. "Our people are so desperate they sell their own children for dog meat. I will tolerate this no further."

The leader of the Visigoths led the group to Durostorum, where he demanded an immediate audience with Lupicinus. They were led through the gates of the fortress into an interior room with a large table and told to sit. Lupicinus kept them waiting a long time, which did nothing to soothe Fritigern's anger.

When at last he arrived, Fritigern's face flushed with rage as he barked, "My people are starving, and I will wait no longer!"

"You must appreciate the situation we're all in," Lupicinus replied calmly in a slightly condescending tone as he took a seat at the head of the table. "So many people in so small an area was bound to create shortages. Surely you realized this when you asked for our aid." His mouth curved into a cruel smile.

Fritigern's face was now bright red with anger. Veins bulged from his neck and temples. "We were promised food!" he demanded with a forceful pounding on the table.

"And you promised not to bring weapons. A promise I hear has not been kept."

"We will not just wait to starve to death! I have been stern with those who rebel, but I will hold them back no longer."

"Is that a threat?" Lupicinus asked calmly as a servant placed a single plate of food in front of him.

"It's the situation we're all in," Fritigern sneered. "Starving people won't stay patient forever. Nor will I. Nor will our brothers across the river!" Fritigern banged on the table again to drive home his point. He was letting himself show his temper more than he had previously. He wanted Lupicinus to understand things were unhinging.

"I will do the best I can, but you should not expect a miracle," Lupicinus said dismissively as he began to eat. "I'm afraid the logistical problems are far more complex than you can imagine."

Fritigern bolted to his feet, knocking his chair over backward, and glared intently at Lupicinus. The other Visigoths rose as Fritigern pointed menacingly at the Roman commander, who feigned surprise at the reaction.

"The blood that will be spilled stains your hands!" Fritigern barked and stormed out with the others following him. Lupicinus simply continued to eat his meal.

Alaric frantically sought his older brother. "Theoric, we must save Ungmar! His father is selling him to the Romans."

Theoric's eyes grew wide at the news, but his face softened. "My brother, I'm afraid we can do nothing."

"We can help Ungmar hide. You can tell his father he's not allowed to sell him."

"I'm afraid I can't, little brother. As much as I too would like to save him, this is his father's decision to make. Most families now starve. We barely have enough food for ourselves. This may be the only way his father can keep his whole family from dying of starvation. Otherwise Ungmar himself may starve."

"Ungmar can have half my food. I'm not hungry anymore."

Theoric frowned. "Mother won't allow that. I won't allow it. But there's another way. A better way."

Alaric became excited. "What?"

"After he's sold and his family is fed, we can free Ungmar."

"How?"

"Fritigern will not let us starve without a fight. The time for battle draws close, and we outnumber the Romans. Once we defeat them, we can take what we want, including taking back those they now take from us."

Alaric vowed to free his friend and hurried off to tell Athaulf and the others about the plan.

That evening Fritigern called for a large meeting of elders and officers. He spoke first. "Lupicinus is withholding what was promised us. We can no longer just wait."

"We should take the fortress!" shouted one of the young captains, and many of the young warriors expressed their approval. "We outnumber them with double our numbers across the river, and now we have weapons."

"It's not so easy to take a stone fortress from a Roman garrison," Fritigern replied. "We don't have the equipment, and the Romans are well trained in defending a siege. We're still only lightly armed. They will just retreat within their walls, and we will be powerless to do anything about it."

"We would then be free to roam the countryside," the young man said. "These people are rich! We can take whatever we need."

"We have women and children to defend," Fritigern responded. "The Romans do not. They will summon reinforcements. We cannot let them hide in their fortresses, coming out to attack only when they wish. And letting the others cross while the river's defended will be a bloodbath."

"Then what?" the young man demanded.

Fritigern paused, and Alavivus interjected, "Lupicinus fears a revolt. I see it in his eyes. He seeks to use his smugness to cloak his concern. He knows the situation is untenable. He knows something needs to change. We must force his hand."

"How?" another young man asked.

Fritigern answered, "Alavivus is right. We must put pressure upon him without making it obvious what we're doing. We'll turn a blind eye to attacks on guards, and I'll insist it was just ruffians desperate for food. I'll promise to regain control, but the violence will only grow worse. If small groups of guards are beaten or slain, he'll have to increase the size of each patrol. Larger patrols mean fewer patrols. As the situation grows more unruly, he'll have to keep his men near the fortress. Once he can no longer see all we do, he'll have no choice but to move us farther south. That is when the river must be taken."

The atmosphere in the Visigoths' encampments grew tenser. Theoric and other young men harassed the Roman soldiers whenever possible. Sometimes they just massed large enough groups to cause the Romans to fall back or call in reinforcements from elsewhere. Often patrols were pelted with stones from assailants, who quickly disappeared among the large crowds. A few Roman soldiers moving in small groups were beaten and stripped of their gear.

Alaric wanted to help, but his mother forbade it. She also still forced him to attend Father Ulff's lessons and study Latin, causing him much discontent. If the present circumstances didn't get him out of Latin, nothing would. He lamented the pointlessness of studying another language in such times, but Alenia wouldn't yield.

After lessons one day, Alaric walked back to his family's camp and saw another boy about his age shove Daria to the ground. Alaric yelled and confronted the boy, who claimed justification because of Daria's supposed insolence.

"Get out of here!" Alaric demanded.

"I will go wherever I please," the arrogant bully responded.

"I know you," Alaric said more calmly. "You're the brat Athaulf and I thrashed across the river. Did you not learn your lesson? Where's your rotten brother?"

"Where's your father?" the boy jeered.

The words had not long left his mouth when Alaric connected with a quick left cross to the chin, which dropped him to the ground like a sack of wheat. The boy flipped onto all fours, and as Alaric noticed Father Ulff approaching, the boy rose quickly, throwing a handful of dirt in Alaric's eyes and tackling him around the waist. The two wrestled on the ground, and the priest struggled to separate them. Once he'd pulled them apart, Ulff pulled the bully toward him by the ear, but he squirmed away and ran off. Ulff grabbed Alaric by both arms. "Do you know who his father is?" he demanded.

"I don't care," Alaric responded defiantly. "He shoved Daria."

"One day, my boy, you're going to have to care. He is called Sarus. He is the son of Cniva. Their family is the wealthiest among us, and their father's no better tempered than his sons. I suggest you stay away. Now run along back to your mother."

Back at their camp, Alenia scolded her youngest son over his unkempt appearance. "You've been fighting, haven't you?"

"Just playing. Where's Theoric?"

"Well, son, that's something I wanted to talk to you about." He stared blankly. "You see, Theoric has asked Luca to wed. They'll be married Sunday. Isn't that wonderful?"

"It's just ... it seems odd to have a wedding now. We cannot feed guests."

"No, but even without food, there will still be love. As long as we live, we must keep living our lives. Besides," she said, straightening her back proudly, "I see it as an omen that our fortunes will improve."

"What makes you think that?"

"Do you not remember what your father used to say? 'Fortune smiles upon the bold.'"

Alenia knew what she was doing. She pitched Theoric's wedding as an act of defiance against the Romans, and her youngest son came fully onboard. The ceremony was simple and meager but filled with dignity and love. All who attended felt a sense of hope.

Sarus found a stream and tried to clean up before he went home. When he entered his campsite, his brother saw him first. "Don't let Father see," Sergeric said with much concern.

"It's nothing," the older brother replied. "I fell while climbing a tree."

"Father will not believe that, nor do I. He will beat you worse than last time once he learns you were again bested by Guntheric's son."

"Then he will beat me," Sarus replied defiantly. "I do not fear it."

"Punch me," Sergeric said.

"What?"

"Punch me in the face. Hard. We will tell father that we fought each other. We'll make up some quarrel, and he'll believe I busted your lip but only if I look worse. He'll punish us, but it won't be as bad."

Sarus stood close to his brother and squinted. Sergeric would stand there and take a beating to save him one. "No. I will not strike you because I lost a fight. And I didn't really lose. It just got broken up too soon. I shall face Father and tell him the truth. He may be proud of my courage and spare me a thrashing."

When Cniva returned, Sarus stood before his father and explained what had happened in a calm, dignified tone. Their father's rage was worse than the two brothers had imagined. He punched Sarus in the face, then demanded that the boy stand still and not defend himself. When he'd marked up his son's face, he took a cane to the boy's back, screaming harsh insults with each blow. When his rage began to subside, Cniva forced his son to sit and endure a long lecture.

"You must understand that the house of Balt is a ragged house with no place among our leadership. Whatever nobility may have existed has long since perished. Guntheric had a seat in Fritigern's council only because of their friendship. It is our house with the rightful claim to lead.

"If Guntheric's son is seen as your superior, those who loved Guntheric will cheer his rise. Already many speak of his courage in finding his brother's company. He will become a threat to your leadership." Cniva's tone became less harsh and his body more relaxed. "I am hard on you to make you strong, my son. You must know the pain of defeat to learn to never accept it. I do this for your own good and the good of our house. You understand that, don't you, boy?"

"Yes, Father." Sarus was bitterly angry with himself for shedding tears and summoned all his willpower to stop.

"You must not let this boy surpass you. It is a humiliation not only to you but to our family as well. When you fight him next, you must prevail." Cniva took a deep breath. "It really shouldn't be that hard. His fool of a mother must have given away all their food by now." Cniva began to pace. "Fritigern will not live forever, nor will the folly of bringing us here be forgotten during life. As hunger spreads, people will become desperate, and those with the wisdom and the wealth to still eat will become the new leaders. I must be prepared to rule, and you must be also when your time comes."

When word arrived that Lupicinus had ordered the Visigoths to march to the Roman regional headquarters at Marcianople, Fritigern's heart leaped with joy and relief. He immediately sent word to Saphrax that the Romans would need to pull troops from the river to defend the march south. Preparations were frantic. Almost all the Visigoths were severely weakened by hunger but also desperate for a change, and an invigorating hope spread throughout the camps.

When the time came, the Romans led a huge caravan down a paved road through the woods to Marcianople. Theoric had been ordered to take a place near the front of the column. Most of the other men of fighting age congregated near the back to require the Romans to maintain a robust rear guard. As Fritigern expected, this caused the Romans to pull troops off the river to guard the march south.

Theoric drove one of the wagons filled with the family's possessions, and Alaric sat next to him. As the road narrowed between two steep hills, a rider came up from the rear and whispered a message to Theoric. Alaric asked what had transpired, and Theoric instructed him to mind his own business and take the reins. Theoric then hopped down, jogged next to the wagon, and thrust a spear into the spokes of a wheel. The wooden spokes shattered as the wheel turned, causing the wheel to break and that corner of the wagon to drop to the ground. The horses came to a sudden halt, and the line behind them could move no farther.

When the Romans noticed the column had stopped, riders located the blockage and demanded an explanation. Theoric innocently asserted the wheel had oddly failed, and only after much argument and delay was a replacement provided by another family. Theoric then claimed not to have the tools necessary. In frustration, the Romans finally made the repair themselves, and the column slowly resumed its march.

By the next morning, word had spread of Fritigern's intent, and the column was slow to resume the journey. With great frustration, Lupicinus and his guard cantered down the column, demanding Fritigern's whereabouts. When he finally confronted the Visigoth leader, Fritigern protested that the people were too weakened with hunger to move more quickly. Lupicinus demanded that they quicken the pace, but an assortment of mundane problems continued to slow the march.

While the Visigoths' march proceeded at a snail's pace, Saphrax moved quickly to take advantage of the lightly guarded river. The few Roman soldiers left remained within Durostorum in the face of the Ostrogoths' invasion. The Ostrogoth soldiers were unchallenged as they crossed, and most rode quickly to join forces with Fritigern, with only a small contingent left on the river to protect the civilian crossing. By the time the Visigoths reached Marcianople, Lupicinus's worst fear had been realized—a unified Gothic army of over thirty thousand soldiers inside Roman territory.

Now inside the city's walls, Lupicinus tried a new approach. He invited Fritigern and Alavivus to join him for a dinner party. The Goths were led into a banquet hall while their guards waited outside. This time Lupicinus was prompt and generous. The food was more plentiful and of a higher quality than the two Goths had enjoyed in a long time. As they feasted, Lupicinus turned his head to receive a whispered message from an aide. He whispered a response, then sat silently until the sounds of a loud clash outside the room became apparent. Sensing the trap, Fritigern and Alavivus jumped to their feet and drew swords.

"What treachery is this?" Fritigern screamed. "You invite us to dinner to slit our throats!"

"This violence was caused by *your* people! They riot in the market."

"They're rioting because they're starving! You ordered that they not be permitted to buy food, didn't you?"

"That's no excuse for killing Roman soldiers."

"And many more will die! My people will not keep peace after this betrayal!"

Lupicinus's plan to quickly murder the Goths' retainers didn't go as planned. The battle continued to rage outside, and Lupicinus had only two guards in the room, who now moved to attack the Goth commanders. Alavivus stepped out front to defend Fritigern and killed the first guard to engage him but was stabbed in the arm by the second. Fritigern then thrust forward, stabbing the second guard through the eye.

At that point, beginning to fear for his own life, Lupicinus cried, "Hold, enough! End this violence. You must send word to your people. They must stand down."

"Why don't you send that message yourself?" Fritigern spat angrily as he helped Alavivus stay on his feet. "The only way to restore peace is to let them see we still live. If we leave now, we will lead them out of the city."

Having little choice, Lupicinus agreed, and the Goths walked out with their wounded. Fritigern led the people beyond the gates of the city. The wound Alavivus suffered was serious but not fatal.

Many gathered, seeking to learn what action their leaders would take. Furious at this latest betrayal, Fritigern spoke to his people with much rage. "For too long have we endured the tyranny of the Romans. For too long have we waited for scraps to fall from their table. Tonight we take back our own destiny! Never again shall the Romans command us!" All within earshot roared their approval.

The civilians left first before dawn in a great wagon train on the road west. The unified Goth army stayed outside the city gates, preventing the Romans from leaving. Once the civilians were far enough down the road, the Goth army followed. Fritigern knew Lupicinus would give chase—he had no other choice.

About nine miles from the city, as the road passed through a hilly wooded region, Fritigern stationed archers and infantry deep in the woods on both sides of the road. The rest of the Goth army stopped a little farther down the road and turned back to face Marcianople. When the Romans reached the Goths' lines, they made a forward defensive formation, but Fritigern sprang the trap, and furious Goth warriors simultaneously raced down the wooded hills and into both Roman flanks. The battle quickly became a rout. All the Roman officers were killed, except for Lupicinus, who fled the field early enough to sneak back to Marcianople and Maximus, who had stayed behind to command the garrison. The Goths now had a fresh supply of armor and weapons as well as many more horses from the dead Romans.

The commanders at the garrison in Adrianople were ordered to march to Hellespontus. However, the commanders were Goths themselves, and the Romans feared having a garrison under the control of two Goths during a Gothic rebellion. The commanders delayed, seeking money for the journey and more time to prepare. Fearing a mutiny, the local Romans became violent, and a mob pelted the Goths with missiles. The Goths killed many among the mob and left the city to join Fritigern, whose army now far outnumbered the Romans.

Fritigern led the Goths to besiege the great walled city of Adrianople— now lightly defended. His advisers convinced him its great wealth was worth the risk of an attack, and it certainly felt like their situation was vastly improved when over thirty thousand well-armed Goth warriors surrounded the largest city in the region. But the Goths lacked the equipment or experience necessary to breach the city's towering walls. After watching many of his men felled by arrows and javelins, and seeing the hopelessness of the situation, Fritigern declared before his officers, "I will now keep peace with walls" and quit the city.

With the local Roman soldiers safe only within walled cities and forts, the Goths were free to pillage the countryside. Roman prisoners told them where treasure and surplus food were hidden. Many Goth slaves, prisoners, and laborers living in Roman territory joined Fritigern. The ranks of his army swelled, and they created a huge wagon train to carry their plunder. The people were well fed and content, but Fritigern knew their good fortune would not last long.

Against Long Odds

Valens stood at a window in his lavish chambers, deep in thought. Saturnius sought permission to enter. Valens consented absentmindedly and continued to stare out the window at the bustling city of Antioch.

"Augustus, I'm afraid I have bad news. The Goths have revolted and defeated Lupicinus. They now pillage Thrace."

Valens finally turned to face him with an expression of shocked disbelief. "How did this happen?"

"Most of the food sent never made it to the Goths. When starvation set in, they rebelled."

Valens sat heavily and slumped in his chair, staring vacantly at the floor. "And what of Lupicinus?"

"He lives."

Valens sighed and lifted his head. "This is his fault. He cared more about lining his own pockets than keeping the situation under control. He's as cruel as he is stupid." After a few deep breaths, he continued, "We need new leaders to bring stability while reinforcements arrive. I want General Stilicho to lead an advance force into Thrace. They shall take as many men as can be spared. We must also seek the aid of my nephew. Send word to Gratian that the Western Army is needed to quash this Goth rebellion."

"And what of the Persians, Augustus?" Saturnius asked.

"Send an embassy to negotiate the best terms we can get. The Persians are no longer our primary concern. We must lead the Eastern Army back to Constantinople."

Fritigern, Alavivus, and Saphrax were sipping wine around a campfire when a scouting report arrived. Valens had sent troops from the Persian front under the command of Stilicho. They had learned the day before that a force from the West under General Richomeres had moved to block the western mountain passes and keep the Goths from invading the Western Empire. "The Romans mean to pinch us between the two," Alavivus observed.

"Aye," Fritigern acknowledged. "We must send our people north into the protection of the Haemus Mountains, and we will make defensive fortifications in the southern foothills."

"Will that not leave us trapped between the two armies?" Saphrax asked skeptically.

Fritigern began to clear a space on the ground and draw with a stick. "If our people are deep in the mountains here and we control the southern passes, the Romans can't threaten our people without attacking our fortifications. We'd have the high ground and the ability to force them into narrow spaces. Their advantages would be lessened. I don't think we'll find a more favorable place to fight. And if God is merciful, when they see the situation, they may find it wiser to negotiate."

They spent weeks digging trenches and building barriers. Theoric worked closely by Fritigern's side throughout. The old general wished to protect the son of his fallen friend but was also aware that if Theoric should be seen as receiving special treatment, he would be deprived of the opportunity to move up in the ranks on his own.

When the main fortifications were complete, Fritigern moved most of his army south of the mountain passes to a place called "the Willows" and formed a huge circle of wagons. They'd be able to fight on mostly flat land and retreat back to fortified positions if needed. Fritigern promoted Theoric and placed him in charge of a scouting party that patrolled beyond their lines.

On a patrol in the afternoon, Theoric spurred his horse to the top of a steep ridge. The mountain air was clear, and the sun shined brightly. As his horse reached the summit, he gazed down at the broad valley below, which was flooded with a Roman army marching straight toward him. They were far enough away for him to pause a moment to take in the splendid spectacle. The Romans were clad in shining armor and crimson cloaks. The officers had large colorful plumes on their helmets, and they commanded tight formations of infantry and cavalry. The Roman soldiers were so disciplined that their formations moved in perfect synchronicity. Theoric thought about how this sight contrasted with the Goths' more chaotic style. Still, this force was smaller than Fritigern's army, and having the greater numbers and the higher ground gave Theoric confidence.

The Romans advanced to attack the wagon fort, and Theoric rode with the cavalry from behind the wagons. They raced to outflank the Romans on the right side. Theoric's company was at the forefront of the charge, and he carried a bow as his primary weapon. The effectiveness of Hun-mounted archers was etched in his mind, and he'd spent much time practicing archery from horseback and training his men as well. Theoric's company galloped at full speed to get past the Roman flank. Seeing the danger, the Roman cavalry also raced to keep the Goths from getting to their rear.

As the Roman riders drew close, Theoric twisted in his saddle and aimed his arrow left. He waited to shoot until he was sure he'd hit his mark. His men waited for his first shot. The lead Roman rider had the angle on him and quickly drew close. Theoric fired his arrow into the horse's midsection just in front of the rider's leg. The wounded animal immediately broke stride, and the rider flipped over the horse's head as the beast went down. His men did likewise, and the Romans' best chance to stop their flanking maneuver vanished.

Turning the corner around the Roman flank gave Theoric a soaring feeling in anticipation of a great victory. He continued to shoot horses out from under Roman riders, and the Goth cavalry began to roll up the Roman flank. Roman infantrymen engaged with the Goth infantry were now vulnerable to attack from the rear. But then the Roman formations began to change more quickly than Theoric thought possible. The long Roman line now turned into an L shape to seal off the flank. Many Romans were run down by Goth cavalry in front of the new formations, but the disciplined maneuver prevented the battle from turning into a rout.

The two armies traded charges against each other throughout the day, but neither could obtain a decisive advantage. The battle lasted until dusk. At the end, it was a bloody stalemate.

The Goths fell back to their wagon fort, and Theoric was relieved the fighting was over. Before the battle, he'd felt fear so intense that it made him question his courage. During the battle, he'd felt an intense excitement that gave him confidence. After the drama faded, Theoric felt only profound sadness for the dead. He knew many who'd fallen that day, and many more with grievous injuries wouldn't survive. They worked late into the night and throughout the days that followed, burying the dead and tending the wounded.

Stilicho was livid when he read the order to retreat. He spoke to no one in particular at a staff meeting. "Retreat? Why would we retreat? They're pinned against the mountains. If we retreat, they can go wherever they want."

The young general was almost as irate when he learned the emperor had sent Saturnius to "help" him. The last thing he needed was a politician involving himself in military strategy. Nevertheless, when the entourage arrived, Stilicho graciously greeted his esteemed guest.

Stilicho invited Saturnius to an elaborate dinner on the evening of his arrival. Saturnius announced he had brought a cask of real Italian wine, for which Stilicho expressed much gratitude. The two enjoyed the fine wine and exchanged praise for each other.

"The emperor is quite an admirer of yours, as I'm sure you know," Saturnius remarked.

"I am very grateful for the opportunities he has given me, for the confidence he has placed in me."

"I'm sure you are," Saturnius observed wryly. "You must have experienced much discrimination before coming under the emperor's protection. There are far too many among us who value being full-blooded Roman over all else. Being the son of a Vandal, you've had to strive hard your whole life to attain what is simply handed to the sons of senators." Saturnius refilled their cups. "But it's made you strong. And the emperor has noticed."

"I am indeed grateful for his patronage and for yours," Stilicho said, raising his cup slightly.

The conversation was so pleasant that Stilicho felt comfortable pressing his grievance. "I believe it would be a mistake to proceed too timidly against these Goths. They have chosen the protection of the mountains. That choice gives us certain advantages. They were pinned down."

"My friend, your counsel is wise, of course. None doubt your skill. Yet we must move cautiously. The emperor has sent what force he could while he disengages from the Persians. Soon the entire Eastern Army will be at our disposal. What will the Goths do then? Will they even fight? If they have wisdom, they will submit to the emperor's command. Many lives on both sides may be saved."

"My good friend," Stilicho began cautiously, "I know you speak for my benefit, and I understand we cannot be routed before the Eastern Army arrives, but there are times when an overly cautious approach creates more danger. I believe this to be one of those times."

"How so?"

Stilicho now became a bit exasperated. "As we sit here, the Goths can move anywhere they want, including attacking us here. We should deprive them the freedom of movement. Keep them trapped where they are. We had that, and then the order came to retreat!"

"Be cautious of criticizing the emperor's orders."

Stilicho lifted his head back in exasperation, then took a couple of deep breaths and looked back at Saturnius. "That's good advice," he said calmly.

"Besides, I'm not saying we have to stay here. If you believe it is wise to keep the Goths pinned down, let us march to make it so, but we must not engage them yet in full battle. We cannot afford to risk defeat. Instead, we will wait and see how the Goths like wintering in the mountains. They can't have much food left. We shall starve them out in the winter, force them from the mountains, and then finish them off on the plains."

"It may not be so easy to trap the Goths a second time. They defend the area south of the mountains to keep freedom of movement. When we attack, they will know our purpose."

"But they will not know that Richomeres moves east. He will provide the men we need to seal off the passes so that the Goths must go through us if they are to escape. Once they're committed to defending the mountain passes, we'll build fortifications over the winter and keep them trapped."

The Goths could indeed see what Stilicho's force was doing but struggled to stop it now that Richomeres moved against them from the West. The Romans were smart enough not to follow the Goths too deep into the mountains but drove them deep enough to build defensive

49

fortifications that kept the Goths in. Fritigern tried again and again to break through, but each charge became a bloodbath. The fortifications were too strong. The Goths could not get out. The fear Saphrax expressed had come to fruition, and Fritigern again doubted the wisdom of his decision. Hunger began to set in. Their need was dire.

"Do you remember how old you are?" Thoris asked his friend as they worked together to set up a tent. It was a cloudless, bright, and windy day. The chill of autumn had begun to set in.

"I'm about the same age as you, right?" Hamil responded.

"Yes, but I don't know whether I'm twenty-two or twenty-three."

"Do you not remember your birthday?"

"No, but it was in the summer. I wish I'd asked my mother. I don't think there's anyone alive who knows. I was seventeen when we were taken, so five years later, I must be twenty-two now, right? Or did I turn twenty-three over the summer?"

"I think we've been here longer."

They laughed a bit and worked side by side in silence for a few moments, tying the hides to the tent's poles. "Did you ever use to dream of escaping?" Thoris asked his friend.

"Yes, all the time. Still do. Don't you?"

"Not anymore. I used to dream of being freed by a great Goth army returning to reclaim their homeland."

"Wow. That's ambitious. I just dream of sneaking off."

"It wouldn't be so easy to sneak off. How would you get past the guards?"

"One day the Huns will suffer a defeat. Or perhaps be so pressed by a foe that they become disorganized, and I just slip away."

"Where would you go?" Thoris asked skeptically.

"You used to say the Huns spoke of Athanaric's people in the North. I would seek them."

"I haven't heard talk like that in a long time."

"Maybe they just don't speak of it when you're around."

"Maybe. I didn't let anyone know I could understand their speech for a long time. But when they found out, they didn't seem to hold back what they said around me. Nor do they now. I don't think Athanaric threatens them as he once did."

"I've always wondered. How were you able to learn their language so quickly?"

"I don't know. I just started paying attention to what they said—even when I didn't understand. At first, I began to recognize words and phrases, and over time it started to make sense."

"I can still scarcely understand their black speech. It's easy enough to understand what they want, and I don't much want to talk to Huns. But you picked it up quick, and now you have the honor of translating for the great Hun leader!" Hamil flashed his beautiful smile.

Thoris continued to work and replied ruefully, "It doesn't feel like an honor."

"Better than gutting goats, eh?" The pair laughed.

When they finished the tent, they took a moment to look around and noticed an unusually large number of horses and men congregating near the center of camp. It wasn't long before more guards appeared and hauled Thoris off. As they drew closer to the center of camp, Thoris realized they were taking him to Uldin's tent, and his body grew stiff. Uldin called on him frequently and even seemed strangely fond of him. But Thoris never saw the Hun leader without remembering the day Uldin had killed his father. Uldin's favor had elevated his status and eased his suffering, but he never forgot, and he never forgave.

The guards held him outside the tent for a while and then were beckoned to bring him in. The day outside was bright, but the inside of the tent was dark and lit only dimly by torches. His eyes hadn't yet adjusted when he was forced to hide his astonishment. Before Uldin stood four Goths with swords on their belts; they were dressed in the traditional garb of their people. They stared at Thoris as he entered, as did Uldin and many Hun chieftains and clan leaders. He'd never seen Uldin's tent so crowded.

Uldin spoke first and commanded Thoris to translate. In the harsh, guttural tongue of the Huns, Uldin demanded to know why the Goths had come.

Thoris complied, and the eldest Goth spoke. "We come seeking your allegiance. We bring gifts to show our friendship, and there are many more such treasures awaiting you should you ride with us." As Thoris translated, the Goths began to slowly pull jewel-encrusted gold goblets and jewelry from large sacks. Many Huns made astonished and greedy sounds. Uldin waved them silent.

The eldest Goth then addressed Thoris. "I am called Alavivus. How are you called?"

"I am called Thoris."

Uldin's voice rose, and he demanded a translation. Thoris complied, and Uldin insisted that Alavivus refrain from addressing his slave directly. The Goth leader then addressed Uldin. "When my people crossed the great river, we entered the Roman Empire, a powerful and wealthy nation. But the Romans didn't keep their promises to feed our people when our need was dire, and we revolted and defeated a Roman army in a great battle."

Uldin interjected, and Thoris struggled to translate.

Finally, Thoris said, "He wants to know why the Romans let you cross the river, if they're so powerful."

Uldin stared intently at Alavivus, and the room was silent.

The Goth general raised his head and spoke loudly and with confidence. "Most of their army was fighting a war in a distant land. They didn't have the numbers to keep us out and thought it better to use our warriors to bolster their defenses against your people. After our victory, we found much treasure for the taking. The Romans now bring an army from the West to challenge us. With your aid, we can defeat the Romans and share with you ten times the gifts we bring today."

Again, a low covetous murmur spread among the Huns. Their lust for gold was obvious, but Uldin remained passive, and a long silence ensued. "How many riders do you need?" he finally asked.

"We know well the fierceness of your fighters. Combined with our own forces, only a thousand of your warriors would be needed to turn the tide in our favor."

Uldin stroked his scraggly beard pensively and announced that they would discuss the proposal among themselves. Once the Goths had gone, it was clear all the chieftains were in favor of the proposal, and the dispute was over which of them would be allowed to seize the prize. A contentious argument raged until Uldin declared each tribe would send warriors, and all would split the treasure.

Upon leaving Uldin's tent, Alavivus turned to Thoris and asked, "How long have you been here?"

"Five years."

"How are you treated?"

"I'm still alive."

Alavivus looked at the young man with sympathetic eyes.

"There are more like you?" Thoris asked. "More who escaped the Huns?"

Alavivus smiled as they walked. "Yes, my son—more than a hundred thousand."

Thoris smiled also, more broadly than he had since his mother's death. "Sir, would you need a translator for your journey?"

Alavivus smiled again. "Yes, of course. You would be invaluable."

Upon further reflection, Thoris again turned grim. "I'm afraid it's too good to be true," he replied dejectedly. "Uldin will not give me away."

"But surely he has other Goth slaves who speak both tongues. We'll see what they say, but we have held back some of the gold to sweeten the deal, if needed. I'll see if I can't barter for your services." The old general put his hand on the young man's shoulder as they were led to the tents the Goths would use.

It wasn't long before Uldin summoned the Goth embassy. Thoris translated as the Hun leader announced they would have not one but two thousand Hun riders but would expect twenty times the gold Alavivus had brought, plus whatever they could pillage for themselves. Alavivus made a great show of anxiety over the price demanded to convince Uldin he had made a hard bargain. Before agreeing, Alavivus announced, "With so many of your warriors, we will need more translators. If we agree to such a high price, will you give us this slave to assure communication and knowledge of your ways?" Uldin paused, then announced that he would allow Thoris to ride with them, but he must be returned with the booty, or the alliance would be broken, and the man's life forfeit. Alavivus nodded his agreement.

Thoris prepared for the journey with great excitement and hurriedly told the story to Hamil as he worked.

"I'm going to escape," Hamil declared bluntly.

"What?" Thoris asked in disbelief. He stopped working and turned to face him. His friend stood resolute, and he realized Hamil was serious.

"How?"

"The night before you leave, I'll tell the other slaves that I am to ride with you. With two thousand warriors in camp, it will be chaotic. I'll sneak off when everyone's attention turns to the departure of such a great host. No one will know I've gone until nightfall, and the others will say I rode off with the war party. It will take time to figure out what happened. By then, I'll be too far gone to hunt down."

"You'll be alone on the prairie with no food or water. Where will you go?"

"North. I can make it to the mountains on my own, and there I'll live among Athanaric's folk."

"They'll use dogs to sniff you out."

"I've already thought of that. I'm going to take off all my clothes before I reach the river. The dogs will find them, but I will already have swum across the river. When I reach the other side clean, the dogs will lose my scent."

Thoris laughed in exasperation and frowned. "You're going to walk from the river to the Carpathians with no food or water and without clothes? It's too cold."

"I'll find clothing in one of the looted villages. Besides, if I die, I die. I'd rather die now than be a slave to these people for the rest of my life. This can work, and I'm going to do it."

Thoris breathed deeply. He wasn't convinced of the plan but knew his friend wouldn't be dissuaded. If he was going to try to escape, this probably was the best chance he'd get. The two friends embraced, and both hearts beat fast in anticipation of a new beginning.

It had been only a little more than a year since Theoric last saw his family, but his careworn face made him look much older. An excited crowd surrounded the group he led as they trotted into one of the civilian encampments. Theoric expected to see his brother among the first to greet them but didn't spot Alaric until his gaze reached the back of the group. His younger brother too seemed older though still not quite a man.

Theoric smiled more broadly than he had since their last meeting, and he quickly dismounted and strongly embraced his brother for a long time.

"How's Mom?" Theoric asked.

"Better. She doesn't seem sad *all* the time anymore."

"That's good. And Daria?"

"Same as always. Annoying."

"And Luca?"

"She's all right. She's been eager for your return."

Theoric smiled. "I've been eager for my return."

"What about you?" Alaric asked. "Tell me what you've been doing all this time."

"Fighting the Romans."

"I *know* you've been fighting the Romans. I want details. I want to hear about the battles from someone who was actually there."

"Be patient. I'm only going to tell the tale once. I suspect many will want to hear."

The two approached a woman washing clothes in a cauldron over a small fire. Alenia looked up, put her hand to her mouth to cover her gasp, and cried out in joy as she ran to her son. They embraced, and Daria came running out of a tent and joined their hug. Alenia smiled and wept as she clung to her eldest son until a crowd began to form around them. Theoric spent several minutes shaking hands and hugging various friends and relatives before he could find his wife. Luca beamed brightly to see him and embraced her young husband as tears of joy rolled down her face.

It was agreed that they would all have a feast to honor the returning heroes that night. The rest of the day was spent preparing. They built a huge fire at the center of the camp and slow-roasted a wild boar over a pit.

That night they gorged themselves on pork and even had a little wine from a pillaged villa. Theoric and his men had been pestered since their arrival for news of their deeds, and finally Theoric agreed to tell the tale. A group gathered around a glowing fire, and Theoric paced the perimeter, raising his head and voice so all could hear.

"When we stopped attacking the Roman fortifications, many became nervous. Why were we just waiting? Was there no plan? But then word began to spread. Fritigern had dispatched Alavivus to hire Hun mercenaries, and he rode west with a host of some two thousand Hun riders."

He paused for effect. "The next thing I knew, we prepared for another assault on the Roman positions. The attack was coordinated with a Hun cavalry charge in the Romans' rear. The Romans couldn't defend both fronts at the same time and began to retreat.

"But it was an orderly retreat. Once we overtook a fortification, they always had a second line formed behind it. When the defenders had to retreat, they fell back behind the second line and formed a new line. The Romans retreated like that all the way out of the mountains."

"Where is Fritigern's army now?" a man asked.

"Moving south," Theoric responded. "And we are all to join them."

The crowd was much relieved and comforted by Theoric's tale. Again, Fritigern had led them to victory and safety. But they also knew the Romans would be back in greater numbers, and the mood was serious as they broke camp over the following days and followed Fritigern's army south.

Before they left, Alaric sought to speak alone with his brother. Once they'd walked into the woods, Theoric asked, "What is it, little brother?"

Alaric's demeanor was serious, and he struggled to find the right words. "I ... I want to apologize."

"For what?"

The boy didn't respond.

Theoric teased, "It's probably mother you need to—"

"No. I want to apologize ... for that day ... when you returned and told us of father, and I ..." Alaric began to cry.

"My God, Alaric! That seems like a lifetime ago. You were a young child. You'd just found out your father was dead."

"But still," Alaric stammered, his voice wavering, "I'm sorry I said that. It wasn't your fault, and you'd just lost your father too. You're a hero."

"I'm not a hero," Theoric responded firmly. Alaric stared at him with a puzzled frown as tears continued to stream down his face. "I hope you never come to understand this, little brother, but the real heroes all lie dead on the field. Everyone else found a way to live."

Theoric could tell his brother didn't understand. "Come here." Theoric hugged his brother closely. "Forgiveness is not needed, but I accept your apology. Think no more of it."

Theoric put his arm around his little brother as they headed back to camp. "And I forgive you as well," Alaric announced.

"You forgive me? Well, that's good. What exactly am I being forgiven for?"

"For tricking me into thinking we were going to rescue Ungmar."

Theoric laughed heartily. "Good Lord, Alaric, you'd already defied Fritigern, not to mention our mother. I didn't know what you would do, but I knew whatever it was, it would get you killed. So, yes, thank you for forgiving me."

Alaric smiled. "I'm still going to rescue him."

"I don't doubt you will, little brother."

Valens marched north to Constantinople. The price of peace with the Persians wasn't cheap, but his massive Eastern Army was now free to deal decisively with the Goth problem. His entry into the great city, however, was less than hospitable. As the emperor and his court ceremoniously entered the massive gates on May 30, 378, both plebs and patricians hurled insults. "Why do you hide behind our walls? The Goths are not here!" and similar sentiments made clear the people were furious the mighty empire had been unable to stop the uncivilized Goths from marauding the countryside, and they expected swift action. Even the most prominent citizens complained publicly that Valens had neglected their defense and should leave the city to confront the invaders. Small riots ensued.

The situation became so untenable that Valens left the city after only twelve days and moved his army to the imperial villa Melanthias west of the city. He distributed pay and supplies and sought to boost morale. Valens appointed Sebastianus, a general from Italia, to lead the Eastern Roman Army. Sebastianus sent out small groups to confront Gothic raiding parties. His success caused Fritigern to recall the raiding bands to consolidate his forces.

Valens expected the western emperor Gratian to bring his army through the Alps to join forces. Gratian, however, was delayed by an invasion in Gaul. Warnings of barbarian preparations to cross the Rhine caused Gratian to cross himself and nip the invasion in the bud. Gratian was successful, and news of his victories spread quickly through the

Eastern Empire, creating a poor contrast with the people's view of Valens's dithering.

On August 7, Richomeres arrived at Valens's court with an advanced guard and a message from Gratian. Valens read the note while standing in a well-lit room in his ornate villa with a circle of advisers. "My nephew sends word he is nearing the Succi pass and advises me to wait for him. Gratian, however, does not know that the Goths are moving south to Adrianople." Valens paused in thought for a few seconds and turned to Sebastianus. "What would you have me do?"

"Sire, our scouts report a force of only ten thousand Goth warriors moving south toward Adrianople. If we wait, the Goths will have too long to consolidate their forces—perhaps doubling in size. If we strike now, they will be outnumbered. Victory is within our grasp. We should seize it!" The general's confidence was persuasive.

Stilicho interjected, "If we wait, the combined eastern and western armies will be too large for the Goths to withstand. If both sides fully consolidate their forces, we will be assured of victory. Anything else leaves our fate to chance. The safest route is to wait for Gratian."

"The safest course is not always the best," Saturnius replied with a wry smile at Stilicho. "Further delay will not sit well with those who have endured the pillaging of the Goths. The people will not respect inaction when additional troops are not needed."

"The people will respect victory," Stilicho retorted. "Once we defeat the Goths, people will no longer speak of how it became so."

"They *will* speak of it, and they will say the victory belongs to Gratian." Saturnius turned to face the emperor directly. "If you wait for Gratian's army to move through the pass, it will appear you couldn't defend your own land. It is likely Gratian will do nothing more than provide reserves. Reserves that are not needed. If you act now, it will be clear to whom the victory belongs. A victory that is already in your grasp."

Valens turned to Sebastianus. "Are you so confident in our victory?"

"Yes, Emperor. The Goths are too few and have nowhere to hide. We stand on the cusp of a great victory."

"And where, I wonder, are the rest of the Goths?" the emperor asked.

"They must be far to the north. Our scouts see no signs of them."

Valens still harbored doubts but instructed Sebastianus to begin preparing the troops to march on Adrianople. The next evening, a Gothic embassy led by a senior Christian priest arrived. They brought two letters from Fritigern. The first stated that the Goths wanted only lands in Thrace, and in exchange they would ally themselves with him and become staunch allies. The second letter was privately addressed to Valens from Fritigern. It stated that Fritigern truly desired peace but that Valens would need to keep his army mobilized so Fritigern could keep control of his own people. Valens shared both letters with his council.

"Sire, this is obvious deceit," Saturnius said with great contempt. "Why would he send a second letter in secret to you? Does he seek to deceive his own people?"

"Perhaps he speaks the truth," Valens replied calmly. "Perhaps there are those in his council who have grown overly ambitious—who would demand aggression when they perceive weakness. Would I not keep our forces mobilized anyway? Are the terms he proposes not reasonable?"

"It will not seem reasonable to landowners in Thrace," spoke Saturnius with some agitation. "Will they be expected to pay taxes while their lands are given to invaders who threaten them?"

"I think he's bluffing," Sebastianus offered. "He plays the role of the reasonable peacekeeper holding back barking dogs. He is weak. He knows he lacks the numbers and yet pretends to hold the advantage."

Valens paused in thought for a long time. "Very well. We will proceed with the march and judge the situation as it unfolds." On the morning of August 9, Valens's army marched north to confront the Goths.

The Visigoths created a huge circle of wagons on an open plain near a wooded area outside Adrianople. Some civilians retreated to the north, but Theoric chose to keep his family within the wagon fort. He had risen in the ranks and now commanded an infantry company stationed to the southeast of the wagons.

Alenia was sick with fear and could barely control her trembling hands. She prayed fervently that Fritigern would make peace with the Romans. She spoke sternly to Alaric about staying by her side. But in the early afternoon, as word spread of the Romans' approach, Alaric slipped past his mother's watchful eye and found a tree at the edge of the wagon fort atop a small hill. He climbed the tree higher than a grown man could have, and from that perch he had a better view of the action than even the commanders.

Alaric could see the Visigoth infantry companies arrayed in a double semicircle south of the wagon fort. They were grouped into companies of about five hundred men each. The interior semicircle contained nine companies with twelve outside. There was enough space between each company to allow forward soldiers to retreat behind a defensive formation, regroup, and attack again. Theoric's company was on the outside line on the eastern side, and Alaric intently watched the action on that side. The Visigoth cavalry was stationed behind the wagon fort, poised to strike from either side.

Alaric watched intently as the Roman formations came into view. The Roman divisions were much larger. Four infantry divisions marched straight toward the Goths. A cavalry and infantry division on each side protected the flanks. Just when Alaric thought there couldn't possibly be any more Romans, three more reserve divisions appeared in the rear. It was well after noon by the time the Roman army arrived, and they'd been marching all day under a hot August sun. Fritigern pressed this advantage by ordering his men to light fires, which blew smoke and ash into the Roman ranks.

Fritigern cantered in front of his formations, watching the movement of the Romans. Alavivus rode up next to him. "As we expected."

"Aye," Fritigern replied.

"Any chance they choose not to fight?"

"Maybe. I've dispatched another peace envoy. Valens will have one final chance." The old friends exchanged smiles and looked out at the military spectacle unfolding. The Romans were rapidly forming their ranks, and the window for peace was closing quickly.

Valens watched the deployment while mounted on a pure-white gelding with Sebastianus at his side. "Tell me. What do you think of their strategy?"

"What I would expect, Augustus. Fritigern has deployed his forces wisely, but he's outnumbered. The Visigoth cavalry may come from either side, but our flanks will be well defended. Their cavalry is not large enough to break our lines. And if he chooses to split his cavalry and attack from both sides, the battle with end quickly."

Valens wasn't as confident as his general. When a written message arrived from Fritigern, the emperor seriously considered the proposal.

But Sebastianus spoke with alarm as he pointed. "The right flank is engaging too soon!"

Fritigern's hope for peace was dashed as soon as he saw it. He had never intended to let the Roman army get fully set. This early engagement created an opportunity he couldn't refuse. He ordered the infantry on the eastern side to advance and signaled the cavalry to begin its charge on the west.

Before the Visigoth cavalry had begun their charge, Alaric heard a low rumbling noise behind him. He turned and saw what the Romans could not. A huge host of riders galloped from the north. Alaric's heart leaped as he recognized the banner of Saphrax. The timing of the Ostrogoths was nearly perfect, and now a huge host of Gothic cavalry swung around the west side of the wagon circle and smashed into the Romans, protecting their western flank.

The Roman formations on the west weren't fully formed, and the cavalry protecting the western flank was overwhelmed by the Goths' swift charge. The Roman calvary, caught flat-footed, was now in disarray. The men looked around in panic, unsure in which direction they should form ranks. Goth riders plowed into the Romans with greater numbers and momentum. Alaric saw Goth horsemen use their spears as lances, mowing down Romans on foot. The Goth infantry companies guarding the wagons advanced and engaged the Roman infantry, locking them in place.

The Eastern Roman Army was now stuck, unable to move forward, with an exposed western flank. The Goths drove deep into the Roman ranks. Roman soldiers were packed into a tight phalanx formation, and most couldn't turn to the left to face the onslaught. Goths slashing through the Roman formations from the west used overhand spear thrusts to stab Romans in the necks and sides. Goths rained down blows with swords, axes, and hammers on the heads of defenseless Roman soldiers, packed too tightly to face their attackers. The horsemen wreaked even more carnage. Only when the tight Roman formations begin to crumble did the surviving

Roman soldiers have room to flee the carnage. The field became slick with blood and gore.

The battle was a massacre, and confusion reigned among the Roman commanders. Sebastianus fell. The position of Valens and his personal guard was no longer secure, and he fled the field. Goth soldiers gave chase and cornered Valens in a nearby farmhouse. The Goths lit the house on fire and kept it surrounded as the eastern emperor met his fiery demise.

The battle was winding down, and Alaric left his perch and snuck under the wagons. If he left the wagons during the battle, he'd be severely beaten, but the Goth line where Theoric was stationed had withstood a heavy charge, and Alaric was eager to see his brother. When the fighting was over and the formations started to break up, Alaric decided to take the risk and sprinted out upon the field. He started to pass men under Theoric's command, and their expressions caused a sinking feeling in his stomach. Then he saw it. A group of stone-faced men carried Theoric's lifeless body on a shield back into the fort.

Alaric didn't cry at first. He felt too numb for grief, like nothing was real. Like it wasn't possible his brother was gone. He knew he must tell his mother but could barely force his body to obey his command.

Once he slowly walked back into the wagon circle, he heard his mother scream, "Alaric!" She rushed toward him. "Don't you every again disobey ..." Her voice trailed off, and her rage vanished when she saw the expression on his face.

"Theoric has fallen," he blurted and finally burst into tears. Alenia's tears came quickly, and she clutched Alaric close. They both sobbed until Alenia noticed Daria had walked up. "Honey," Alenia began to say, but Daria turned and ran back to their tent, burying her face in a blanket and refusing to speak to anyone.

Luca had now arrived and quickly realized what must have happened. She ran in a panic until she found Theoric's body lying lifeless on the ground. She knelt over her dead husband's corpse, burying her face in his chest and weeping piteously.

The Goths had won a historic victory. Two-thirds of the Eastern Roman Army lay dead. But there was no joy in the camp that night. Although the victory was lopsided, the Goths had lost too many to celebrate. Fritigern spent the evening consoling and thanking the families who had lost so much.

The family brought Theoric's body back to the campsite that night. Alaric stood there a long time, looking down at his fallen brother's still face. Alaric began to the feel the great weight of responsibility. He knew what his father would have said. Alaric was a son of the house of Balt, now the only son. He must protect his mother and sister. It wasn't until all had lain down to sleep that he could hold the grief back no longer and sobbed aloud. His mother and sister came to comfort him, and they all cried and held each other as exhaustion overtook them.

Chapter 5

A Hard-Won Peace

On a chilly night late in the winter of 379, Fritigern held counsel to hear word from Father Ulff, who had returned from Constantinople. The leaders exchanged greetings and settled in around a roaring fire. They began the meeting, as had become their custom, with loud grumbling over the evil deeds of Julius, who had seized temporary command of the Eastern Empire after Valens fell. Julius had ordered the massacre of many Goths, including civilians, who had long lived within the Eastern Empire. Even some Goths serving in the Roman army had been slaughtered. After hearing the latest news of the continuing massacre and much discussion of what they would do to Julius if captured, Fritigern invited Father Ulff to speak.

The priest stood and formally spoke. "I bring word that Gratian will now name Theodosius as Augustus of the Eastern Empire."

"Theodosius?" Fritigern asked with great surprise. "The one who commanded the Eastern Army after Adrianople? *He* will accede to the purple?"

"Yes."

"Why him? From where does he come?"

"He was an unlikely choice," Ulff replied. "He is from Hispania—the son of a renowned general. Theodosius served as the governor of Moesia and led a Roman army against the Persians. However, his father fell victim to court intrigue. Theodosius then thought it wise to retire to his estates in Hispania. After Adrianople, the East's need for military leaders brought him out of retirement. His men are very loyal, and Gratian was pressed to choose him. He will now serve with Gratian as co-emperor."

"At least it's not that butcher Julius," Fritigern said while rubbing his beard. "His first task will be to rebuild the Eastern Army."

"Yes. He's set up headquarters in Thessalonica and is recruiting new soldiers. He's drafting farmers and laborers and hiring mercenaries."

The old general scratched his head. "That's an army that may not fight when the time comes."

"Indeed, there are already stories of those who mutilate their own thumbs to evade service. Some try to hide. Theodosius responds harshly to deserters and forces even those who mutilate themselves to serve."

"Then we must make them fear us more than Theodosius," Fritigern observed, and a low murmur of approval came from the group. "And Theodosius must fear us also. If he does, he may find it wiser to just let us live in peace."

The council debated long into the night. Some wanted to attack Theodosius before he could construct a new army.

Saphrax, however, felt there was no need. The Ostrogoth general argued, "The Eastern Empire remains in turmoil. It takes a new Augustus a long time to consolidate power, even among his own court. All the more after such a defeat. Once Theodosius rebuilds his army, he will not want to risk using it, especially if there is no need. We should ride north. We can find a new home, a quiet place far from the politics of Constantinople. By the time Theodosius can fight, he will see that we are no longer a threat. We will be out of sight and out of mind."

The group grew quiet, and only the crack of the fire could be heard. "I do not believe peace will come so easily," Fritigern replied somberly. "If we ride north, we will be too far from Thessalonica or Constantinople for our scouts to inform us of the Romans' movements. We could face a huge army with little warning. And what if Gratian gives aid to his new co-emperor? Riding south keeps us closer to the action—allows us to strike before Theodosius builds a new army we cannot defeat."

The judicious Saphrax remained skeptical. "Being close to the action is exactly what drives the Romans to view our presence as a problem. If we're not pillaging the villas of aristocrats in the emperor's court, if we're not troubling those who pay taxes to the empire, Theodosius will not face pressure to confront us. Left to his own devices, I believe he will find it wiser to simply let us live in peace."

Fritigern didn't wish to offend his old friend and spoke in a kind, measured tone. "Unfortunately, my brother, your plan relies on the benevolence of the Romans. I will not put myself in that position again. The Romans are wealthy beyond imagination, highly organized, and skilled in the art of war. If we give them long enough to prepare, they will build an army that can impose its will upon us. Only by keeping our enemy close can we choose to strike before the danger becomes too great. And only by keeping that power for ourselves can we force the Romans to agree to a peace we can accept."

Throughout the winter, many similar debates were held. There was no anger between the two sides, but Fritigern and Alavivus were not swayed by the Ostrogoth's arguments. The next spring, the Goths split, with the Ostrogoths moving northwest into Illyricum and Pannonia, and the Visigoths moving south into Greece.

A young Goth maiden diligently washed laundry on the stony bank of the broad creek. She heard something on the far bank and looked up quickly. Screaming in terror, she abandoned the clothes and raced back to camp. She screamed as soon as she was close enough for anyone to hear. "A man! A man! There's a naked man across the creek."

Her parents rushed forth. "A naked man?" her father asked incredulously. "Is he armed?"

"I don't think so," she replied breathlessly. "He's so skinny. He looks like a skeleton with flesh."

"Did he seek to harm you?" the mother asked.

"No," the girl responded. "He just stood there. He almost looked lost. I was just so frightened. I ran."

"It's okay, honey." Her mother embraced and consoled her. The father armed himself, as did several other men, and they went to the creek to investigate.

The men returned with a filthy, emaciated man, who could barely walk. He was covered in dirt and wore only a coat one of the men had given him. He was led to a fire, and a woman wrapped a blanket around him. He was very appreciative of the hot stew offered to him, and a bit of life returned to his face after only a few bites.

After giving some time to let him compose himself, the leader said, "I am called Gerad. How are you called?"

"I am called Hamil. I escaped the Huns' captivity." Those in the group began to murmur and look at each other.

"The Huns you say? How close are they?" the leader asked with evident concern.

"You needn't fear. They were camped south of the river when I escaped. They sent warriors across the Danube and will stay there until their riders return." Hamil continued to eat his stew.

The man frowned. "How were you able to come so far?"

"I buried myself under the ground at night for warmth. Fear drove me to do things you wouldn't think possible."

"You're lucky you found us. We do not often venture this far south."

"God has smiled upon me," Hamil said with a broad grin.

"Indeed," the man responded, and the rest made sounds of agreement.

"Are you Athanaric's people?" Hamil asked. "I come to pledge my allegiance."

"Well, then you've come to pledge allegiance to a dead man. Athanaric fell out of favor when the winters in the mountains became harsh and hunger set in. They say he felt guilt over the predicament of our people and sought redemption by riding south to reclaim land we could farm. His intentions were noble, but he rode to his doom."

"Who leads now?"

"Our people are divided. Some follow Odothesius. His people use the protection of the river valley, as Fritigern once did. But they are hard pressed by the Huns, and some say one day they will have to invade the empire. If they do, they will have to overcome strong defenses."

"We follow Radagaisus. We are safe from the Huns in the mountains and come south to the plains in search of food. Life is hard, but one day we will move northwest. We will unite Goths along the way. We will seek to live in peace with the other tribes and remain safe from the Huns. If need be, we can invade the empire from the north, where their defenses are weak. Which path will you choose, Hamil?"

All listened intently to the response. Hamil put down his cup. "Long have I dreamed of an army uniting those like me scattered by the Huns. I would march proudly with Radagaisus." The folks smiled, and he was warmly welcomed to the group.

When word reached Theodosius that the Goths had divided their force and the Visigoths were invading Greece, he moved his new army to confront them. He wanted more time to build and train his army, but Fritigern's action had forced his hand. The two armies met on a sparse, hilly plain in Macedonia. The new Eastern Roman Army was a splendid sight to behold. The soldiers wore the typical crimson cloaks, and the sunlight shone brightly off their polished armor. The Roman formations moved in perfect synchronicity, as Fritigern observed atop his horse on a hill before rows of Visigoth infantry.

Alavivus rode up next to Fritigern. "What do you think, my old friend? Has this army come to fight?"

"That is what I want to know also. They certainly look the part," Fritigern replied while still surveying the Roman formations. "For many, this will be their first battle. Let us see if they have the stomach for it." Fritigern gave orders for his troops to maintain a defensive formation. He wanted to make Theodosius commit to the first move. The Romans, however, drew close and formed their own defensive formation. Each of the two huge armies waited passively for the other to act. Fritigern concluded that Theodosius questioned his hold over his own troops and ordered the reserves to move up and reinforce the right side of the line. The Visigoths then all marched straight forward.

The Germanic mercenaries in the Roman auxiliary were stationed in front of the main line, looking somewhat apprehensive. The regular Roman soldiers were arranged in tight formations. Most were clean-shaven with bald heads or hair trimmed short. The Goths were a more ragged but fiercer-looking group. Some had various pieces of Roman armor, and their cloth was poor. Almost all were bearded with long, unkempt hair, sometimes partially braided. No two looked alike. As the two armies faced off, the Goths began to beat their swords and spears against shields, stomp their feet, and scream furious war cries.

Before the two armies made any contact, many barbarians in the Roman auxiliary began to flee the field, and a few even joined Fritigern's men. At that point, Fritigern signaled the charge, and the Goths advanced quickly. When the two armies finally clashed, the large numbers of Visigoths on the right side of their line overwhelmed the Romans' left flank. As the Visigoths rolled up the Roman flank, the Roman infantry men could see the danger, and many fled the field. Those who didn't faced the difficult choice of giving their lives for a cause that appeared lost or joining the flight themselves. Enough chose survival that the Eastern Roman Army began to simply melt away. Theodosius, recognizing the futility of further combat, cut his losses and ordered a fighting retreat while he still had the ability to do so. The battle had been another clear victory for Fritigern, though Theodosius avoided a rout.

Gratian, hearing of yet another military disaster for the Eastern Empire, moved his army back east and met Theodosius with what was left of the Eastern Army. This combined army was large enough to dissuade Fritigern from another direct confrontation. Small skirmishes were mostly drawn and allowed Fritigern only to avoid disaster and slowly move his army back into Thrace near the lower Danube by the summer of 381.

After two decisive victories over the Eastern Roman Army, the Visigoths were back where they had started. With the immediate crisis averted, Theodosius retreated to Constantinople. Fritigern was now contained, but Gratian could keep the Western Army at the eastern edge of the empire for only so long. A rough military parity had been established. Unable to defeat the Visigoths on the field, the Romans had no choice but to open negotiations with Fritigern.

Fritigern thought the bright crimson tent was made of a material too fine for use as a tent. It was as if the Romans sought to demonstrate their wealth through waste. The smell of incense was strong many paces from the entrance. He and Alavivus were asked to remove their boots before entering. Unlike the Goths' tents with grass or dirt floors, they entered a tent adorned with plush carpets and ornate furniture. Fragrant candles and torches created dramatic lighting. Richomeres and Saturnius invited the two Goths to sit, and all four took seats facing each other in fine wooden chairs with cushioned seats. The Goths feigned indignation the Romans had arranged for a translator.

Saturnius began with an eloquent monologue about how it served the interests of all to have peace, but that would be possible only if certain conditions were met.

Fritigern interrupted, "And what conditions are those?"

"We have a long tradition of incorporating new populations into the empire—a certain way of doing things. An exception was made to save your people from the Huns. There wasn't time to do things properly."

"Valens let only half of us in and then only because he lacked the troops to keep us out," Alavivus shot back.

Richomeres retorted angrily, leaning forward in his seat, "Valens was generous with you and too trusting. He paid for that with his army and his life."

"If you know of Valens's demise, then you also know I sought peace with him," Fritigern said calmly. "Several times. We sought only what we needed to keep our people safe. In return, we offered to become loyal allies. He could have kept his army and his life, and gained a powerful ally."

"And that's what we want to talk to you about now," said Saturnius diplomatically. "We can discuss the past all day, but we now face the future. We too want to reach an agreement all can accept. We understand your people seek peace and prosperity. You can have that. But it must be done, as much as possible, the way we have always brought in new groups."

"You want to split us up into small groups and disperse us throughout the empire," Alavivus said contemptuously. "We won't agree to that. We've beaten the Eastern Roman Army twice, plus several other Roman forces, and we'll do it again if we must. We know what it's like to live under Roman subjugation. We know what it's like to see our people selling children for dog meat, to see Goths in small groups massacred." He had begun angrily, but Alavivus's demeanor now turned calmly resolute as he folded his arms and leaned back in his chair. "Never again will we leave our people at your mercy."

"What you want is an army to breach the peace and start pillaging again whenever you want," Richomeres replied sharply, earning a fierce look from Fritigern.

"So what you want is to stay together?" asked Saturnius, seeking to defuse the tension.

"Yes," Alavivus replied, "and live by our own laws and customs."

"And those laws and customs would be enforced by your own leaders?" the wry politician noted.

"Yes."

"But then you wouldn't really be part of the Roman Empire," Saturnius replied. "You'd be a sovereign state within the empire. *Surely* you understand we can't have an outside group coming into our borders and just taking a piece of our territory. If you want your own country, why don't you go back across the Danube?"

"You know why," Fritigern replied dismissively. "The Huns will be the death of us all if we ignore the threat. We can fight them together and win, or we can fight each other, and the Huns will conquer whatever's left. You know we can be a strong ally."

"Yes, but will you be a *dependable* ally?"

"Are you questioning our honor?" Alavivus demanded.

"I'm not questioning your honor. And I'm not questioning your courage. I'm questioning whether a foreign group with its own laws and leadership can truly be trusted to answer the call when their own interests lie elsewhere." Saturnius leaned forward in his chair and used his hands for emphasis as he calmly spoke. "We need allies who are loyal to the emperor, not their own tribal leaders. And there is another concern also."

Saturnius paused, his tone becoming a bit conspiratorial. "A political concern. Many in the Senate oppose a treaty with you at all. Many senators and citizens take a hard-line view. They think those who have taken up arms against the empire should be vanquished. They think making peace is weakness."

"How is that my problem?" Fritigern asked.

"It's your problem because if we don't reach a deal that I can sell politically, we won't reach a deal at all. Let's not forget you sit with your back to the Danube and the Huns on the other side. The appearances are important, and allowing the general who destroyed the Eastern Army to sit like a king within the empire is not something I can sell."

"I am not a king."

"But you're a leader who has brought your people victory against the empire, and your people clearly follow your command. What's the difference really? Whether you're called a king or not, that's the way you will be perceived."

"So, what do you want from me?"

"I don't have authority to commit to anything now, but I'm wondering if I could get approval for a deal that would allow your people to stay together, where they are now, provided your young men enlist in the Roman army and provided further that all Goth men of fighting age answer the emperor's call. But for that to work, you'd have to agree to step down."

"What do you mean, 'step down'?"

"I mean simply disappear. We don't care what you do, as long as you're no longer the leader of the Visigoths. But that's a critically important term of any agreement, and if it's violated, we would no longer have peace."

"You want me to disappear?"

"Call it what you wish—retirement perhaps. Spend time with your family. Grow old. Whatever you want. But your career as a general—as a leader—must end."

Fritigern and Alavivus asked for privacy to discuss the matter among themselves. They generally agreed Saturnius's proposal was reasonable and wondered how the Romans would even know whether Fritigern had truly "disappeared" from leadership. They were reluctant to make a firm commitment while Saturnius was speaking in hypotheticals, but they indicated conditional interest in the deal he had outlined. It took time for Saturnius to communicate with Constantinople, and Fritigern and Alavivus were well treated during the delay. Additional details were worked out, and the final peace deal was agreed to on October 3, 382.

It was still autumn that year when Fritigern and Alavivus rode with their retainers back into the Visigoth encampments. There was much excitement about the peace but much concern about Fritigern's treatment. Many were insulted. A leader of a large group pledging allegiance to the empire should receive titles and a formal position within the Roman command structure, but the Romans seemed to go out of their way to insult Fritigern. Many saw no need to make peace with the Romans at all—they'd be better off settling disputes on the field. But the old general took a different view. He knew he could still do what was needed behind the scenes. How could the Romans know who participated in their councils? Spies, perhaps, but he understood Saturnius's point. As long as he didn't flaunt a continued role, he should be free to do as he had been, and the Romans wouldn't care. He'd be out of sight and out of mind. And besides, Fritigern was starting to feel his age. It was time for a new generation.

The following spring it was time for the Visigoths to live up to their commitment to provide new recruits for the Roman army. Alaric was then eighteen and would be among those enlisted. He was excited, proud, and terrified. All the young men knew the training would be brutal, but they were proud to serve their people, and Alaric was eager to learn what the Romans had to teach about warfare. As the day of his conscription approached, Alaric was surprised to see Fritigern walk up to his family's encampment.

"Will you walk with me?" Fritigern asked.

As the two walked alone down a dirt path through a meadow toward a small stream, Fritigern spoke somberly. "Long did I know your father and brother—good, loyal, and courageous men. I see the same traits in you." He paused, glancing quickly at Alaric and drawing a deep breath. "You're going to be surrounded by Romans. You'll live with them, eat with them, train with them, even bathe together. There's much you can learn," Fritigern said as he put his hand across Alaric's shoulder. "But be careful you do not become one of them." The two exchanged glances. "The Romans are organized and efficient and prosperous, but many are cruel, and all will see you as an unclean, uncivilized barbarian."

Fritigern paused in thought for a moment and continued, "They will know you come from a noble family. They will see you speak good Latin. That kind of thing matters to them very much. They will look to you to provide leadership. But they will look to Sarus and his brother as well."

"I'm not worried about Sarus," Alaric said.

Fritigern chuckled. "I understand why you feel that way, but I'm not talking about a fight between you and Sarus. I'm talking about what he says to the Romans when you're not there. I'm worried what he might do out of your sight to promote his own ambition."

"What can I do about that?"

"Just keep your eyes and ears open and remember flattery and mutual benefit can be as important as skill with a blade. Alliances are important, even among your own people. Athaulf rides with you, yes?" Allaric nodded. "Good. I think you'll be able to rely upon at least one friend in the Roman army."

With that, their conversation turned to lighter fare as they walked back to camp. "Do you leave a girlfriend behind?" Fritigern asked.

Alaric blushed and said, "No."

"No? A strapping young lad like you? And with so many pretty girls in camp?" Alaric made no response. "Well, watch out for the women who hang around the bathhouses. They—"

Alaric cut him off. "Mother's already told me all about that."

"And you must beware of strong drink."

"Yes, she warned me about that also."

They reached Alaric's camp again, and Fritigern smiled fondly. "Your father would have been very, very proud." He placed his hand on Alaric's shoulder a final time and took his leave.

The young men had packed what they would take, and their horses were ready. But before Alaric left, there was one more goodbye he wanted to say. His sister's best friend had blossomed into a lovely young woman with blonde hair and big, beautiful brown eyes. He found Brechta washing clothes near the creek. She worked with her back toward him as he approached.

When she turned to greet him, he strode up confidently and smiled. "I've come to say goodbye."

"So, you're off now?" she said coyly.

"Yes. We ride shortly."

"You're going to become a Roman general after all?"

"Yes, I shall be Alaricus, *generalissimo*," he replied facetiously. She laughed a bit too hard.

"When you come back, will you have time for a simple Goth girl?" she said with a flirtatious smile.

"I will always have time for you," he said seriously. It was clear what he meant, and Brechta blushed, tucked her hair behind her ear, and looked up at Alaric with wide eyes.

He took a small step toward her, placed one hand gently on her waist and another behind her back, leaned his head toward hers, and pressed his lips softly against hers for a few seconds.

He straightened, and they smiled at each other as Alaric held both of her hands. "Will you wait for me?" he asked.

She paused for a moment, then blurted, "Yes!" with evident emotion and a big smile.

"Yes?"

"Yes!"

He smiled. "I'm going to hold you to that."

"OK," she said, nodding enthusiastically.

"I have to be off now. I'll see you again by winter." They smiled at each other one last time as he slowly backed away.

With a new spring in his step, Alaric strode back into camp and mounted his horse. He received much grief from those who'd been waiting but endured their taunts with a good nature. His thoughts remained of Brechta as the company of young men made their way to report for duty and a new way of life.

Chapter 6

Life in the Roman Army

The young Visigoths reported to a camp not far from the Roman fortress of Novae—one of the great Roman strongholds on the Danube, far upstream for Durostorum. The camp had many buildings, including barracks, packed together tightly and surrounded by a stone wall around the perimeter. Roman soldiers greeted the Visigoths outside the main entrance. A group of older men bearing the insignias of sergeants immediately barked orders.

"You will dismount and lead your horses to the stable hands!" one sergeant yelled loudly.

As the new recruits began to comply, he bellowed, "We don't have all day! When I give you an order, you do it immediately!"

The sergeant was speaking Latin, and Alaric knew many who rode with him wouldn't understand. He translated the sergeant's orders in a low tone. The sergeant immediately took notice. "What are you saying? What did you just say?" the sergeant demanded, walking up very close to Alaric.

Alaric responded in Latin. "Not all these men speak Latin. I translated what you said."

"So, you're a translator, eh? Who else here speaks Latin?"

Alaric calmly identified Athaulf, Sarus, Sergeric, and a few others.

"Fine. You will each be squad leaders, and you will be responsible for making sure that every man in your squad knows exactly what I say. You will each be responsible for making sure all the men in your squad learn Latin."

The sergeant then addressed the group, and Alaric translated. "I am Sergeant Linus. I am your direct superior. You will be divided into squads of eight. I have selected your squad leaders, and each leader will take turns selecting the other members of his squad. Each squad will then report to the quartermaster, who will take your possessions and these ragged, foul-smelling clothes and issue you a proper uniform and equipment kit. You will then report to the clerk, who will enter your names on the rolls. You will form ranks on the mustering field and await further instructions. Do it now!" At that, Linus and the other sergeants and corporals began shouting at the recruits to move quickly.

Linus gathered the squad leaders and, beginning with Alaric, ordered them to each select a member of his squad. Once the squads had formed, their possessions and even clothes were confiscated, and they were ordered to form lines before wooden tables, at which sat clerks who inscribed their names and possessions in large scrolls. The squad leaders then ordered their men to stand in rows in a field near the center of the camp. The Romans inspected their ranks and were clearly displeased.

"You no longer suckle at your mother's tit!" Linus bellowed. "This is not a barbarian army. You are in the Roman army now! You will stand straight. You will form straight lines. You will learn to move as a group—without hesitation, without confusion." He and the other Romans ordered the squads to form two rows of four and stand slightly apart from each other. A group of twenty squads lined up with a gap in the middle.

"Everyone on this side is in my company," Linus announced, indicating the side on which the squads led by Alaric and Athaulf stood. He indicated the other side, on which Sarus and Sergeric stood, and announced that Sergeant Lupis would lead the company.

The two groups separated farther, and the sergeants ordered the men to make various formations. Sometimes they formed groupings of various depths with separations by squad; sometimes they formed ranks irrespective of squad. They practiced forming squares, rectangles, and circular defensive formations. The sergeants never seemed satisfied with the quality of the formations or the speed at which they were formed. Even minor imperfections provoked howls of displeasure. It quickly became apparent no room for error would be tolerated. The drills continued until well after dark, when the exhausted men were finally provided a small meal and led to their barracks. All slept soundly except the miserable few who drew guard duty.

The next morning, the men were awoken before dawn and provided a small amount of goat meat and boiled barley. They formed ranks to hear the orders for the day. Linus introduced the camp's commandant, a

Roman general named Jovius. The commandant came forth surrounded by his honor guard in an elaborate show. The guards wore bright-red tunics and were adorned with medals and helmets, with fancy plumes signifying their importance. Jovius welcomed the men and spoke of their purpose in his camp.

"You come here as raw recruits from the far corners of the empire. We've seen many like you. You come in rags, unwashed, speaking strange tongues, and following barbaric customs. You lack discipline. You lack training. You are nothing more than a group of individuals, each following his own interests." The portly commander took a moment to survey the group. "But that is *not* how you will leave this camp. You will learn discipline. You will learn to use weapons, yes, but more importantly, you will learn to fight as one. You will leave here as Roman soldiers!"

Jovius paused and looked around, as if expecting a cheer. When one didn't come, he continued, "Although you are here to become Roman soldiers, we understand maintaining your own customs is important to you. When you become part of the Roman army, you will serve together in the auxiliary, with your own people and your own officers. Who among you will rise to become officers in your own ranks? Well, that is among the questions we are here to decide. This will be a training ground but also a proving ground. Those of you who show your merit will rise up in the ranks. And one of you will rise to lead the entire company! Your training will be a contest of sorts. Whoever excels above all others will be named company leader."

Alaric and the other Latin speakers had been translating Jovius's speech, and a general murmur spread throughout the ranks when the translation was complete. Jovius continued extolling the virtues of the training the men would receive and took his leave.

Once his formal procession had quit the field, Linus screamed, "Don your gear and form ranks!" When there was no immediate movement after the translation, Linus screamed, "Now!" The men scrambled to comply without need for further translation.

The ranks quickly reformed, and the sergeants berated the men about how long it had taken. They screamed they'd all be dead if they took that long to respond when the camp was under attack. The sergeants led their groups out of the camp one by one, and they began running in full gear and at full speed. An hour went by, and many thought a break must be near. They thought the same thing after the next hour. Many vomited. The sergeants used cudgels to beat any who attempted to stop. It quickly became apparent that stopping was more painful than pushing forward. After the third hour, the sergeants ordered a stop, and all were gasping desperately. Some dropped to their knees.

After only a brief break to catch their breath, the men were ordered to set about the business of building a camp. They were each given various entrenchment tools and assigned particular tasks. Most were required to work on creating a wall of turf around the camp's square perimeter. A trench just inside the wall was dug to serve as a latrine. Rows of tents were put up in the four corners of the square, leaving roads bisecting the square north to south and east to west. Similar to the fort they had come from, the commanding officers' quarters, food storage facilities, and a large meeting area were located near the center. They were all exhausted by the end of the day. Alaric wasn't the only one amazed the whole camp could be built in less than a day. Those who hadn't been selected for guard duty collapsed in their tents at sundown.

Each squad slept in its own tent. Eight men in a single tent sounded crowded, but they were all so exhausted that they slept soundly next to one another. The last two Alaric had selected included two he didn't know. One was called Thuruar. He was an enormous man with red hair. Thuruar identified as neither a Visigoth nor an Ostrogoth; rather, he had been living in Roman territory prior to the Danube crossing, and his parents had joined Fritigern's group after the Goth massacres began. Alaric also selected the smallest of the new recruits, a man named Diminimus.

The recruits were again woken before dawn and were again required to run in full gear until midday. In the afternoon, they received instruction in the proper use of their shields and were called forth to demonstrate their proficiency against attacks by sergeants wielding wooden swords. Linus called Thuruar forth first and immediately began a furious attack. He used overhead swings to induce Thuruar to raise his shield high, at which point Linus stepped deftly to the side and swung his sword low, hitting Thuruar behind the knee and bringing down the large man. Thuruar cried out in pain.

"Be quiet, you big oaf! If this was a real sword, you'd only have half a leg. In a real battle, I wouldn't even bother to kill you. I'd just move on to the next fight while you bled to death."

With a tinge of disgust, Linus ordered Thuruar to limp back in line and engaged his next victim. And so it went. Few of the recruits were able to defend themselves. Linus and the other sergeants were brutal with their wooden swords to drive home the lesson.

Unlike most of the recruits, Alaric, Athaulf, Sarus, Sergeric, and other sons of the Visigoth upper class had already received weapons training. The Goths tended to be taller than the Romans, and Alaric was taller than most Goths. When his time came, Alaric strode forth confidently and grasped his shield with his right hand.

"Ah, a lefty, ay?" Linus remarked. "Very well. Let's see what you can do with it."

Linus came after Alaric with a variety of attacks, but Alaric had little difficulty fending off the blows. His calm demeanor seemed to enrage Linus.

The other groups began to take notice. Lupis, seeing his compatriot struggle, joined the attack, forcing Alaric to defend against two assailants. Linus sought to engage Alaric's full attention with repeated overhand blows, while Lupis circled around to his rear. Alaric quickly moved to his left to step out of their trap and turned to face both as they tried again to outflank him. This, however, caused the space between the two to grow larger, and Alaric seized the opportunity to charge Linus, who again swung overhead. Alaric blocked the blow with his shield and side-kicked Linus's knee, bringing him to the ground. Alaric pivoted quickly, sidestepped Lupis's charge, and tripped him, sending him tumbling into Linus, who struggled to regain his footing. The entire company watched, and low laugher spread among the men.

Enraged by this insolence, Linus and Lupis again charged Alaric. Moving to his left, Alaric fended off Linus's blows, while Lupis was helplessly stuck behind his comrade. Lupis tried again to get behind Alaric, but Alaric repositioned himself to defeat the strategy. After the wild melee had brought both Romans to the point of exhaustion, Linus managed to touch Alaric slightly on the calf and quickly claimed victory. The claim was unconvincing, but Alaric thought better of protesting. The whole company knew what had happened.

Alaric was conspicuously placed on both latrine and guard duty that night. The rest of the men were given time off late that afternoon and milled about the camp, socializing, shooting dice, and wrestling. Sarus used the opportunity to approach Linus, who sat on a barrel away from the other men.

"The only wonder is that it took Alaric so long to show off his arrogance," Sarus said to the sergeant in a low voice.

Linus shot back a sideways glance. "You two are rivals then? I might have known. I take it you must both be from noble houses among your own people?"

Sarus adopted the tone of one trying to be generous. "Alaric's from a remote area. A noble house for that part of the world but …"

"But not as fancy as yours? Well, guess what?" Linus stood and turned to face Sarus. "I don't give a shit where you're from. You're in the Roman army now, and all I care about is that the men under my command fight and win when the time comes. That golden-haired prick may be prettier than half the whores in town, but he knows how to fight—and how to keep his mouth shut. You want to prove how noble your house is? Win on the field."

"Of course … I …," Sarus stammered.

"Go on. Slither off now!"

The training went on week after week. Three- and four-hour runs in full gear were common. They changed locations and built new camps frequently—not out of necessity but just for the value of the repetition. They trained with weapons heavier than normal to make real weapons seem lighter in battle. After three months, they had traveled a great distance but circled back to the fort they had started from.

When they arrived back at Novae, the men were given a half day to relax and enjoy the lack of need to build yet another camp. During announcements the next morning, the troops were advised the time had come for a war game. The men would wear full armor but be armed only with wooden swords and rags dipped in red dye tied around the tip.

Jovius explained the rules.

"You will be divided evenly into two groups. We will select a leader for each group. Boundaries will be marked with red flags, and any who venture beyond the boundaries will be considered slain. Roman soldiers will judge whether any man stained red should be removed from the competition. Any man told to leave the field will do so immediately. The game will end when one side eliminates all the others' men, or I decide the contest has been decided." The Romans selected Alaric and Sarus as team leaders. The Roman general Stilicho, previously unfamiliar with this group of recruits, came to watch.

Sarus won the flip of a coin and was permitted to choose first. He selected one of the camp's more physically gifted recruits, who was given a helmet with a red plume. Alaric selected Athaulf as his first pick, who was then given a helmet with a blue plume. The first few rounds of choices were fairly predictable based on the men's performance in training exercises. However, as the group of the unchosen dwindled, Alaric began making choices based on friendships and loyalty rather than on demonstrated weapons proficiency. Athaulf voiced concern when Alaric chose Diminimus sooner than warranted to save him the indignity of being chosen last. Once the teams were chosen, Sarus exhibited an arrogant smirk, believing he had chosen the superior team.

As they huddled to devise strategy, several bemoaned the physical superiority of the other team. Alaric was undaunted. He already had a strategy in mind and drew lines in the ground with a stick to illustrate his plan. Sarus also huddled with his squad leaders to devise a plan.

Jovius and Stilicho watched the action from atop a wooden tower on the edge of the field. Jovius was a relatively short, balding Roman, who still wore the traditional toga. He was one of the few remaining pagans to hold the title of general. Stilicho was lean and hungry looking, with sharp eyes and an intimidating bearing. His talent was recognized by Theodosius, who had brought him back into a leadership position in the Eastern Army.

Each team formed ranks, facing each other. Alaric's team formed a long line with a supporting line behind the front line on each end but not in the middle. Diminimus and some of the other weaker members were stationed in the center, and Alaric, Athaulf, Thuruar, and six others stood behind the line in the center. Sarus's team made a wedge-shaped formation. Alaric's formation allowed for a longer line but was weak in the center.

As the men formed ranks, Stilicho asked, "Who's this blond fellow?"

"His name is Alaric," Jovius replied. "He's been a standout from this class. Well educated, well trained, respected by the men. He'd likely be the first choice were the men allowed to choose. And yet there's something about him that concerns me."

"What might that be?" Stilicho asked with a sideways glance.

Jovius continued to watch the formations. "He definitely carries the arrogance of youth. That wouldn't concern me so, but I also suspect that, although friendly and likeable, he carries unseen anger and resentment over the treatment of his people."

"He's cocky and loyal to his people. Can you blame him? Yet we must know where his allegiance will lie when the time comes."

"Aye."

"And the other captain?"

"That's Sarus. He and his brother, Sergeric, are from a prominent family. He's also well educated and trained but not so well liked. His team respects him, though, and fears him."

"Well, we need men like that too," Stilicho observed. "And if he feels slighted by his own people, that can be useful as well." Jovius nodded his agreement, and Stilicho gave the sign to begin.

Sarus immediately ordered a charge, and his men sprinted forward with fierce cries. When the wedge hit the center of Alaric's line, Diminimus and those around him gave ground, but their line held. Alaric and Athaulf waited to see where the line looked weak, then charged forward to fill the gaps. At the same time, the longer line allowed those on the ends to outflank and then surround Sarus's team.

"This is starting to look like the battle of Cannae," Stilicho observed. "It seems your fair-haired boy has a nose for strategy."

Alaric's men, who had gotten around the flanks, were able to quickly eliminate many of Sarus's men from behind. As the Romans ordered men off the field, the noose tightened around Sarus. He ordered the rest of his men into a defensive circle, but they were too few at that point, and Alaric's force wore down their outnumbered foe until the circle crumbled and Sarus was eliminated. It had been a rout.

Once the action was done, men on both teams milled about the field, joking and laughing. Alaric warmly embraced men on the opposing team, participating in the good-natured banter. Sarus wasn't amused.

Watching the social interactions from the sidelines, he commented to his brother, "Now he seeks to weaken my leadership with his false good humor. I see his scheme. He seeks to appear gracious in the hope of winning more support when time comes to select a leader. Two can play at that game."

Stilicho also observed Alaric's magnanimity following the clash. Turning to Jovius, he asked, "Have you decided who will lead?"

"Not yet, but Alaric's a clear favorite at this point."

"I would think so," Stilicho replied. "I want you to get to know him better. Invite him to socialize. When he is relaxed, ask about his past. Explore further how he feels about the empire. And do the same with Sarus."

Jovius sent word to Alaric to join him later that afternoon in the officer's bathhouse.

The bathhouse was an impressive stone structure just outside the gates. The path allowed a view of the edge of the town, and women frequently congregated on the outskirts, soliciting business. Alaric hadn't seen any women in many months, and his eye was drawn to several. They were from the south, darker skinned and more exotic than he was used to.

One woman was particularly stunning, and Alaric's gaze fixed on her. She was tall and thin with raven-black hair and large, dark eyes. She'd put something around her eyes—something dark that gave her an even more intriguing look. She seductively beckoned him to come to her, but he was now startled to be at the entrance of the bathhouse.

Alaric entered and disrobed, washing himself with cold water. Once clean, he was provided wooden sandals and led upstairs to a hot, steamy room. There he met Jovius, also naked, who introduced himself and invited Alaric to sit.

"Quite a performance on the field today. Congratulations!"

"Thank you. The victory belongs to the men who fought."

"I saw good men on both sides. Good men get slaughtered when their leaders lack wisdom."

Alaric grunted vague agreement.

"I understand you were a child when your people crossed the Danube."

"Yes."

"And your father was a follower of Fritigern?"

"Yes. He died in the war with the Huns."

"Have you ever met him?"

"Fritigern? Yes."

"You know him well?"

"Not really. We've met a time or two. He spoke at my brother's funeral."

"I'm sorry about your brother. He must have been quite a hero to earn such an honor."

"Yes."

"And you view Fritigern as a great leader, I presume?"

Alaric had grown suspicious of the purpose of these questions and sought to limit the information he provided. "He led us ably from defeat by the Huns. He won a great victory at Adrianople and had the wisdom to negotiate the peace we have now."

"Yes, well, that's really what I want to talk to you about. I can see your loyalty to your people. I respect that. But you're now part of the Roman army. We need leaders whose first loyalty is to the empire."

"I swore allegiance to the empire the day I arrived, and to that I hold."

Jovius didn't react, continuing to stare intently at Alaric, who continued, "My people now live within the empire. We cannot survive the Huns otherwise. If I serve the Roman army loyally, I serve my own people as well."

Jovius seemed more satisfied. "You've done well, son. I will follow your career with great interest. Come with me. I have something for you." Alaric followed Jovius back down to the main level. They used wooden rods to wipe the water from their bodies and began to dress. Jovius bore a small leather purse and produced a few coins, which he gave to Alaric. "Tonight, your company will have its first leave. Venture into town. Leave your cares behind!" Jovius said with a smile and slap on the back.

Alaric thanked the general and began the walk back to the barracks. As he left the building, he saw Sarus going in, who passed him with a sly grin.

The number of women seeking his attention had grown, but he resisted their temptations and made his way back to the barracks. The men had now received their first pay, a few coins of little worth, and were anxious for their leave to commence so they could explore the town for the first time. After dinner, with great excitement, groups of young men began to make their way to the village.

Before they entered, they were greeted by many beautiful women. The one who'd caught his eye earlier approached Alaric, stood very close, and began to gently caress his chest and arms. "I've been waiting for you, handsome," she purred. "You can have Jeda for only two coins."

The smell of her hair was intoxicating and her gentle touch highly arousing. Alaric immediately thought of Brechta. He would rather be with her, of course, but she wasn't here, and this woman was. The logic seemed unassailable. Would anyone even know? Surely his comrades wouldn't betray him. And yet, what of his soul? Was she worth damnation? The question was just, but yet the answer seemed to be yes. She continued her seductive caress, knowing exactly what she was doing.

What of the other men? Alaric thought. *Will they not think that, if I indulge this temptation, it is right for them to as well?*

He began to stammer a polite declination but was cut short as Sarus took the woman by the arm. "Don't waste your time with him," Sarus snarled as he pulled Jeda toward an inn. "He prefers to lay with men." She maintained her eye contact with Alaric for a moment, then shrugged and turned to walk with Sarus.

Alaric stood there, watching his rival walk off with the beautiful woman.

"You're a virtuous man, brother," Athaulf said, walking up from behind and placing his hand on Alaric's shoulder. "But, you know, not all men are so—"

"Go, my friend," Alaric said with a pleasant smile. "I will judge you not."

Athaulf eagerly set off in search of a companion for the evening. Alaric was left with only a small group who either didn't feel the temptation or feared eternal damnation even more. They made their way to a tavern, where Alaric used his additional coin to buy the men a round of wine. They had a weak, sour wine as part of their rations on occasion, but this was much different. Not since a band of Visigoths had returned from looting a Roman villa had Alaric tasted wine of this quality.

The men were mostly drunk as they made their way back to the barracks. Alaric, feeling more than a little loopy, climbed up to the clay-tiled roof and lay down with his hands behind his head. He looked up at the bright stars shining down from a clear sky. His thoughts turned to Brechta. Perhaps she too gazed up at the same sky. He smiled, thinking about the last time he had seen her. Her movements had been so graceful, so calm—such a contrast to the rough belligerence of the men who constantly surrounded him. Her gentle femininity was worth even the sacrifice of the village temptresses, who had sought his coin.

But his thoughts turned dark also. Would Brechta wait for him? Why should she? She couldn't know whether he would even return. And she was surrounded by many men, who would seek her favor. Men too old to be drafted would covet such a lovely, young wife. The men her own age were still too young for conscription. As the wine began to wear off, Alaric became tired and grumpy.

Climbing into his bunk, he thought, *She will have many suitors. I was a fool to turn down the woman in the village. The men now think me a prude, and I denied myself my own desires for a woman likely now betrothed to another.*

Chapter 7

Reunited

Most afternoons, Brechta tended a garden along the road leading into the camp. Following the harvest, some whispered questions about the reason for her toil. Before sundown, she usually walked down to the river to meet Daria, who finished her job of washing clothes for hire when the sun set. The two friends walked back to the encampment of Brechta's family. Daria had moved the wagons of her family close by. After greeting the family, the girls walked over to the privacy of Daria's small camp.

"How much longer are you going to pretend to garden a fallow field?" Daria asked.

"I'm not!" Brechta protested with obviously false indignation. "I'm just preparing for the spring."

"Winter has yet to come. I know why you watch the road."

Brechta looked down.

"Don't worry. I won't say anything," Daria reassured her friend. "But you should know people are starting to talk. We all look for their return."

Brechta looked up sheepishly. "Is it that obvious?"

"Yes!" Daria said with a laugh. "You will not see them that much sooner. Everyone will know when they arrive!"

"I look to their return for you as well," Brechta said sadly.

"I know. I try not to think about it too much. I can't wait for his return, but I dread having to tell him."

"You shouldn't have to. It should be someone else. I'll do it!"

"I would see you have a happier greeting with him. It should be me."

"Once he's back, you won't have to be afraid anymore," Brechta offered.

"If he arrives soon. The old man calls daily. He tells others a young woman shouldn't live alone—that my mother's possessions don't belong to me. And he is not alone."

"My father will protect you. He will keep the hungry wolves at bay."

"Thank you, my sweet friend. Your father is a good man. But he can fend off the vultures only so long. The truth is, I would watch the road with you all day, if it wouldn't just make more talk."

"Do not despair," Brechta said. "The days grow short and the nights cold. Soon they will come!"

Winter began, and Brechta had ceased her vigil. Instead, she helped her friend with the laundry and avoided others in the camp. Callers sought her attention as well. Her father wouldn't say to whom he might offer her hand. She had the support of her mother, but she could only hope her father knew her heart and wouldn't condemn her to a miserable marriage. They were finishing their work late in the day when they heard an unmistakable sound. A host of riders approached. The two friends smiled gleefully at each other, dropped their baskets, and raced to the wagons.

Now that the moment she had longed for had finally arrived, Brechta became afraid. She lingered on the fringes as Daria rushed to find her brother. Brechta peeked around one of the tents. She saw Alaric embracing his sister and spinning her around. He looked as if life in the Roman army had suited him. He must have been well fed—he was even more muscular than when he'd left. She felt ashamed of her cowardice as she lurked on the fringes, watching Alaric and his sister make their way back to Daria's camp; she was too afraid to make her own greeting.

She watched from a distance as the two siblings sat on stools outside Daria's tent. Alaric wept and buried his face in his hands. Brechta couldn't hear the words but knew Daria had just told him of their mother's passing. She wanted to go to him to give him comfort, but now wasn't the time. Then, as the siblings continued to talk, she saw Alaric grow very angry. He walked over to Brechta's family's camp and exchanged angry words with her father. He then stormed off. Now was definitely not a good time for the reunion she'd dreamed of.

When she returned home, her father ordered her in the tent and refused to speak of his business with Alaric. It wasn't until the next morning that she saw her friend by the river.

"Are you all right?" she asked gently.

"Yes," Daria replied with a soft smile. "Alaric was very angry. Still is."

"About what?"

"About how our mother was treated. About suitors calling on me without his permission. About our family's servants abandoning me after Mother's death. About the men saying I own no possessions and must be wed."

"Will they listen to him?"

"I don't think they'll have a choice. The Romans made him captain of his company. He's now an officer and may rise further next season."

"Well, that's good, isn't it?"

"Yes. But he thinks I must wed before he leaves next."

"Who?"

"I wish I knew! I don't think he's decided yet."

"Where's he now?"

"Probably still arguing with the elders. He'll be back at our camp soon. Come. We should go and be there when he returns."

Brechta's eyes grew wide with excitement. "What about the laundry?"

"It will still be here when we get back!" They laughed and ran off, hand in hand.

When Alaric returned to camp, Daria and Brechta were seated on stools around the firepit.

"Brother, you remember my friend Brechta?"

"Yes, of course," Alaric responded, gazing into Brechta's eyes. "I've thought of you often."

Brechta blushed and looked at the ground. Desperate for something to say, she finally blurted out, "Are you a general yet?" No sooner had the words left her mouth than she realized how silly they sounded.

"Not quite. Maybe next season," he replied with a wink. He then proceeded to tell the girls tales of his time in the army, and they shared stories of life in the camp since he'd left. They laughed and enjoyed the conversation until Athaulf came striding up.

"Ah, you ladies remember my friend Athaulf," Alaric declared. Athaulf smiled broadly as he joined the group. They chatted casually, and Alaric made a point of extolling Athaulf's valiant deeds in the army. On her mother's plates, Daria served some aged cheese she'd been saving. Alaric produced a flask of wine, and Brechta drank from his cup out of fear of being seen by her father. After a time, Alaric invited Brechta to join him on a walk by the river. Athaulf remained and chatted with Daria.

As the winter wore on, Alaric built a much-improved campsite for his sister. Those who had served their parents now helped construct a proper camp. One evening, as the siblings prepared for sleep, Alaric asked his sister, "What do you think of Athaulf?"

"He's nice. He's been a loyal friend to you. Why do you ask?"

"I mean, what do you think of *him*?"

"As?"

"As a husband."

"Are you asking me if I want to marry him?"

"Yes."

"I'd be honored, brother, but they will say I'm too young."

"Too young to wed now, perhaps, but not too young to be betrothed. If you are promised to Athaulf, no one else will seek your hand. I think it would be a good match. And you could marry after the next campaign season."

"Well, if that's your decision."

Alaric scowled. "I'm not your father. I'm asking you."

Daria smiled and began to cry.

"Why do you weep, sister?"

"I'm sorry … it's just … I'm happy."

"You cry because you're happy?"

She nodded as Alaric gazed on her with a puzzled look. "Yes." She wiped tears away and forced a smile. "I'm fine."

"There's still a little wine, if you need to calm your nerves."

"No, I'm fine," she insisted. After a pause, she asked, "And what of you, brother?"

"What of me?"

"Will you not wed also?"

"Who do you think I should wed?"

"Whoever you want. I'm sure you can have your pick."

"Hum," Alaric huffed. "A difficult decision."

Daria stared at her brother, then flared her eyes and bobbled her head. "Are you really that dense?"

"You question my wit?" he asked with a laugh.

"No. I question your … whether you think of anything beyond army formations and horses and weapons."

"Those are all things we need to survive."

"I understand, but they are not all we need to live our lives." She paused and continued to cast an exasperated look at her brother. "How can you not know?"

"Know what?"

"That Brechta is totally, completely in love with you."

"Brechta loves me?" Alaric asked with a smile, beginning to blush.

"Yes, she's been infatuated with you since we were children. She's looked for your return since the harvest."

Alaric turned toward his sister and grasped her hand, growing serious. "I have thought of her every day since I left."

"Then what are you waiting for?"

"Her father won't consent. She's too young."

"She's almost as old as me! By the time you return next, she'll be just a bit younger than me when I wed."

"Still, her father will not agree. He will—"

"Are you afraid?"

"I do not fear Brechta's father!" Alaric declared.

"Shh." Daria frowned as she put a finger to her lips, glancing sideways at the next camp.

Alaric composed himself. "Very well. I shall speak to him in the morning."

Daria beamed and giggled.

"You're very proud of yourself, aren't you?"

"Oh yes." She smirked. They both laughed and continued to talk until late into the night.

Brechta was surprised to see Alaric at her camp after breakfast the next morning.

"Hello! What brings you here?" she asked coyly as she began playing with her hair.

"I've come to speak with your father," Alaric announced in a surprisingly formal tone.

"Oh, I shall fetch him." Brechta disappeared and returned with her father, a gruff old man with a dingy gray beard and a bald crown.

"Yes, what is it, boy? What business have you with me?"

"Will you walk with me, sir?"

The father didn't respond but began walking with Alaric, who spoke at length about his gratitude for the protection provided to his sister during his absence. "I was wrong to speak harshly with you. I was angry but should have checked my temper until I knew the truth. I am sorry."

The man glanced sideways at Alaric and said, "Well, my boy, no one likes to be barked at, but I understand how you feel. I too was upset when I learned Daria had to dig your mother's grave herself. Alenia helped so many, and yet when illness began to take her, few offered aid. I would have been angry also had I returned to such news. Think no more of it."

"Thank you," Alaric replied and started to stammer something else.

He began to trip over his words, and Brechta's father interrupted. "Well, what is it, boy? What is it you seek?"

"I ... I seek your daughter's hand."

The father rolled his eyes. "Half the men in this camp seek her hand. I'll tell you what I told them—she's not yet old enough."

"I do not seek to marry her now but when I return next. Will she not be old enough by then?"

"Well, yes, but do you expect her to wait for a return that may never come?"

"If she would ... if you will ..."

"You expect me to believe you would remain chaste while you gallivant around the empire? I know what goes on around those forts. The brothels ..."

"No ... sir ... please. I will be true. I give my word."

The father stopped walking and wiped the entirety of his face with his hand. "I've watched you since you were a boy," he said. "I knew your mother. Your father too. If you're half as honorable as them ... then ..."

Alaric raised his eyebrows and leaned forward. "Then?"

"Then, yes. You may marry my daughter but only when you return. *If* you return."

Alaric beamed with joy and lavished the old man with elaborate promises of his virtuous intent.

Daria was waiting to inform her brother that Fritigern's messenger had summoned him to a meeting. Alaric quickly prepared to depart, and Brechta's father pulled her aside for a private chat. He gruffly said only that she was to marry Alaric in a little more than one year hence. She suppressed her joy and waited for an opportune time to sneak off to Daria's camp once Alaric had left to join Fritigern's council. Alone together, the two friends squealed in excitement.

Alaric alone had been summoned, but he asked Athaulf and a few other men to join him and remain just outside the council. Fritigern looked like he'd aged more than just a year. His beard was grayer and his face careworn. The two embraced as old friends, and Fritigern was anxious to hear Alaric's tales of life in the army. They walked and talked for a long time before Fritigern took his leave to greet the other guests at his council.

As usual, the meeting was held around a campfire, with the men seated on benches around the firepit.

Fritigern rose and spoke first. "Welcome, my friends, and welcome to our sons, who return from their first year in the Roman army!"

A murmur of general approval rose from the older men.

"We are blessed by their service and their safe return. But we continue to send more and more of our young men to serve, and I become troubled by how the Romans will use their new recruits. We have word the villain Maximus, who profited from our hunger, now leads a rebellion in Britannia and Gaul. The emperor Gratian is slain—murdered in his own home. The pretender Maximus now calls himself Augustus. Will Theodosius seek to avenge Gratian's death? Will our people be caught in the middle of a Roman civil war? Father Ulff rides to us from Constantinople with tidings. I ask that he now share his wisdom."

The priest rose. "Thank you. I do not know the emperor's mind, but many in his court believe he will sue for peace if he can. He fears war with Maximus will leave the East too weak to defend against foreign threats. Gratian had fallen out of favor with many Romans. They say he showed preference for barbarians over native Romans. He was likely murdered by guards angry that foreign soldiers were being promoted over natives of Italia.

"The rightful heir to the Western Empire is Gratian's younger brother, Valentinian II, who is still a child. Now does not appear an opportune time for a civil war so that a child can be called Augustus. Many expect Theodosius to mobilize forces to check Maximus's ambition, but few see him waging a full war to oust the usurper."

Ulff took his seat, and Fritigern rose again. "These are good tidings, but if war does come, you can be sure Theodosius will put our men on the front lines."

"I think he will wait," Alaric declared. The other members of the council looked at him, surprised such a young man would speak.

After a pause, Fritigern frowned and asked, "And why do you think that?"

"It is as Father Ulff says, and also Theodosius has now but one crop of Goth recruits. Next year that number will double and more the year after and the year after that. All the while the earliest recruits become better trained, more seasoned in the Romans' ways. In a few years, Valentinian will be a more suitable age, and Theodosius's hand will be strengthened."

"Boy, you know not of which you speak," said Cniva. "You should learn to trust the wisdom of you elders and learn your place. I will not have my sons sacrificed in some Roman power struggle. We should refuse to fight in this civil war."

"And break the peace?" Alaric shot back, rising to his feet. "What happens then when the two halves of the empire are again united? When we again face both the Western and Eastern Armies? Better to maintain allegiance to half the empire than confront the whole."

Cniva also rose. "Boy, you are too young to understand how ridiculous you sound."

Alaric began walking toward Cniva.

"Being made captain has given you delusions of grandeur," the old man sneered.

Alaric swiftly drew his sword and pointed it at Cniva's neck. No one moved.

"Call me 'boy' one more time," Alaric said.

"What?"

Cniva's guards and Alaric's men had all now drawn swords, and Fritigern bellowed for peace.

"Call me 'boy' one more time," Alaric repeated.

"Alaric! Lower your sword! Now!" Fritigern demanded as the two groups of guards drew close. Alaric stared at Cniva for another moment, then complied, showing no emotion.

"Everyone will sheath their weapons and sit back down! I have brought you here for a council, not a bloodbath." Fritigern calmed himself. "Will we turn on each other just as the Romans weaken themselves?"

Walking toward Alaric and pointing, he barked, "Alaric, you ever draw a sword again at one of my councils, and I promise it will be your last." Fritigern returned to his seat and said over his shoulder, "Cniva, stop being such a pompous ass."

A low, suppressed chuckle spread among the group. Fritigern turned the conversation to more mundane governance issues, and Alaric remained silent. The council eventually dissolved, and Fritigern bade Alaric to remain.

"Son, I don't expect you to remain silent at a council, but my God!"

"I'm sorry. He … I … he provoked me."

"Well, you're going to have to learn to pick your battles. Cniva is the wealthiest among us. His family is one of the most prominent." Fritigern sighed. "Look, I know you don't care about his family, but many are in his debt. You're becoming a leader, but that doesn't mean just glory on the battlefield. To lead, often you must learn to accommodate even those you don't respect. And you must think how the others will perceive such a display."

"How will they?"

Fritigern sighed again. "Many will think you rash and reckless. Others will see strength and courage."

"What do *you* see?"

The old general paused for a moment. "I see both. What you did was reckless. What would you have done had blood been spilled? Were his insults really worth turning us against each other?" Fritigern allowed the question to hang in the air before he continued. "I see in you much potential, but courage alone is not enough. You must also learn wisdom." The two sat in silence for a moment, until Fritigern spoke again. "Go, my friend, and cool your temper. And *if* I summon you for another council, leave your sword behind."

As winter drew to a close, Alaric prepared to report back for duty. His engagement to Brechta and Athaulf's engagement to Daria were well known. The time apart would be difficult.

Chapter 8

Oaths Fulfilled

They waited until the last minute to leave their families, then rode hard for Novae. They now had coin for accommodation and no longer slept beside the road. Their arrival was a decidedly less hostile reception than they had received as raw recruits. After settling into their barracks, the men milled about leisurely. Athaulf and Alaric made their way to the gates to watch the new recruits streaming in. The pair stood at the top of the wall, leaning over the edge and watching the scene unfold.

"My God, please tell me I didn't look that scared," Athaulf asked, pointing at an awkward-looking young man.

"I'm afraid we all did, brother. Well, maybe not that one," Alaric replied, indicating a particularly ashen-faced new recruit. They laughed, and Athaulf began to ridicule a newcomer with a particularly prominent nose. "Wait, that's my cousin," Alaric said, growing more serious.

"Your cousin? He looks nothing like you," Athaulf replied with evident surprise.

"That side of the family does tend toward unfortunate appearances. It's mostly the nose, I think." The two friends chuckled. "But they also tend to have the virtuous qualities that matter most. This man is called Wallia. I think he'll make quite a soldier—once he gets that panicked look off his face."

They continued to laugh but stopped abruptly and snapped to attention at the appearance of Jovius. He returned their salutes and ordered Alaric to walk with him.

"I trust you enjoyed your time with your people?"

"Yes, sir. Very much. And you?"

Jovius ignored the question. "We don't have much time. You've heard of Maximus's usurpation, no doubt."

"Yes, but I don't know very much."

"You need only know that war is a possibility, and we need to prepare. You will lead your company to Viminacium. There you will train with the cavalry. If the Goths are to honor their oaths in this fight, you must be able to get to the action quickly."

"Then why another fortress on the Danube?"

"From there you can march west or be transported by barge south into Dardania and then ride to Doclea. Ships can then carry you anywhere in the Adriatic. I'll give you tomorrow to prepare. You ride at dawn the day after."

Theodosius sat on his throne in the palace in Constantinople as he received word from messengers who had sailed from Italia.

"Augustus, General Bauto sends word that his force stopped Maximus in Italia. Maximus declined to engage. The two armies now face one another. The young emperor Valentinian remains safe. Bauto awaits your command."

Theodosius dismissed the messenger and summoned his council.

As was his custom, Saturnius was eager to speak first. "Augustus, the fact that Maximus declines to engage implies a desire to negotiate. We should—"

"It implies only that Maximus surveyed the field and didn't like what he saw before him," Stilicho interjected. "This is the man who has slain Gratian and named himself—"

"No one defends his actions," Saturnius interrupted, "but the question is, what is to be done now? We must consider the risks. What if Bauto is defeated?"

"What if Bauto stands on the verge of a victory you have not the courage to seize?"

Theodosius lifted both hands with irritation. "Your bickering serves me poorly. I will hear from Saturnius first and then you, Stilicho."

Saturnius cleared his throat. "We should propose a peace with Maximus that allows him to claim Britannia and Gaul. In return, he will recognize young Valentinian II as Augustus in Italy, Hispania, Pannonia, and Africa. The crisis will be averted for now, and our strength grows as Valentinian enters manhood and we integrate our new Gothic allies into the army."

Theodosius turned to Stilicho, who stepped forward and spoke forcefully. "He's talking about giving half the Western Empire to a usurper. What message does that send to other would-be pretenders? Can anyone lead a rebellion and claim their piece of the empire?" Stilicho looked directly at the emperor. "Even if you do not order Bauto to attack now, he must stand his ground while we muster reinforcements. We can call upon all Goth men to serve as an army. We needn't wait to train new recruits. The longer Maximus is allowed to call himself Augustus, the more people will wonder why it should not remain so. Time is against us."

Saturnius spoke as soon as Stilicho paused. "The general speaks of noble ideals, but I speak of practical realities. If a deal is possible, it will buy us time to prepare for a definite victory. If Maximus is content with Britannia and Gaul, the full strength of the rest of the empire will bring him to heel in time."

Theodosius announced his decision. "As usual, my friends, you both speak wisdom. Stilicho, I am no happier of this than you, but we must think of what is possible. It is too much a risk to retake Gaul and Britannia now. We should recognize reality and use it to bargain assurances from Maximus—for whatever those are worth. Stilicho, I want you to lead our efforts to build an army to overwhelm Maximus. We will bide our time, but when the moment is right, we will bring justice to him."

The fortress at Viminacium was even more impressive than Novae. It was a huge complex that housed an entire legion. Embedded in the higher stone walls were periodic guard towers standing above the landscape, with narrow windows too high to be reached by arrows. The surrounding town was also much bigger. The large metropolitan center became known as Belgrade, whose citizens came from many places within the empire and beyond.

The cavalry training was hard but not nearly as intense as the infantry training. Alaric was formally made centurion and selected Athaulf as his optio. By the end of their training, Sarus also was elevated to centurion, although still junior to Alaric. As new Gothic recruits continued to arrive, their numbers grew beyond even what the large fortress could handle, and centuries were dispatched to marching camps farther south.

Late in the summer, Jovius arrived to inspect the troops. After an elaborate formal parade, the general summoned Alaric to his quarters. Sitting at a table laden with fruit in a stone courtyard, Jovius greeted Alaric and asked him to sit. The day was bright and mild with a gentle breeze.

"Good to see you, my boy," Jovius said with a friendly smile. "Please, eat." Jovius summoned a young, olive-skinned woman and grasped her by the arm when she arrived. "My dear, bring us some of the smoked fish and," he said, turning to Alaric, "would you care for some wine?"

"Yes, please."

The young woman smiled at Alaric before she left. "Well, Alaric, I'm glad you're joining me. I just don't trust men who don't drink. It's as if they don't trust themselves." Alaric smiled, not knowing what to say. Jovius poured the wine.

"Umm! Good this," Alaric said with conviction.

"Yes, one of my favorites. Not like that watered-down swill they serve you men. Have you ever had any proper wine?"

"Well, yes. I had a fine cup last year."

"Pillaged from a Roman villa, no doubt!"

Alaric didn't know how to respond, then opted for candor. "Oh yes, no doubt at all."

Jovius burst out laughing. "Ha! I do like you! Honesty. That's what I'm talking about—and a sense of humor." He took another sip.

The woman returned with the food and looked mostly at Alaric as she served the plates and poured more wine.

As soon as she left, Jovius leaned forward and said in a low, conspiratorial tone, "I think she likes you." Alaric blushed. The old general continued, "You know I could arrange for you—"

"Oh no," Alaric protested. "That's very kind, but no, I am betrothed."

"No? Youth really is wasted on the young," Jovius said wistfully. "Very well. I was told you're an honorable man, which is good—to an extent. But about your wedding. I'm told you've requested leave this winter."

"Yes, I wish to return home for my wedding and—"

"You know war with Maximus may come at any time. I can't have centurions gone if we're called upon. Although I do want to help you, and if you trust your optio to serve in your stead, I think we could arrange—"

"Actually, I also sought leave for my optio. He's—"

"Well, I certainly can't have a century with no leader!"

"I understand, but we needn't be gone all winter or at the same time."

"Why don't you just order your optio to stay?"

"He is to wed also—my sister."

"Ah, I see. Well, that is difficult. But I still can't have you both gone. Sends a bad message. I'll grant leave for one of the two of you but not both. You choose. And if you change your mind about the girl …" Jovius raised his eyebrows and poured more wine.

Alaric agonized for days over writing letters to Brechta and Daria. He felt he lacked the skill to express his love and disappointment. The words couldn't be beaten into submission. He couldn't intimidate or outflank them.

He was the only family member Daria had left, other than her aunt. Now she would stand alone at her own wedding. Would she be angry? Would she understand his sacrifice? Would Brechta continue to wait for him? His anguish was only somewhat lessened when he finally completed the arduous task and entrusted the letters to Athaulf.

Although his decision weighed heavy on his heart, remaining in the camp carried clear benefits for his career. The men respected his sacrifice and his loyalty. He spent many long hours that winter socializing with the troops, sharing stories, and making many new friends. He formed alliances with many of the other Goth centurions, including a particularly brash fellow called Gainas, whose family had long lived in the empire. Gainas had spent much time in Constantinople, and Alaric never tired of hearing his tales of the magnificent city.

Alaric also benefited from the time he spent with Roman officers, attending many feasts at Jovius's invitation. He realized he had become adept at navigating Jovius's guests. The Romans were easily flattered, and he checked his temper at their arrogance.

His thoughts turned to his mother. Much had he scoffed at her rigid insistence on table manners. Many times had he cursed her demands that he master the nuances of Latin. Not anymore.

The separation was also difficult for Brechta and Daria. Brechta was unable to hold back bitter tears when she heard that Alaric wouldn't return again for another year. Daria wasn't angry but still sad she would have no immediate family at her wedding. Both sought to suppress their sadness and instead celebrate Daria's marriage to Athaulf.

When the wedding day arrived, Brechta spent the morning helping her friend prepare. She was brushing Daria's hair when the two were surprised by the sounds of many riders approaching.

Fritigern rode into her encampment with his guard. He had brought a beautiful, young filly, which he offered to Daria as a wedding gift. He and his guard then escorted her to the ceremony. The riders formed a square with the young bride riding bareback in the center. They cantered dramatically into the meadow in which the ceremony was to take place. As they arrived, the riders broke off, revealing Daria astride her beautiful filly. Fritigern helped the bride dismount and walked her to Father Ulff.

Many had come. Daria wore a long, white, sleeveless dress bound at the top of the shoulders by bronze hoops. Some of the older women thought it immodest that her dress barely covered her knees. The bride's hair was worn in elaborate braids and adorned with beautiful white wildflowers. Daria's eyes grew wide in amazement as Athaulf appeared with the first clean shave he had ever had—his long, brown hair pulled back in a neat ponytail. Strange, it seemed, that she'd never realized how handsome he was.

Father Ulff presided, and few understood the Latin. But the gist was clear enough. As the ceremony drew to a close, Ulff loosely wrapped a silk ribbon around their joined hands, declaring in the Goth tongue that their marriage was complete.

After the nuptials, Athaulf's family procured a barrel of mead and invited the guests to a feast to celebrate. They roasted a pig, and Fritigern had casks of wine brought in. Occasions for joy were rare, and the group celebrated until well into the evening. The young couple spent their first night together in a wooden structure Brechta's father had constructed. Just a single room with a dirt floor, but it seemed almost lavish to a couple so accustomed to sleeping in tents.

Brechta had the letter Alaric wrote read to her so many times that she was almost able to read it herself. She kept it among her most prized possessions. There was much she wished to convey to Alaric, but she couldn't write. Father Ulff agreed to take her dictation, but his presence constrained her ability to truly speak from the heart. Still, she took comfort in knowing he would soon have her letter and know that she prayed each day for his safe return.

As the following year progressed, it seemed the peace with Maximus was likely taking hold. Alaric's dedication was rewarded with a promotion to First Centurion, and he was reassigned back to the fortress at Novae.

By spring, all the Goths were granted leave, but the regular Roman troops were not. Strange, he thought it was, that they should all be released at the beginning of the season. Even though the peace with Maximus likely meant a reduced need for troops, why would the Goths all be released rather than continue training? It weighed on Alaric's mind that he didn't know the answer but was overjoyed to be going home.

When he rode unannounced into the camp, his arrival created a great commotion, and Brechta dropped the basket she carried when she saw his approach. He rode directly to her, deftly swung down from his horse before it had fully stopped, and strode toward her. She leaped into his arms. They kissed passionately, and those around them forgave the immodesty in light of the circumstances. The young couple resolved to wed as soon as possible.

After the ceremony, Alaric and Brechta received many well-wishers in a large meadow. The gathering was even larger than Daria's wedding. The families provided food and drink for the festive occasion, and the new couple was occupied by handshakes, hugs, and greetings. Once Alaric felt like they had greeted all, he snuck up to his bride, whispered in her ear, and led her away by the arm.

"Where are you taking me?" Brechta asked with happy curiosity.

"You'll see." Alaric led her far from the camp to a small glade near a babbling brook. He had chosen this spot with great care and laid thick animal skins and woven blankets on the soft ground. The perimeter of their bedding was adorned with wildflowers. The night was warm and clear, and the bright starlight of the galaxy's center shone straight overhead. The fresh smell of spring was heavy in the warm, gentle breeze.

He led her into the glade by the hand, and she looked around, her eyes wide with wonder. "What is this place?" she asked softly.

He faced her, holding both hands, and looked down into her wide, beautiful eyes. "I wanted to spend one night alone with just you. Away from the camp. Away from the screams of the children and the smells of the beasts."

Brechta laughed sharply and buried her face in Alaric's chest. She drew back a couple of small steps. Maintaining her gaze with Alaric, she slipped her dress slowly off each shoulder, letting it drop to her feet. The soft starlight flattered her curves, and she sank down gracefully onto the blankets, smiling seductively as she beckoned Alaric to join her. He disrobed also. Long years in the Roman army had left him lean and muscular. He lay down and embraced his new wife. They rejoiced in each other throughout the night. Only at first light did it occur to them to dress and rejoin the group.

Brechta blushed and cast her eyes downward as they reentered the camp. The newlyweds endured much good-natured teasing. Athaulf joked he was about to send out a search party. The new couple returned to their camp and began married life together.

Alaric and his men were summoned back to Novae during the summer. No explanation was given as to why they were released and now called back. The fortress was lightly manned and rife with rumors of troops transferred to Durostorum because of heavy fighting along the lower Danube. Roman officers refused to speak of the matter. Alaric knew it must concern the Goths who remained east of the river.

When finally a company returned from Durostorum, Alaric and Athaulf took leave to visit a tavern in town and looked around for a Roman drunk enough to have loose lips. They had many options. The tavern was dark and dramatically lit by torches and a fire that reflected only dimly off the stone walls. The darkness created a private feel, and the pair soon spotted a particularly drunk soldier drinking at a table alone. They cheerfully introduced themselves and offered to buy the returning hero a drink.

They kept his glass full and cheered on his tales until Alaric asked, "You have seen much, my friend, but I hear few know of the recent fighting along the lower Danube.

"Few Gothss know!" he slurred. "And for good reason. I was there. I know everything," he said with an exaggerated swing of his arm. "They don't want to tell you because ... well ... you're Gothss!" The man seemed to lose his train of thought.

"The Goths east of the river tried to cross," Alaric offered.

"Yes, yes. You know there's still Goths east of the river?"

"Yes, they follow Odothesius and shelter from the Huns in the river valley, correct?" Alaric urged.

"Not anymore," the man said, beginning to hiccup. "They tried to crosss, and Odothesius fell. Total ... total bloodbath." He began to sway and continued to hiccup. "They didn't want to tell you because ... well, because they're Gothss and you're Gothss. They didn't want Gothss in the fortresses while other Gothss tried to invade."

Alaric and Athaulf feigned indignation. "We are Roman soldiers!" Athaulf declared proudly. "We swore the oath!"

"I know. I know. Just what I heard. Some people don't like Gothss. Not me. I like Gothss just fine." He smiled, and the pair nodded and smiled reassuringly.

"What of the civilians?" Alaric ventured.

"They didn't try to cross. No. But ... but ..."

"But they're now at the mercy of the Huns."

The man pointed at Alaric. "Exactly right. That's exactly right."

"Did they stay on the banks of the river?"

"No ... no ... they moved upstream, northwest. They're trying to get to ... to ... His name is ..." The man began to look around as if searching for the name.

"Radagaisus?"

"Yes!" he said with the snap of his fingers. "That's it."

"Radagaisus still holds the mountains?"

"And the lowlands to the northwest. They're creeping, always creeping north and west. And they're being chased by ... by ..."

"The Huns," Alaric stated flatly, amazed this man could still function at all.

"Yes, yes, by the Huns."

Athaulf smiled broadly and cheerfully offered to buy the man another drink. Alaric elbowed his friend in the ribs, got the man some water, and walked him back to the barracks.

Leave was allowed again that winter, and Alaric was eager to return home. He'd received word from Brechta and rushed to make it home before she gave birth. Before spring had come, the couple rejoiced in a beautiful baby girl. Alaric proudly displayed the new baby around the camp, and many well-wishers came by to express their congratulations and admire the child. They named her Alonia in honor of Alaric's mother.

By the spring of 387, Alaric was ordered to lead his men to Viminacium. From there, they made preparations to march west but weren't told the reason. Twenty-two years had now passed since Alaric's birth, and Brechta was pregnant with their second child.

As they awaited the order to march, Alaric was much surprised by word that Father Ulff was in the city and wished to speak. Alaric made his way down cobblestone streets to the cathedral near the city's center and warmly greeted the priest just outside the grand entrance.

"It's good to see you, my son," Ulff said, grinning. "How are you?"

"I am well and glad to see you also," Alaric replied, begging to walk with the priest. "I must say I was surprised you'd come. What business brings you to Viminacium?"

"I come from Constantinople. I want to speak with your privately. Come, let us pray together." Ulff led Alaric into the dark but beautiful sanctuary, and they lit candles and knelt before the altar. The scent of incense was heavy in the air. An old woman kneeled in the back pew, praying silently, and a group of monks chanted repetitively in Latin, rocking back and forth. Otherwise, they were alone. Kneeling beside each other in the front pew, Ulff began to speak their native tongue in hushed tones as they both looked toward the altar. "The court in Constantinople buzzes with rumor. War is upon us."

"What happened?" Alaric asked.

"Maximus invaded Italy. He crossed the Alps under the pretense of reinforcing the Rhaetian frontier. He then treacherously turned his march south to Milan. Young Valentinian and his mother, Justina, fled to the fortress of Aquileia and escaped by ship to Thessalonica."

"Did the army of Italia not defend Valentinian?" Alaric asked. "Was there some treachery?"

"Justina had alienated many in Italia by refusing to convert to Nicene Christianity. Her Arianism offended important people, as did her conflicts with Bishop Ambrose of Milan. Few in Italia were willing to risk their lives for a sixteen-year-old ruler, whose mother they consider a heretic."

"Will Theodosius now attack?"

"I believe so. Long has he feared war with Maximus and his Germanic auxiliaries. Maximus has amassed many mercenaries and also the forces of Britannia, Gaul, and Hispania at his command."

"Theodosius can no longer afford to allow Maximus to gain more power," Alaric observed.

"He is swayed also by his great love for Valentinian's sister, Galla. Justina was happy to wed her beautiful young daughter to the emperor, and now I fear he will wait no longer. War is coming."

"The Eastern Army is strong," Alaric responded. "Theodosius has also many ships. He can land troops anywhere in the Mediterranean any time he wants. He can invade Italia behind Maximus's march. Not to mention Goth auxiliaries are now near forty thousand men."

"It's the last part that has me worried," Ulff whispered. "I fear the Romans will use our blood to settle this conflict, saving their own troops to dominate the peace that follows. You must use caution. Do not be led into a slaughter."

"Of course, but it's—"

"What?"

"It's not as easy as you might think. The auxiliaries march first. The main Roman force is behind us, so we're trapped between the approaching force and the rest of the Roman army. Retreat is not an option. And abandoning the field, even if we could, just makes the battle a rout." Alaric paused, lowering his head and his tone. "Do you expect any more kindness from Maximus? I remember the stories. At least Theodosius—"

"We're better off with Theodosius, yes, but it is his generals you must watch."

"Always do they seek assurance of our loyalty and that we will fulfill our oaths."

"I know this puts you in a difficult position. I am here only to warn of what comes. Be on your guard and speak to no one of our meeting. I will soon travel to Rome and see what tales are told in that court."

Within days the order to march finally came. They moved west along the road near the Danube to a point close to where the great Save River feeds into the Danube. The forces of Maximus defended the other side. Roman forces from the Danube region were gathering southeast of the Save, awaiting the arrival of Theodosius's army, which was moving up the Adriatic coast.

Jovius summoned Alaric and led him to a group of Roman officers standing outside the many tents clustered in the center of camp. Jovius ignored most of the officers but addressed a gaunt, intense man wearing the uniform of a general.

They exchanged salutes. "Stilicho, my friend, this is the boy I spoke of. Alaric, may I introduce General Stilicho, one of the great generals of our time."

The two clasped forearms, and Stilicho asked Jovius and Alaric to step into his tent. Stilicho pulled back the flap on a flamboyant bright-red tent and invited the two to enter. The smell of incense was strong, and the tent was dramatically lit by many oil lamps. The three sat at a round table at the center of the tent.

"Alaric, Jovius tells me you are one of our most promising Goth recruits. He tells me one day you may lead the Gothic auxiliary."

"I'm flattered," Alaric said modestly. "I really just wish to serve—"

Stilicho cut him off with a rough laugh. "You don't need to pretend to be modest with us, boy. We understand ambition."

"You can speak freely here, my friend," Jovius assured.

"I have heard tales of your actions. How you're admired by your own people. Such a man can go far."

"With the right friends, of course," Jovius interjected.

"Leading my people would be a great honor," Alaric conceded.

"Yes," Stilicho continued, "but to be worthy of such an honor, you need to understand what we need, what this army needs in battle. When the fighting starts, we are not Goths and Romans but rather soldiers in one army. Brothers in arms. Trust becomes as important as sharp swords."

"Of course."

Jovius reached out to grasp Alaric's forearm. "We've spoken of this before, my son. We need to know that those we choose lead well and loyally and do not mislead their people into disaster."

Alaric turned back to Stilicho. "Then I shall tell you what I've told Jovius. I've been a soldier too long to think one part of an army can go off on its own. An army fights together or suffers defeat. I don't see conflict between serving my people and serving the Roman army. These are one. Victory on the field serves all."

"Well said, Alaric." Stilicho rose to retrieve a map and retook his seat as he spread it on the table and turned it toward Alaric. "Maximus's forces are deployed along the Save River, with reinforcements in the rear. He intends to stop us at the river. Theodosius will be here in two days. He brings most of the Eastern Army with him as well as Hun and Alan mercenaries. The crossing of the river will likely be bloody. The auxiliaries will be our first line of attack."

Alaric interrupted, "Have you heard of the Huns' victory on the Dniester?"

"Excuse me?" Stilicho's brow furrowed.

"The Huns crossing the Dniester. Have you heard the tale?"

Stilicho and Jovius exchanged glances.

"No, my lad," said Jovius. "Do tell."

"The Ostrogoths hoped to hold the Huns at the Dniester. They had plenty of time. All the bridges and fords were well guarded. Many thought the crossing would be a bloody disaster for the Huns. But they didn't cross where expected or in large groups. They split up and simply remained mounted while their horses swam across the river. Then they regrouped on the other side and forced a hasty retreat."

Stilicho and Jovius looked at each other again. Stilicho turned back to Alaric, leaned forward, and said with a frown, "So you suggest that, instead of Goth infantry leading the attack, we should send Hun cavalry?"

"I'm suggesting you let Huns be Huns."

"Sounds awfully convenient for the Goths," said Stilicho with great skepticism.

"I don't think you'll get any argument from the Huns. They're bloodthirsty, vicious, and exactly the sort you want for this. Goths will fight too, of course, and I will be among them, but by the time we cross the river, the Huns should already be harassing Maximus's rear. That will weaken their defenses enough to allow us a stronghold on the other side and allow the rest of the army an easy crossing."

After a pause, Jovius looked again at Stilicho. "I told you this one's special!"

Stilicho smiled. "I admit you're quite persuasive and have an eye for strategy, but the emperor will decide who leads the attack. If he orders the Goth auxiliaries to cross first, you must not hesitate."

"I understand," Alaric responded confidently. "When the time comes, we *will* not fail you."

Theodosius arrived with his vanguard. As the rest of his army was still marching, he convened a war council and asked Stilicho for advice. The young general wore a grand chest plate over chain mail.

Stilicho gave his advice swiftly and with great confidence. "Augustus, we must seize the advantage of surprise. Our men show force along the river at locations well known to the enemy. I would send the Hun and Alan mercenaries across where the river is deep, where none will expect a crossing. They will attack the defenders from the rear, while we cross in greater numbers than they think we have. I would attack the very day your forces arrive."

This strategy was well received. Hearing no objection and disposed toward the boldness himself, the emperor agreed and ordered that it be made so.

That evening Jovius summoned Alaric and advised him that the strategy he suggested had been more or less agreed to. They would attack the next day. Alaric was much relieved. He had anguished over how to respond had he been ordered to lead an ill-advised attack on the far bank of a fortified river.

When the time came, the crossing was much easier than expected. Maximus's troops were stationed opposite Stilicho's forces. When Theodosius's army arrived, it never stopped. The emperor deployed his troops directly to undefended portions of the river and pushed straight across. Surprised by the speed of the crossing, Maximus's forces were spread too thinly and outflanked in many places. The Goth auxiliaries fought on the front lines of Stilicho's force. With Hun and Alan mercenaries behind his lines and Theodosius leading his army straight across the river, Maximus was forced to retreat in a disorganized and costly fashion.

The usurper was forced to flee to the great fortress at Aquileia on the northern edge of the Adriatic. Theodosius's troops trapped the traitor. The emperor himself encamped not far outside the fortress.

Early one evening, Athaulf commanded the Goths posted outside the main gates. He sat atop a sable stallion just outside the main entrance, when, much to his surprise, the gates began to open without apparent reason. He gave orders, preparing to defend an assault from the fortress, as unlikely as that was. When the gates swung open, however, there was no assault. Instead, the torches approaching from inside the fortress dramatically lit the shadowy profile of Maximus being led from Aquileia in chains. The soldiers formerly loyal to him yanked the chains, cruelly pulling him forward. They boasted they had avoided bloodshed by bringing the pretender to justice and begged for their own forgiveness.

Athaulf watched this dramatic scene unfold with mixed emotions. Shouldn't he feel a greater sense of vengefulness? Of satisfaction? The man who had starved his people as a child was now being dragged before him in chains. If he didn't feel the glorious wrath himself, should he not feel it for the many who had fallen from starvation? For those who had lost loved ones to Maximus's greed? Athaulf realized that all he really felt was pity as he watched the usurper being dragged naked through the mud, suffering many indignities from his former subordinates designed to prove their rejection of their former leader.

Theodosius sat stoically on a wooden throne in a large pavilion when word arrived that the gates of Aquileia had opened. He ordered Maximus brought before him. The fallen leader bore many cuts, bruises, and swollen eyes. He was thrown on the ground before the emperor's feet.

"Augustus, I beg your forgiveness!" Maximus pleaded. "Whatever punishment you see fit, I beg you spare my life. I could still serve." He crouched in a prostrate position and began to grovel.

Theodosius was unmoved and gravely motioned to a soldier wielding a large ax. Maximus struggled as his neck was forced over a wooden block, and he continued to beg shrilly even as the ax fell. His head rolled across the ground, and blood spurted from his neck as his heart continued for a few more beats.

After the victory, Theodosius adorned Alaric with medals and heaped much praise on him in an elaborate ceremony, at which the Roman leaders were also decorated. Alaric, however, wasn't elevated to a position with authority over how the Goth auxiliaries would be used.

Chapter 9

The End of an Era

It was a somber gathering. The large meadow was overfilled, so many crowded into the woods. On this clear, pleasant morning, Alavivus, now elderly and frail, struggled to make his voice heard to the multitude present. Finally, as the crowd settled, he started over and let his voice boom from his chest.

"We gather here to pay tribute to our fallen leader. A great warrior who fell not on the battlefield but here with us, among friends and family." Alavivus began to move around, shifting the direction of his voice for all to hear.

"How many leaders would have relinquished power and slipped into obscurity to ensure the safety of his people? Would the greatest of Roman emperors have shown such humility? Such selflessness?" Alavivus's pause let these questions sink in.

"Fritigern never sought power or fame. He didn't seek to promote his own ambition or establish a dynasty. Everything he did, from the time the very first Hun darkened the eastern horizon, he did to secure the safety of our people. He led us into the empire because he knew we couldn't live outside it. He fought valiantly to force the Romans to accept us, and he agreed to disclaim his leadership, all for the purpose of securing the peace we've enjoyed these last ten years. Years filled with peace and plenty—with new children and the natural passing of the old."

Alavivus paused again. It was so quiet, even the insects could be heard. Alaric had secured for his entourage an honored place near the burial site. Brechta stood next to him, holding their new baby girl, and Alaric held Alonia, who buried her face in her father's chest.

Alavivus continued, "Some ask who will lead us now. For whom shall we look to for guidance? Some even ask if I will now lead." He paused again, taking time to look around him. "I am old. It will not be long before I join my old friend in heaven. Fritigern knew we do not need to be ruled by a dictator. Our way has always been the way of each free man making his own decisions. A leader is needed in times of war, yes, but we are not at war. If the time comes, I say we choose the one among us most like Fritigern, a man driven not by his own ambition but by the same desires that drove Fritigern. Loyalty to our people, respect for each of us, and humility over arrogance. When the time comes, I believe we will have the wisdom to choose such a man."

Alavivus now motioned toward Father Ulff, who spoke out clearly. "I now ask each of you to join me in prayer for our beloved leader. Let us pray to God that Fritigern be admitted to the kingdom of heaven and that he might watch over us still."

The assembled throng all bowed their heads. Father Ulff raised his head and loudly sang a prayer in Latin. He switched to the tongue of the Goths and chanted a prayer in his native language. When he had finished, the body of the old warrior was slowly lowered into the grave. The crowd remained silent. As the hole was being filled, a chorus sang a traditional lament for the fallen leader—a rhythmic, chant-like dirge as somber as the moment. When the song was done, the crowd slowly began to disburse, none speaking a word.

After the ceremony, Alaric invited Father Ulff to join his family for dinner. The priest rode up to Alaric's enclave, a modest wooden structure with many carts, a large garden, and much livestock. Before dinner was ready, Ulff asked Alaric to join him for a walk. The pair strode down a well-worn path winding through a beautiful forest.

"I sense you have news you wish to share," Alaric said with a good-natured smile.

Ulff returned the smile. "Yes, a visit to Constantinople is always enlightening, and this more than most. Trouble again brews in the West. Emperor Valentinian is now dead."

"Dead? How?"

"That's a matter of some controversy. General Arbogast now leads the Western Army and claims Valentinian took his own life. But Empress Galla does not believe her brother would have committed suicide."

"Nor would I," Alaric responded. "Arbogast murdered him, and—let me guess—he now claims the purple for himself."

"No. Arbogast is a Frank and would have difficulty finding acceptance among the patricians in Rome. He knows this, and word arrives he has now elevated Flavius Eugenius to the title of Augustus. Eugenius is a native Roman and senior civil servant in Italia. His ascension is backed by many in Rome, particularly the pagan senators who distrust the Christianization of the empire. He has already begun elevating pagans to key positions, and it is said he will begin restoring pagan temples."

"Will Theodosius march against him?" Alaric asked.

"It's too soon to say. His young wife craves vengeance, but Theodosius is cautious, as you know. He has little interest in who rules the West, and I do not believe he would risk another civil war only to avenge Valentinian. But Eugenius's pagan sympathies give Theodosius natural allies in the West and a cause larger than grievance. I suspect Eugenius will send an embassy to Constantinople. It is upon the success of that embassy that war will turn." He looked back at his former pupil. "You may be called on for a campaign in the spring."

Alaric inhaled deeply. "You do not believe Theodosius learned his lesson last time?"

"I fear the lesson he learned was that the Goth auxiliaries are a powerful ally. Your small rebellion let him know Goth blood cannot be taken for granted, but when the need is great, he would prefer to defeat Eugenius on the field and deal with a rebellion later, if need be."

The two made their way back to Alaric's encampment, and just before they arrived, Father Ulff announced that he had a gift for Alaric. He presented him with a leather-bound book.

"What is it?" Alaric asked, flipping through the pages.

"It's a collection of the works of Seneca."

"You want me to become a stoic?"

Ulff smiled. "What if you already are and just don't know it yet?"

Alaric smiled back. "Well, I shall read it with great interest."

Later that evening, after Father Ulff had departed and the children were in bed, Alaric sat at their table, reading his new book. After a time, Alaric put the book down, watched his wife tidying up, and asked, "What is it?"

"What?"

"The reason you sulk."

"I'm *not* sulking."

"You haven't said a word since Father Ulff left. What's wrong?"

"Nothing," she said curtly, returning to her chores.

"If you tell me what's bothering you, I might be able to help, but if you keep it a secret, it is certain that I cannot."

"That's right!" she snapped. "You cannot. You cannot help what the Romans do. You cannot help when you will be called away. You cannot help how long you will be away. A year? Two? More?"

"Where is this coming from?"

"Do you think I'm stupid? Do you think I do not notice when you grow grim after a long walk with the priest just back from Constantinople? Do you think I have not come to learn what your distraction means?" She burst into tears and buried her face in her hands.

Alaric rose and embraced his wife. "My love. You have no need to despair. We have not been called. Father Ulff speaks only—"

"Only of what?"

"Only of rumors. Gossip in the royal courts. He tells me what he knows so I can prepare. You needn't burden yourself."

"I'll be burdened plenty if you make me a widow!"

Alaric spread his arms and lifted his palms upward. "I'm here now. Can we not enjoy the time we have?"

"Why do we have to stay? We could ride off with the girls. We could hide from the war. Why must we always bear the burden? Wealthy Romans pay to keep safe—"

"We're not wealthy Romans," Alaric replied. "Where would we go? Nowhere safe. There is strength in numbers. That's what's kept us safe all these years. Alone we would be at the mercy of others. And you underestimate my skill."

Brechta regained her composure and looked in her husband's eyes. "Promise me you won't get killed. Promise me our daughters will not grow up without a father."

Alaric's stomach churned as he imagined his girls grieving for their father as he had. He reassured his wife, and they talked at length about plans for the future. Alaric played down the prospect of war and speculated that the crisis would be resolved peacefully.

Although her demeanor was now calm, Alaric knew there was more on his wife's mind and grew frustrated that she wouldn't divulge her concerns. "Woman, why will you not just speak your mind?"

"Well, I'm sorry, but I am not a Roman sergeant. I just thought ..." She began to get choked up.

Alaric sought to console his distraught wife. "I am sorry. I didn't mean ..."

She began to weep, and he pulled her close. After a time, her mood calmed again, and she ventured, "I was just wondering. I didn't want to interfere, but I wondered if one day Thuruar would wed."

Alaric howled in laughter. "Thuruar? That's what troubles you? Whether the huge man would wed? I don't know if he even—"

"Even what?"

"Even ... would be fit company for a woman."

"And why should your friend be unfit company for a woman?"

"Well ... I don't know ... he ... he eats meat nearly raw. He *never* says no to strong drink. He belches as if it were an art. I've never thought of ... Do you think there is a woman who would ...?"

Brechta pulled her husband close and lovingly put her cheek to his chest. "I think there is someone for everyone."

"Do you have anyone in mind?"

"What of Luca?"

Alaric pulled back and looked at his beloved wife. "Theoric's widow? That seems ... it's just ..."

"She's mourned the loss of your brother for years. She's lonely. Should she not one day find love again?"

"Well, yes, but ... Thuruar? Would a woman not see him as ...?"

"Women may not see him as you do!" Brechta said.

Alaric grew wise. "You must know something I do not. Does she—"

"She sees him as loyal and brave. Do you not also?'

"Yes. Of course. It's just ... I didn't think women would see ... Anyway, he's one of the largest men I've ever seen, and she's ... tiny."

"Does it matter? Should love be arranged by size?"

"Well, I would think ... Wait! If you already know ... if this is ..."

Brechta smiled knowingly. "Could we not, at least, invite them both to dinner?"

The great military leader felt as if he'd walked into an ambush. His wife clearly knew more than he, and why would he not wish love for his friend?

An embassy from the West awaited an audience with the eastern emperor, and Theodosius prepared to first meet with his own council. As he dressed, his beautiful, young wife grew grave.

She faced her husband. "You know they will seek to flatter you. They will praise your wisdom even as they think you a fool and a coward for tolerating my brother's murder."

The emperor smiled gently and took up his wife's hands. "My love, if I could do whatever I wanted, I'd have the lot executed right now. You know I can't make decisions based on my own passions."

"You're the emperor." She pouted.

"Yes, but with that comes great responsibility. I have to think of the needs of the empire, not just myself."

"And what of your sons? Will they be safe if it is known there is no penalty for murdering an emperor?"

"They may become emperors themselves one day. My rule is secure because people believe I have ruled well. If I'm seen to be risking the empire for a personal vendetta, all that is lost. I may well ride to war against Eugenius, but you must trust me to make that decision."

Theodosius kissed his wife gently on the cheek and made his way into a large hall, in which his counsel sat at a long, rectangular table. The emperor took his seat at the head of the table and asked Richomeres to speak to the readiness of the army for a campaign in the spring.

"It will take time to fully reconstitute our auxiliaries. If we must march by spring, we would have only about half the number that marched against Maximus."

"Would twenty thousand be enough?"

"I'd prefer forty thousand, of course, but yes, with twenty thousand Goths and the full strength of the regular troops and better generals, we would ride to victory."

The group smirked at Richomeres's confidence.

"Richomeres, my friend," interjected Saturnius, "is Eugenius's general Arbogast not your nephew?"

"He is. I'm ashamed to say. But that matters not."

"Saturnius, what do you think of all this?" the emperor asked. "Would you not have me ride to war against this pretender?"

"I would, Augustus. Eugenius alienates our Christian allies in the West. He has removed from positions of authority those you installed after the death of Maximus and replaced them mostly with pagan sympathizers. The church grows wary of his direction. Already he has restored the Altar of Victory and the Temple of Venus and Rome. His list of enemies grows long, and his strength wanes."

"I hear none among you who disagree. Why then should I receive the embassy of this usurper at all?"

"Because we want to keep our enemies guessing as long as possible," Saturnius replied. "Why communicate your intentions? Wiser it would be to receive them and speak only generally of a desire for peace. Keep Eugenius blind to your true intent and delay further his own preparation."

"Ahh. You are cunning, my old friend," the emperor said with a smile. "I shall greet these ambassadors warmly with presents and vague talk. We will then make our own preparations for a campaign this spring. Richomeres, I do not doubt your loyalty. However, in light of the circumstances, I will have you retain your charge over our cavalry. Stilicho, I look to you to lead our army against Eugenius."

"You honor me, Augustus," the general replied with a broad smile.

The Visigoths enjoyed a time of peace and relative prosperity. Thuruar and Luca were soon wed with Alaric's blessing. By winter, Daria midwifed Luca through a difficult delivery. Thuruar was much relieved to have a healthy baby and wife. His worry next turned to a suitable name for his baby boy. He sought Athaulf's counsel.

"Why do you worry over a name for your own child? Call him anything you want."

"I wish to honor Theoric, but I fear what Alaric might think."

"Oh, you want to actually call him Theoric?"

"Would that not honor the fallen hero? Or would it be deemed … I don't know … inappropriate? I've always lived in the empire. Romans often name many descendants after honored ancestors."

Athaulf smiled pleasantly at his old friend. "I see. Our way is not to call another as someone else was called. Would it not take from Theoric's memory to also call another Theoric? When you wish to honor another's memory, it is better to choose a name that's similar but not the same. Think of all the sons whose names are only a little different from their father's."

"Ahh, perhaps something like Tharic."

"I'm not sure that's close enough."

"Theo … Theodesius? No, too Roman. Theo … Theodoric?"

Athaulf lit up. "That has just the right ring, my friend."

Despite Athaulf's assurances, Thuruar still harbored deep anxiety about speaking with Alaric. He approached his friend in such a grim and somber mood that Alaric feared some ill had befallen the child.

"Is everything all right?" Alaric asked with a frown.

"Yes, yes, Luca and the baby are fine. It's just … I just … I wanted to ask your permission … about the name."

Alaric was relieved that he didn't stammer over something more serious. "My friend, you do not need my permission to name your own child."

"It's just, I wanted to choose a name … to honor Theoric."

Alaric stiffened a bit. "What did you have in mind?"

"I was thinking Theodoric."

Alaric smiled and put his hand on Thuruar's shoulder. "I think it a splendid name, and I'm grateful you honor my brother's memory in this way. In all the time I've known you, I've never once doubted your loyalty."

Thuruar smiled, and the old friends embraced. They continued to chat, but their pleasant conversation was cut short by a cry from Brechta. She labored in the garden and warned of riders approaching. Alaric walked outside with his sword drawn, Thuruar just behind him. A small company of Roman horsemen galloped close to Alaric's dwelling, and the leader dismounted and saluted Alaric, who sheathed his weapon and returned the salute.

"I bring word from the emperor. You are to begin mobilizing your troops. Commanders are to report by the first day of March. All troops must report by the first day of April." The Roman soldier handed over a small scroll with the emperor's message. By this time, Athaulf, Wallia, and several other men had gathered.

After the Romans left, Alaric took only a day to say goodbye to his family and get his affairs in order. His company rode through the various encampments, spreading the word and gathering an ever-larger horde. Many were discontent. Some asked why they should again leave their families to fight another Roman civil war. All found this to be a just question.

The Eastern Army marched west from Constantinople in May of 394. At the age of twenty-eight, Alaric was leading the twenty thousand Goths who would march first into battle. Theodosius led the campaign. Their advance through Pannonia was unopposed. As they approached the Alpine passes, they discovered that these, too, were undefended. The men didn't know whether to feel relieved or apprehensive.

Only once through the mountains did they encounter Eugenius's forces, in a valley on the far side of a river called Frigidus, due to the cold meltwater it carried from high in the mountains. It was a relatively small space for two such large armies to clash. Alaric sat mounted in the vanguard on a plateau with a view of the entire valley. Stilicho and his guard arrived with word that the emperor had ordered an immediate attack, with little reconnaissance of the field. Alaric was ordered to lead the Visigoths to attack the rebel line on the far side of the river.

Before Stilicho had even finished relaying the order, Alaric shook his head vigorously. "That's exactly what they want us to do! Men struggling to get out of the river will be slaughtered by soldiers waiting for them."

"The river is shallow in many places," Stilicho replied stoically. "You will be able to cross where the water is only knee deep."

"Do you think they do not also see where the water is shallow?" Alaric shouted with great exasperation. "They will see us coming and be ready wherever we seek to cross. They will have the high ground and the greater numbers."

"You must seek to cross in more than one place," the general continued resolutely. "Spread out their forces. The emperor's full plan will not be known until you see it unfold on the field. You need only puncture their line, and the full strength of the Eastern Army will join your assault."

Alaric continued to protest, and Stilicho could only insist that Alaric's orders had been given. When Stilicho rode off, Athaulf nudged his horse forward to privately consult with his friend. "He sends us into a death trap," Alaric said in a low voice.

"Do we have another choice?" Athaulf asked, looking over his shoulder. "If we break the peace, we're caught between two Roman armies."

"You are right, my friend," Alaric said with grave reservation. "The only path is forward. We must find a way to break their lines." He feared the moment Ulff had warned of had now come.

Alaric motioned to move the Visigoths toward the river. They formed a line back far enough to avoid archers on the other side. Alaric's horse paced on high ground. Seeing the river shallowest in two places, he ordered two large groups to attack in unison.

Many Goths were felled by arrows as soon as they started to cross. By the time they neared the bank, javelins began to take more lives. Those who made it across struggled to fight their way up the bank, with a row of defenders thrusting spears down from above. The few Goths able to bring their weapons to bear did little more than dent shields. Rarely did Goth arrows find their mark. The fighting was too lopsided. Alaric recalled his forces.

Alaric now knew crossing in large groups was too dangerous. They would have more success in small groups crossing at many places. The Romans became spread too thin. A broad grin came to Alaric's face as he saw Diminimus lead a company up the far shore. Alaric motioned for reinforcements to take advantage of the opening. Arbogast also saw the danger, and his reinforcements were much closer. Roman reinforcements came running in great numbers, furiously driving Diminimus's company back into the river.

Alaric spurred his horse into a gallop across the shallow bank. His horse slowed to a swim in the deep water, and he almost reached Diminimus before a javelin pierced his thigh. Diminimus collapsed into the river, writhing in agony. Alaric leaped from his horse and pulled his friend from the current. Alaric pulled Diminimus to the shore as the wounded man screamed.

Many healers held him down while one pulled the javelin from deep in his thigh. They couldn't stop the bleeding. Diminimus gasped and shook. Alaric knelt and held his hands as the healers worked. "My friend," Alaric said, "you will soon be healed and return to your wife a hero."

Diminimus's pained grimaces gave way to a momentary smile as Alaric spoke. His body heaved and shook a final time, then he went limp, as if his soul had suddenly left his body. The healers stopped working. Alaric knew he must return to the battle.

The second wave of attacks had been costlier for Arbogast, but still, his lines held. A third and a fourth wave had much the same result. Only late in the afternoon, after many failed charges, were the Visigoths able to get across the river upstream. Their position, however, allowed Arbogast to use the mountains to protect his flank and pull his forces back only a little to maintain his line.

Alaric and his officers made camp close to the river, and Stilicho rode forth with much praise of Alaric's success. It had come at a great cost, though. Nearly a third of Alaric's force had fallen. The river ran red with the blood and gore of the Visigoths. They were able to recover only some of the corpses that floated downstream. Alaric was angry and bitter. He demanded Stilicho support his troops and threatened to quit the field if he did not. Stilicho remained calm and assured Alaric his men would be supported.

Only after Stilicho departed did Athaulf share more bad news. Scouts reported Arbogast had sent troops to close off the mountain passes behind Theodosius and trap his army. This had been his plan all along.

Alaric and Athaulf helped dig Diminimus's grave and somberly lowered their friend. When the rites ended, Alaric would take no food. He waited until he was alone in his tent to weep bitterly.

This was the disaster he had feared. So many dead. If this was the price of peace, it was too high.

The next morning, the forces Arbogast sent to block the passes behind them defected and joined Theodosius's army. Alaric surveyed the field and saw a favorable wind blowing along the valley from the east, creating a cloud of dust that blew into the faces of the western troops. Men would later say God intervened against the pagans.

Theodosius ordered another charge, and this time Alaric agreed with the decision. The high dusty wind obscured the movements of the attacking troops and made it difficult for the western troops to face their attackers. Their arrows were ineffective in the high wind, and some even blew backward. Alaric ordered additional crossings at multiple places. Finally, the western lines broke. Once the Goths had penetrated the line, Roman regular troops flooded through the openings and rolled up the flanks. An eastern cavalry charge through the gaps devastated western soldiers already engaged with the Visigoth infantry. The battle turned into a slaughter, and western troops began to surrender.

Eugenius was captured and brought before the emperor. Like Maximus before him, Eugenius pled for his life, but Theodosius was unmoved and had him beheaded. Arbogast escaped and committed suicide alone in the woods.

Theodosius celebrated the victory with elaborate ceremonies to honor the battle's heroes. He lavished Alaric with praise and medals to commemorate his valiant leadership but failed to promote him to a rank that would allow him to prevent such a heavy toll on his people. After the ceremony, Alaric walked off with Athaulf grumbling loudly.

"Theodosius heaps honors on Roman officers never close to the action."

Alaric spoke loudly, but Athaulf responded in a low tone. "I heard one of the Roman officers say Theodosius won two victories today: one against the usurper and another against the Goths."

Alaric's face flushed with anger. "This will not happen again. The Romans can't keep their own house in order, and we pay the price. How many more usurpers will they call upon us to defeat? We must force a new agreement on the Romans while we still have the strength to do so."

Chapter 10

A New Beginning

Alaric's horse trotted briskly near the front of the vanguard. The road home had been long and the mood somber. The Visigoths now entered Thrace and approached the civilian encampments of their people. Bitterness toward the Romans was widespread. They all knew the victory of Theodosius had been paid for with the blood of their people, and there was no reason to expect a different result the next time a usurper made claim to the purple. A spirit of revolution dominated the mood. Alaric gave orders that the Visigoth soldiers should return home as an army, and none questioned his authority.

This new army camped outside the civilian settlements, and Alaric granted leave for family visits only in small groups for limited periods. To set the example, Alaric waited many weeks before again visiting his own family. Brechta and the girls were overjoyed at his return, and the family spent many days rejoicing in their reunion and sharing stories of their time apart.

Within a couple of months of their return, Father Ulff returned from Constantinople, seeking an immediate audience with Alaric. Ulff wasted no time. Immediately upon entering Alaric's pavilion, he announced, "Theodosius is dead."

"Dead?" Alaric asked. "How?"

"By all accounts, he died of natural causes."

Many voices erupted in anger and concern.

"We should not fight in another civil war," Wallia said above the din.

Alaric continued to look at the priest. "Will the East really accept Arcadius as emperor? Will they really call a sixteen-year-old Augustus?"

"No one knows," Ulff replied. "Honorius is even younger, but Theodosius called him Augustus in the West, and they've accepted that."

"But Stilicho serves as his protector. No one expects the boy to actually lead."

"Stilicho claims that on his deathbed Theodosius also made him protector of Arcadius."

Gasps filled the room.

"Stilicho will call himself Augustus," Wallia declared. "Why would he not?"

"Because the Senate and the other patricians probably wouldn't accept it," the priest responded. "Just as I do not believe the eastern court will accept his claim to be protector of Arcadius. Naming Stilicho protector in the West was made during Theodosius's lifetime, and no one questions the decision. But no one really knows what Theodosius said on his deathbed, and the eastern court has too many vested interests to just take Stilicho's word for it."

Alaric began to pace and looked down as he spoke. "Honorius gives Stilicho legitimacy, and yet he has the real power. Why overplay his hand now? He has no need. Maybe Honorius dies before adulthood, or maybe he does something that makes him unacceptable. Either way, Stilicho has no incentive to claim power now. He can afford to wait for a more opportune time if he does have designs on the purple himself."

"Whether sooner or later," Wallia responded, "he will seek power for himself. The question is whether we're better off with Stilicho or the children of Theodosius."

Ulff turned to Alaric. "You served under Stilicho. What do you think? What kind of man is he?"

"He's definitely ambitious," Alaric said. "He's half Vandal but as much like a Roman as any I've seen. I don't truly trust him, but he's a military man at heart and seems to have a sense of honor. I think we could make a deal with him but only if it serves his interests. I'd rather not face him in battle."

"For now, Stilicho is a reality in the West," Ulff said. "The question is, what will happen in the East? The court in Constantinople will do everything possible to keep Stilicho from power. They will pledge loyalty to Arcadius and set his mind against Stilicho. Arcadius is easily influenced. If there is to be another civil war, it will likely be over Stilicho's quest for power."

"I'll tell you this," Alaric announced authoritatively. "We are no longer bound by Fritigern's peace with Theodosius." A loud murmur of agreement arose. "We must seek a new agreement, one that treats us as equals. One that does not subject us to slaughter at the whims of Roman politicians. And we do not need an agreement with both halves of the empire. Only one."

"Who would you seek to treat with first?" Athaulf asked.

"Stilicho has no need to treat with us now. But Arcadius is vulnerable. His advisers know this. An alliance with the Goths could be a powerful counterweight to Stilicho's ambition."

"And you believe the people will follow you?" Ulff inquired.

"The time has come for a choice, as Alavivus said." Alaric paused and looked around the room for any dissent before continuing. "If we are to rebel, we must all be united. We must choose a leader."

"And you intend that leader will be you?" Ulff asked. The atmosphere was tense as all awaited Alaric's response.

"If that is what the people choose."

"And what if they don't?" Athaulf demanded. "An election sounds noble, but what if the people make a bad choice? What if they select Sarus?"

"Then he will lead, but I don't think that will happen. Sarus wouldn't be the choice of the army."

Ulff paused for a moment and pressed Alaric further. "Whoever wins, will they be made king?"

"That's not our way. In the West, we have never had kings. Fritigern didn't make himself king."

"We're not in our homeland anymore," Athaulf noted. "We need strong leadership. Only a king has that kind of power. And you could always trade away the title, as Fritigern did."

Alaric paused for a long time, then announced, "This too is a decision the people should make."

Stilicho invited young Honorius to walk with him on a cool morning late in the winter. The boy was royally dressed in fine purple robes and wore a golden crown. His garb was finely tailored, but his frightened expression gave the royal attire an ill-fitting look. Stilicho was used to speaking bluntly and giving orders but knew a softer touch was needed for this conversation.

"I've been waiting for the right time to talk to you about the death of your father," Stilicho began. The boy looked up at him with a wide-eyed, innocent expression. "I didn't want to burden you with these matters when your loss was too near, but you are emperor of the West. There is much we must discuss."

They strode through a marble courtyard in the center of the castle. The courtyard itself had no roof, but they walked along the covered perimeter, supported by majestic columns.

"Trouble brews in the East," Stilicho continued. "As your father lay dying, he summoned me to his bedside. With his last breaths, he asked that I serve as protector for your brother Arcadius, as I do for you. But the court in Constantinople is filled with many ambitious schemers, who will not honor your father's wishes."

"Why not?" the boy asked.

"Because it doesn't serve their interests. A young emperor creates many opportunities for them to enrich themselves. They know that I wouldn't tolerate this."

"I want to see my brother," Honorius said. "We can go to Constantinople and make the court behave?"

Stilicho smiled mildly. "I'm afraid it's not that simple. Your life would be in danger and perhaps Arcadius's as well."

"Why?"

"Many usurpers have tried to claim the purple for themselves. Emperor Gratian was murdered, as was Valentinian. I am sworn to protect you. I couldn't do that in Constantinople without bringing an army. If we approach with an army, I fear those who control the Eastern Army would provoke battle."

"My brother wouldn't. If he knew I was coming, he would welcome me, and he wouldn't allow his advisers to harm me." Honorius had become agitated and had to use his hands to keep the crown from falling off his head.

"I know he would. That's not the problem. The problem is, he does not yet truly control the Eastern Army. We must be patient. We must allow Arcadius to consolidate his control over the Eastern Empire, and while he does so, we will always stand ready to render aid. Being emperor is not easy. You must always think of not only what you want to do but what your enemies will likely do. You must project wisdom as well as strength and courage."

"What if I don't want to?" Honorius asked innocently.

Stilicho frowned. "Don't want what?"

"To be emperor."

Stilicho smiled kindly and placed his hand on the boy's shoulder. "I'm afraid you don't have a choice. I know this is hard on you. Being emperor at such a young age deprives you of a childhood. It places many worries on your head that no child should have to bear. But there is no other option. If you tried not to be emperor, those who wish power for themselves would still kill you to make sure you made no claim later in life. But do not despair. I swore an oath to your father to protect you from all harm. If you will trust me as he did, I will make sure you and your brother are safe and your rule is secure."

The Visigoth leaders agreed that on the first day of spring, they would choose a king. Soldiers took black rocks from a creek and placed them in a pile in a large field. They also made a pile of white rocks from a nearby mountain.

At sunrise, hundreds of Alaric's most senior soldiers marched with him to the field. As they neared, Athaulf and Thuruar snuck up behind Alaric, each holding the edge of a large, round shield. They pressed the bottom edge of the shield behind Alaric's knees, forcing him to fall back into the shield, which they raised above their heads and took up the chant. "King Alaric! King Alaric! King Alaric!" Soon nearly the whole army joined in as Alaric was borne to the rock piles.

Father Ulff stood between the two piles. It had been decided that he would judge the vote. Cniva demanded that Sarus be allowed to speak. Father Ulff announced that Sarus and Alaric would both be allowed to speak. Then all free men would form a line south of the rock piles. Ulff would stand in the middle, and each man in line would come forward and pick either a black rock for Alaric or a white rock for Sarus, march past Ulff, and then place their chosen rock in one of two piles north of the priest. Once all men had chosen, the size of each pile would be counted, and the one with the most votes would be made king.

Sarus was anxious to speak first, thinking he would convince many before Alaric could speak. The crowd was so huge that it spread far beyond the large field. Many were out of earshot and could rely only on those closest to relay what was said.

"Long have I and my family sought to serve our people," Sarus began in a loud, clear voice that carried across the field. "We've earned great prosperity and always used our wealth to help the people. During the great famine at Durostorum, I remember as a boy that my family was generous with those who were starving. My brother and I entered the Roman army to honor Fritigern's peace. We could have paid to be exempt, but we chose to serve." When Sarus paused, only the sound of a soft breeze could be heard.

"And we should think also of who has been loyal to our people. I know many men follow Alaric and think him their leader. But ask yourselves, how did Alaric come to this position? What promises of loyalty did he make to the Romans? Would they have picked someone to lead the Visigoths they didn't believe would serve their interests? I say to you that I will be loyal *only* to our people. It's well known that Alaric seeks a Roman generalship for himself. His own ambition is most important of all. Shall we call him Alaricus? Too close has he become to the Romans. Alaric's leadership did nothing for the thousands who fell at Frigidus."

Some of the soldiers who fought at Frigidus began to grumble, but Sarus continued, "I will not bring further death to our people. We can build our strength to a point the Romans will not challenge. We can continue to live as we have, with no need to ride to war. Call this rebellion if you will, but the Romans will not. They will see us living peaceably, and they will have no quarrel with us. Make me your king, and I promise I will serve you loyally and deliver to our people peace and prosperity." The crowd remained quiet as Sarus concluded his remarks and walked back to his family.

Alaric stepped forth boldly, and his voice rang out clearly. "The peace Sarus speaks of will not come for nothing. We may live here in peace for a while longer, yes, but that peace will not last." He paused as his words sank in.

"Think what has happened. We've won many battles, but new Roman armies always come. A boy is now Augustus in the East. Whether led by

Arcadius or someone else, the Eastern Roman Army will grow stronger, and the Western Army will come to aid the East, as it did under Gratian." Alaric's voice carried clearly across the field as he walked back and forth. "Why do you think the Romans have been content to let us live in Thrace? It is because they know the Huns keep us from crossing the Danube, and on its banks, we are most easily contained. They have us cornered, and when the Huns invade—I say *when* not *if*—we will bear the brunt of the invasion.

"The Huns not only threaten us, but they also move north and west. Their numbers grow north of the Carpathians. Soon they will be plentiful in Germania also. Other peoples are forced by their advance to cross the Danube and the Rhine. Odothesius was forced by the Huns into a disastrous crossing. He will not be the last. As the Hun scourge spreads, others will also become desperate. A common purpose we have with the Romans, but we must demand our own place within the empire, equal to all others."

Alaric glanced at Sarus before continuing. "I do know the Roman way. I know it well. The Romans respond only to strength. We have now an opportunity. The East is weak. We should not wait for the young emperor to become a man. We should not wait for the Romans to sort out another leadership dispute. If we act swiftly, we can seize land, and we can seize treasure to pay for what our people need and hire mercenaries also. We can make the Romans treat while the advantage is ours.

"Like Sarus, I too want peace. But we will find peace only through strength. I wouldn't trust hope in the kindness of the Romans. I too remember the great famine. My family too was once wealthy. But we weren't wealthy after our people starved. We prized life over possessions. If we are to live, we must live together. We must fight together; we must move together." The crowd began to stir and sound agreement.

"And for any who might question my loyalty, I say only this—" Isolated cries of "No! No!" could be heard throughout the group. "Should you choose Sarus, I will serve him as best I can. I will serve all of you as best I can. I have been in the council of the Romans. I do know what they think. And our best strategy is to take what we can now and use that position to negotiate a true peace with the Romans.

"Would that include them making me a Roman general? Yes. Roman generals have many privileges. Generals have control over the armories. We would be better armed were I a Roman general. That I promise. But more, I would have control over who is first in battle, when we fight, and how we fight. I wept for every man who fell at Frigidus, but I knew also far fewer would have fallen were I the general in charge. Stilicho is half Vandal. Arbogast is a Frank. Roman generals need not be natural Romans, but they all decide how their battles are fought.

"Choose me, and we will rebel against the Romans now. Choose me, and we will force Arcadius to make peace. Choose me, and we will wield an army the Romans cannot defeat!" Alaric lifted his fist above his head, and most of the crowd let out an enormous roar. Chants of "King Alaric! King Alaric!" became overwhelming.

Through a combination of effort and sheer patience, Ulff eventually calmed the crowd. When at last silence was obtained, he announced that the entrance line was to be formed. The huge throng began the lengthy process of forming a line south of where Ulff stood. Not all men were permitted to vote, but even those who could numbered well over a thousand. Once all men were south of his position, Ulff allowed the voting to begin. It started slowly at first, but the pace quickened over time. Fewer than a quarter of the men had been through when Cniva began to complain. Black stones predominated. Ulff implored Cniva to wait as the vote progressed, and over time it became clear the pile of black stones was growing much larger. So lopsided was the final result that an exact count wasn't needed. All present could clearly see the larger pile favored Alaric. Indeed, the total was so skewed that it proved an embarrassment to Cniva and his clan. They left the field in humiliation and disgust.

Again, Athaulf and Thuruar hoisted Alaric on a shield, and again the men took up the chant. "King Alaric! King Alaric!" The throng was louder this time—now unanimous in its view. Alaric was thus paraded through the troops and the densest parts of the civilian encampment.

For the first time, the Visigoths had chosen a king.

As soon as he pulled back the flap of his tent, his girls screamed with excitement. "Tata! Tata!" They rushed toward him, and he bent down to lift them both. He was smothered with hugs and kisses. Brechta walked toward him, and he put down the girls to embrace his wife. She wiped away tears and smiled.

"Your sister tells me you are now our king."

Alaric blushed a little and smiled. "Yes. It's true."

"Does that make me queen?"

"I suppose so, and these little darlings are princesses."

The girls cheered excitedly.

"And how long will the king stay with his family this time?"

"Forever."

"Forever? Really? Daria says you're going to attack the Romans."

Alaric rolled his eyes. "Her husband talks too much. I will no longer separate our army and our people. If I ride south with just the army, there would be nothing to stop the Romans from attacking the encampments."

"Do you really think they'd do that?"

"Yes," the new king said gravely. "We must move as a group—all of us—until we find a new homeland."

"And where will that be?"

"Somewhere safe. Somewhere we're not caught between the Huns and the Romans. Somewhere the Romans will be forced to accept."

"And how will you find such a place?" Brechta asked innocently.

"We're moving south. Eventually into Greece. We will raid and pillage rich Roman towns and give them need to treat with us. The eastern court is weak. We can offer them strength and peace."

"I'm just glad we will not be separated again!" Brechta said brightly.

"I as well." Alaric pulled his wife in close, and his girls joined the hug.

Hamil felt oddly nervous on the day he would pledge fealty to Radagaisus. He wasn't truly afraid. He knew no harm would come to him. Indeed, it would be a joyous occasion he'd looked forward to. And yet he felt anxious.

Heather attended his grooming and sought to soothe his worries while he sat looking forward blankly.

"There will be many who take the oath with you," she assured him while combing his hair, "so you needn't worry about forgetting the words. You look very handsome!"

He put his arm around her waist and pulled her onto his lap. "Do I look more handsome than the day we met?"

"Ha!" She laughed. "Yes! Much!"

"You've been so kind to me," he said, looking into her eyes and stroking her hair. "You and your family. I've been so blessed since—"

"Don't even think about that. You're safe with us now."

"But Thoris is not."

"He has a high position as translator for the king of the Huns! Surely he's well cared for."

"No, he's not. He bows and scrapes before the man who murdered his father and siblings. I know hatred still burns in his heart as hot as the day it happened. Whenever I feel joy here with you, I feel guilt also."

"There is nothing you could have done for him, my love. And there is always hope. You will march with Radagaisus to victory! One day we will conquer Italia and use the wealth and power of the empire to defeat the Huns. You march to free all our people, including Thoris."

He flashed his bright smile. "That's why I wanted to take the oath."

"Then stop worrying!" Her cheerfulness brightened his mood.

He looked and sounded confident as he stood side by side with many others before the great Goth leader and pledged his loyalty. Not long afterward, he rode with Radagaisus many times to fight the constant encroachment of Hun raiders, who were penetrating deeper and deeper into Germania.

Alaric met with his council as the people prepared to march. Sarus and Sergeric were included as well as Wallia, Thuruar, Athaulf, and other leaders. They discussed the preparations, and Wallia addressed the king. "Before we break the camp, there is another matter you need to address."

"What's that?"

"Many people have disputes."

"What kind of disputes?"

"All kinds. Whatever people disagree about. You're king now. People need to see the king make decisions."

Alaric reluctantly agreed, and an open wagon was rolled into a flat meadow. An ornate chair, pillaged from a Roman villa, was placed on top. Guards patrolled the meadow, and Alaric's war council and many civilian leaders crowded in front of the wagon. This throng numbered around fifty, with many more commoners clustered behind them. At first, Alaric heard petitions from leaders about mundane matters, such as military promotions, civilian responsibilities, and generally how issues not warranting the king's attention should be handled. Alaric saw little reason to handle these matters publicly but heeded Wallia's advice that the people should see their king being a king.

When the public business was concluded, individuals were allowed to come forth with grievances. The first was a young military leader known to Alaric, who stepped forward with his father in front of the crowd now numbering well over two hundred. The young man was nervous and stammered something about not knowing how Alaric was to be addressed.

"My God, man, I've seen you look more calm marching into battle. You're among friends here. Speak."

"King Alaric, my family and I, like many others, follow the old ways. We do not disturb the Christians, but our rituals have been disrupted. Some have been threatened."

"How have your rituals been disrupted?"

"Sometimes by intruders hurling insults. Sometimes idols have been stolen or damaged—altars have been defiled."

"Worshipping false idols is a great offense to Christians," Alaric intoned gravely.

"We know this and have sought to keep our practices secret—outside the sight of the Christians."

Alaric paused in thought, and the crowd was still until the king continued. "I hope you and all pagans will come to accept Christ's salvation," he announced authoritatively. "But no one can command this. What I can promise is that any who harms you for your beliefs will face my justice." Alaric rose from his chair and spoke loudly. "All gathered here, understand that we are not so strong that we can fight ourselves and still defeat the Romans. We invite our brothers and sisters to accept Christ, but we cannot force salvation upon them. Those who still worship the old gods will be allowed their customs. And any who threaten them will answer to me."

The king sat again, and the two men thanked him and bowed repeatedly as they backed away into the crowd. Next came forth a ragged-looking woman with a prominent black eye and broken lip. She looked down at the ground with her hands clasped before her as she spoke. "My king, I ask your protection. My husband—he threatens to kill me. I try to be a good wife, but when he drinks …"

"Where is this man?" Alaric demanded. "I will hear from him as well."

There was a general commotion as two of Alaric's guards located and produced the man. He stumbled when brought forth, then straightened himself and looked up at Alaric.

"Is this your wife?" Alaric asked.

The man nodded in agreement.

"How did she come by these marks?"

"You might say she did it herself. She's constantly harassing me about things I've already told her to leave me alone about. Sometimes I can't even hear myself think."

"That might be easier if you weren't drunk. You've been drinking today, haven't you?"

"Well, just a few drops."

"It's not even midday yet. If I catch you drinking again while the sun shines, I'll have you tied to a tree for two days. If I catch you beating your wife again, I'll have your head." The king paused and stared intently at the drunkard. "Do you understand?"

The man stammered his agreement and sulked away.

And thus it went. Alaric decided disputes about payment for work and ownership of property. He freed a slave who had been mistreated and required two men who had quarreled over the ownership of a horse to wrestle for it.

He was ready to declare an end to the day when an old woman in a black-hooded cloak was brought before him. As she was brought forth, many hissed and cried, "Witch!"

Two burly men clung to each of her frail arms. One of the men announced, "This woman is a witch! All those she curses turn ill or suffer bad fortune. Her witchcraft will bring doom to us all!"

Many in the crowd shouted agreement, and the hisses continued. One voice cried, "Only fire will rid us of her evil."

"How are you called?" Alaric asked sternly.

"I am called Ordu."

"Do you have children?"

"No."

"Do you have a husband?"

"Not anymore. He was killed in the battles between Athanaric and Fritigern," she said ruefully.

"Did your children die also?"

"No. I had no children."

"Her witchcraft left her barren," shouted a voice from the crowd.

"How do you answer those who call you a witch?"

"I am not!" she said as loudly as she was able. "I am just an old woman."

"Why do so many accuse you?"

"You'd have to ask them. The world is a hard place for an old woman with no family. They look for someone to blame for their troubles."

"You deny cursing anyone?"

"I've had quarrels, yes, but none have suffered misfortune because of my doing."

Alaric looked at the crowd. "If there are any here who accuse this woman of witchcraft, let them speak now."

One of the men who held the woman's arm spoke. "She argued with my wife while she was pregnant. My wife demanded to know where she sleeps. She wouldn't answer. Instead, she cursed us, and our child was stillborn."

"Did she say that?"

"Say what?"

"That your child would be stillborn?"

"No. But she told us we would be cursed!"

Another man came forth and announced that she had cursed his family, and his son then fell at Frigidus.

"What other weapon do I have?" the ancient woman lamented. "Only when those who torment me think me a witch will they leave me be."

"Until they bring you here." Alaric stared at the women for a few moments. "Where do you sleep?"

"I sleep in the woods. I hide so I will not be harmed in the night."

"What work do you do?"

"Once I was a weaver. Now I do chores for scraps."

Alaric was struck by the lack of fear in her eyes.

She blurted out, "I also knew Alenia."

"You knew my mother? How?"

"She fed me when we starved on the Danube, and I helped her as much as I could."

Alaric now remembered an old woman doing odd jobs for his mother, but surely that woman could no longer be alive. He again surveyed the crowd and announced, "This woman will be spared."

Groans and other displeased sounds grew louder. Alaric exchanged glances with Athaulf and Wallia. He was unwilling to gainsay his decision.

"I shall keep a watch over her," he announced, and the crowd grew silent. Alaric now looked again to Ordu. "Why should you not do chores for my family and sleep under my protection?" She agreed, but Alaric concluded with a warning. "You shall never again curse any among us."

After holding court, Alaric walked away with Athaulf by his side.

"Well, that went well," Athaulf said cheerfully. "You're a natural."

"Thank you. I think," Alaric said with a sideways glance.

"I do wonder though. How did you know what sentences to give? The Romans would have crucified the lot."

"Crucifying a man's a lot of work," the king replied facetiously. "Carpenters have to build the cross, guards have to stand watch, and many are needed to hold the condemned down. You've got to really want to set an example to order a crucifixion." The two exchanged amused smiles. "Tying a man to a tree is easy. It can be done quickly, and, if done properly, no guards are needed."

"Ah, but how did you decide how long they should be tied?"

"One day tied to a tree is hardly any punishment at all. You wake up one morning, spend the day tied to a tree, doing no work, and then sleep well that night. But few slumber while tied to a tree. By the second day, most are exhausted and so stiff they can barely walk. Still, most can hold their bowels for two days, although they all smell of urine. By the third day, many have soiled themselves, all are dehydrated to the point of begging, and almost none can stand or walk again until the following day."

"So why did the goat thief get two days and the cow thief three?"

"The goat thief confessed his crime and professed remorse. The cow thief was a liar also."

Athaulf laughed. "A judge indeed!"

Brechta was uncomfortable having the old woman around but declined to even acknowledge her frosty demeanor. Daria had no such compunctions. "Are you really going to bring that woman around your children? Around our families?"

"Do you *really* believe she's a witch?" Alaric asked.

"Are you so sure she's not?"

"I'm sure the man she cursed fell at Frigidus because Theodosius attacked as soon as we arrived without regard for Goth lives. I was there, my sister," Alaric said, placing his hand gently on her shoulder. "It wasn't witchcraft that decided who lived and died. Nor do I believe she can cause a stillborn child."

"Still, she makes me uneasy."

Chapter 11

On the March

Alaric's horse walked slowly around a curve, bringing Constantinople into view. He'd heard it described many times before, but the splendor of the massive city was even more striking than he'd imagined. They approached from the west toward the great outer wall stretching across the wide peninsula from shore to shore. The walls stretched off beyond the horizon in both directions. Towering walls also rose along the shore, protecting the city from attack by sea.

No city in the world was better defended.

Athaulf pulled his horse up next to Alaric and, as they both looked ahead, asked his old friend, "What are you thinking?"

"I think of when we were children." Alaric paused a moment. "Do you remember when Fritigern laid siege to Adrianople?"

"Just barely. We were very young."

"Yes, but I remember it well. Soldiers tried to scale the walls. They tried to ram in the gate. They just made targets of themselves for missiles from above."

"You think we'll suffer the same fate?"

"I think I too will keep peace with walls. We are not here to sack the city. We are here to put on a performance. Have the cavalry parade before the walls. Put infantry formations outside the gates. I want the citizens to know only the gates stand between them and our army. Let them begin to wonder how long we will remain—how long their food will last. Then we shall send an embassy."

Athaulf nodded his agreement and set off to make it so.

At the palace in Constantinople, the young emperor Arcadius sat on the throne in the great hall with his step-aunt Grata standing in the shadows behind him. Grata was one of the sisters of Theodosius's second wife, Galla. She had become a confidante of Theodosius after Galla's death and swore on his deathbed to protect Arcadius. Saturnius, Rufinus (prefect of the East), and the eunuch Eutropius were now the primary advisers to the western emperor. They came to the great marble throne room for an audience with the new emperor. Also with them but walking behind their procession was the Goth, Gainas, who was now the most senior general in the Eastern Army.

As they approached the marble stairs leading up to the throne, Arcadius welcomed them somewhat awkwardly and asked about their purpose.

"The Goths are coming," Eutropius announced dramatically. He was a bald and portly man who kept his hands clasped before him under brown robes.

"How many?" Arcadius asked.

"All of them."

"Their army marches first, maybe thirty thousand strong," Rufinus clarified, "and their people move behind them in a vast wagon train."

After a pause, in which faint whispering could be heard, the emperor asked, "If they come to make war, why do they bring women and children?"

Rufinus responded, "To protect them, most likely. They have appointed Alaric as their king. He led the Goths at Frigidus. He feels the agreement reached with your father didn't survive his death. Alaric likely fears an attack on his people if his army is not nearby."

"And where is *our* army?" the emperor asked, looking at Rufinus.

"The Eastern Army is split in two. Half fends off a Hunnic invasion in Asia minor. The rest fight the Huns in Syria. Neither can get here quickly."

"Then how do we defend the city?"

"We just close the gates and wait them out, Augustus. The Goths lack siege equipment. We will stay safe within our walls for a long time. Long enough even for our armies to return."

"Then why does Alaric come?"

Eutropius stepped forward and took the question. "He comes to seek peace."

"Why does he need an army? Why not just send messengers?"

"He wants to negotiate from a position of strength," Eutropius continued. "Having a large army of Goths just outside our walls is an effort to intimidate you, to use fear to drive an advantageous bargain."

"What does he want?"

"Something more than what your father agreed to, I'm afraid. They reject the peace of 382. Alaric must want something more. Lands, riches, titles—we don't know his mind."

Again, faint whispering was barely audible. "What response do you propose?"

Rufinus responded confidently, "We should not negotiate with a knife at our throats. We should wait out this siege. Force Alaric to lead his people elsewhere. But still, we should know the price of peace. The Goths were a powerful ally to your father. Perhaps again they could be useful. But the people will reject a peace with barbarians at the gates. Only when the Goths have moved on should we send an envoy."

After another pause filled with indistinct whispers, Arcadius consented to this plan, and Rufinus continued, "Augustus, there is another matter to discuss. Now that you are emperor, it is proper for you to take a wife. The people will expect it. As you choose a bride, I offer for your consideration my own daughter Eudoxia." Eutropius cast a hard stare from the corner of his eyes as Rufinus continued, "She is very beautiful and would make a loyal and devoted wife. It would be my pleasure to introduce you to her. Perhaps at a dinner? And your aunt would be welcome, of course."

After another pause, the emperor smiled. "You are very kind, Rufinus. I would be happy to have your family as my guests. I will ask Grata to make the arrangements."

In a dimly lit stone hall, the eunuch Eutropius held a secret council of elders, eunuchs, and officers. After Alaric's overtures were rebuffed, the Goth king grew angry and began pillaging the countryside.

Eutropius rose to address the gathering with a three-pronged candle in hand. "My friends," the eunuch began in a low voice, "we gather here tonight to address a grave threat. The ambition of Rufinus threatens us all. He seeks to marry his daughter to the young Arcadius. The father will control the daughter, and the daughter will control her husband. Now we learn Rufinus rides to meet Alaric in secret. Will he return with Alaric's army at his back? Dare we wait to find out?" The eunuch slowly slumped back in his seat.

"I will not wait," declared an elderly man. "Long have I said the Goths need to be dealt with forcefully—harshly even. It is all they understand.

They are not like us—unshaven, unwashed, uncivilized. They befoul our streets and now threaten our lands. But ever does Rufinus speak lovingly of them. 'They must have a homeland; they can be powerful allies,' he says. I say Rufinus can become one of them if he wishes. He can stop shaving, stop bathing, and sleep in the dirt like a dog!"

Loud sounds of general agreement filled the dim hall. None spoke kindly of Rufinus. Many expressed fear of the power Gainas now held. Saturnius stood in the shadows and didn't speak.

After more discontent, Eutropius rose again. "My friends, we do not have much time. Rufinus intends to wed his daughter to Arcadius before he leaves. This we must prevent."

"Who then will the emperor wed?" asked a voice from the shadows.

"Does it matter?" Eutropius responded. "If you will support me, I will find a suitable bride for our beloved young emperor.

The day Arcadius was to wed his daughter, Rufinus dressed formally and awaited the nuptial procession in his residence near the palace. It never came. He instead received word that the emperor had wed Aelia, daughter of the general Bauto. His initial anger and humiliation quickly subsided into fear that the ground was shifting beneath his feet.

Aelia made her way through the palace, seeking the remote room in which she was to meet Eutropius. She looked beautiful in an elegant blue dress made of the finest silk and adorned with silver trim. She was very young and felt overwhelmed by the weight of the responsibilities she now bore. Uneasy about whether she should have even come, she finally located the meeting place and came in through a large oak door she could barely move. The stone room had only a small, narrow window, and Eutropius sat alone in a shadowy corner lit by a candle.

The eunuch stood to greet the young empress with a low bow and asked her to join him. She sat upright with her hands together in her lap.

He leaned forward with a serious look, placed his hands atop hers, and asked, "How are you? I know the speed of recent events must be overwhelming."

"I'm fine," she said curtly, skeptical of his concern.

"And how is it being married to such a young ... man?"

"Arcadius is kind and sweet. I do love him."

"I'm sure you do, my dear. Still, it must be a challenge—him not quite through the journey to manhood. You so much older. But it is an opportunity as well."

"An opportunity?"

"A chance to help guide our beloved emperor. He's so pious and innocent. What a cruel fate that he should be thrust into the most important position in the East. We must help him. Protect him from those who would seek to use his innocence for their own advantage. Rufinus was such a person—God rest his soul—and I fear his ambition led to his demise. You know he was trying to force Arcadius to marry his daughter, and I was able to play a small role."

"I know what you did." Aelia stiffened, and Eutropius released her hands and leaned back. Her suspicion grew.

"We could be allies, you know."

"About what?"

Eutropius feigned surprise. "About the future of the empire, my dear. You know what transpires in Greece?"

"I know the Goths rampage and pillage the countryside."

"Oh, it's gone far beyond that, sweetie. The Goths not only pillage and loot whatever treasure they can find; they have now sacked Attica. But that's not the worst of it. The worst is what this destruction invites. The Goth Gainas gains ever more power, and our defenses rely more and more on Goth mercenaries. And now Stilicho marches east with a huge army. The Vandal claims to be guardians of Arcadius as well as his brother Honorius in Rome. Stilicho uses Alaric's invasion as a pretext for his own invasion of the East. Do you want to have to take orders from Stilicho?"

"No."

"Then we must work together to help your beloved husband see the danger of allowing Stilicho's army in the East. Arcadius must order Stilicho to leave. Only a direct order from the emperor himself will do."

"What makes you think Stilicho will listen?"

"Stilicho cannot defy the emperor without showing his hand. He's not ready to claim control over the East. He would lose the support of the Senate and bureaucracy in Rome. He has to pretend to be working in the interests of Arcadius. In the face of a direct order to leave, he can pretend no longer."

"What do you want me to do? I'm … a woman. I can't just tell my husband to order the Western Army to leave."

"No, my dear. You must be far subtler than that. Use your charm. Make him comfortable and happy. Then you can just casually ask questions. You must take care never to appear to be expressing your own opinion, but the questions you ask can help guide his thoughts. 'Is Stilicho to be trusted? What will people think should it appear *he* is the savior? What will he do when the Goths are defeated?' And I will raise the same questions myself. When those he trusts most are of the same mind, he will see the wisest path." Eutropius rose and walked the young woman to the door. "We'll speak again soon."

Alaric strode confidently to his family's compound of tents and wagons. The eastern court had indeed demanded that Stilicho return to Rome. This allowed the Goths to have their way throughout Greece, and he now prepared to sack the storied city of Athens.

Then Athaulf, Brechta, and Daria all confronted him. "Brother, you cannot ride into Athens wearing *that*," Daria said emphatically.

"I thought kings could do as they liked."

His sister persisted. "Even kings need to be aware of how they look. When you ride into Athens—one of the great cities of the world—the citizens will be on the streets. They will all want to see the great Goth king. You can't just look like—"

"Like a Goth?"

"Like an ordinary person with dirty, patched clothes."

Alaric took a deep breath. "So you want me to look like a perfumed lord clad in silk who's never been dirty. What good does that do?"

"Brother," Athaulf interjected, "being king does involve keeping certain appearances—a certain image."

"We're here to intimidate the eastern court into making peace. Dressing me as a woman hardly inspires fear in the local population. I want them to feel gratitude that the barbarian king has spared their city, not amusement that I seek to appear as a pampered patrician."

Brechta stepped next to her husband and touched his arm softly. "You don't need to dress like a woman or a patrician. We have very manly garments and adornments you can choose."

"We want you to look kingly," said Athaulf with a smile. "We want the citizens of Athens to be impressed."

"Why should I care what they think?"

"You shouldn't care what they think, my friend. You should care what they say. You know how the Romans are. They think we're dirty, that we roll in the mud as animals. But what if the Greeks see something different? What if they see a proud, splendid king, adorned in finery obtained through noble conquest?"

"And with a haircut," Daria blurted.

Alaric looked sternly at his beloved sister. "So on the eve of our people's conquest of the great city of Athens, you would have me spend my time as a bride before her wedding day? Do you think I have no more serious matters to attend?"

"It won't take long, and I will handle anything that comes up while you're away," Athaulf assured him. "Go with the women for just an hour or two." Each woman grasped one of Alaric's arms and led him off.

The next morning, Alaric was greatly vexed to be mounted atop a horse not his own. He had been cajoled into foregoing his spirited stallion for a pliant, pure-white gelding. His blond beard and hair were neatly trimmed, and he wore a golden helmet, which gleamed brilliantly in the sun. A chainmail shirt made of silver was worn over a white silk tunic. His splendid appearance and that of the honor guard around him made a royal sight. The citizens of Athens were awed by the military spectacle, and even more, awed to hear Alaric speak. Few expected the Goth king to speak Latin, and they were even more impressed when he said a few lines in Greek. He didn't appear or sound like the beast they had been led to expect.

Brechta and the girls were brought to a splendid home in the city that one of the elders had offered to Alaric. They were amazed by the fine home and took great pleasure in the bathhouse and other amenities. After a few days, they didn't want to leave, but Alaric decided the time had come to march north.

The king's premonition proved prescient. Near the city of Pholoe, scouts began to report a huge force led by Stilicho arriving by ship. Stilicho divided his force, with different elements landing in different locations, and Alaric began to fear they would be surrounded. After frequent skirmishes between the two armies, Alaric summoned the captains, who had recently fought Stilicho's forces for a private meeting.

"Tell me, what type of men march with Stilicho?"

The men looked around at each other, and then one brave soul spoke. "They mostly looked like mercenaries. A few Goths I saw. Others looked to be Germanic tribesmen." The other men looked around and nodded in agreement. Alaric went around the room, asking each his experience. When their tales were told, Alaric dismissed the group, and Athaulf sat next to him.

"You think this army will not fight for Stilicho?" Athaulf asked.

"They might. We carry enough treasure to make it worth their while—if they think they can win. I wouldn't trust hope that they abandon the field, and yet Stilicho must have his own doubts." Alaric stroked his beard and looked up pensively. "I want to try to meet with him."

"With Stilicho? You think he'll agree?"

"I think it's worth sending a messenger to find out. See to it. Send also a messenger to Constantinople. We must know what the eastern court thinks of this. Will they again order Stilicho out of their territory? We must meet before he knows the answer to that question."

Several days later, word arrived that Stilicho agreed to meet in secret. None should know of their meeting, and each leader would bring only a personal guard. Both groups sailed to a small island in neutral territory. Alaric's vessel sailed around the rocky island to verify only one ship had come. The island's shores were steep, ensuring no ship could land except at a single pier, at which the Roman ship had already docked. Stilicho commandeered a villa on the island, and when they landed, Alaric's troupe was bidden to join the Roman general inside. Alaric strode into a large dining room, and Stilicho greeted him with a broad smile.

"My friend! It's good to see you again," Stilicho announced jovially with a firm clasp of forearms and a vigorous pat on the back.

"And you as well," Alaric replied.

"Come, let us sit." The two leaders took seats in simple wooden chairs on opposite sides of a rustic table. "You know why I'm here, right?" the old general asked.

"Of course. You come because the Eastern Empire is powerless to stop me from pillaging Greece." Alaric appeared confident and calm; he added slyly, "Do you know why I'm here?"

"I do. Because you seek a homeland for your people, and what better location than the Greek isles?"

"We do not come to occupy Greece. We come to extract concessions. Concessions that would see us live in peace and equality somewhere within the empire."

"And you would leave Greece to obtain these things?"

"Of course."

"Alas, my old friend. This is not within my power to give. I am guardian only of the western emperor. Many in the court now have his ear. Many oppose allowing a foreign king to impose his own conditions upon us."

"Tell me, what other choice do I have?" Alaric looked Stilicho directly in the eye.

"I understand you're in a bad position, my friend."

"And that's why you should avoid battle," Alaric responded pointedly while Stilicho sat with a puzzled expression. "My men will fight to the death. We have no other choice. Those who fight for treasure have other options."

"You haven't seen my men in battle," Stilicho replied smugly. "We've already won great victories against invaders across the Rhine. Victories against tribes these men are much closer to than the Goths."

Alaric was undaunted. "If you fight now, you may lose. Always difficult to know what an army of mercenaries will do. Even if you win, what do you get? If the eastern emperor does not order you out as soon as he hears of your arrival, he will surely do so as soon as he hears of your victory. Why wouldn't he? Without the threat my army poses, what business have you in the East at all?"

Stilicho's eyes narrowed, and he asked suspiciously, "How do you know Arcadius didn't ask me to come?"

"I have ways of knowing what happens in the Eastern court," Alaric replied cryptically. Stilicho stared at him for several seconds, and Alaric continued, "We both gain more from friendship."

"How?"

"You said it yourself. You come to protect Greece from our raids. All we want is to force a deal with the East. We're leaving this place anyway." Alaric paused and leaned forward to emphasize his point. "What if you just let me continue my march? You accomplish your goal without a drop of blood. I intend to sack Epirus. Once I do, I will continue to march north and seek permission to settle in Illyricum. Arcadius will have no choice but to make peace with us. What's more, I'll still be a counterweight to ambition in the eastern court. A reason they still need your friendship. And who knows? One day you may welcome me as an ally. Someone you can trust." Alaric leaned back confidently.

"Can I trust you?"

"You can. You know me. I'm a simple man. Not like the schemers in the eastern court. My ambition is a safe homeland for my people. No more, no less. I do not aspire to titles or treasure."

"Treasure? I hear you've amassed quite a bit."

"Yes. Treasure I can use to feed my people or pay mercenaries, if need be. You want it? Find me a province where my people can settle as citizens, and it's yours. All of it."

Stilicho rose and walked to a window, looking out over the sea. He thought for a time while staring at the sea, then turned back to Alaric. "You are persuasive, my friend. And I do trust you and value your friendship. If you march north, I'll sail my army back to Italy. But if you betray me, you'll be caught between my wrath and the Eastern Army."

"I understand," the king of the Visigoths replied without hesitation.

Stilicho walked toward Alaric, and they looked each other in the eye as they again clasped each other's forearm.

Arcadius attended religious rituals, while Grata and Aelia awaited the arrival of Eutropius and Saturnius. The old man and the eunuch didn't keep them waiting long.

Saturnius announced, "Alaric's people marched out of Greece and now occupy eastern Illyricum. He's sent an embassy to negotiate for peace."

"What does he want?" Grata demanded.

"That his people be allowed to live in Illyricum. He also wants to be placed in charge of the Eastern Army for Illyricum."

"Why would we agree to that?" Aelia asked. "He lays siege to the capital, ransacks Greece, and now we're to reward him with lands and title?"

"My dear," Eutropius responded, "Alaric now occupies Illyricum. A fact that at present we can do nothing about. He controls the military situation there, whether we like it or not. Agreeing to his terms is just a recognition of the current reality. Wiser it would be to avoid further bloodshed for the moment, at least until our situation improves. In time, the strength of the Eastern Army will return. And if the Huns were to invade, Alaric may make a useful ally."

"Let me get this straight," said Grata. "You have Rufinus murdered on suspicion of making peace with Alaric, and now—"

"My lady!" Eutropius declared indignantly. "I don't know what you might have heard, but I can assure you—"

"I can assure you that I am not blind to your machinations. I'm not going to advocate your desires to Arcadius just so you can eliminate a rival." Her face flushed red with anger.

Saturnius interceded. "My ladies, we didn't come here for a confrontation. We merely came to be sure you hear from voices who seek peace. Arcadius will be beset by many who want war. There is no greater danger to the rule of an emperor than a military defeat. Strengthening the Eastern Army before another war with the Goths makes sense, no matter what you think of anything else. We just wanted to make that point, and now that we have, we will wish you two very distinguished ladies a blessed day."

Saturnius turned to leave, and Eutropius followed, leaving the two women alone.

Aelia took a deep breath. "Eutropius is as trustworthy as a poisonous serpent, but that doesn't mean he's wrong about peace with the Goths."

"Peace with Alaric makes sense, but that doesn't mean it will be popular. The city is rife with resentment of the Goths. People fear Gainas controlling the city's defenses."

"But what other choice is there? We can't do anything about it now. Why not make peace and gain an ally?"

Grata rose and looked out a narrow window at the sprawling streets of Constantinople below. "I fear a revolt. I was there the night Gratian was murdered. Loyalties change quickly. We must be vigilant to protect Placidia."

Aelia shook her head slowly. "Do you really think anyone in the court would murder a little girl?"

Grata turned quickly. "Yes! The daughter of Theodosius would be a grave threat to any usurper. They wouldn't hesitate to slit her throat to leave no heirs. We must be quick to send her to Rome should a threat to Arcadius arise."

Chapter 12

Between East and West

On Easter Sunday, Alaric and his family attended Ulff's service at a church on a plateau with a majestic view of the Adriatic Sea. After mass, tables were brought out into a flat meadow nearby, and many families congregated for the midday feast.

Alaric was served a plate of goat meat with boiled barley and slices of cooked carrot. As he prepared to eat, he noticed his guards detaining a woman, who was trying to get his attention. He motioned that she was let through, and she approached most humbly with her daughter behind her. She bore a wooden plate with two shallow cups and a small spoon in each. When she neared his side, she explained the cups contained spices for his meal. One was sea salt, which Alaric had sampled before. The other was a black powder. He inquired, and she explained it came from India and was called "pepper." She produced some small black peppercorns from her pocket and explained that these were ground into a powder. He sprinkled a little of each on his food and sampled the result.

"Umm. This really does make a difference," he declared. "Everyone should try some." He nodded to the woman, who was clearly pleased that she liked it. She cheerfully served the spices to the other guests. The adults were all happy with the discovery, and Alaric took a moment to be grateful for the beautiful day, the peace his people enjoyed, and the time spent with his family.

Ulff had made it back from Constantinople just in time for the Easter celebration, and Alaric was eager to speak with him. After dinner with his family, Alaric invited Athaulf, Wallia, Thuruar, and Ulff to meet with him in the headquarters he had established in an old Roman villa in the suburbs of the coastal city Salona. They met in a stately room with a polished wooden table strewn with maps. Ulff spoke of dire news from Constantinople.

"The eunuch Eutropius has been executed," the priest declared. "He was corrupt and viewed as a Goth sympathizer. A great hostility to Goths spreads throughout the city. Citizens blame their troubles on Goth immigrants, who take work for little pay and offend local customs. Too many have been allowed to enter the city, and many come illegally, they say. The royal court is unstable. The emperor's weakness breeds a dangerous chaos."

The room was quiet and tense as they considered the grim news.

"Who now takes the place of Eutropius?" Alaric asked.

"Aurelianus is now prefect in the East. But the empress Aelia remains the real power behind the throne."

"Will Arcadius strip me of command in Illyricum?"

"I think it's inevitable."

"And such a perfect day I thought it was," Alaric said wistfully as he rose and paused in thought. After a few moments, he announced, "We cannot remain here." The king then turned to his military leaders. "If the Eastern Army appears and the west blocks the Alpine passes, we will be trapped." He sat again and tuned to Ulff. "What news from the West?"

"Stilicho deepens his hold on the young emperor Honorius. He has now married his daughter Maria to the eleven-year-old emperor."

"How old is she?"

"I don't know exactly, but she's an adult."

"Unbelievable. The Romans wed children to adults and call us barbarians. Does the church have nothing to say about this?"

"The pontiff in Rome faces certain … practical realities."

Alaric leaned back in his chair and rolled his eyes in disgust. "What of their army?"

"Stilicho's army of mercenaries has largely disbanded. The Western Army now consists mostly of troops in Gaul, Britannia, and Rhaetia. Italia itself is left with few mobile troops."

"Stilicho will go north to gather more men," Wallia observed, locking eyes with Alaric.

"Yes, and we may have little time to march before the trap is set. If the Romans move against us, we must be prepared to act quickly. By the time the Romans learn of our march, time must be our ally."

The conversation turned to more mundane matters, and Alaric asked a servant to bring wine. The group retired from the table and pulled chairs around a large stone hearth housing a roaring fire. The men stared into the warm glow of the fire, sipped their wine, and discussed their families, domestic concerns, and hopes for the future. The good-natured banter turned more serious as Alaric began to lament the weight of the crown.

"Often I wonder if the path I have put us on is best. Would it not be better to just disperse as Saphrax did? Are his people now safer far from the cares of the world?"

"Their people are defenseless," Wallia said emphatically. "Those who moved too far north are pressed by the Huns and must rely on Radagaisus for protection. Those who remain in the empire are subjugated by the Romans. We can defend ourselves."

"But such a large army makes us a target also," Alaric responded vacantly, still staring into the blaze.

After a moment, Athaulf offered his view. "Brother, it is a great burden to decide for so many. But you are wise to follow the path of Fritigern. Athanaric was foolish to stand alone against the Huns, and now his people are scattered and defeated. Many came into the Eastern Empire not as a formidable group but as individuals or in small bands. They lack the strength to defend themselves or insist on fair treatment from Constantinople. I don't envy them."

All in the group made sounds of agreement, and Wallia raised his chalice. "I'd rather die defending my people than just run and hide. Here's to Alaric's rule! Long may he lead us against our enemies!"

All joined the toast, and Alaric smiled slightly, heartened by the support of his closest friends. "We face many threats," he said. "Let's hope I have the wisdom to lead us past them." He raised his glass again.

"Wisdom?" Wallia asked. "I think sharp swords and greater numbers are all you'll need!"

As the group's laughter died down, Athaulf ventured, "Do you not get enough wisdom from that book you're always reading?"

Alaric smirked. "Seneca is master of many pithy quotes. Whether it all adds up to wisdom is a question I still ponder."

"So, you're not convinced by the stoics?" Ulff asked.

"I think it easy to advocate freeing yourself from the bonds of desire when you're a rich Roman patrician."

The group chuckled, and Ulff continued, "But should it damn the philosophy to be advocated by a flawed messenger? Would it be true if urged by someone who is not a hypocrite?"

Alaric smiled broadly. "Perhaps not, but still I question the wealthy telling plebs and slaves they need only stop wanting what they do not have."

"Aye!" Athaulf declared. "We've spoken of this philosophy. A tool for the Roman aristocrats to control the masses, I think it is."

A few grumbled agreement. "Perhaps the philosophy can be misused," the priest offered, "but is it not also true that clinging to desire begets disappointment? Does coveting wealth not increase the pain of its absence?"

They all stared into the fire for a bit longer until Alaric spoke again. "I've thought much of that as well. As with many things, the truth lies somewhere between two extremes. Accepting your lot in life may make suffering easier, but it does not justify accepting fate without fighting for change. We could all just be satisfied as Roman slaves or mercenaries, abandoning hope for a better future, but do any of us want to live that way? We must strive for what we truly need while avoiding the temptations of avarice."

"Well spoken," Ulff conceded, raising his glass again. Only when the fire burned low and the cask ran dry did the men part company and return to their families.

Aelia walked down a dark marble corridor with a high ceiling and towering columns on both sides. A voice in the shadows startled her. "My God! Saturnius, you scared me half to death."

"I have urgent need to speak with you, Empress." He led her into a small, dark room used for storage and lit only by the candles he had brought. "The Goth situation spins out of control. Gainas now seizes control over the city.

Aelia's heart sank, and she slumped down on a bench. "Is there nothing we can now do?"

"That's why I've come," Saturnius whispered. "The city is ripe to rebel. Great mobs will rise up against the Goths, and Gainas will be forced to flee the city."

Aelia looked ill. "Is there no other way? What of the Goth women and children? Will the mob spare them?"

"This uprising is coming, whether we welcome it or not. I come only to warn you. You and Arcadius must remain inside the palace. You must be sure he does nothing rash. Aurelianus will help you.

When the rioting began, horrific screams moved even the placid Arcadius to act. He demanded the immediate presence of his prefect.

"What happens outside the palace?" the young emperor demanded. "I've heard screams for hours."

"I'm afraid the Goths have finally pushed their welcome beyond the breaking point," Aurelianus replied passively. "They are—"

"The empress says even women and children are being slaughtered."

"I can assure you, Augustus, the guard is acting to ensure peace."

"I will not allow a slaughter of Christians."

"Yes, but we should remember most Goths are not true Christians."

The emperor's face grew red. "I said I will not have a slaughter. You will go forth and stop the violence."

"Of course, Augustus." The slight sneer in his voice was apparent only to Aelia, who lurked in the shadow of the drapes behind the throne.

The screams continued until nightfall, unabated by Arcadius's orders. Few Goths in the city survived. Some escaped through the gates or on ships. A few found protection among the scarce Romans with the compassion to grasp the inhumanity of the moment. The city's sewers ran full with blood. Thousands of corpses were stacked on the street like firewood. Gainas escaped with a portion of his force, but they were now too few to stand their ground outside the city. In desperation, he was forced to flee across the Danube into Hun territory.

News of the massacre was received with great bitterness in Alaric's camp. Ulff dropped to his knees when word arrived. Even the Goth clergy hadn't been spared. Among the military leaders, only Alaric failed to join in the angry calls for vengeance. Some began to quietly question the king's temperance. He tolerated the insubordinate whispers for a time and then called the leaders together to announce his decision to march.

They gathered on a soft, flat meadow near a bend in a gentle creek. In addition to his normal council, Alaric summoned also Sarus and Sergeric, leaders of other prominent families, and high-ranking officers.

Alaric welcomed each to the gathering, then stood on a log and began to speak. "My friends, I gather you because the time has come for us to march. The slaughter in Constantinople cannot go unanswered. Those who drove this massacre are now more powerful. Only the threat of the Huns keeps the East at bay. Should Stilicho block the Alpine passes, we would be trapped between East and West, between the sea and the mountains.

"The West fights its own battles along the Rhine. Should they prevail, those troops will soon be brought to confront us. But Italia is now lightly defended. We will march deep into Italia before an army from the East or West can arrive. The Romans would give much—"

"And what if they don't?" Sarus questioned.

"Don't what?"

"Don't agree to a deal. What if the Rhine frontier is stable and they bring troops from Gaul, from Rhaetia, from North Africa even? How can we be sure such a large group in Italia will be safe?"

In near unison, all the faces solemnly turned back for Alaric's response.

"None know the future, but if Stilicho could move troops to defend the mountains, they would already be there. Should we wait for them? We will seize the advantage of speed. It is because we are so many that we must not give away the first move. The Romans don't have time to defeat the Rhine invaders before we control Italia. We must all prepare to march."

As they began the march toward northern Italia, a captain made little effort to keep his rage quiet. "The streets shall run thick with the blood of the Romans! I shall avenge ten times over the violence done to our people!"

Alaric could endure such comments no longer. "I grow weary of calls to do unto the Romans as they have done unto us!" the king roared in anger. "Do you lack the wit to think what your vengeance will bring? Will you tell God you murdered civilians because the Romans did the same? I tire of being the only one who thinks beyond tomorrow morning.

Filling Rome's streets with blood will change nothing." His outburst was sufficient to quell the complaints but did little to change the sentiment.

In Milan, Stilicho convened with the West's young emperor. They met in a private chamber within the royal palace. Honorius sat alone with only his new bride, Maria, at his side, and several civil officials standing along the walls. Once Stilicho sat next to the emperor, he began to explain that the eastern court had stripped Alaric of his title, and the Visigoths now marched toward Italia.

Stilicho drew a breath to continue, but Honorius finally spoke. "If Constantinople strips this barbarian of his title, why does he march west?"

"A just question. Should we block the Alpine passes, the Eastern Army could trap him. Alaric's a military man. He knows this and will not allow himself to be surrounded. He knows also that our forces are occupied defending the northern borders. Italia itself lacks the strength to repel him. Alaric will invade and demand a western province for his people."

Another pause ensued, then Stilicho spoke urgently. "Let me ride north, Augustus. Our troops are tied up in Gaul, repelling an invasion by the Alemanni. I shall either defeat the invaders or make peace with them. Either way, I will return with an army able to crush this new threat."

"You would leave me now?" the emperor asked with evident fear.

"Only briefly. The rivers of Italia will slow the Goth advance. I will leave and return with a mighty army before they arrive. Else I stay only with a force that cannot protect you." Honorius looked at his wife, and she nodded her approval. He consented to Stilicho's plan, and the old general set out.

Aelia was the first to be notified that a gift had arrived from the king of the Huns. She entered the throne room with a few attendants and immediately noticed a putrid smell. She summoned the courage to look inside the basket sent by Uldin but gasped and stepped back quickly, horrified at the sight of Gainas's head.

Saturnius had just arrived in the chamber and knew what was in the basket without looking. "The Huns never tire of reminding others of their savagery," he remarked. "A woman need not concern herself ..."

The intensity of her stare cut his words short. "We'll all be concerned when Uldin decides to cross the Danube," she noted as she walked slowly toward him.

"If … if he crosses the Danube, Empress."

"Why should he not? The Eastern Army is spread thin. We've massacred our Goth mercenaries. Your advice has left us at the mercy of the Huns."

"My advice?" the old politician asked incredulously.

Aelia spoke with clarity and confidence. "When you convinced me to use Gainas against Eutropius, you said he would be banished only. When his head rolled, you said it was an unfortunate mistake. Then you unleashed a great massacre of the Goths, and now our defenses are depleted. The only thing that seems to have improved is your position."

"Empress," Saturnius pleaded, "you know I have always sought—"

"I don't care what you've sought!" she snapped.

"Uldin sent this head as a gift. He wishes to curry favor—"

"What concerns me most is that you actually believe what you're saying. You're quite content to think the Huns will show us kindness. Gainas once led the Eastern Army. Now his head's in a basket. Forgive me for not sharing your optimism over the message Uldin wished to send."

The Visigoths' advance was easier than expected. Dry weather made for easier crossings of the many rivers lying in their path. They passed south of the Alps in November, and the winter was far milder than any they had endured. The Western Empire provided little resistance. By the time Alaric threatened to besiege Milan, the young emperor had fled the city. Honorius retreated to a smaller town on the coast, and Alaric moved in to surround him.

Thuruar returned from the rear guard with an urgent message from the scouts.

Still struggling for breath, he announced, "Stilicho approaches with a vast army. He convinced the Alemanni to join him, and he marches south with legions from Gaul as well. They'll be upon us in two days."

Alaric's stomach churned, and his appetite disappeared. He didn't have the men to fight both the Romans and the Alemanni.

"Send word to the civilians," he commanded. "We must move west at once. We cannot be caught between Stilicho and the sea."

"And then what?" Athaulf asked. "A fighting retreat all the way back to Illyricum?"

"No," Alaric responded, still lost in thought. "The civilians cannot move quickly enough. We would be trapped in the mountains, with no room to maneuver. It would turn into a massacre. We must face Stilicho here."

"We do not have the numbers," Wallia observed incredulously.

"Running won't change that," Alaric snapped back. "If we let this army arrive fully, if we let them get set and attack when Stilicho chooses, we won't stand a chance. His men will be weakest when they first arrive. Some won't yet have completed the march. All will be weary. That will be our best chance. How much stomach will the Alemanni have after a defeat? After a draw even? We must press the issue now."

The Goths moved west near the town of Polenta. But Stilicho too saw the benefit of a first strike. On Easter Sunday, April 6, 402, Stilicho attacked the Goths, seeking to catch them observing the holiday while unprepared. Alaric was notified immediately. He skillfully rallied his troops and rode out to confront the Alemanni's cavalry.

The fierce counterattack took the Alemanni by surprise. Alaric was able to outflank them on both sides. Unable to fall back due to the Roman troops behind them, the Alemanni had no room to maneuver, and the Goth's attack turned into a slaughter. The Alemanni cavalry was defeated, and their king slain.

Daria and Brechta put on brave faces for the children. The young ones ran and squealed without a care. The women noticed each other's hands tremble. They sought to console one another, but neither would find solace before news of the fighting.

A heavy sound on the wind brought all to silence. Then the noise became unmistakable.

Veins burst forth from Daria's neck and face. "Run!" she screamed. Women and children shrieked in terror as they fled. Daria clutched her friend's forearm. "You must take the children! Lead them into the woods." Brechta clutched her baby and yelled for the children to run with her.

Terrified screams rang out as Roman soldiers marched into camp. They strode quickly behind great curved shields, with sharp spears clearing the way before them. Daria moved deftly through a sea of refugees streaming the other way. She could hear the growing sound of galloping horses. They would soon be surrounded.

Buying time for others to escape was the best Daria could hope for. She strode toward the line of spearmen. The commander's horse walked slowly before the line. She stepped forth to confront him. A soft wind blew the hair from her face—fair and unyielding.

The commander raised his hand, and the march stopped. Silence came abruptly. Daria drew a long dagger. She lifted her head, and her voice rang out. "Do you not have the courage to fight our men?"

The commander smiled mildly and dismounted. He was surprised a Goth woman could speak Latin at all. He now had all the hostages he needed. This one seemed special. He made sure she wasn't harmed.

It wasn't long before the Goths repelled the Roman attack and again controlled their camps. Alaric clutched his sword tightly and strode quickly toward his family's encampment. He bellowed for Brechta and the girls. The closer he got, the louder his calls and the quicker his pace. He was in a full panic by the time he arrived.

He saw there only Ordu. The king of the Goths dropped to his knees, lifted back his head, and let out an anguished scream. Ordu offered comforting words—telling him Brechta, Daria, and the others had been unharmed when taken prisoner, and two of his daughters had escaped. His grief turned hopeful, and he commanded a search that soon retrieved his girls. Both were found hiding in a tree not far from the camp and were reunited with their father. Athaulf's children were also found hiding in the woods, as was Thuruar's son, Theodoric.

That night Alaric's council worked late, plotting their strategy. There was a heated discussion about the merits of a counterattack. Athaulf and Wallia favored an attack designed to rescue the prisoners. Thuruar wanted to focus on defeating Stilicho first and worrying about the prisoners later. Sarus and Sergeric favored an immediate retreat, arguing that they should never have come. Alaric remained silent as the debate raged. He knew as well as any that their plan couldn't just be about retaking his family. The Romans would expect such a plot. The survival of thirty thousand other souls was paramount. Still, an immediate retreat offered little, and a second attack held the prospect of a victory that solved all problems. Alaric remained convinced they had a better chance fighting out in the open than they would if trapped in the mountain passes.

"Thuruar is right," the king finally announced. "At dawn we will attack again. Even a draw buys time for the rest of the civilians to gain a day or two's march." Alaric's characteristic confidence was drained and his anguish apparent. With a somber mood, they made preparations and took a little sleep.

Alaric returned to his camp and lifted the flap of a tent back to check on his girls. Alonia was awake and sobbing quietly. Alaric lay down and embraced his oldest daughter. He couldn't provide the assurances she sought and felt a sense of hopelessness foreign to him.

Before first light, Alaric and his captains mustered the troops and prepared to charge the Romans. Alaric rode with the scouts, quietly probing the enemy lines. Even as the sun began to rise, a dense fog made it difficult to see. If he could just learn how the Romans were configured, perhaps he could order the perfect assault. So much depended on it. Then he saw something move. A Roman messenger appeared out of the misty darkness. He declared that he bore a note from Stilicho, which Alaric hurriedly read.

Turning his horse quickly, Alaric galloped back to Athaulf and the other commanders.

"Stilicho offers an exchange of prisoners provided we retreat back to Illyricum," the king announced with great excitement.

"I knew he liked you," Athaulf quipped.

"He must have seen you would attack again," Thuruar mused. "He fears this. Perhaps the Alemanni will no longer fight."

"Perhaps," said Alaric, "but this remains our best choice. We can move our women and children to safety without a fight."

"Almost too good to be true," Athaulf said suspiciously.

Alaric frowned and stared ahead vacantly. "Stilicho would fear the possibility of a defeat here. If he loses, what stops us from sacking Rome? Even a small risk may be more than he can afford. He may still also desire to use us as a shield against the East."

"Or maybe he just knows we'll be more vulnerable in the mountains," Wallia observed.

"Still, we have little choice," the king concluded. "Lose on the field, and we condemn our people to death and slavery. Take the deal and we might leave without further loss. If Stilicho does strike in the mountains, we will have bought time for most to escape." Alaric stroked his beard as he pondered his decision. "I will send word to Stilicho now. We must be prepared to fight should he betray us."

Late in the afternoon, Alaric stood again on the front lines, watching the Roman infantry arrayed against them. This time he could clearly see the Roman front. The infantry was arrayed in a tight formation two rows deep just outside a densely wooded area. It wouldn't take much to provoke another clash.

The tense silence was broken by the happy and chaotic sounds of women and children nearing the front. Between Roman companies, the civilian prisoners came flooding, then ran fast toward the Goth lines. Alaric spied Brechta in the crowd and ran toward her, gripping her tightly in his burly arms and swinging his wife around with great joy. Tears streamed down their smiling faces as they kissed passionately.

Alaric brought Brechta and their young daughter back to their compound, where the older two girls awaited. Their joyous reunion was a common scene as the other captives were reunited with their families.

The civilians broke camp swiftly and marched by morning. Alaric kept his army in a standoff against Stilicho until the civilians had a few days' head start. The Visigoths began a slow retreat north across the Po Valley and into the Alps, with Stilicho's army hard on their heels. Goth spies in Stilicho's army sent word the general was convinced Alaric planned to circle back and invade Italia again. Alaric was thus not taken by surprise when Stilicho's force ambushed them in the mountain passes.

Most of the civilians were still a few days ahead when Alaric's army entered a mountain valley near the town of Verona. The two old friends rode slowly north, surveying the mountain pass before them. A cool mountain wind swirled through the valley.

"Stilicho betrays us," Athaulf observed without much concern. The old friends looked north at a flood of Roman soldiers pouring down the mountains ahead of their march.

An attempt to block the passes before them wasn't a surprise. Only when the Romans began to attack their flanks did Alaric's heart sink. The Romans had the high ground all around them.

Stilicho's men blocked the passes on both ends. They were surrounded. The assault on their flanks split the Visigoth army in half. Alaric was trapped on the south side closest to Stilicho's main force. The Visigoth soldiers sensed the battle turning into a disaster. Many sighed in despair, knowing they were divided and surrounded.

Deathly silence was broken by the sound of Alaric's horse galloping behind them. They turned to their king. He screamed as he rode, "The Romans are weakest on the north. Fight your way to our brothers, or we all die here!" The king turned his horse north, leading the charge.

Visigoths trapped on the north end of the valley rallied to their king. The ferocious attack from two sides broke the Roman lines. Alaric had reunited his army.

No longer surrounded and with the mountains near the northern pass protecting their flanks, the Goths were able to fight their way back through the pass and enter terrain too steep for the Romans to set another trap. The Romans were the ones who now feared an ambush.

As night fell, the Visigoths moved a safe distance from Stilicho's force, reinforced guards on the passes, and tended the wounded. Alaric took no rest. Many of the wounded wouldn't long survive. Some wouldn't live out the night. Few could sleep amid the tortured moans and screeches.

At daybreak, they moved again, driven by fear of the Romans. By the next night, they became more confident in their position, and grumblings of discontent began to grow. Some questioned why they had come at all. What had been gained by the invasion of Italia?

Alaric found Brechta putting the girls to sleep in one of their wagons. She smiled and pleaded with him to take some rest. They lay together in their own wagon, warm under blankets on a frosty night. Brechta caressed his brow, which still bore a frown.

"What troubles you, my love?" she asked.

"The men now question the wisdom of invading Italia. I question it myself. I should've known the Romans could use their wealth to buy more armies. Stilicho is a great general."

"And so are you!"

"Am I? Every battle I've fought against him has been a draw, except for this one, and I barely escaped with my army intact. We return to Illyricum no better off than we left."

Brechta lay on her side, gazing on her husband as he stared upward. "I hear the people speak," she said softly. "They do not blame you for our loss. Everyone knows the Romans are powerful. How many generals have invaded Italia? Stilicho respects your skill. You should not despair." Brechta smiled as her husband turned to face her. "Our fortunes will again brighten."

In the shadows of the outskirts of camp, Sarus and his brother watched the glow of the far-off fires and spoke in hushed whispers.

"The rumblings grow louder, brother," Sergeric said. "The time comes to challenge Alaric's rule."

"I hear the same voices, but those who see the truth are still too few." Sarus didn't face his brother but looked toward a small group huddled around a distant fire. "Alaric's arrogance and false graciousness still enchant most. It would take another defeat to weaken his grip on power."

"Should we then do nothing?"

"No, my brother, we must bring these grievances to light. All must hear our warnings and then remember who spoke wisdom when disaster arrives."

"Should we then remain in Alaric's service? Would it not be better to join with the Romans?"

"It is difficult to know which path to follow. If we join the Romans, we would prove our loyalty to them and move up within their ranks. If the Romans then win on the field, we would be positioned to govern our own people—to lead them to peace."

"Would the people not call us traitors?"

"Perhaps that is why we need not walk the same path. After I speak, I could lead those who would follow to Stilicho's camp. You could remain in Alaric's council—hearing all that transpires. We would then be able to unite our followers once Alaric's foolishness is exposed."

The next evening, Alaric held council with all senior officers. He knew Sarus would give voice to the discontent and called on him to speak first.

"Is it not now plain for all to see the folly of blindly pursuing one man's ambition?" Sarus asked. "Have I not long counseled against risking the safety of our people so Alaric can maintain his Roman title?"

Thuruar shot up and growled, "Long have you brooded that Alaric was chosen king and you were not!"

Alaric quieted the grumbles of approval. "Let him speak."

Sarus continued, "We marched into Italia because the Eastern Empire stripped Alaric of his generalship."

"And slaughtered thousands of Goths," Athaulf interjected.

"But we weren't attacked. Nevertheless, all of us, every last one, upended our lives and marched into Italia. Then we were forced to retreat right back where we had started. For what gain? What did those who fell buy with their lives?"

Athaulf stood. "All who served in the Roman army understand the foolishness of allowing them to decide when and where we fight. Waiting around for the Romans to strike would bring disaster. All who live outside the empire suffer at the hands of the Huns. To live within the empire means we must find a way to fit in. Having our king as a Roman general is the only way to truly be safe."

After much bickering, it became clear only a few shared Sarus's view. Alaric wanted to give the discontented a chance to air their grievances. After many hours, the council was concluded, and Alaric urged the leaders to take rest and reflect on what they had heard. In the morning, Sarus rode off with two hundred of his followers, but Sergeric pledged his loyalty to Alaric and remained in his council.

Stilicho rode into Ravenna as if a conquering hero. He had saved the Western Empire from destruction and was welcomed with much gratitude and praise. Young Honorius was so shaken by Alaric's invasion that he had moved the capital to Ravenna, a well-defended fortress surrounded by swamps and close enough to the sea to allow for a quick escape. Many prominent Romans worried the emperor's seclusion would weaken the Western Empire beyond Italia, but most also saw the opportunities a weak emperor could open for them.

At a ceremony honoring Stilicho for his victory, Honorius asked, "What gift can I bestow upon the Roman who delivered us from the barbarian invaders?"

"Augustus, you honor me. I would ask nothing for myself. It was my great privilege to defend the empire. I would ask only, for the benefit of the entire empire, that you indulge me in one request," the general paused, leaving the whole court hanging on what followed. "I would see you name Alaric again as head of the military for Illyricum."

A stunned silence ensued, followed by gasps and frantic whispers. Even the young emperor was stuck by the irony of Stilicho's request. "And why would I bestow such an honor on the man who took up arms against me? The man you just drove out of Italia?"

"He can be a useful ally. Many in Constantinople claim Illyricum as part of the Eastern Empire. That province has always been fertile ground for new recruits. Arcadius is now surrounded by many schemers, who seek to enrich themselves by claiming part of your empire. But it is Alaric who in fact controls Illyricum. Make him your ally, and Illyricum remains part of the West. Should the schemers succeed in tricking Arcadius into invading Illyricum, Alaric will defend it for the West without need to deplete your own troops."

"How do you know Alaric will not betray us? How do you know he wouldn't make a deal with the East?"

"I don't. I just know he's less likely to do so if you make him your military commander. The Goths have no love of the East after the slaughter in Constantinople. And I have known Alaric to be an honorable man. He seeks a homeland for his people. If you give him one, I believe you will have his allegiance."

Some in the court spoke out against Stilicho's request. They objected to the idea of using a barbarian warlord as a shield against the Eastern Empire. Honorius was sympathetic to their concerns but ultimately unwilling to deny the victorious general's request. With the emperor's consent, Stilicho again named Alaric *magister militum per* Illyricum.

Chapter 13

Betrayal

A smile spread across Hamil's face as soon as his column marched within view of the walls of Florence. They had covered much distance through Italia in little time. After ceding ground to the Huns for so many years, it felt good to seize the initiative, to be winning. He marched with an army twenty thousand strong and with thirty thousand civilians following.

In light of the disaster that befell Odothesius, many feared to cross into Roman territory, but the invasion of Italia was successful, and they stood on the verge of a great victory over a fabled Roman city only ten days' march from Rome. Once they occupied Florence, the Romans wouldn't be able to dislodge them. Hamil felt more confident than ever before and took great joy in marching around the walls as they took up positions for a long siege.

Stilicho recognized the danger as soon as Radagaisus's invasion began. When he read the order to break the siege at Florence, he pounded the table in rage. "Do they really think it's that easy? I'm supposed to break an entrenched siege with less than half the men. No one but Honorius actually thinks it is possible. They look only to blame me for the failure." Stilicho spoke to himself but wasn't alone in his tent.

"You need more men," Sarus observed.

"Do I?" Stilicho asked sarcastically, still fuming over the impossible task. Stilicho had no great love for Sarus, finding him much as Jovius had described.

"Is it not possible to pull troops from elsewhere in the empire?"

Stilicho didn't look at Sarus, who stood near the tent entrance. Instead, he stared ahead vacantly. "The Eastern Army looks to its own borders. I could go to Gaul and rally more troops, but it will not be enough."

"If you cannot defeat Radagaisus, perhaps you can make peace with him."

"That would never be accepted. The court's control over Honorius is now too strong. They've convinced him it would be treason to make peace with an invader. Many believe our problems result from Valens's decision to let the Visigoths cross the Danube."

"You do not?"

"It wasn't the crossing that caused the problem, and we didn't have the men to keep them out. It was the greed of Maximus and the vanity of Valens that created disaster. Valens attacked before he understood the situation. This I will never do. I must know everything that will affect the outcome." He paced the room before continuing. "Radagaisus judged the Huns a more dangerous foe. He believes he's gained an advantage by escaping them. But what if we take that from him?"

"What do you mean?"

Stilicho now looked at Sarus directly. "Tell me, friend, when Fritigern enlisted Hun mercenaries to break the siege in the Haemus mountains, how did he arrange it?"

"He sent Alavivus with a few Alans who spoke both languages, but now there is no need. The Huns have long had many Goth slaves who speak both tongues."

"I imagine not many of those Goths speak Latin."

"Probably not."

"But you do." Stilicho's mood brightened. "My friend, this is a time when one predisposed to bold action can gain much."

"An embassy to Uldin will take time. What if the city falls?"

"The Goths don't have the equipment to breach the walls. They're trying to starve the people into opening their gates. Instead of a large force easily noticed, we will send small bands to smuggle food and supplies into the city. If properly provisioned, it will not fall."

When Thoris realized he'd been summoned to translate for a Goth leader, his heart leaped at the prospect of peace between the Huns and his people. Sarus had not long addressed Uldin before that hope was brutally dashed. Thoris found it difficult to conceal his rage as he translated. This man wasn't a leader of the Goths; he was a traitor who had sold his sword to the Romans and now schemed to wield the Huns as a weapon against his own people.

Since the Huns had pushed Radagaisus's folk farther and farther, Thoris began to feel guilty about the service he had provided Uldin. Now he felt more like a collaborator, who abetted the persecution of the Goths. Was he even better than this man? Only after he'd been dismissed could he truly ponder what he had become. Would it not be better to do as Hamil did and escape the Huns' torment, even if it meant death? At least dead he could no longer be forced to aid the enemy of his people.

Hamil sat down to enjoy another hearty meal just before sundown. The Goths had eaten well off the rich countryside during the siege. Hamil loved the weather in Italia and looked forward to watching another beautiful sunset.

Frantic riders galloping into camp shattered the tranquil moment. He stood up quickly, dropping his plate. The men were bloodied and panicked.

"The Huns, the Huns!" one rider screamed as he galloped straight through the camp on his way to the next. Another rider pulled back on his reigns sharply, causing the horse to rise up on its hind legs, kicking wildly with its front legs.

"Hun cavalry attacks from the North! Stilicho's army marches from the South!" he announced to Hamil's commanding officer. "We must quit the city!" The man galloped off.

It wasn't long before foot soldiers began flooding into the camp. Many were badly wounded.

Hamil didn't sleep that night; instead, he attended to wounds, one after the other, until he was surprised to see the sun had already risen.

Despite the beautiful weather, the days that followed were dark and foreboding. Stilicho used the Hun cavalry to break the siege but didn't move to provoke a major battle. The camps were rife with rumors of what had transpired in the councils of Radagaisus. All agreed they had too many civilians to try to flee both the Huns and the Romans. Making defensive formations around the civilians was obviously not a long-term strategy, yet no other options were plausible.

Hamil was greatly concerned that he seemed to see the danger before the senior commanders did. Every time he marched on patrol of the perimeter, he saw more and more signs their enemies were entrenching themselves. The Goth leaders had waited for Stilicho to attack, hoping their defensive fortifications would provide the advantage leading to victory. But for weeks and weeks, Stilicho never attacked—his men just kept digging in.

The only good news for Hamil was that, as the Goths pulled in closer and closer, he was now able to live with Heather when not on duty. Their circumstances were too grim to be truly happy. They could be thankful only to have each other and their small children for a little while longer.

Only when the problem became too apparent to ignore did Radagaisus begin ordering attacks to break out of the tightening noose. By then, however, the clans had begun to turn inward, each wanting to act only for its own interest rather than risking death for the sake of others. Radagaisus lost control of the army, and the attacks he was able to order were too small to punch through. Each day the fortifications of the enemy became stronger and stronger. Radagaisus rode the perimeter, seeking a weakness they could exploit. He never found it.

Hamil would never forget the day it happened. It was August 23, 406. His sadness overwhelmed him as he watched the mighty king, to whom he'd pledged allegiance, walk out of camp alone. Hamil didn't know what had been said in Radagaisus's council, but the fact that the king walked without his guard and that he had such an expression on his face made clear what he meant to do. Hamil followed behind him all the way to the front. He saw the king turn himself over to the Roman guards, who handled him roughly as he was led off.

Rumors had circulated for days that Stilicho offered equitable terms for a surrender and that the Goth people would be spared. This offer must have struck Radagaisus as his best option. But in the days that followed, word began to spread that Radagaisus had been beheaded as soon as he arrived in Stilicho's tent. What the Romans had in mind for equitable terms was that the Goth men would have the option of joining the Roman army. If they did, their women and children would be dispersed to towns throughout Italia and used as hostages to ensure the loyalty of the men. Those who refused or had no men to offer the Romans would be sold into slavery.

Thoris never saw the great Roman general until after the battle was won. He knew the Huns had been successful because of their joyous mood and boastful tales of triumph. The gold they'd been promised was flowing in, and even the most cantankerous chieftains were effusive in their praise of Uldin's wisdom. They had been paid handsomely to defeat their old enemy and expand their conquest even further. Now the time had come to conclude the alliance, and Stilicho came to pay homage to Uldin.

Thoris was more impressed with Stilicho than he anticipated. He expected a pompous and cruel Roman, not much better than the Huns. What he actually saw was a general able to exude strength and confidence without arrogating authority or making threats. Stilicho had Sarus translate Thoris's words into Latin. He took the time to ask about Thoris, and this time Uldin tolerated the general's personal interest in his slave.

Stilicho had come to thank Uldin for his service and lay the groundwork for another alliance in the future.

"I hear twelve thousand of Radagaisus's men are now under your command," Uldin said. "Eight thousand more will be your slaves. You have profited much from our alliance."

"Yes, my friend, your service to the empire will not be forgotten. We look forward to future alliances that would benefit both, but we do not have many among us who speak your beautiful language. As you can see, it takes two translators for us to communicate. I wonder if you might be willing to sell me this translator to facilitate future communications. I would pay you handsomely, of course."

Thoris's hopes were lifted only for an instant before Uldin abruptly dismissed the suggestion. Uldin knew Stilicho sought not only a translator but also someone who knew his mind. Uldin had also come to trust Thoris, more so even than his own kin.

When Thoris had been dismissed and walked out of Uldin's tent, the sun was so much brighter than the dark tent that he could barely see for several seconds. As his eyes adjusted, he could see a large column of Goth prisoners being led away to service in the Roman army. Their plight saddened him, but he always enjoyed seeing the faces of his people. He took a moment to watch the scene unfold, then heard a familiar voice.

"Thoris! Thoris! I knew I'd see you!" Hamil's voice sounded cheerful, and Thoris was overcome with joy. He could see his old friend marching toward him in the middle of the column.

"Hamil! My God, you're alive! All these years, I never knew."

"I made it!" Hamil declared triumphantly. "And now I'm going to be a soldier in the Roman army!"

The commotion had caught the attention of Roman guards, who began to crack whips as a warning.

Hamil turned as he passed his old friend. "Be well, my friend! We'll meet again!"

On the last day of 406, a huge group of Vandals, Alans, and Suebi crossed the Rhine and overran northern Gaul. They were driven by desperation to escape the encroaching tyranny of the Huns. The Romans' depleted forces were nowhere near sufficient to stop the huge groups from crossing the frozen river.

Alaric's people had migrated to east Illyricum—far enough from Rome and Constantinople to give them room to maneuver if attacked from either direction. Stilicho recognized a need for more men to counter the Rhine invasion and sought an alliance with Alaric. But what could he give in return? Giving the Visigoths a permanent homeland in west Illyricum meant taking land from citizens of the Western Empire. The Roman Senate would never allow this. But Alaric's Goths already controlled most of east Illyricum—claimed by the Eastern Empire as part of its territory. Why not force the East to give Alaric what he already held and thus buy his allegiance to fend off the Rhine invasion?

To this end, it was agreed that Alaric would move his army east to threaten Constantinople. Stilicho would cross the Adriatic with an army from Italia, and before the gates of Constantinople, the combined army would force the East to yield. Stilicho also coveted the opportunity to at last break the hold the eastern court held over Arcadius and fulfill his oath to Theodosius.

To cement their alliance, it was agreed that they would ostensibly exchange young men to learn more of each other's culture but in reality, more as hostages. Alaric debated which of the young men to send. They had to be sons of the high ranking—people influential enough to object to any treachery that might endanger their children. Although his son was an obvious candidate, Athaulf argued the boy was too old and already a leader in the army. Many suspected Athaulf just wanted to protect his son.

The debate grew contentious until Thuruar finally declared, "Theodoric will go."

The group grew silent. Theodoric was well liked but seen as a timid lad. Some whispered the boy grew weak under the protection of his huge and influential father. Would sending him send the right message? Some worried Theodoric's mild demeanor would embolden the Romans to greater aggression. Alaric would say only that he would consider the matter.

After the meeting, Alaric obtained Thuruar's consent to speak with his son directly. Theodoric was summoned, and the two walked together on a dirt path on the outskirts of camp. Alaric was friendly and sought to put the boy at ease.

"I suspect your father's already told you about—"

"He's told me. He wants me to go to Rome."

"Is that what you want?"

The young man paused and breathed deeply. "I want to serve my people. I want to make my father proud. If this is the—"

"But is it what *you* want?"

Theodoric didn't respond, and the two continued to walk in silence for a while. "You know, it's all right to be afraid. We all are at some point. Sometimes it helps to talk about it. Dark fears often lose power when exposed to light."

"I fear many things. I fear being so far from my friends and family. I fear not fitting in among the Romans. I fear disappointing my father. I fear my first battle. I fear even what others will say if they learn I've been chosen."

"What will they say?"

"They will say it was a poor choice, that I will make the Romans think our people are meek."

"And why would they say that?"

"Many already say I do poorly in training, that I wouldn't stand and fight when the time comes. Above all else, I fear being a coward."

They came to a log at the edge of a peaceful meadow, and Alaric bid the boy to sit with him. "I've seen much in many battles, Theodoric. Many things I didn't expect. Sometimes the fiercest in training turn soft on the field. Sometimes the meekest of men find their courage when it matters most." He paused. "Tell me, if you did flee the field, what would you do? Become a Roman slave? Starve alone in the wilderness? Come back to live in shame?"

"No. I'd rather be dead," Theodoric replied.

"You come from a noble lineage. Your father's not a coward. What makes you think you'd be? And you know what the Romans would do to our people if we don't defend them?"

"Yes, I know."

The two locked eyes. "Theodoric, cowardice is a luxury for those who have other options. I'm afraid courage is the only choice any of us have."

Alaric turned his gaze back to the green field in front of them. "You will feel fear as the battle approaches. What sane man would not? Fear is not cowardice. It's the beginning of courage." Alaric put his hand on the boy's shoulder and looked him in the eye. "Long have I watched you. When the time comes, you will find your courage and make us *all* proud.

The king's gaze again turned distant. "Theodoric, Rome may be different than you expect. I've never been there myself, but I know many from there. They tend to be well educated. They speak highly of Rome as a place of art and learning and commerce from all over the world. I'm not sure sending the most intimidating Goth sends the right message. Perhaps it's better to send someone they do not expect, someone they come to trust rather than fear. Those who most covet this role may be the exact wrong sort." Alaric turned back to the boy. "Would you be less afraid if I told you your mission was to make friends?"

Theodoric looked the king in the eyes. "Yes, I would. And yes, *I do want to go.*"

The next day, Alaric announced his decision to send Theodoric to Rome.

For his part of the bargain, Stilicho sent Aetius, the young son of a prominent Roman politician. Aetius made quite an impression on the Visigoths, including Alaric. He had a proud and noble bearing. Despite his young age, he projected strength and confidence and never appeared afraid or resentful of his fate. He seemed likely to become an influential leader among the Romans, and Alaric's people took care to make a favorable impression.

By late spring, Alaric's army was in position and waiting on Roman reinforcements. Alaric grew increasingly frustrated they had not come. He was forced to spend his time attending to military matters, leaving concerns in the civilian camps largely unattended.

Alaric left Brechta in charge of civil matters. They weren't starving, but food was scarce. Having so many men away created hardships. As resources dwindled, disputes became more common. Brechta fretted over whether the judgment of the queen would be accepted, especially with few soldiers to enforce compliance.

When the need grew dire, Brechta announced, "I shall hold court tomorrow afternoon. Afterwards, we shall hold a public feast and feed those who are hungry."

Daria praised her wisdom and courage.

Brechta held court just as Alaric had. She sat in the same chair placed atop the same wagon he had used. The guards, although much younger or much older than usual, were formidable enough to defend the queen. They surrounded her wagon, leaving her well protected from those who had come to plead their cases.

A thief was brought before her. She struggled to remember Alaric's rules for how long criminals should be tied to a tree for various offenses. She wasn't sure, and this man seemed remorseful, so she ordered him tied to a tree for only one day and also allowed that he should be given water, which many men found overly lenient. She began to feel the weight of opinion shifting against her and was well aware of the bias toward viewing her sentences as too light. But should that affect her judgments? She was determined to remain unswayed by such prejudice.

Finally, a badly beaten woman appeared and pled for protection from her husband. She told tales of severe beatings and consistent abuse. Brechta's anger flared, and she ordered that they should no longer be wed. A hush fell over the crowd.

The most senior priest in attendance climbed into the wagon and spoke in her ear. "My queen, you are not permitted to break the holy bonds of matrimony. This is a decision for the church only."

Her blood ran cold. If she backed down now, she would be viewed as weak. Without a strong leader, life in camp would become chaotic and violent. All would suffer if she couldn't command authority.

"Since our blessed father reminds me that only the church can terminate a marriage," she announced clearly and with confidence, "this man shall be tied to a tree. None shall feed him. None shall give him water. And none shall free him, save his wife. Only when she decides his sentence has been served shall he be untied. If he dies tied to a tree, so be it."

The crowd approved.

Many disputes concerned ownership of animals or other property. Brechta knew Alaric often made claimants wrestle over disputed property when there was no other basis to decide. She chose a different path. Absent a clear winner, she ordered both sides to contribute food for the feast. Those ordered to contribute were furious, but others were pleased, and fewer seemed anxious to bring petty disputes before her. At first, some men complained of the decisions as arbitrary. However, before she began holding court, Brechta had ordered the lighting of a firepit nearby. The men were now beginning to cook the meat Brechta had provided. The smell filled the air. Most appreciated what Brechta's fines would provide and the wisdom of her decision.

By winter, it was clear Stilicho's army wouldn't honor the agreement. Alaric convened a council to discuss their options.

Athaulf spoke first. "The Western Empire can no longer ignore the threat of the Huns. They push ever to the West. Those in their path grow desperate enough to invade the empire in larger numbers. And why should they not? The Roman forces were depleted fighting us, and now the Rhine invaders. Both halves of the empire continuously fight themselves. And the eastern court remains unstable following the death of Empress Aelia."

"Aye," Alaric responded. "But both empires will now unite, if only for a while. They have no other choice."

"Can they set aside ambition even for a while?" Wallia asked. "Do we ever see them act for a common purpose?"

"This time is different," Alaric responded. "The Romans in Gaul now rebel against the lack of protection from Rome. They unite behind yet another pretender called Constantine III. Stilicho must now seek to reconcile with the East. And when he does, we will lose our value to him. I most fear a union of both halves of the empire, and that is what they must now do to survive."

"Is there not also an opportunity for us?" Athaulf offered. "Would it not make most sense for Stilicho to treat with us? We could be in Gaul much faster than the Eastern Army."

"True," Alaric conceded. "But do we ally with the Romans again? They would be quick to use our blood to fend off another usurper ... to defend the empire from foreign invaders and then break faith with us once more. Stilicho asked that we maintain an army for an invasion that never came. Will he now enlist our aid and again give nothing in return? They must pay the costs of pulling our men from their work to form an army for their benefit. Many families struggle with a poor harvest because too many are gone from the fields."

All the men nodded in agreement.

"And so, brother, what shall we demand in payment?" Athaulf asked.

"I understand every Roman senator receives four thousand pounds of gold a year. Why should we not have at least that for the efforts of our army? And if they will not pay, can we trust them to honor another alliance? Perhaps our best option is to just let the empire fail and claim our own homeland when it does. If Rome values our allegiance, let them show it."

Honorius sat on his throne in Ravenna, dressed lavishly in purple robes and seated at the top of marble stairs high above the advisers summoned to his court. Now a handsome young man of twenty-three with dark, curly hair, Honorius had become more assertive than his older brother in the East, but he was still wary of acting against his advisers. Stilicho pled the case for the gold Alaric had demanded. Olympius, a portly and graying politician who enjoyed hearing himself speak, objected to Stilicho's request.

"Augustus, why should we pay ransom to these barbarians? It wasn't so long ago that we were forced to drive them out of Italia. Then we were told they would become allies. Now they demand the emperor pay them tribute? I shudder to think what the Senate and the people will think. How can you govern if your own subjects think you are too weak to stand up to these intruders?" Many other members of the court sounded their agreement.

Feeling he was beginning to lose the emperor, Stilicho interjected, "Augustus, there will be a time to consider the politics, but it is not now. Our need for allies is dire. And Alaric does not call this tribute but rather compensation for the costs of mobilizing his army to aid our ambitions. The amount also is not great."

"Four thousand pounds of gold not great?" Olympius asked and received laughter throughout the hall. "Stilicho must be a far richer man than I."

The general pushed forward. "Alaric thinks of this as the amount paid to each senator annually."

"Is Alaric now a senator?" Honorius asked to growing laughter.

"Of course not, Augustus. My point is just that the situation in Gaul is dire. Some, who are not trained in military matters," Stilicho said, looking pointedly at Olympius, "may not see the danger, but we do not have the strength to subdue the rebellion in Gaul while defending Italia. If I march to defend Gaul, Italia will be unprotected. What would then stop Alaric from invading again? If I stay here, the invaders of Gaul will eventually turn their ambitions to Rome. Perhaps this new usurper will lead them, or perhaps they'll all be content to just divide Gaul up for themselves. If your advisers are so concerned about you appearing weak, they should address what it will look like if you lose a province that's been part of the empire since the time of Julius Caesar."

Honorius didn't like the idea, and the atmosphere in the room was clearly against it. Yet no one had a better strategy for retaking Gaul. Honorius refused to grant Stilicho's request without the consent of the Senate and ordered Stilicho to travel to Rome to seek the Senate's approval. The idea was no more popular in the Senate than it had been in Honorius's court, but again the absence of a practical alternative led to begrudging consent.

Before the payment could be made, however, word arrived that on May 1, 408, the eastern emperor Arcadius had died. He was succeeded by his young son, Theodosius II. Stilicho returned to Ravenna to influence Honorius's response.

When Stilicho arrived in the throne room, the atmosphere was tense. He made an elaborate show of expressing condolences for the emperor's deceased brother. Honorius's response was stiff and unmoved. He interrupted Stilicho. "You agree then that Theodosius should be called Augustus in the East?"

"Yes, of course," Stilicho replied with a bit of feigned surprise. "This is the promise that I made to your father, an oath I will always fulfill, to protect both his sons and their families as well. But we must act swiftly. The court in the East is treacherous. Many will see this tragedy as an opportunity."

"That's why I've decided to go to Constantinople myself. To ensure the proper succession of my nephew."

"My emperor ..." Stilicho was at a loss for words. "I understand your desire and admire your courage, but this is not wise. You'd be walking into a den of vipers. Those with designs on the purple would see an opportunity to slay you and claim both halves of the empire." This statement drew gasps, but Stilicho continued. "I can barely stand to think of the tragedy that would befall us were you to be betrayed by the eastern court. I beg you, send me in your stead. I will sail for Constantinople at once with as many men as can be spared. I will assure that young Theodosius is called Augustus in the East."

Honorius stared intently at his general. "And what of Eucherius? Will your son sail with you?"

"Yes, Augustus. I would take him as well," Stilicho replied, somewhat puzzled. Only now did it occur to him that Olympius and the other advisers had remained strangely silent.

After a few more moments of thought, Honorius announced, "So be it."

"I shall make preparations at once, Augustus."

Stilicho had barely left the room when Olympius stepped forward and spoke gravely. "It is as I feared, Emperor. Stilicho means to betray you."

"How can you be so sure?"

"Did I not tell you he would insist on going himself? Did I not say he would take his son? He means to call his son Augustus in the East and return to claim the West for himself. And what could stop him? He would control the Eastern Army through his son. He already controls the Western

Army—a force full of barbarians loyal only to him. And his friend Alaric moves north into Noricum, ready to invade Italia again once Stilicho gives the word. We must act now before it is too late."

"What would you have me do?"

"Nothing. You don't need to do anything at all, other than allow me to solve this problem for you. Stilicho has many enemies in his own army. Those who are truly Roman despise his coddling of barbarians. They know we rely too heavily on an army filled with foreigners."

"How can we change that?"

"We can't, but we can teach them a lesson. Only if we show a firm hand will these barbarians understand that the price of disloyalty is death."

"What are you proposing?"

"Some things are better left unsaid, Augustus. Soldiers in the Western Army who may be tempted to join our enemies need to understand their women and children are vulnerable to our vengeance. Give me authority to do what must be done, and all will know disloyalty is not worth the price."

As Stilicho prepared for the voyage to Constantinople, he began to hear stories of mutiny by Roman soldiers against his most loyal supporters. The barbarian troops under his command offered to strike back. Stilicho forbade this, knowing his biggest problem was the rumor that he planned to betray Honorius. To put this concern to rest, Stilicho returned to Ravenna to meet with the emperor himself. Honorius, however, had now come to believe Stilicho planned treason and ordered him arrested.

When confronted by Honorius's guard, Stilicho fled to a nearby church, in which he claimed sanctuary. Stilicho's troops followed and threatened conflict. Honorius's guard wouldn't enter the church but lured Stilicho out by promising he would be safe and taken to Honorius for judgment. Wishing to make his case directly to Honorius, Stilicho walked out. Roman soldiers seized him. His heart sank, and his vision grew narrow as the captain announced he was to be immediately executed. His men drew swords, but Stilicho lifted his voice and demanded his followers shed no blood. Even in the face of death, the old general sought to maintain his honor and defend his family and followers by refusing to act against the emperor.

He was executed on August 22, 408. Olympius replaced Stilicho as the primary adviser to Honorius.

Hamil sprang to action as soon as he heard the first of the shrill cries. The noises were faint and distant, but he well knew the sounds of terrified people. It seemed strange that all morning they had been ordered to remain inside the fortress while most of the regular Roman troops were being deployed outside the gates. For what purpose? As he rushed around to find out what was happening, Hamil realized the remaining Roman troops weren't guarding the walls; they were positioned to keep the auxiliary troops from getting out.

His thoughts immediately turned to Heather and his children, and a dark terror gripped his soul. The sounds had the high-pitched quality of women and children in distress. He could only imagine what the Romans were doing. His mind raced through options. There was no chance to escape such a mighty stronghold without being seen, at least not quickly.

"My friends!" Hamil cried above the din of the other auxiliary troops. They were mostly Goths and members of other tribes that had marched with Radagaisus. "I am not the only one among us with a family in town. Roman troops leave mysteriously, and then we hear the cries. Will we just sit here while our women and children are murdered? When the Roman troops return, it will be too late. Now, their numbers are few, and we can break free of the fortress and save our families."

One spoke out against his plan. "We do not know what happens beyond the walls. Mutiny will be the death of us all."

"I will not wait!" Hamil yelled passionately. "I will not find out later that my family was butchered while I did nothing! We are too many for the remaining guards to keep in. I will storm the gates with all who have the courage to act!" The horrific screams grew louder, and almost the entire auxiliary charged and overcame the Roman guards. Many were slaughtered, but some now had weapons.

They flooded into the town. Blood stained the streets. The natives of Italia barred their doors and hid within their homes. The homes of foreigners had been ransacked.

Hamil rushed into his house and dropped to his knees. Heather lay dead in a pool of blood near the door, her throat slit, her forearms slashed by swords as she had sought to fight off the Romans. The children lay dead behind her—their throats slit as well. Bitter tears burst from his eyes, and he struggled to breathe. He sat in the blood and pulled their bodies close to him. They were still warm, and he would never again have the chance to hold them, to feel their touch. He rocked slowly and wailed in agony as he held his family one final time.

Hamil's head swam. It was hard to focus on what to do next. *Does it matter?* he wondered. But he knew the answer was yes. Would the Romans desecrate their bodies? Would the men wait to be slaughtered as lambs when the Romans returned? Already, the piteous sounds of grief outside turned angry. They must do something.

Hamil found a cart in which he gently placed the bodies of his wife and children. He allowed others to use his cart to transport their dead. Other men gathered horses and what weapons they could find. The Roman troops remained on the outskirts of town. They had fewer numbers and knew their own women and children were now vulnerable to vengeance. Mounted criers rode through the outskirts, announcing that those who laid down their arms and returned to service would be granted amnesty, but those who didn't would suffer the fate of their families.

Rage filled the men, and none would return to the subjugation of the Romans.

Hamil was among the oldest, and many looked to him for leadership. "We must take what we can and march north," he cried while standing on his wagon. "Alaric's army occupies Noricum. This is what the Romans fear. We should pledge our allegiance to him and march with his mighty army to avenge our people!" The men roared their approval.

Before nightfall, they marched north together. The Romans shadowed their march for a few days but lacked the men to engage and returned to fully garrison the fortress.

Alaric was so shocked by the news of Stilicho's death that he didn't believe it at first. He held council in a pavilion in a military encampment late in the afternoon.

"Honorius faces a usurper and an invasion of Gaul, and so he decides to execute his best general?" the king asked.

Athaulf and Thuruar were just as puzzled, but Ulff responded. "Honorius is still a young man. He relies heavily on advisers. When Arcadius died, a power struggle was inevitable."

"Maybe our old friend's ambition finally got the best of him," Alaric said. "Still, the Romans now lack a proven general. Will Radagaisus's men fight for Stilicho's successor? We must learn that answer."

As the group continued to discuss their plans, distant screams and commotion became audible. They left the pavilion and strode through the army encampment in search of an explanation. They approached a large bonfire near the center, and several of the captains were speaking excitedly.

As Alaric approached, the man responsible for security in the camp addressed the king. "Many of Radagaisus's followers have come from Aquileia. They tell tales of Romans butchering their women and children."

Alaric's heart sank, and his body tightened. He could only mutter, "Why?"

"They say there was no provocation. The Romans just started slaughtering civilians. Young children, even babies, were put to the sword." The man's voice cracked, and he began to cry. Tears came also to Alaric's eyes.

As word spread, intense emotion hung like a storm cloud over the camp. The grave silence was punctuated only by the anguished cries, which periodically rang out. Alaric ordered that scouts be sent forth to determine whether this slaughter was happening elsewhere.

Honorius summoned Olympius to the throne room.

"Why am I hearing that women and children are being massacred?"

Olympius struggled to portray a calm demeanor. "With Stilicho's treachery, I'm afraid it created some very hard feelings toward the barbarian troops loyal to him. As you know, we all fear the consequences of disloyalty among them."

"You think murdering their women and children will make them loyal?"

"No, I think it will make them afraid. Barbarians don't understand loyalty. They understand strength." Honorius stared at his adviser skeptically. Olympius continued, "I understand this is difficult. I understand you don't want to see more bloodshed, but you must understand there is much animosity toward barbarians in the military. You know what happened to Gratian."

"You needn't always remind me what happened to Gratian," Honorius said. "How many more women and children are you going to kill to make your point?"

"No more than necessary. I assure you, Augustus, I will get control of this situation. You will have an army loyal to you."

Honorius did nothing to stop the massacre.

At the Visigoths' encampment, large groups of Goths arrived daily. Most had been followers of Radagaisus. Some were Goth mercenaries or from other Germanic tribes who had long served with the Romans. Their families had been dispersed to cities throughout Italia. Each day brought news of slaughters in more places. Each day more and more men abandoned their Roman posts and made their way to Alaric's camp. Many didn't know the fates of their own families until they arrived, if even then. Pained and rage-filled screams were common. As the days passed, the number of defectors grew well into the thousands. Those who hadn't lost loved ones were respectful and silent. Those who had alternated between expressions of despair and intense rage.

Alaric strode through camp surrounded by his guard. He heard many cries for vengeance. One man struggled to get past the guards. They forced him back, and he screamed in a loud, desperate voice, "Alaric! King!" The man's voice cracked in a piteous mix of rage and sorrow. He waved his arms wildly. "They killed my family. They murdered my wife and children. I have nothing."

Alaric was moved by the man's pain and stopped to hear his plea. The guards let the man through, and he dropped to the ground prostrate at Alaric's feet.

"Please. I will do whatever you ask. I beg only to be led against the Romans. To give my life to avenge my family!" The man sobbed uncontrollably.

Alaric kneeled, brought the man to his feet, and looked deeply into his eyes. "How are you called?"

"I am called Hamil. I escaped the Huns and followed Radagaisus. I had a wife and two young children. The Romans butchered them like animals. My little girl … they slit her throat. I wasn't there." Hamil broke down in tears, and Alaric put his hand on his shoulder. Hamil regained his composure, lifted his head, and said gravely, "I beg you to lead us against them … to avenge my wife and children!"

Alaric took a deep breath. "I understand your thirst for vengeance. No man should suffer as you have. Before the sun sets, I will speak for all to hear. Come then, and you will know what you must do." The king began to leave but turned back and said, "Hamil, you will be with your family again in heaven."

Late in the afternoon, Alaric called a large gathering in a wide, stony valley. The air was cool and clear, and the smell of pine hung heavy in the air. All officers not on guard duty were present, and thousands of regular soldiers gathered on the valley floor and both slopes. Alaric stood on a large boulder near the top of the eastern slope as the sun began to set, and the full moon rose behind him.

"Brothers!" His voice rang out clearly throughout the valley. "Each of us now faces a choice. We have been loyal allies to the Romans. We have fought their battles and honored their treaties. We have waited patiently for lasting peace, but they have not kept their promises." The king's words held the men in rapt, silent attention. "They have left our people refugees without a home. Now their hatred has grown so intense that they murder innocent women and children by the thousands!"

The crowd let forth a thunderous roar. The primal rage of thousands of voices filled the air. "For what?" Alaric screamed over the crowd. "Do they think we will be intimidated? Do they think we will not defend our people?" A deafening roar echoed throughout the valley. When it began to fade, Alaric's voice soared again above the din. "I do not see frightened men!" The crowd became so loud Alaric could barely be heard over the thousands of fierce cries. "I see an army the Romans will now flee before!"

The king had to pause for the crowd to quiet again before continuing. "Our numbers grow by over ten thousand, and the Romans have lost the same. They can no longer defend Italia. Our time has come!"

The men became even more raucous with screams, foot stamping, and weapons pounding against shields. "But know this. If you would march with me, you must follow my orders. Many of you come from the East.

You didn't choose me as your king. You have taken no vows to heed my command. And even those who have I will not command to bring their families with us. The road will be dangerous. The Romans may abandon Gaul to defend Italia. The Eastern Army may sail to aid Honorius. Even if we sack Rome itself, new Roman armies will appear.

"Know too that if you follow me, I will not tolerate the murder of Roman people. We are not murderers of women and children. We will not rape. We will not burn. We will not slaughter. When I joined the Roman army, the great Fritigern told me that although I would learn to walk among them, I must not become one of them. I will honor that advice until my last breath." The crowd turned somber. "I fault no man for craving vengeance against this evil, but you must follow orders, or you must walk your own path.

"We all face a dilemma. The Huns prevent us from living outside the empire. Yet we cannot live within the empire without making peace with the Romans, a peace that provides us a homeland where we can live and prosper.

"I bid each of you to take tomorrow to think about what I have said. On the morning of the second day, you must tell your captains what you've decided. We must know who stands with us!" The crowd roared again, stomping feet and banging shields. The king's voice rose again even louder, his tone more excited than before. "Never again will we be dominated by the Romans. Our time is now! Join me and march to victory!"

The crowd roared louder still and continued long after Alaric had stepped down. Eager men swarmed to pledge their allegiance. His guard forced the crowd back to provide the king space as he moved through the throng, receiving well-wishes and thanking his followers. Late into the evening and the next morning, Alaric and his advisers met with the leaders of the newcomers. He offered to allow the Ostrogoths to have their own companies and leadership. Many different ethnic groups held their own councils.

On the morning of the second day, Alaric summoned all captains to a mustering ground near the center of camp. The men stood in a large circle. Alaric called first on his own captains. In turn, each stepped forward and reported that his company had chosen to march with Alaric, and none had dissented. When Alaric called on the first of the Ostrogoths, the men stepped forward and announced they wished to join Alaric's army—without need for separate groups or leadership.

"We all follow Alaric!" All the other Ostrogoth captains said, "Aye!" in unison.

The hair on the back of Alaric's neck stood up, and his chest filled with pride. After a brief and somber silence, they began to break camp. The king would lead the main force south with most of the civilians. Athaulf would remain with a smaller force to defend the Alpine passes from any Roman army seeking to enter Italia.

Thoris was summoned to the tent of a particularly fierce, young Hun chieftain. He was aware of Attila's reputation for violence and feared being alone with him but was anxious about crossing him even more. It was rumored that Attila and his brother had murdered their own father to take charge of their clan at a young age.

"I have a task for you," Attila said. "If you do it, you will win your freedom."

Thoris frowned. "How?"

"You are Uldin's slave?"

Thoris nodded.

"Once he's dead, you will be free."

"You want me to kill Uldin?"

Attila didn't respond. His intent was clear.

"I'd be slaughtered by his guards."

"I've taken care of the guards," Attila replied.

Thoris was much aware of the danger he was now in. If he refused, he'd never leave the tent alive. "How would I escape camp?" he asked.

"I will give you a horse and this." Attila handed him a pouch with a few coins—not much but enough to bribe his way into the empire. Attila also handed Thoris a curved knife used to butcher animals.

Thoris nodded agreement and made his way to Uldin's tent. He was so afraid that he struggled to breathe. Uldin retained many supporters. If Thoris failed or got caught, he wouldn't receive a quick death. But what was the point of living only to serve the enemy of his people? If he really could kill Uldin, that would at least create a bloody power struggle and weaken the Huns, if only for a while.

As Attila had predicted, the guards didn't stop him. Uldin was sleeping and was startled by Thoris's entry. He started to dress, and Thoris stepped up behind him, reached around his neck, and slit his throat. Uldin grasped his neck and began to gurgle and choke as he turned to face Thoris. His eyes were wide with surprise. He couldn't speak, but his disappointment was obvious. Blood spurted from his neck as he dropped to his knees and looked up at Thoris.

"You murdered my family. Burn in hell."

Chapter 14

The Siege of Rome

Alaric rode with the vanguard as he led his army south through northern Italia on the road to Rome. The remaining troops in the army of Italia declined to engage such a large force. The small towns and hamlets they passed looked deserted; most civilians fled before the huge horde of Goths. The king carefully looked down the road ahead, ever watchful of an ambush.

In the Po Valley, just before crossing the river, Alaric squinted to make out a small band approaching. Far too few to be a threat, but who would ride toward such a large force? As they drew closer, Alaric could tell they were Goths, mostly young men. A smile slowly spread across his face even before the image was clear. Could it be? Indeed, it was.

Alaric spurred his horse to a gallop as soon as he recognized Theodoric's face. The two met just in front of the slow-moving army, their horses circling each other, the two men grinning broadly.

"You're late," Alaric declared.

Theodoric laughed. "I am sorry, my king. I've been delayed."

Alaric's smile vanished. "We've heard many tales of slaughter throughout Italia but few from Rome itself."

Theodoric drew a deep breath. "When word spread, the emperor ordered Stilicho executed, and the Senate also accused Stilicho's wife and son. It was said they conspired with you to overthrow the emperor. The Senate ordered them beheaded."

Alaric scowled. "Only Roman politicians would execute a woman and a boy I've never met for conspiring with me."

"Everyone panicked. None would speak for those accused out of fear they too would be suspect. Peasants also were put to the sword but not like elsewhere. Most Goth slaves in Rome were spared because the Roman masters insisted their property not be harmed."

Alaric pulled back on the reins, and his horse stood still. The king solemnly looked down the road ahead. "They will be property no more."

Alaric summoned his council in a large building near the port of Rome, his makeshift court. His advisers had gone to great lengths to transform the building into a throne room fit for a king. They had used the finest chair they could find as a throne and built a platform so Alaric could sit high above his audience. Far more ostentatious than Alaric's normal council rooms, the scene was carefully set to project authority to the Romans who would eventually come in pursuit of peace.

Alaric's army now surrounded Rome. Instead of attempting to breach the city's walls, Alaric created a strict blockade, preventing food and other supplies from entering. Ships laden with grain from North Africa were intercepted. The Goths were well fed.

Not long after the blockade began, Alaric received word that Pope Innocent wished to meet with him. Alaric was uncomfortable sitting high above his old friends. The formality of the setting seemed to have an impact on all.

Theodoric sounded nervous as he spoke. "My king, I worry over meeting with the pope. I see risk but no gain."

Alaric smiled. "What are you worried the pope will do to me with thirty thousand soldiers at my command?"

"I don't worry what the pope will do. I worry over the tale he will tell."

"You think he will not be suitably impressed?"

"I think he will seek assurance you will not slaughter and pillage. How will you answer him? Will you tell the pope you will put Christians to the sword? If not, will you tell him the Romans are safe? If you do, why would they make peace?"

"He's right," Ulff responded. "But I don't think that means you shouldn't meet with him. The Romans need to fear you. But you can also promise peace as long as your demands are met. You should present yourself as the barbarian the pope thinks you are. Make him ask for mercy and leave him with the impression you can be merciful but only if you get what you want."

"But ... I ... I mean no disrespect," Theodoric stammered.

"Get on with it." Alaric demanded impatiently. "I invited you to my council because I want to hear your opinion. If you have something to say, say it."

"It's just … that's not you. What if the pope doesn't see you as a barbarian? What if he sees who you really are? What if he leaves, knowing you're not the type of man who would slaughter the defenseless?"

Alaric looked back at Ulff, who persisted. "I think our young friend may overestimate the ability of the Romans to see the good in people. Even the pope. Long have I lived among them. Most see us as brutal savages. Such prejudice runs deep. It will not be easily dislodged."

Theodoric's words concerned Alaric, but he decided to meet with Pope Innocent anyway. Alaric was amazed by how long it took to arrange a meeting the pope himself had requested.

"It's easier to meet a hostile general while two armies face each other than to meet with unarmed clerics!" Alaric declared. He was concerned even more that Ulff had been summoned to meet with the Bishop of Milan first. Surely Innocent sought information about Alaric. And now he wanted to meet on a field before Ulff returned. Theodoric's concerns seemed increasingly warranted.

When the time came, Alaric rode into a broad meadow with his honor guard numbering more than a hundred. Pope Innocent and his staff had already made camp in colorful tents. Formally dressed high church officials lined both sides of a path leading toward the central pavilion, in which the pontiff awaited Alaric's arrival. The Visigoth horsemen surrounded the meadow, and Alaric's personal guard dismounted and surrounded their king.

Alaric's horse walked very slowly toward the pavilion. One of the priests stepped forward and smiled as he greeted Alaric. Alaric looked around cautiously and dismounted slowly. He motioned for Wallia to dismount as well, and the pair strode into the pavilion.

They were both surprised by how many were inside. The floor was covered with plush carpets, and they could smell the heavy incense before entering. All stood except Pope Innocent, who sat in a rich chair near the back of the pavilion. Innocent rose as they walked in, smiled, and invited them to come forward.

"Welcome, my son." He addressed Alaric without acknowledging Wallia. He held forth his hand, inviting Alaric to kiss his ring. Alaric complied but grew increasingly suspicious the pomp and circumstance was intended to intimidate.

Innocent introduced the bishops in attendance, then announced, "We've been praying for your soul, Alaric."

"And for that I am grateful, Holy Father."

"But we pray also for the thousands of souls who now starve because you deprive them of food. This is not the way Christians—"

"What of the followers of Radagaisus?" Alaric cut in.

Several priests gasped.

Alaric's voice rose defiantly. "Do you also pray for the souls of the women and children who were murdered? Is that the way Christians treat each other?"

The atmosphere tensed as the pope paused. "No," he finally conceded, "but you must understand. The sins of others will not cleanse the blood from your hands."

Alaric looked around the room slowly. "Every day I pray as well. I pray that I will have already fought my last battle. I pray that without a single drop of blood spilled, I will lead my people to a new homeland. A place where children no longer lose their fathers to battle. A place where women can raise children in decent houses. A place where we can lay down our weapons and take up the tools to build new lives. I pray the emperor will see the wisdom of allowing us to live in peace, and we will become loyal allies. I pray that together we can defend all Christians from the threat of the Huns."

The room went silent again. Alaric wasn't what they had expected. Innocent took a few deep breaths. "We all pray for your people, of course, but you must understand the sentiment … many believe … After all, you are not Romans and have forced your way—"

"Does God care where we were born?"

"My son, Christ teaches us to render unto God that which is God's and render unto Caesar that which is Caesar's."

"Forgive me, Holy Father. It is not my place to argue theology with the pope, but was Christ not referring to paying taxes? If we had our own land, we would happily pay—"

"You know I cannot grant what you seek."

"Of course, but if you would seek to convince me to avoid bloodshed, will you not deliver the same message to the emperor?"

Innocent paused again and smiled. "I will do all in my power to avoid further death."

Alaric also smiled. "Then we share a common purpose."

Alaric gazed out a window, lost in thought, as he watched Roman soldiers patrolling atop the mighty stone walls protecting Rome. He had eagerly awaited the return of Father Ulff and straightened when he saw the priest striding briskly toward his hall. The old friends cheerfully greeted each other as the council gathered.

"I must know," Ulff said. "How did your meeting with the pope go?"

Alaric remained silent and allowed Wallia to respond. "It was far better than I expected. Alaric spoke the truth with great moral authority, and the pope himself was forced to acknowledge the worthiness of our cause. I think he will become an ally in our quest to force a negotiation."

"But tell me," Alaric interjected. "What did they want from you before we met? What does the church now say?"

"They wanted to interrogate me about you. I never met Innocent himself, but his aides questioned me about you at length. They wanted the pope to be fully prepared. I did my best to make you sound Christian but still threatening."

"I think Alaric did enough of that himself," Wallia added.

"But what do they say now?" Alaric pressed.

Ulff sighed. "I'm afraid they say Innocent convinced the barbarian king to avoid bloodshed."

"What?" Alaric asked in disbelief.

"That's not what happened," Wallia added.

"Perhaps I was wrong to advise you to meet with him," Ulff replied.

"No," Alaric said. "He may yet play a useful role."

Food stocks within the city ran dangerously low, and the citizens became desperate. Receiving no help from the emperor sitting safely in Ravenna, the Roman Senate decided to take matters into its own hands. The Senate sent an embassy to treat with Alaric directly. They were escorted into Alaric's court under heavy guard and there found a king in no mood for generosity.

Without introduction or pleasantries, Alaric gruffly demanded, "Why have you come?"

The lead ambassador was a lean, middle-aged man with a clean-shaven head and face. He adopted a proud and defiant manner, and held forth on why the conquest of Rome wouldn't be as easy as Alaric might think. "The citizens are desperate enough to fight for their lives. They are packed densely within the city and will pose a bigger threat than you suppose. Such a crowd in tight quarters—"

The loud and genuine laugh bursting from Alaric's chest interrupted the ambassador. When his laughter subsided, Alaric spoke. "The thicker the hay," he boomed, his smile fading into a stern frown, "the more easily mowed." The king stared at the ambassador in stony silence. Thinking better of his efforts to intimidate, the Roman ambassador switched tactics.

"As you know, we do not have the power to give you what you seek. We cannot force the emperor to make peace with you. And yet you lay siege to our walls, forcing starvation upon our people."

Alaric smirked. "My army surrounds Rome. Your emperor does nothing, and now you say your plight is my fault? You must be desperate indeed."

The ambassador was out of tricks. Finally, in an exasperated tone he asked, "Is there nothing the Senate can do to dissuade you from this blockade?"

Alaric continued to stare intently at the ambassador as he thought. Finally, he announced, "Because your emperor has abandoned Rome, if my conditions are met, I will end the blockade long enough for the city to restock its food supply. To obtain this reprieve, you must free all the Goth slaves in Rome or elsewhere in the empire. We were also promised four thousand pounds of gold. Now eight thousand must be paid for our trouble. Plus, fifty thousand pounds of silver." Alaric paused in thought.

The ambassador turned his head slightly. "Anything else? Dare I ask?"

"Yes," replied Alaric, "five thousand pounds of pepper."

The ambassador arched an eyebrow and spoke again in a confident and courtly manner. "Tell us, if we give you all this, what would the citizens of Rome have left for themselves?"

Alaric drew a deep breath before roaring, "Their souls!" The king let his words sink in for a few moments, then glanced at the captain of his guard, who brusquely escorted the Romans from Alaric's hall.

The Senate sent subsequent messages, protesting Alaric's demands but extending counteroffers. After much negotiation, it was agreed that the Senate would free most of the Gothic slaves in Rome and pay five thousand pounds of gold, thirty thousand pounds of silver, four thousand silken tunics, three thousand hides dyed scarlet, and three thousand pounds of pepper. In exchange, Alaric temporarily lifted the siege and allowed food to flow into the city.

When payment was finally received, Alaric was true to his word and withdrew his guard from the area around the Salarian Gate. The gates opened, and thousands of former slaves began to pour out of the city. Alaric watched the scene while mounted atop a black stallion beside the road leading out of the city. The king was finely adorned and wore a golden helmet. He made a kingly sight easily visible from the Roman ramparts.

Behind Alaric, the sides of the road were lined with thousands of his followers, many looking for loved ones among the former slaves. Several of the recently freed paused to bow before and praise Alaric, but his guard quickly ordered them to move along. As the procession passed, isolated screams of joy rang out as Goths were reunited with family members not seen in years. Some of Radagaisus's soldiers were lucky enough to find wives and children who had survived the slaughter.

After more than an hour, the stream of Goths continued. Alaric struggled to contain his emotions. A king shouldn't be seen weeping, so Alaric turned his horse away from the procession and dismounted, as if he had somewhere else to be. Moving away from the road, a messenger told him Brechta wished to speak with him.

The messenger led him to his wife, who smiled through tears streaming down her face.

"Look who I found!" she said. She pulled a middle-aged man dressed in rags from the crowd. The man looked at him and smiled weakly. It took a moment for Alaric to place the face; then his eyes grew wide.

"Ungmar! It cannot be!" The man nodded, and Alaric strode quickly toward him, grasping his childhood friend in a strong embrace. "I thought I'd never see you again," Alaric exclaimed, still in disbelief.

"Nor I you," Ungmar replied. Both men wept openly. Ungmar attempted to kneel, but Alaric brought him to his feet.

"It's been so long. How've you fared? Did you ever wed? Do you have children?"

Ungmar nodded and smiled. He turned around and brought forth his wife. "My boys are grown now and have families of their own. I'll introduce you."

"Of course! You shall all be my honored guests at the feast tonight. We shall honor all those taken from us."

It took many hours for the former slaves to flood out of the city. The gate remained open long after as food was brought back into the starving city. That evening the Goths feasted and rejoiced in camps all around Rome. Days later, the liberated were still finding long-lost family and friends.

The blockade was reinstated, and hardship again befell the citizens of Rome. In January, 409, the Senate sent an embassy to Ravenna to urge the emperor to make peace with Alaric. They advised that if his demands were met, Alaric would resume his alliance with the empire. Honorius was silent as the ambassadors made their case. When they finished, he thanked them and advised them that he would consider their request and send messengers with word of his decision.

When the embassy left Honorius's court, Olympius was quick to speak. "Augustus, the Senate worries for their own fortunes, but you must concern yourself with the whole of the empire. How will men speak if you allow this barbarian to dictate terms to you? Will it not appear that Alaric, rather than Honorius, in fact controls the empire? We should wait out this dark hour. Be patient until more forces can be brought to bear."

Sarus, now a regular member of Honorius's council, interrupted, "Would you allow Alaric to sack Rome for the first time in eight hundred years? Should the emperor sit by idly while Alaric parades triumphantly into the Eternal City? How will men speak of that?"

"Of course, we should not abandon Rome," Olympius responded. "There are five legions now stationed in Illyricum—some six thousand men. Alaric has moved most of his force north of the city. These legions could cross the Adriatic and enter Rome from the south. Once the city is so garrisoned, it will not fall."

Then the old general Jovius, now second only to Olympius in his hold over the emperor, stepped forth. "Augustus, these men both speak wisdom, but there is benefit also in negotiating with Alaric. I know him. He served under my command at the Battle of the Save. He can be reasonable. I wouldn't abandon hope of an agreement to your liking. It is wise to keep the option alive."

"I know him too, Augustus," Sarus said. "We grew up together. Ever does he seek to appear gracious and just, but when it matters most, he will seek his own glory above all else. Only when he is gone will it be wise to make peace with the Goths."

Honorius, trying to please all his advisers, was loathe to cut off the possibility of negotiating with Alaric, but he agreed to send the legions from Illyricum to defend Rome. Those legions were led by a man named after the fallen eastern emperor Valens. His force landed on the east coast of Italia and made their way west toward Rome. Valens was counseled that a southwestern march would likely avoid detection by the Goths, but he found the indirect route too time consuming and cowardly. Instead, he marched directly toward Rome—and directly into Alaric's army. Almost the entirety of Valens's force was killed or captured. Only one hundred made it to Rome.

Athaulf spent most days riding from post to post and hearing scouting reports. His force was well positioned to block the Alpine passes from any direction. He abided his duties with more difficulty than usual. His closest companions rode with Alaric, and Daria had taken ill, as had many.

Athaulf and his oldest son performed the domestic duties usually handled by the women but made poor substitutes. One cold evening, he sat by Daria's side, caressing her forehead, which felt hot to the touch. She held his hand and uttered encouraging words. He spoke of sending the civilians south. Perhaps the warm weather in Italia would break her sickness. She assured him she would improve in time, but he worried she might not survive the journey south. The road would be long and cold. After agonizing reflection, he decided the ill would fare best remaining in place, surrounded by warm fires. Winter wouldn't last much longer, and it would be safe to move south by spring.

The stalemate in Rome persisted, and the Senate sent another embassy to Ravenna to again plead with Honorius to accept Alaric's demands. This time the embassy was accompanied by Pope Innocent, who made a personal plea to the emperor. Again, however, Honorius was swayed by Olympius and Sarus to reject peace.

Word also arrived in Ravenna that Athaulf's force now moved south to reunite with Alaric's army. Honorius gathered all the Roman forces available, including Hun mercenaries from his imperial guard, and placed them under the command of Olympius, who led them to intercept Athaulf. Jovius and Sarus both stridently spoke out against this plan, but Honorius placed his faith in the persuasive orator.

Olympius's force clashed with Athaulf near Pisa but was badly outnumbered. Olympius himself had no prior combat experience. Athaulf considered it only a minor skirmish, which scarcely slowed his march south.

Olympius returned to Ravenna with an audacious tale that his force had slain over eleven hundred Goths and lost only seventeen of his own men. The remainder of his troops, however, were nowhere to be found. It became obvious Honorius didn't believe him. Shortly after being summarily dismissed from Honorius's court, Olympius fled for his life to Illyricum.

Jovius now became the power behind the emperor and arranged a meeting with Alaric in a city called Ariminum on the Adriatic coast. Before his meeting with Jovius, Alaric wished to consult with Athaulf, whose force had now reunited with his own. When Athaulf arrived, Alaric met him at the stable. The two old friends warmly greeted each other, but Alaric could tell something was amiss. They walked together into the city.

"Tell me, brother, what troubles you?"

Athaulf had trouble speaking. He took a deep breath, and his voice trembled. "It's Daria," he said at last. "She's dead."

The shock caused Alaric to look up and breathe deeply. His little sister was too young to be dead. "How?"

"An illness of the winter took her. It afflicted many."

"And your children?"

"They're fine. They're with the others now."

Alaric struggled to breathe. The last of his family was now gone. He was the last of his parents' children. Brechta would be heartbroken at the loss of her best friend. He had no words.

Athaulf put his hand on his friend's shoulder. "We will mourn Daria for the rest of our days, but we must now face the Romans. Your old friend Jovius rides to hear your demands. We must have a plan. Take the night to mourn your sister."

"No. You're right," Alaric insisted. "We must address the business at hand. Summon the others. We will hold council tonight."

Alaric's council gathered in a small church. Pews were moved out of the way, with four arranged in a square near the altar. Athaulf announced that they must decide what demands to present to Jovius.

"What is there to speak of?" Alaric asked. "Our demands are unchanged. If Honorius will give us land we can defend and include us as part of the empire, he will have peace and our allegiance. I've made clear—"

"But what land should we seek?"

"Well, I don't expect him to give us Italia," Alaric replied, and laughter followed. "I assume he'll want us somewhere on the outskirts of the Western Empire. Somewhere between Ravenna and the Huns. Being on the Danube has advantages for us, if the Romans turn treacherous."

"Whatever you ask, he'll think you'll take half," Wallia offered. The others nodded agreement.

"It's true," Athaulf continued. "We can sack Rome at will. We can sack any city in Italia. Honorius can do nothing. On the other hand, our allegiance would mean the end of the latest usurper. We should make demands equal to our strength. If the Romans were in our position, they would demand the whole world."

After more discussion, it was agreed that Alaric would demand the provinces of Noricum and Venetia as well as Illyricum, plus an annual payment in gold and grain. They knew the demand would be rejected. The land was more than they needed. Plus, occupying Noricum and Venetia would give them control over the Alpine passes and thus entry into Italia. The Goths would remain a dagger pointed directly at the Roman heart. Alaric was troubled to demand more of Honorius than he could give but agreed it made sense to project strength in their opening offer.

When Jovius arrived, Alaric greeted him as an old friend. Jovius was far older than when they had last met, but he was as jovial as ever. One passing by would have thought it a social gathering. Jovius had been a supporter of Stilicho and now enjoyed the support of those who mourned the loss of the great general. In light of the unfortunate events that had transpired after Stilicho's execution, Jovius now held much political clout.

The group retired to a hall laden with food and drink, and the good-natured mood continued until the discussion turned to the business at hand. When Jovius heard Alaric's demands, he expressed concern about how they would be received in Honorius's court. Alaric knew Honorius was heavily swayed by his advisers but was alarmed to hear of Sarus's treachery. Jovius explained that the offer would inflame passions and be a gift to those who favored conflict. Alaric wouldn't retract what had already been demanded but did agree to let Jovius write separately to the emperor, indicating that if Alaric were named head of the military, his other demands could be lessened. After sending his letter, Jovius remained in Ariminum while they awaited the emperor's response.

Alaric, Wallia, and Jovius were relaxing together in the local bathhouse when word arrived that the emperor's response had been received. The men hurriedly dressed and walked to the church, where the messenger awaited. Most of the rest of Alaric's council had assembled, and Jovius excitedly read the letter aloud for the first time.

The letter was addressed simply to Alaric without recognizing him as king or even leader of the Goths.

Jovius skipped over that part and began reading the body. "'Your demands for land and tribute are rejected. It is with hope for the safety of your people that I urge you to flee from Italia while you still can.'" Jovius paused, clearly regretting his decision to read the letter aloud.

"Go on," Alaric insisted.

"'I have enlisted over ten thousand Huns, who now march with legions from the East. I remind you of what happened the last time you were foolish enough to invade Italia. The same fate awaits you now, only this time your wife and daughters will not be spared. Instead ...'" Jovius stopped and looked at Alaric. "My friend, I cannot—"

"I've heard enough," Alaric growled as he stood. "If Honorius wants to be the emperor who let Rome fall, so be it." The king began to pace. Athaulf snatched the letter from Jovius and read it to himself. He then handed it to Alaric.

Jovius spoke again. "It is as I feared. Sarus and the like have convinced the emperor that the rest of the empire will reject peace with you and that the current military situation is only temporary. I must return to Ravenna."

"Go then," Alaric said gruffly.

Alaric walked alone down a stone path, his hands clasped behind his back and his head lowered. Being among his family brought Alaric's feelings to the surface. In Ariminum, he had sought to keep his attention fixed on striking a deal with the Romans. He had also sought to lift Athaulf's spirits by keeping his grief private. Now, alone with his family, he felt free to experience the pain of his loss in full.

His little sister had loved, supported, and even nurtured him since they were children. Strong of spirit, wise, and intensely loyal—it was hard to imagine she could be gone. He regretted having failed to spend more time with her—having failed to take the time to express his love more fully. The king spent long hours praying for her spirit. Much of the rest of his time was consumed with worry about whether Honorius's threat of ten thousand Hun mercenaries was real.

One afternoon, Brechta asked her husband to join her for a walk. They proceeded down a stone pathway from the port. Rome's majestic walls could be seen in the distance. They held hands, and Alaric waited for his wife to speak her mind. Eventually, she asked, "Have you thought yet about who Alonia should wed?"

"Alonia? She's far too young."

"She's the same age we were when we wed!"

"That was different. I was in the Roman army, and there were hungry wolves seeking your hand. We had to move quickly."

"What makes you think hungry wolves don't seek Alonia's hand?"

Alaric turned toward his wife. "Is there something I should know?"

"Well, no. It's just … Alonia likes a boy."

"What do you mean, she likes a boy?"

"I mean, she seems fond of Theodoric."

"Theodoric? He's not much older. I sent him to represent us, and he sought to return early from Rome because he said he was homesick. Did Aetius seem homesick to you? And what do you mean by *fond*?"

Brechta flared her eyes and said, "You know what *fond* means. And you speak highly of him often. You even said he might one day lead."

"He's a good man. Someone I trust. But that's not the point. We're talking about our daughter!"

"Will there be none good enough?"

"Why does it have to be now?" he asked. "Why not wait?"

"She wants to start a family."

"Start a family?" the king asked. Brechta smiled as her husband declared anxiously, "I need time to think this through."

The couple found their way back home, and the girls and their servants were engaged in various domestic tasks. Alaric sat at the dining table, writing in a diary. Ordu began to clean the table and mumbled, "The boy is honorable."

Alaric looked up. "And how are you able to judge his honor?"

She continued to look down while cleaning the table. "I watch. I listen. I know."

She moved on, and Alaric continued to watch her, perplexed by her comment. She had long served him loyally. Still, she sometimes made odd comments, and it was strange the old woman was even still alive. She had survived long marches, harsh winters, and diseases that claimed the lives of many far younger, and yet she seemed no worse for the wear.

Within a week, Theodoric, son of Thuruar, came to speak with Alaric. The king knew Theodoric would come seeking permission to court his daughter. He at first planned to greet him sternly. But when Theodoric arrived, the young man was so nervous that Alaric lacked the heart to follow through with his plan. The king had spoken to his old friend and decided to give his blessing. Once the boy was able to stammer out his request, the king smiled and granted him permission to begin courting Alonia.

Hamil struggled to get the king's attention. He didn't look like someone who would have business with the king, and he had to shout to be heard. Once his attention turned, Alaric remembered him well and took time to pay respects.

"I have someone I want you to meet!" Hamil said cheerfully. "This is my friend Thoris. We were held captive together by the Huns. He has a gift for languages and served for years as Uldin's translator—before he escaped."

Alaric's eyes grew wide. "You come now from the Huns? You are a most-welcomed guest. Come, I have many questions."

Alaric led the pair to his hall and summoned his advisers. Thoris and Hamil were treated as honored guests and served wine as they all sat in a circle. Alaric sought to avoid getting to the point too quickly and took pains to inquire about Thoris's capture, family, and life as a Hun slave. They were all amazed to hear he had translated when the legendary Alavivus procured the Hun mercenaries so critical to breaking the siege in the Haemus mountains.

Wallia then got to the point. "We hear word that Uldin is dead and the Huns vie for power among themselves. What can you tell us?"

"Yes, Uldin's dead."

"Are you sure?"

"Yes, I killed him myself."

A stunned silence fell over the room. None knew whether to believe this outlandish tale.

"You killed the Hun king?" Wallia persisted. "How is it you escaped alive?"

"As he grew old, his support waned. A power struggle was brewing. A supporter of one of his rivals—a particularly fierce Hun named Attila—gave me money and safe passage, so I slit his throat."

Another awkward silence ensued. "You killed the man you served all these years?" Athaulf asked.

"He murdered my father and siblings; he enslaved my mother," Thoris replied coldly. "No man has harbored more hatred than I have these many years. I even came to hate myself for aiding him. So, yes, I waited for my time, and when the opportunity arose, I avenged my family."

None now doubted his tale. "Where did you go?" Wallia asked.

"Constantinople. I labored there until I heard of the great massacre and Alaric's march into Italia. I then bought passage on a ship that brought me here."

"What can you tell us about Uldin's dealings with the Romans?" Wallia demanded. "Did they form an alliance?"

"Roman embassies were common. They came to pay tribute. They sent a young Roman nobleman as a hostage."

Alaric's advisers exchanged glances. "How was he called?"

"He was called Aetius. An intense young man—even some Huns seemed to fear him."

"Thoris," Alaric said, leaning forward in his seat and looking deathly serious, "Honorius threatens to have ten thousand Hun mercenaries on the way. We must know if he's bluffing."

"I can't say for sure, but I doubt that many would now come. After Uldin's death, the Hun chieftains fought for supremacy. Word in Constantinople was Donatus succeeded Uldin. I would be most surprised if he allied with the Romans."

"Why?" Alaric wanted to know.

"He was among those who criticized Uldin for failing to drive a harder bargain with Stilicho. Uldin brought the Romans a great victory for little treasure, they say. What if Radagaisus had sacked Rome? Would there then not be more lands for the Huns to conquer? Donatus believed that without the threat of the Romans, none would have the strength to resist them."

Alaric leaned back in his chair and breathed a sigh of relief. "Thoris, your tale comforts us greatly. But we must be sure." The king leaned forward again. "I have a task for you. Any guilt you carry for your aid to Uldin will wash away with this service. You must ride to Noricum immediately. We've left some who understand the Huns but none with your skill. I need you to cross the border again into Hun territory. I need you to talk to the Huns you encounter and learn if a great host approaches. If it does, we need warning and an embassy to promise the Huns wealth beyond their wildest dreams should they change allegiance."

"Can I take Hamil with me?"

"Of course. You can take as many men as you need. We have relay stations positioned from here to Noricum. Guides will take you there directly." Alaric stood. "Thoris and Hamil, you do us all a great service." He breathed deeply and announced, "You ride at dawn."

In the autumn of 409, Alaric gathered a group of Roman bishops and sent them to Honorius with new demands. Although Honorius had made no offer of peace, Alaric now demanded only lands in Noricum, which were far enough from Italia to remove the military threat and close enough of the upper Danube to put the Goths on the frontline of a Hunnic invasion from the North. Alaric sought no gold or other subsidy beyond as much grain as the emperor himself saw fit to provide. Even the Romans were surprised by the reasonableness of the proposal and Alaric's own moderation in light of the prior insults. Honorius, however, wasn't swayed. When that became clear, Alaric renewed his assault on Rome in late 409.

Faced with the renewed prospect of starvation and having no hope of help from Ravenna, the Senate met again with Alaric. This time the Senators themselves came to Alaric's hall and pled that he not punish them for the emperor's intransigence.

Alaric heard their laments and then spoke sternly. "You call this man Augustus, and yet he hides in a swamp while his people suffer. You haven't starved because I was willing to be reasonable. Yet Honorius will make no accommodation at all—even as I have Rome surrounded and can pillage at will anywhere in Italia." The king paused, slowly making eye contact with the most prominent senators. "Tell me, is an emperor who will not defend his people an emperor at all?" Alaric paused again, and the senators looked around at each other and mumbled general agreement with the sentiment.

Alaric continued, "If you seek mercy from me, you must choose a new Augustus. The Senate must elect a new emperor who is one of you and will act in Rome's interests. Do this, and much can be yours. You can prevent the sack of Rome and see the siege lifted. As I have offered Honorius, I would agree with a true Augustus to form a military alliance. I would protect Italia from Constantine and the Huns." Alaric paused again, and the senators began whispering among themselves.

One of the eldest asked, "Who then would you have us choose?"

"The choice is yours," Alaric replied. "A man like Priscus Attalus would be suitable." A few heads nodded agreement, and the senators obtained Alaric's consent to discuss the matter among themselves.

After lengthy deliberation, the Senate decided to follow Alaric's advice and name Attalus emperor of the West. It wasn't an easy decision. They knew the decision would be viewed as treason in Ravenna. But between the threat of over thirty thousand Goth warriors surrounding their city and an absentee emperor, the Senate chose to address their most pressing problem first.

Attalus was a thin, older man who still wore the traditional toga and was an old hand at Roman politics. A pagan who had permitted himself to be baptized, he had many friends and few enemies. He was crowned emperor at a ceremony in the Senate, attended by Alaric and his court. In a separate ceremony in Alaric's hall, Attalus made Alaric commander of the Western Roman Army and appointed Athaulf to a high civilian position in the Roman government. Alaric then lifted the blockade, and food again began to flow into Rome.

Chapter 15

The Fall of Rome

O nce his trusted advisers had gathered in the great hall, the king spoke. "Heraclian blocks grain shipments to Rome. The Senate panics. Attalus now prepares to send his own force to bring Heraclian to heel."

"Why would we not send our own men?" Wallia asked. "What kind of soldiers could Attalus possibly have capable of retaking North Africa?"

"I offered to send our troops. Plenty to ensure success. But Attalus begged me to allow him to act alone. He fears appearing only as my puppet. The Senate also argues that to be legitimate, he must not be seen to unleash barbarians on a Roman province. I agreed."

"You sound as if you regret your decision," Athaulf said with a hopeful smile.

"I do not regret my decision to let Attalus make his own decisions. If the Romans see him as only our tool, they will not accept him, and a peace with him will be without value. But now I think North Africa may be a better homeland for us than a province on the Danube or the Rhine. I see now how important Africa is to the Western Empire. I see how quickly withholding shipments can bring the empire to heel. I also see how difficult it is to invade North Africa. It's well defended by the sea and far from the Huns. Yet could we not conquer the province? Especially if Heraclian is weakened by war with Attalus? Would our people not be safe and prosperous there?"

"Perhaps, but how would we get there? Do you mean to invade?" Wallia asked skeptically.

"If Attalus is able to subdue his renegade province, I will keep faith with him. But if he cannot establish himself as a true ruler and if Honorius continues to cower and concede nothing, the time may come when we need to choose for ourselves where we will settle and force the Romans to accept our choice. If we chose Africa, we will use the plunder of Rome to

211

buy ships to carry us across the sea. While we await tidings from North Africa, I will ride with Attalus to Ravenna and seek Honorius's surrender."

Alonia walked innocently past two covered wagons bearing a basket of wildflowers. Someone grabbed her around the waist and pulled her between the wagons. She started to scream but then turned and recognized the face.

"Oh, I've missed you so much!" She reached up and put her arms around his neck. Theodoric looked down, put his nose next to hers, and kissed her gently. Her body relaxed and seemed to melt into him as she kissed him back.

He pulled her still closer and became more passionate, but she stopped and stepped back slightly. "We must wait."

He placed his hands on her hips. "I'm ready," he announced.

She looked up with wide eyes. "Ready for what?"

"Ready to ask your father."

"Oh," she whispered, gently placing her check on his chest and pulling him close. "I so want to have a family with you."

"Then why should we wait? Why should we not be wed? I am *so* in love with you."

Her heart soared, and she smiled sweetly. "You know it's not that easy. My father is king."

"So, he is king. Does that mean his daughter can never wed? He gave me permission to court you. Why should he not consent to our wedding? If I must confront the king to be with you, so be it!"

"Oh my love. Just be careful. He is very … protective."

Attalus marched with Alaric's imposing force toward Ravenna. Along the way, Alaric was able to force several cities in Northern Italia to pledge allegiance to Attalus. Although Ravenna was well protected by impassable marshes and the sea, Honorius had few troops to defend his fortress—his guard having been depleted by the misadventure of Olympius. When they arrived, Alaric recognized the deficiency and immediately began preparing for a frontal assault.

As the king discussed strategy with his captains, messengers brought word Honorius had sent an embassy. Alaric summoned Attalus, and soon

Jovius and other members of Honorius's court arrived. Jovius greeted Alaric and Attalus with great enthusiasm.

"My friends!" the old general shouted. "Long have I waited to see you again. I congratulate you both!"

The mood was optimistic. Alaric had no need to state their purpose, as Jovius made no pretense of defending the emperor's intransigence. "You may be close to getting what you've long sought," Jovius said directly to Alaric. "The emperor now panics. He wishes to discuss a possible division of power with Attalus."

"I shall discuss with Honorius only the place of his exile," Attalus interjected.

Alaric winced at Attalus's arrogant words. He sounded very much like a Roman emperor—just not a very good one. Alaric knew blood would be spilled if Honorius wasn't given a way out. Yet he remained wary of contradicting the new emperor in front of such a distinguished group. Alaric held his tongue and waited for the reaction from Honorius's ambassadors. To his surprise, they didn't recoil or show disappointment. Indeed, Jovius made no protest at all. Perhaps the emperor expected such a response? Some of the ambassadors were dispatched to convey Attalus's stark terms.

Free of the company most loyal to Honorius, Jovius made it clear he no longer maintained faith in the emperor. He recalled at length the many times Honorius had failed to heed his advice and the hopelessness of the situation he had now put himself in. As the conversation wore on, it became clear Jovius wished to switch sides, and in appreciation of his loyalty, Attalus immediately named him patrician. Alaric was encouraged by what he heard but also concerned by the apparent ease with which his old friend switched allegiance. That evening they feasted and drank the fine wine Jovius had brought as a gift. Jovius accepted Alaric's offer to stay the night as his guest, confident the morning would bring good news.

At Honorius's court in Ravenna, Attalus's demand of surrender was grimly received. Honorius had made his offer to share power only in the hope of buying time to raise an army to crush this latest pretender. Faced with the prospect of exile or an attack he couldn't repel, Honorius prepared to flee. He summoned the harbor master and explained his need to sail to Constantinople at once.

"But Augustus, what of the ships that now arrive?" the harbor master asked humbly, hat in hand.

"What ships?"

"Do you not know? Many ships arrive from Constantinople. The captain of the first to dock told me they bring some four thousand eastern Roman soldiers to garrison in Ravenna."

Honorius breathed a noticeable sigh of relief, and his body relaxed. Seeking to appear to take this news in stride, he spoke confidently. "Bring this captain to me at once. I wish to speak with him."

The harbor master complied, and Honorius quickly confirmed he now had the troops he needed to defend Ravenna, at least for long enough to learn the outcome of the conflict in Africa. He sent his ambassadors back to inform Attalus his offer was rejected. No counter proposal was made.

When Alaric learned Ravenna was now well defended and the emperor wouldn't likely negotiate further, he again urged Attalus to permit him to send enough Goths to make victory in Africa certain. The two men argued this point extensively, but Attalus refused to budge. It appeared Attalus had grown suspicious of Alaric's motives, perhaps realizing the benefit the Goths would derive from holding such an important province. Hearing this lengthy argument, Jovius privately counseled Alaric to dispense with the pretense of Attalus as emperor.

On the ride back to Ariminum, Alaric considered Jovius's advice. Attalus had not made much progress outside Rome establishing himself as a true emperor, and his refusal to heed Alaric's advice created only problems. What good is a puppet who refuses to do your bidding?

Once in Ariminum, Alaric summoned Attalus to a great hall filled with his most senior warriors. Before this fierce audience, Alaric loudly proclaimed that Attalus had been stripped of the tile of emperor, and he ordered his men to ritualistically strip him of his imperial regalia. After this humiliating ceremony, and much to Alaric's surprise, Attalus asked for permission to remain in the king's service as an adviser. Mindful that his former puppet would likely be unwelcomed in Roman circles and desiring his insight on matters of Roman politics, the king agreed.

Alaric then sent messengers back to Ravenna to restart negotiations directly with Honorius. Honorius agreed to negotiate and arranged to personally meet with Alaric a few miles outside Ravenna. Alaric waited on horseback with his guard at the appointed meeting place, but Sarus, leading a small Roman force, ambushed him. The attack was easily repelled, but Alaric was furious about the treachery and Honorius's steadfast refusal to negotiate a reasonable compromise. In a rage, Alaric marched back to Rome and once again laid siege.

On the morning of August 24, 410, Alaric dressed in a white silk tunic and shining armor. Accompanied by his best cavalry, he sat mounted before Rome's Salarian Gate. Long rows of infantry filled the road behind them. Goth soldiers were similarly stationed outside Rome's other gates. They stood patiently outside the range of archers, showing no signs of attacking the walls.

Then, without provocation, the Salarian Gate began to swing open. Whether by fear or bribes, or with the help of slaves still in the city, the gates were opened wide without need for a bloody assault. Alaric's vanguard cantered through the open gates, and soon Alaric paraded majestically through the streets of Rome. He led his honor guard into the heart of the city as the rest of his army flooded in behind. The Goths quickly took control of the city's walls, additional gates were opened, and thousands of Goths entered from all directions. The speed and decisiveness of the sack precluded any serious resistance.

Goth criers rode through the streets, announcing that the basilicas of Saint Peter and Saint Paul would be places of sanctuary. Alaric continued to trot proudly through the city, demonstrating his authority to the Roman citizens who dared to come out and observe the spectacle. He carefully watched his troops to ensure they followed orders and that no violence would come to citizens who didn't resist. Alaric was pleased to see a pair of his warriors gently escort an elderly woman to a safe place before pillaging her house. Buildings and monuments were stripped of valuables, and the houses of the wealthy were raided in search of riches.

That evening Alaric convened his council in the old Senate building. They brought in fine chairs and sat in a circle on the ancient marble of the Senate floor. Tables outside the circle overflowed with food and wine.

It was a festive occasion, and all were joyous over their historic feat and the great wealth they now held. As the wine flowed, some asked why they shouldn't continue to occupy Rome. Why should they not now call Alaric Augustus?

Alaric smiled and indulged this banter for a time, then spoke. "My brothers, you flatter me with such talk. None could be prouder of our accomplishments than I. In our lifetimes, we have gone from starving refugees to a mighty people, now victorious over the world's most powerful empire!" A proud and boisterous cheer broke out.

"But we must now look to the future. The usurper Constantine will attempt to legitimize his claim by driving us from Italia. He will attack from the North. The Eastern Empire will send ships bearing an army that will attack from the South. And even if we defeat these forces, more will still come. We cannot wait until confronted by these threats. We must act decisively while the advantage is still ours."

Athaulf stood and strode a few paces into the circle with his hands clasped behind his back, looking down at the marble floor.

The room grew silent, and Athaulf looked to Alaric. "Do you still mean to lead us into Africa?"

"I do. Already we use our plunder to buy ships that will carry us across the Strait of Messina. On Sicily we will be protected by the sea and have a foothold to invade North Africa."

"Are you sure that's wise?" Athaulf asked, still pacing.

Alaric paused. "I am. But I can tell you are not." The group chuckled nervously. The festive atmosphere turned tense. "Tell us. What troubles you?"

Athaulf spoke reluctantly. "We've always fought on land. It's how we were trained. It's what we know. Naval warfare is different."

"I do not intend to fight ship to ship. We will merely use ships to bear us to new lands and fight there. We can move more quickly by ship—arrive where the enemy does not expect."

"True, but it's still something new. Something untried."

"Why should we fear the unknown?"

"It reminds me of trying to cross a well-defended river. Except now the river is so wide the enemy has plenty of time to know where we would cross."

"Ships are faster than men. We can change our landing site quicker than they can change their defenses. And we now number almost thirty-five thousand good warriors. We would land at many places."

Athaulf lacked passion in his opposition but remained skeptical. "We have many fine craftsmen among us but no sailors. Most of the seafaring Goths were slaughtered at Constantinople."

"We will hire sailors," the king replied calmly.

"And what if they betray us? What if the weather turns treacherous?"

"I cannot promise it will not rain, my friend." The hall was silent, and Alaric scowled. "And what other path would you see us take?"

Athaulf's tone brightened. "We could march north, defeat Constantine, and settle in southern Gaul."

"It may not be so easy to defeat Constantine. He will ally with the tribes pushed from their homes by the Huns. He will promise them land and have us fight each other. And even if we are victorious, we will have the same problem he does. The Huns will push to invade across the Rhine. Eventually, the West will raise a new army. We'd be farther from the reach of the East, but the Eastern Army could just sail to Italia or southern Gaul, join a Western Army, and trap us with our backs to the great Atlantic."

"If that happens," Athaulf shot back, "we could sail to Hispania. A great mountain range separates Hispania from Gaul. A land-based army couldn't easily cross. We could even invade Britannia, if needed."

Alaric rolled his eyes and sighed. "Our people cannot constantly run. We must be able to stay in place long enough to farm, raise families, and build great structures, as the Romans have. In North Africa, food is abundant, and controlling the flow of grain gives us control over the Western Empire."

Athaulf said no more.

Finally, the king announced his decision. "I appreciate your counsel, my friend. But the time comes now to act. At first light three days hence, we will begin our withdrawal from Rome. We then march south. We will sack the cities of southern Italia and carry great wealth onto ships that will bear us across the sea. Heraclian is now weakened by his victory over the force Attalus sent. We will destroy his army and conquer the province. We will then control the flow of grain into Rome and use that power to force

Honorius or Constantine or whoever wears the purple to accept reality and make peace with us."

The assembled were generous with their praise of the new plan, and even Athaulf acknowledged the benefits. Alaric ordered more casks of fine wine meant for Rome's wealthy to be distributed to the Goths occupying the city and those camped beyond its walls. They celebrated late into the evening, and a feeling of invincibility spread among them as they continued to pillage the Eternal City.

The next morning, Alaric held public court in the old Senate. His throne was placed high on the risers, upon which Roman Senators had once sat. Those with business before the king were led onto the Senate floor. As he decided disputes, Alaric noticed Theodoric waiting with a beautiful young Italian woman. He motioned them forth. Theodoric led the young woman to the center of the floor.

She made a stunning sight. Her olive skin and dark features were highlighted by the flattering white silk dress she wore. She had large eyes and full lips, and her face seemed strangely seductive, even when she made no expression at all.

"My king, allow me to present Princess Galla Placidia, daughter of Theodosius," Theodoric announced formally. "She showed me much kindness during my stay in Rome."

The king straightened a bit and smiled. "Welcome, Galla Placidia. Know that no harm will come to you under my protection."

The princess stepped forward and expressed eloquent gratitude. She appeared poised and confident despite the intimidating setting.

Alaric sympathized with her plight but couldn't leave behind such a valuable bargaining chip. He informed her that she must accompany them when it came time to march, but she would be treated well. She was allowed to bring her personal attendants and many belongings.

After a few days, the Goths prepared to quit the city. The occupation was brief and far more civilized than any Roman could have expected. The city was thoroughly looted of valuables, but there was little violence. Some buildings, particularly pagan temples, were burned or otherwise desecrated, but overall, the damage was minimal. By the time the Goths departed, the city was calm and quiet.

Alaric marched out of Rome and into the rich lands of southern Italia, followed by a huge caravan of over one hundred thousand people. His original followers, defectors from the Roman army and now former slaves freed from servitude throughout Italia, all joined. Alaric soon had more than forty thousand warriors at his command. Worries of attacks from Gaul or Constantinople seemed distant concerns.

As they rode south, Ulff rode up to the king's guard. Seeing his old friend, Alaric ordered that he be let through. The priest rode alongside Alaric, and the two smiled at each other and chatted pleasantly as their horses walked calmly down the road.

"Tell me," the king said with a smile. "What does the clergy now say of the sack of Rome? Have we not laid to rest their concerns that we are ruthless barbarians?"

"I'm afraid not," Ulff said somberly.

Alaric scoffed. "Please don't tell me the Romans still believe we didn't murder and rape because I met with the pope one afternoon."

"It's not the pope they credit but rather God himself."

Alaric took a deep breath. "So, the church believes God allowed the Romans to murder Goth women and children by the thousands but protected the Romans from our wrath?"

Ulff thought for a moment before responding. "During the long siege, many pagans argued that it was the old gods who had held the city safe for eight hundred years, and they had now abandoned Rome as it turned to Christianity. Some in the church now make the opposite argument. They say it was only faith in God that protected the city from destruction. The Bishop of Hippo has been making this argument forcefully."

"The Bishop of Hippo?"

"Yes, his name is Augustine. His writings have become influential among the clergy."

"Well, I do feel I played some small role," the king replied with a sideways glance. The two laughed heartily.

"I wouldn't worry," Ulff remarked. "He's an obscure bishop from a remote area. I doubt his writings will be widely read."

They sacked many cities along the way. Their wagons could barely carry all the plunder they had collected. At last, the huge group entered the region of Calabria, near the southern coast. Alaric had made arrangements to acquire ships to carry them across the sea.

Feeling confident and cheerful, Alaric walked through camp with Brechta, accompanied only by a few guards. They took time to watch the children play and their parents make camp. Brechta took her husband's arm and smiled as she leaned her head toward him and whispered, "You have brought us much joy."

Alaric smiled too, surveying the domestic scenes around them. "I'll rest much easier once we've crossed the sea."

They held hands and walked slowly back to their compound. Alaric spent the rest of the day playing and joking with his daughters, and the family enjoyed a delicious and exotic meal. Locals offered the king a feast of smoked fish, fruit, and grilled octopus, a delicacy they had never tasted. They spent much of the meal discussing how good the food was, and Alaric joked that he enjoyed the food in Italia even more than the plunder.

When the children were asleep, Brechta lay with her head on her husband's chest. She caressed his arm and asked softly, "Do you think it is time for Alonia and Theodoric to wed?"

Alaric's body stiffened, and he looked down. "If Theodoric wants to wed my daughter, why doesn't he ask?"

Brechta looked up at her husband. "Maybe he's intimidated."

"Intimidated? That didn't stop me."

"My father wasn't a king."

"No, but I still did it. I wouldn't have asked another to do it for me."

"He didn't ask me. I just know—"

"What?"

"That Alonia is ready."

"She wants to have a wedding while we march? Why not wait until we settle in North Africa?"

"Because she's lived most of her life on the move, and she doesn't want to wait. Besides, we'll be here for a while until the ships arrive, won't we?"

"Yes."

"Well then, why not?"

He took a deep breath. "If Theodoric can muster the courage to ask, he will have my answer." Alaric put both arms around his wife and held her tightly.

After a few moments, she ventured further. "Do you think Athaulf will remarry?"

"*That* is not my decision."

"But do you think he will?"

"I don't know. Why do you ask?"

"I see how he looks at that … Italian woman."

"Placidia? He's not the only man who looks at her that way."

"I know. She's very beautiful. It's just that—"

"You think it's too soon."

"Don't you?"

"Probably. But you needn't worry about her. She'll likely be returned to her brother as soon as he comes to his senses." The king's eyes were now closed, and his voice grew sleepy. The two slept soundly until after first light the next morning.

A few days later, Alaric noticed Theodoric was shadowing him. Alaric knew why he had come, yet he didn't wish to make it easy for him. *Why?* he wondered. Perhaps some paternal instinct to test the mettle of one who would claim his daughter's hand?

"What is it you want?"

Theodoric straightened his posture and held his head high. "I love Alonia, and I seek your blessing to marry her. I swear to be a good and faithful husband for as long as I draw breath. I swear upon my honor to—"

"I know your intentions." Alaric was surprised by his earnest poise and lost the desire to make the boy sweat, and yet he didn't want to get to the point too quickly. "Come, walk with me." The two began to stroll down a stone path near a small village.

Alaric glanced sideways at Theodoric as they walked. "The older you get, the more you remind me of him."

"Who?"

"My brother. Your mother's first husband. The man you were named to honor."

"I've heard many tales of Theoric. I'm honored by the comparison."

"Indeed. He was a kind and devoted man. The type of man who appears ever calm and gentle in camp but fierce on the battlefield. I see the same qualities in you. That's why I've included you in my council. But my memories of Theoric aren't all happy. The sadness in his eyes after our father's death—it never went away. I know it was difficult for you also."

"I wish Theoric had lived. I wish …"

Alaric put his arm around Theodoric's shoulder. "I've never been very good at speaking of such things. But it's not that I don't …"

Theodoric smiled. "I know your intentions. You need say no more, other than that I can wed your daughter!"

Alaric threw his head back and laughed. "Yes, Theodoric, son of Thuruar, you may wed my daughter."

Brechta and Alonia feverishly planned a grand event, and Alaric saw to it that they had all they needed. Alaric didn't concern himself with the planning, other than ensuring proper security was provided. Sergeric offered to have his men stand guard. The offer made sense. Although a senior member of Alaric's court, Sergeric didn't often socialize with Alaric or his closest friends, including his regular guard, who would all want to attend. The king thanked Sergeric for his kindness and accepted his offer.

When he arose on the morning of the wedding, Alaric found the black-cloaked figure of Ordu waiting patiently. He was startled by her presence. "Do you need something?"

"I have come to beg a favor. Have I not served you loyalty all these many years? Have I sought any favor beyond the protection and sustenance you provide? I beg you to allow me to continue to serve you and your family."

Alaric frowned. "Are you in some danger?

"I do not fear for myself. I beg that on this day you remain in your compound. Do not leave this place until the sun rises tomorrow."

"Why?"

The old woman just stared at him.

"Are you aware of some treachery? If you know of some danger, I would have you tell me."

"I do not know the source of the threat, my king. I know only that on this day you face a threat to your life you can avoid only by remaining here."

Alaric rolled his eyes. "Woman, when people tell me you're a witch, and many still do, I always defend you. But talk like this doesn't help. I have conquered Italia. My army has doubled in size. There is no army south of the Alps that can challenge me, and we wait only for ships to bear us to North Africa, where no army can touch us. I'm not going to cower in fear on my daughter's wedding day because of the ramblings of an old woman."

Ordu continued to stare at him, concerned. Finally, Alaric tired of the conversation and walked off.

It was a huge festivity, and even those not invited celebrated in camps across the region. After the ceremony, the guests enjoyed much feasting, wine, and dancing until well after sundown. The finest musicians performed, and Alonia beamed with joy. Alaric watched the joyous scene unfold from a seat in the middle of a grand table set atop a short, wide platform. The king laughed and clapped as he watched his eldest daughter dance with her new husband.

Servants passed in front of Alaric's table, bringing more food and drink. The king held out his cup for a servant holding a flask of wine and noticed a shadow cross the table from behind. He turned to look over his left shoulder and saw a man holding a dagger over his head.

The man brought the dagger down hard with his right hand, and Alaric twisted away. He wasn't quick enough to block the blow, but by the time the stroke fell, his back was turned to the side, and the knife glanced off his right shoulder blade. The king deftly rose while spinning left, caught the man by the back of the neck, and pushed him facedown on the table. By that time, the guards had pounced and pressed the point of their spears against the man's back. Alaric released his grip and stepped back.

Brechta and Athaulf were at his side almost as quick as the guards. Alaric couldn't see the wound but knew it was superficial. He insisted he was fine and refused to sit or allow the celebration to be disrupted. Brechta pleaded, and he finally agreed to allow a healer to examine the wound and clean it with a damp cloth. The king was fierce in his demand that the musicians play on, and some dancing continued. The mood was somber, however, and the festivities continued only because the king had so commanded.

Athaulf strode in a great rage to the compound of Sergeric, accompanied only by those who had failed in their oath to protect the king. He cursed them as traitors and cowards; they could only reply meekly that they had seen no danger and had become distracted by music and dance. Athaulf's pace didn't slow as a guard stepped before him at the entrance. Rage burst forth from Athaulf's chest as he shoved the man to the ground and demanded Sergeric's presence. Sergeric's stunned visage appeared out of the darkness into the glow of torches.

"You offer to defend the king, and he is stabbed at his daughter's wedding!"

"What?"

"Don't play stupid with me. The king was stabbed while your men did nothing."

"He was stabbed? Is he all right?"

"No thanks to your treachery. He had to fight off the attack himself!"

"Is this true?" Sergeric demanded in a menacing tone. Those who stood closest to Alaric stammered their excuses.

Athaulf stepped forward and stuck his finger into Sergeric's chest. "I'm not going to stand here and let you pretend your guards were just too distracted. You'll pay for this treachery!"

Sergeric continued to profess his innocence and promised to punish the guards as Athaulf turned and stormed off.

That night Alaric's restlessness woke Brechta. She was alarmed by his fever. Alaric also awoke and insisted he needed only water and more rest. By the morning, his condition appeared worse, and Brechta summoned a healer. Little could be done, and Alaric insisted on attending a meeting of his council. As soon as he entered the tent, he encountered many concerned faces.

Athaulf spoke what they all thought. "You do not look well, my friend."

The king sweated profusely, despite the mild weather, and his eyes were red and glazed.

Athaulf insisted that he return to bed and helped him to do so. That evening Alaric's condition worsened further. He could no longer rise. Brechta and the girls wouldn't leave his side. Athaulf came frequently and spent the rest of his time responding to concerns among the leadership.

Alaric awoke in a cold sweat. He couldn't stop shivering. Trembling, he struggled to rise, shocked at how weak he'd become. Had the dagger been dipped in poison? How else could he have been laid so low by a superficial wound? It no longer mattered. Alaric knew what must be done. He lay back down and called for aid.

The members of Alaric's court came to his bedside one by one, even Sergeric. The king thanked each graciously for their service. Most protested that his sickness would pass, but Alaric insisted on discussing his wishes after his death. He said the people should choose their next king but should also be told that he believed Athaulf would be the best choice.

Alaric called last for Theodoric and spoke privately with his new son-in-law. The king motioned for something across the room and attempted to rise but was overcome by a fit of coughing. It was obvious what he wanted. Theodoric rose slowly and brought Alaric his sword with great reverence.

"I have carried this sword since Adrianople. It belonged to my brother." Alaric again attempted to rise as he extended the sword to Theodoric.

The young man quickly moved forward to take the gift before Alaric collapsed back into bed. "This is a great honor. I will hold it until you are able to wield it again."

Alaric shook his head. "That is not why I give it to you. I believe one day you too shall be king, and you will reign in our new homeland." He forced a smile over a pained expression.

Theodoric looked down. "I'm not sure I want to be king."

Alaric summoned what strength he had left. "That is why you would be a good one. Long have I watched the Roman way. The schemers think nothing of the lives their ambitions cost. We must not follow their path." He twisted to grab a book lying on the table near his bed. "This I also want you to have."

Theodoric began to flip through it and looked puzzled. "This is your diary."

"This is not my story. It's the story of our people. There are still many pages. Do not let the story end with my death."

Alaric coughed a little more and took some water. "I dreamed I looked down upon you from the heavens as you were troubled by great decisions. You sought my council but couldn't hear me. I say to you now, keep the defense of our people your first priority. We are only a single defeat from death and slavery. Do not be ruled by vanity or ambition. And remain ever wary of the threat of the Huns."

"I have learned much from you." Theodoric smiled and touched his father-in-law's arm. "I will learn even more when your strength returns."

Brechta put on a brave face and received many visitors with dignity. She also reassured her daughters and insisted that they show courage for their father. Only when all others had spoken with Alaric, and they were alone together late in the night, did she lose her composure. Tears streamed down her face, and she couldn't repress her sobs as she sat by his side.

"I don't want to live without you!" she cried.

Alaric took his wife's hand and steadied his voice. He looked her in the eye and said calmly, "We will be together again in heaven." He smiled affectionately, and she forced a smile through bitter tears. "You must stay strong for the girls. You must stay strong for yourself." He raised his hand and gently wiped tears from her face. "I would not see you fall into despair as my mother did. You must promise."

She nodded and looked at him with another forced smile. Regaining her composure, she announced confidently that he should get some rest. They would speak again in the morning. She then lay next to him, placing her head on his chest as she had so many times before.

Before dawn, she awoke and realized he was no longer breathing. A sick feeling overwhelmed her when she touched his cheek and his skin had no warmth. Even so, she tried to wake him before accepting reality.

Alaric now lay dead.

Grief spread quickly throughout the camp. The silence among such a large group was eerie. Almost no sounds were heard other than sporadic weeping and anguished laments. Alaric's body was placed on a table adorned with fine fabrics and flowers. Huge lines formed to walk past and pay respect to the king one final time.

Word spread that Athaulf would speak, and crowds clustered around a hillside on which the eulogy was held. Athaulf stood atop the hill and spoke loudly to the crowd.

"I'm not very good at speeches," he began. "That was always Alaric's job. He was good at it. Not because he was a great orator, like some Roman senator trained in rhetoric but because he always spoke the truth in a simple way all understood. Let me honor him now by following his example."

Athaulf took a moment to survey the sea of mournful faces. "I knew Alaric since we were children. We served together in the Roman army, fought many battles together, held more councils than I can remember, and raised our children together. Many a time, I was asked how it was decided that between the two of us Alaric would lead."

Athaulf paused and smiled. "He was always the bravest and most honorable man I knew. By far. Yes, I would have competed against lesser men, but with Alaric, I always knew he was born to be king. Every act he took, every word he spoke, was for the benefit of our people. When the Romans became our oppressors, he fought them with courage and skill, and won. Yet he had also the wisdom to see that we could not survive outside the empire. He spent his whole life pursuing a just peace with the Romans, a lasting peace that would see us become a respected and important part of the empire.

"Many times, he could have obtained riches, lands, and titles from the Romans—if only he would abandon his people. Yet it never crossed my mind that he would do so. It wasn't him. He was a devout and loyal man who united our people. He brought us victory, he brought us riches, but he always cared more about our families … and our souls." Tears came to Athaulf's eyes, and he paused to take a deep breath.

"Let us each now honor our great leader by seeking to become more like him." Athaulf again surveyed the grim crowd, as if he might speak further, but then he cast his eyes downward and walked back to his children, who stood next to Alaric's family.

The crowd was moved by Athaulf's words but remained silent. Brechta and the girls wept throughout the eulogy and long after. While the crowds continued to pay homage, Athaulf summoned the first council without their king.

Before meeting with the full group, Athaulf pulled Wallia, Thuruar, and Theodoric aside. They stood between two tents and spoke in hushed voices. "We must speak of Sergeric's role in Alaric's death," Athaulf began. "I saw the wound. It was minor."

"They say it became infected," Thuruar responded. "What do you suspect?"

"That the blade was poisoned. That the man acted on Sergeric's orders. That he instructed his guard to let the man through."

"We should question the attacker," Wallia asserted.

"We cannot. Sergeric had him beheaded that night."

Thuruar drew a deep breath. "I believe it in my heart, but can we convince the others?"

Athaulf thought for a moment. "Now is a treacherous time. We must select a new king. Many are now loyal to Sergeric. We cannot risk discord. We must speak to the others in private and only after a new leader is chosen."

"Alaric told me before his death that he would see you crowned king," Thuruar said to Athaulf but then turned to face Wallia.

Wallia frowned. "Why do you look to me? He told me the same, and I agree."

Thuruar and Athaulf seemed relieved, and they made their way to the council. Athaulf assumed the leadership role, and none objected. "This has been a dark time indeed," he began. "Now we receive word most of the ships we bought have been damaged or destroyed by a storm. We need new ships and more time to make the crossing."

After a brief silence, Wallia spoke. "Just sitting here is unwise. We're at the end of a peninsula with no ships. A large enough force attacking from the north would have us trapped. Word of Alaric's passing will reach the Romans. They will be emboldened to act."

All in the group agreed, and Athaulf proposed a new strategy. "If we cannot sail, we must march north. There is no force in Italia now to stop us, and if we are to meet the usurper Constantine in battle, let us do it before his army can fully cross the Alps. From northern Italia, we can choose to move into Gaul or back to Noricum or Illyricum. If we can get into southern Gaul, that is where we should settle. We would be far from the Huns, too far west to be threatened by the Eastern Empire, and the Western Empire will be long occupied putting down Constantine's revolt."

Hearing no dissent, Athaulf continued, "There are other matters that must be addressed. First, we must decide where to bury our king."

"He must be buried in secret!" Thuruar demanded. "The Romans will desecrate his grave at first chance."

"How could such a thing be secret?" Athaulf asked skeptically.

"We should divert the river. We then lay Alaric to rest in the bed. Once the river returns to its normal course, Alaric's grave will be forever safe from Roman pillage."

The group was silent for a few moments until Athaulf asked, "That's a lot of work. Who would complete this task? We must choose a new leader and prepare to march."

"The Roman prisoners should do it," Thuruar retorted.

Athaulf laughed. "You said we should keep his tomb secret from the Romans!"

"We slay the prisoners once the work is finished."

"Wait," Ulff began to protest. "Does anyone believe this is what Alaric would want? His burial is to conclude with a slaughter?"

Thuruar was resolute. "What other choice do we have? Athaulf is right. Our people need to prepare for the long march. Are we going to take the Romans with us? Will we set them loose to face them again on the field? Only this makes sense."

The group discussion broke down into individual conversations. Athaulf allowed this for a time, then announced that they must first choose a new leader, and the new king would decide.

All captains were ordered to ask the men under their command who should be made king. The next day the captains appeared on a large field. The crowd was boisterous, with many loudly proclaiming Athaulf should be the new king. Ulff quieted the crowd and instructed the captains to form a large circle. When this was done, Ulff turned to his left and asked each captain to speak the choice of his company.

The first declared, "Athaulf!" loudly and with great enthusiasm. Then one after the next all around the circle each, including even Sergeric, declared Athaulf the choice of his company. Thus, Athaulf was unanimously made king. The men raised him on a shield and chanted and paraded him through the camp. Word spread quickly, and some cheer again returned to the Goths.

Athaulf held court that night, again addressing Alaric's burial. After further discussion, he announced his decision to follow Thuruar's plan and bury Alaric in the river. He declared the decision wasn't easy and acknowledged Alaric wouldn't have wanted blood spilled in his honor. But his greatest concern was the danger of their current location and the need to march such a large group north. The most expedient choice was Thuruar's suggestion.

So it was done. The great king was buried at the bottom of a river. Only a few were allowed to witness the burial. When the dam was released and the prisoners slain, Alaric had been laid to rest, and Athaulf led the march north.

Chapter 16

Homecoming

Theodoric attended Athaulf's council in the forum of a small Roman town just south of the Alps. Priscus Attalus was invited as well. They spent a year south of the Alpine passes, waiting on word of the conflict between the usurper Constantine and the newest Western Army. Honorius now entrusted General Constantius to put down this rebellion.

The elderly Attalus retained many contacts among the Romans and reported the tales they told. He brought tidings from the stronghold of Arles.

The old statesman, still clad in a traditional toga, rose and announced dramatically, "Finally, Constantine surrendered after the lengthy siege brought starvation and revolt." Many gasps and whispers erupted.

"Where is he now?" Athaulf demanded.

"After he surrendered, he traveled to Ravenna to pay homage to Honorius. I don't know who gave the order, but only the heads of Constantine and his son arrived in Ravenna."

"And now Constantius turns his attention to us," Athaulf observed. "I've heard many tales of this new general. He doesn't sound like the kind of man we can make peace with."

"I beg your pardon," Attalus said, "but I do not believe Constantius intends to risk war with you. He does not have the numbers, especially now that his force is depleted by conflict with Constantine. A defeat would leave you unchallenged in the West. The Romans fear this."

"Then why does he provoke skirmishes? Why does he maneuver for advantage over us? Why will the emperor still refuse to make peace with us?"

"All just questions. But the answer is simply that you remain in Italia. This the Romans cannot tolerate. I think you would be wise to ignore Constantius and press forward your march into southern Gaul.

Constantius would gladly trade places with you and end up in a position to once again allow the emperor to control Italia."

"We should continue to push for peace with Honorius," Theodoric declared.

"What more could we possibly do to pursue peace with the emperor?" the king asked.

"You could send his sister back to Rome," Wallia countered with a fierce stare. Alaric's cousin knew this was a sore subject but took pride in having the courage to say what everyone else thought. Athaulf often spent time with Placidia, and suspicions of his romantic interest were widespread.

"I will not return her for nothing. If Attalus is right, we can march unopposed into Gaul. From there, our position will be greatly strengthened. That is a land where we can finally settle. Our people can farm, build real homes and fortifications. The Romans will know they cannot easily dislodge us from such a place."

The advice of Attalus proved sage. Indeed, the Romans did avoid conflict with the huge Goth army and allowed them to pass unchallenged into southern Gaul. Once there, the Goths found fertile land, with easy access to Mediterranean ports near the protection of the Pyrenees Mountains.

Alonia walked alone on a beach along the coast of the Mediterranean. She was pleased to have been in the same place so long. Many insisted they must be ever ready to march again. Yet people were building, planting crops, and raising livestock. It brought her great joy to walk along the coast, admiring the progress and chatting with common people. The bump in her abdomen was now noticeable. She couldn't wait for Theodoric's return to share the good news in person.

When she heard the familiar sound of many riders approaching, her heart pounded, and her breath quickened. It was too soon. How could Athaulf have completed his embassy already? Did an enemy draw near?

She raced back toward the encampment. But soon Theodoric came galloping toward her. His smile was reassuring as he dismounted swiftly and hurried to embrace her. She resisted his tight squeeze.

"What's wrong?" he asked.

"Nothing, it's just …" She looked down and touched the bump.

His eyes widened. "You're …?"

"Yes!" She smiled sweetly and blushed.

He looked shocked. "I can't believe I'm going to be a father."

"Well, you are, so don't go getting yourself killed!" She elbowed him playfully.

He laughed. "I'll do my best."

They began to hold hands and walk slowly next to Theodoric's horse. "This is the best news I've heard in a long time," he said.

"Was there some trouble? You're back so much earlier than I expected."

"I was ordered to lead my company back with prisoners. Athaulf still pursues his mission. You won't believe who we encountered."

"Who?"

"Sarus."

"No!"

"Yes. It was a chance encounter. He led a group of about three hundred men—a scouting party. Spying on us for the emperor, no doubt."

"What happened? Was he captured?"

"No. Athaulf executed him."

"Executed him? Why not take him prisoner?"

"It was quite dramatic actually. We had far greater numbers, but still it was a fierce fight. Athaulf was angry. Sarus flew into a rage once taken. He called Athaulf a false king and vowed vengeance. When his rant began to disparage your father, Athaulf drew his sword and proclaimed, 'You have betrayed your own people, I condemn you to death.' Then the stroke fell, and his head rolled down a hill. Blood gushed from the neck—it was really gruesome."

"Sounds horrible. What of Sergeric? Does he know?"

"He was there. He pleaded with Athaulf to no avail. Afterwards, he had to be led off in restraints."

"Oh my God!" Alonia put her hand over her mouth. "Do you think Sergeric will revolt?"

"Not now. He doesn't have the numbers. But his followers won't be happy. I sense Athaulf now regrets his decision. He knows disunity is dangerous."

They came to a place where the road ran alongside a sandy beach. "Shall we linger a while and watch the sun set?" Theodoric asked.

She looked at him adoringly. "That sounds lovely. What will we do with your horse?"

"Let's take off the saddle. We can both ride bareback."

The horse walked slowly across the white sand as the sun began to set over the sea. Alonia sat in front, and Theodoric reached around her waist to hold the reigns.

"What else troubles you?" she asked.

He chuckled. "How do you know something else troubles me?"

"I just do."

"Well, I worry we may need march again."

"No!" she protested. "Why would we leave this place?"

"Same as always, the Romans. Athaulf is angered Honorius will not make peace with us. That he demands the return of his sister but will give nothing for her."

"I think Athaulf's perfectly happy having her here."

"You're not the only one who thinks that."

"Don't you?"

"He lusts for her, yes. But I don't think he'd place his own desires above the needs of the people. She's like a beautiful treasure to him but one he'd trade for peace. Honorius must agree to the trade but shows no signs of giving in. Athaulf helps the Romans put down revolts in Gaul, yet his loyalty goes unrewarded. I fear he will do something rash to force the emperor's hand."

In January of 414, Athaulf was clean shaven and adorned in fine silk robes. Surrounded by his honor guard, he strode confidently into the great cathedral in the city of Narbo. The cathedral was a majestic stone structure, filled with all the most prominent Goths and many dignitaries native to Gaul, all dressed in their finest attire. Brechta and her children were seated in a place of honor near the front. Her disapproval was well concealed.

Athaulf stood at the altar as Galla Placidia entered. She looked even more stunning than usual in a long silk dress and a thin silver crown atop her finely braided hair. Attalus gave the wedding speech, and the marriage was celebrated with high Roman festivities. The bride was gifted many fine jewels from the plunder of Italia as well as fifty handsome young men to serve as her guard. The new couple celebrated merrily and received many well-wishers.

This beautiful wedding wasn't well received in Ravenna. General Constantius sought ever to poison Honorius against Athaulf. It was an insult, he said, that a barbarian king had now wed the emperor's own sister. The insults of the Visigoths could no longer be tolerated. Lacking the strength to defeat the Visigoths by land, Constantius obtained the emperor's consent to begin a naval blockade of Mediterranean ports.

The blockade was successful, and Athaulf was forced to lead his people into northern Hispania. The Alans, Vandals, and Suevi who had invaded across the Rhine in 406 now controlled the Iberian Peninsula. The Visigoths were able once again to buy what they needed with the treasure they had amassed during the sack of Rome. Constantius was too occupied with reasserting control over Gaul to pursue the Visigoths.

Alonia and Theodoric were enjoying dinner in their home while their young son Thorismund played on the floor. A fierce pounding on the front door disturbed their tranquil evening. Guards admitted a messenger from Wallia. The man burst breathlessly into their dining room.

"The king! The king is slain!" the young man panted. "He was murdered by a servant while he bathed."

Their blood ran cold. Alonia stammered in disbelief. Theodoric quickly strapped on his sword and led his guards to Wallia's house. By the time he arrived, his father was already there, speaking with Wallia in low tones, their heads bowed.

"Is it true? The king has been murdered?"

Thuruar turned toward him. "Yes, son, I'm afraid it's true."

"And what of his children?"

"Sergeric slaughtered them as well," Wallia responded.

The blood left Theodoric's face, and the room seemed to spin. He sat heavily. "Sergeric did this to leave no heirs."

"Yes," Wallia responded, "he's declared himself king."

Thuruar put his hand on Theodoric's shoulder. "I know this is difficult for you. The murder of those we loved demands vengeance, but we must be cautious also."

"What of Placidia?" Theodoric asked.

"Sergeric has taken her prisoner. He seeks to humiliate her by parading her through the streets in bondage," Wallia responded.

"Sergeric will expect us to seek vengeance quickly. We must be wary of walking into a trap," Thuruar cautioned.

"We have the greater numbers. He knows this. Sergeric will try to lure us into personal combat before we can bring our advantage to bear," Wallia observed.

Theodoric rose and took a deep breath. "I know what we must do." The two older men turned toward him. "If he was going to kill Placidia, he'd have already done it. Instead, he uses her as bait. You two should rally our full strength. I'll lead a smaller force to rescue the princess. I'll shadow them but avoid conflict until you arrive. Then I'll attack first, but you must wait to see the battle unfold."

"Why would we wait?" Thuruar asked.

"He's right," Wallia interjected. "Once we see the battle develop, we'll know where best to attack. We won't need as many men, and it won't take as long. He'll spring the trap. We'll crush it."

Within a few days, Theodoric's company found Sergeric's men dragging the princess behind a donkey. Theodoric watched from atop a hill just outside town.

The remnants of Placidia's clothes were torn and filthy. Even from a distance, he could see her face was bruised and bloody. One of the guards seemed to take pleasure in pulling the rope that tied her hands to the donkey's neck, dragging her down into the mud. Another guard cracked a whip behind her each time she fell.

Sergeric's purpose was to show strength by humiliating Athaulf's wife, the daughter of Theodosius. Yet each time Placidia was brought to the ground, she rose calmly, her head held high with a dignified expression. Loud cries from the people protested her mistreatment.

Theodoric waited until the procession left town on a road through a grassy pasture. He led his cavalry charge into the meadow, quickly cutting down Placidia's tormentors. Theodoric's personal guard surrounded the Princess. Sergeric, however, had many more men both in the town and stationed in the woods, ready to ambush a rescue attempt. Theodoric pushed into town in search of Sergeric. Now alerted to their presence,

Wallia and Thuruar cut off the reinforcements from the woods before they could arrive.

By the time Wallia and Thuruar found Theodoric, he had trapped Sergeric with a few of his followers in Athaulf's throne room. A bloody fight ensued. Thuruar sought to defend his son and took on two foes at once. The large man, now in the twilight of his fighting years, was no longer as quick as he had once been. His first blow was blocked, and his other opponent used the opportunity to stick his sword below Thuruar's chest plate. The old warrior didn't miss a beat as he turned his sword to swiftly stab that man in the throat.

His assailant dropped his sword and clutched his throat as blood spurted out with each remaining heartbeat. He'd dealt a mortal blow, but the exchange allowed the first assailant to stab Thuruar in the neck. Theodoric was now behind his father's attacker and decapitated the man with a clean stroke. Theodoric comforted his father during his last breaths as the fight raged on.

Wallia insisted on fighting Sergeric himself. Sergeric swung his sword from overhead, but Wallia only slightly deflected the blow. Deftly moving to his left while spinning around rightward, Wallia stuck his foe hard just behind the knee, cutting off half of Sergeric's right leg. The wounded man made a feeble stab back toward his enemy while collapsing. He writhed in agony on the ground and made a futile effort to stop the blood gushing from his leg. Sergeric's remaining men lost heart and surrendered. Wallia stood over the enemy of his family and cursed Sergeric as he bled to death.

Wallia was next selected king. His first decision was to return Galla Placidia to her brother.

Placidia received a royal welcome in Ravenna. Soldiers in immaculately shining armor lined both sides of the road as her carriage rode through the gates. The carriage pulled up to the palace doors, and the princess exited and the crowd roared. She was greeted first by her brother, who embraced her firmly, twisting side to side and kissing her firmly on the lips. The emperor allowed his sister to mingle with a great many members of the court and well-wishers before leading her off for a private conversation in a dimly lit and empty marble corridor.

"I've missed you so, sister! There are no words to express how awful it's been without you—how much I worried. I'm overcome with joy that you're back, my love." Honorius caressed his sister's arm as they spoke. "But I shouldn't just speak of my own troubles. It must have been awful for you as well to be surrounded by those barbarians for so long!"

"It wasn't ... actually they're not ... they're not all bad. I made many friends."

"Really? The Goths I've known are all dirty brutes without any manners at all."

"Some are. But many are wonderful. Their hygiene is often poor, but that's because they live outside mostly. Besides, not all Romans are such good people. I do wish you would find a home for them. I'm certain they would make loyal allies."

Honorius lifted his head and breathed deeply. "It's not as easy as you think, sister. Giving land to the Visigoths means taking it from someone else. Who do you think deserves to have their land taken? There are also political risks to crossing such wealthy landowners."

"What about just the Garonne Valley? It's out of the way. On the extreme west of the empire, and they would have no access to Mediterranean ports. You could still use a blockade to bring them to heel, if need be, as Constantius did."

"You should be careful talking like this, sister. They will start calling you a Goth sympathizer and question your loyalty to the empire. I can't even recall how many times I've been reminded of Gratian's fate for coddling barbarians."

"Of course, brother. I speak only in confidence to you."

The emperor grew more somber. "There are certain other matters we must discuss. Certain practical realities that need be addressed."

Placidia could tell he was being pressured into something not of his choosing.

"Well, go on," she prompted. "What it is?"

"I'm afraid you must wed. It's not that I want to send you off. I'd rather have you all to myself. But it will be expected that you will marry, and your marriage offers an opportunity to solve a problem."

"How so?"

"There are many who now fear Constantius will proclaim himself Augustus. He has the loyalty of the army, and many believe my standing was weakened by the sack of Rome."

"You are the emperor who faced down the mighty Alaric!" Placidia protested. "A lesser ruler would have bowed to his demands. You stayed strong!"

Honorius smiled. "You don't know how good it is to be with family again, to be with someone I trust. The schemers and flatterers at court ever seek to advance their own interests. I believe they would all stab me in the back had they the chance."

Placidia gasped. "Then you must allow me to watch your back! I will learn who the traitors are—what treacherous plots they cook up."

Honorius smiled again and embraced his sister. After some time, she pulled back and looked up into his eyes. "You need not fear," she said, "and you need not wed me to Constantius."

"He's become a very powerful man, and he's a great general. Why would you not want ...?"

"Because I don't love him."

"But you loved ... Athaulf?"

"Yes."

"Now he's dead."

"Yes, and I know I must wed again ... eventually, but not Constantius. Please, allow me some time ... time for us to be together ... time to adjust to being home."

Constantius sent messengers to Wallia, seeking an alliance to subdue the Rhine invaders occupying Hispania and to return the province to Roman control. He held out the possibility of granting the Visigoths their own province and the peace agreement they had long sought. Wallia relayed the message to his council, and many spoke out against the proposal. The king himself was skeptical.

"I have a lot more trust for the tribes now in Hispania than I do for the Romans," Wallia announced. "Did they not help us when the Romans tried to starve us into submission? Are we not natural allies against the Romans?"

Theodoric stepped forward. "They gave us food because we paid them with much gold."

"Yet we've lived together in peace," another council member replied.

Theodoric was resolute. "Hispania is a Roman province, and eventually it will be returned to Roman control. Alaric understood when a Roman army is destroyed, a new one always appears. It's only a matter of time. Alaric also knew we must find a way to fit within the empire. If we do not, we shall be forced out and face the tyranny of the Huns. What Alaric offered in return was to become a strong ally of the Romans. This is what Constantius now suggests we can have. We should not abandon our dream now that it is within reach."

The debate raged for days. Eventually the king and council became convinced Theodoric's plan was their only realistic option. Wallia accepted Constantius's overture, and when a great Roman force arrived, the Visigoths marched with their new Roman allies in a brutal campaign that forced the Rhine invaders to flee to southern Hispania, returning most of the province and the major cities to Roman control. Half the Vandals were wiped out.

Constantius's success in subduing Gaul and then Hispania increased his standing at court even further. Honorius was now under great pressure to reward the victorious general, and the reward he wanted was Placidia. The emperor couldn't bear to tell his sister what she must do. At court one day, Honorius arose from his throne, took Placidia by the hand, and ceremoniously walked her over to Constantius, placing her hand in his.

She endured the unhappy marriage with dignity and decided to focus on the advantages she now enjoyed. Her new husband quickly came to value her counsel. Placidia first gave birth to a girl they named Justa Grata Honoria and then a boy they named Valentinian. She was respected among the court, although many rumors spread about her relationship with her brother, stoked by his many public shows of affection for her.

The influence Placidia wielded attracted much jealousy and suspicion. Honorius appeared in her chambers when he knew she would be alone. Her heart sank when she saw his grave expression.

"My beloved sister," he stated, "I'm afraid I have some unpleasant business to discuss. Word has reached my ear of some nasty rumors circulating in the court ... and the Senate. There are those who now say our relationship is ... unchaste."

"Traitors spread these lies!" she blurted through sudden tears. "They seek to weaken you by driving a wedge between us!" Placidia lowered her head into her palms as tears flowed.

Honorius sat next to his sister and patted her back. "I'm so sorry you must endure these indignities, my love." He began to stroke her hair. "The court is filled with vicious vipers. I'd send them all off if I could. What I fear most is what would happen to you if I die."

Placidia lifted her head and wiped the tears from her eyes. "You mustn't speak like that," she whispered as she placed her head on her brother's shoulder.

"It's true, sister. You would be vulnerable. Because I have no children, there would be a bloodbath to decide my successor. That is why ... I have decided to name Constantius co-Augustus and call you Augusta."

"Really?" she asked. "Is that wise? Would the Senate accept the leadership of a woman?"

He pulled her close. "I don't know, sister. But I know no one else would be better suited than you. If the three of us lead together for long enough, they'll have no choice but to accept it. If I die first, Constantius will not be challenged. If he dies first, I will not be. This is the only way."

Thus Honorius, Constantius, and Placidia shared power together. Placidia continued to use her influence to persuade her husband and brother to award the Visigoths their own province in the Garonne Valley. Not a huge province—only part of the valley between the cities Toulouse and Bordeaux—but a rich, beautiful land through which a great river flowed, providing access to the Atlantic Ocean.

Wallia received the news as he lay dying. He had become ill of an infection much like the one that had taken the life of his revered cousin. When the Roman embassy entered his chambers and read Honorius's proclamation, Wallia struggled to hold back tears. Then he decided he just didn't care. Joyous tears streamed down his smiling face. Smiles came even to the faces of the stern Romans, who continued to read Honorius's requirements. When they finished, Wallia was proud to call Honorius Augustus and pledge his allegiance to the Roman Empire. He summoned his closest family and friends to share the good news as soon as the embassy left his chambers.

That evening, the king of the Visigoths summoned his closest adviser. Theodoric sat beside his bed with a concerned look.

"There is much we have to discuss, my friend. My days come to an end, and I would have you know my wishes."

"You have much strength left," Theodoric said. "You will defeat this illness and again …"

"If I've already seen my last sunrise, I'll die a happy man. I wish only to be sure our people do not fail now that we've come so close to achieving our dream. We must not allow a succession struggle to divide our people. I have spoken to the other members of my council, and our view is unanimous. You shall be crowned king upon my death."

"Wallia, I'm honored and humbled. But even I question whether I'm the best choice."

"Your humility will be a great asset. Think of how many Roman emperors and politicians allowed their arrogance to lead their people to disaster. But you must also be seen as strong. What the people say of your rule is important even to a king."

"I already know what they will say."

The old man smiled. "Do you think I do not also hear the whispers? I looked up to Alaric since I was a small child. I followed him without hesitation. He was a brilliant general, a loyal friend, and a wise king. Yet even the great man himself couldn't live up to the immortal legend he's become. He looks down upon us from heaven now, and he wouldn't see his legacy become an obstacle to our success. The battles Alaric decided *not* to fight were as important as his victories. Trust your judgment. Your wisdom will guide our people well."

Wallia passed peacefully in the night. The members of his council all pledged their loyalty to Theodoric before the funeral even concluded. He decided he wanted his coronation to take place in Toulouse—deep within the Visigoths' new homeland. He went there ahead of his family to make land allocations and deal with the local landowners.

As Alonia's horse crested the ridge and began to descend into the valley, she gasped at the beautiful scene. The homeland they'd all dreamed of was even more beautiful than she imagined. She looked around at dark, rich soil; old, majestic trees; and gentle creeks flowing into a large, navigable river. The spring air was fresh and the morning cool and moist. She smiled at each natural wonder and quaint hamlet they passed. Brechta rode up beside her, and the two exchanged knowing smiles. Neither needed to mention how proud Alaric and the others would have been to finally realize such a long-held dream.

Their horses' shoes clicked rhythmically as they trotted across an elegantly arched stone bridge and onto the path leading to the castle. Once through the gate, Theodoric came running. Alonia swiftly dismounted and rushed into her husband's embrace. Theodoric also embraced his mother-in-law and her other daughters, and he began to eagerly show them around.

The next morning, Theodoric strolled casually with his wife through the town. "You look happy," he observed.

"This place—it's so beautiful. Do you really think we'll be able to stay here? Forever?"

He smiled broadly. "I don't see why not. It would be hard for any army to drive us from here. We have access to the great ocean. We control the Pyrenees passes into Hispania. This is a place where we can grow our own food and raise livestock. Athaulf was wise to recognize the many advantages this place offers. I can't help but wonder if Placidia had a hand in all this."

"Please don't mention that around my mother. She—"

"I know," Theodoric replied with a gentle smile.

They walked silently hand in hand, admiring the architecture and bountiful food market. They enjoyed the beautiful surroundings and each other's company for most of the day before returning to the castle.

The morning brought new waves of Goth refugees settling throughout the valley. They came in huge wagon trains, day after day. Filthy, weary, and gaunt, they rejoiced at many happy discoveries in this rich and bountiful land. Many wept joyous tears. A generation of refugees familiar only with war and endless marches had finally arrived home.

Chapter 17

An Old Enemy

Theodoric's reign was prosperous and secure. As the years passed, the Visigoths grew powerful, and the might of the Romans waned. The Huns now threatened the Eastern Empire. Theodoric was eager to hear tidings, ever worried Attila would turn his ambitions west.

The passing of Brechta was hard on Theodoric's family. She had been a leader of the family and had been most adored by her many grandchildren. After days of mourning, Theodoric sought to cheer his boys by wrestling in a meadow near the palace. Their fun was interrupted when a messenger arrived with news of a large group of Goths arriving from Italia. Theodoric also learned that Hamil was among the company. The king was eager to hear his tidings and summoned Hamil to walk with him.

The two embraced warmly. Long years of near-constant travel wore heavily on the old man's face. Theodoric inquired as to his well-being.

"My body begins to fail me, but my spirit soars every time we complete the long journey."

"You've led so many of our people from the East. It must be gratifying to see their faces when they're finally home for the first time."

Hamil smiled. "It is, but my joy is tempered by grief for Thoris. He was murdered by Huns as he sought to free Goth slaves."

Theodoric placed a hand on Hamil's shoulder and expressed his sympathies. They walked in silence for a few moments. "I hear the latest usurpation in the West has been put down. What tales can you tell?"

"It is true. The pretender was executed at Ravenna."

"Who rules now?" Theodoric asked.

"Young Valentinian is called Augustus, and his mother serves as regent until he reaches eighteen. I spoke with her in Rome."

"You spoke with Placidia?"

"Yes, she spoke quite highly of you."

"We're old friends. Her rise to power will be a great boon for us."

"She said you were in Rome together during the massacre. That must be quite a tale."

"Yes, but a story for another time. I worry now about her grip on power. I'm sure ruling an empire is especially difficult for a woman."

"No doubt," Hamil replied. "There are many who would seek to supplant her. Some are suspicious she keeps the Goth guards, which Athaulf gifted her. They question her loyalty and spread nasty rumors that she has a taste for Goth men."

"We must support her however we can. Our biggest threat may again be the Huns. Only with the help of the Romans would we defeat them."

"I fear the strength of the Huns grows as the power of the Romans diminishes. Attila is more fearsome than any Hun I've encountered. He believes it is his destiny to conquer the whole world, and his control over the Huns is unchallenged. His army swells with troops from the people he's conquered. It's only a matter of time until he invades the empire, and I fear the Romans are now too weak to repel him."

Theodoric sought peace with the Vandals and wed his eldest daughter, Dariana, to Huneric, son of the Vandal king Geiseric. The Vandals, however, weren't satisfied with their position in southern Hispania. Geiseric led his people by ship across the straights of Gibraltar and into Africa. The Roman general Boniface confronted the Vandals but suffered a defeat and was forced to retreat to Hippo, which also fell to a ferocious Vandal siege. Reality forced the Romans to accept Vandal control of North Africa.

However, the Vandals became dissatisfied with the land they had received through their treaty with Rome, and they began to seize more and more land from wealthy Roman landowners. Aetius, now the most powerful of the Roman generals, assembled a mighty joint eastern/western force in Sicily that would go to Africa and put the Vandals in their place. The expedition never sailed. Instead, the eastern force was recalled to face an invasion of the Eastern Empire by Attila's Huns. Even with the recalled troops, the East lacked the power to check Attila's ambition. A string of defeats left the Eastern Empire able to make peace only by paying a large annual tribute to the Huns. Attila boasted he had made all Romans his slaves. Aetius had no choice but to agree to a second far more generous treaty with the Vandals.

Theodoric received word of the grim news before Dariana arrived. It was even worse than he had feared. Bitter tears stung his eyes, and he strode quickly to embrace his eldest daughter. Alonia also wept and joined their embrace. Their eldest son, Thorismund, didn't weep but instead angrily cursed the Vandals and vowed revenge.

To seal the new treaty, the Vandal prince Huneric was offered the hand of Eudocia, daughter of emperor Valentinian. Huneric, however, was already married to Dariana. To remedy this, he falsely accused Dariana of plotting to kill him, cut off her nose and ears, and returned her to her father. Thorismund, a fiery redhead as large as his father's father, demanded retribution. Theodoric didn't answer but sought only to console his daughter.

That evening Thorismund found Theodoric in his study. "What are you reading, Father?" he asked.

"It's Alaric's diary. It's a history of our people. He asked me to complete it."

"Will you now write that the Vandal prince mutilated the face of his granddaughter?"

The king rose and walked to his son. "I know it's difficult to bear this horror done to Dariana."

"Will you do nothing?" Thorismund asked with great disappointment.

"What would you have me do?"

"I'd have Huneric's head for a start. His father's too."

"Should we just set off now to Carthage and claim it? We would not sail to victory."

"The men say Alaric once embraced the bold vision of taking Africa for ourselves. They say the Romans now bow to their old enemy because they control the grain all Romans depend on. Why should we not seize that prize for ourselves?"

Theodoric's bearing grew stern. "Men say many things. Not all are wise. Alaric's time was different. The Roman forces in Africa were weakened by conflict with Attalus. Our people were already on the move and fully united. It would have taken the Romans a long time to even attempt to dislodge us. Now is different. The Vandals' hold over the key provinces in Africa is very strong. The new treaty means the Romans would come to their aid. Invading Africa by sea would be a disaster and leave our people defenseless."

"Doing nothing makes you look weak!" Thorismund roared.

Theodoric remained calm. "If I let that change my decision, I would think myself a fool. Do you think the same rage does not burn in my heart? Do you think I don't also lust to avenge a hundred times over this violence against my precious daughter?

"But I must think beyond my own desire. Men older than your friends—old enough to have their own families—would ask how many daughters are to grow up without fathers that I might avenge mine. And they would ask a just question. You speak of what Alaric would have done. I can promise you that he would not have risked an invasion of Africa now. Alaric didn't win every battle, but he made sure he never got routed, and that's why we enjoy the peace we have today. I will not be shamed into a foolish decision, not when the safety of our people hangs in the balance."

Placidia was sitting at her vanity, attending to her face, when she spied her beautiful young niece, hands clasped before her, appear in the corner of the mirror.

Placidia twirled on her satin seat and smiled. "Pulcheria! I'm so glad you've come." The two embraced. "Please, sit."

Placidia wore her age gracefully and with much dignity. Her direct authority had ended when Valentinian came of age, yet her influence remained undiminished. She wished now to educate her niece to navigate the treacherous politics she would soon face.

"There's so much I have to tell you," Placidia said, grasping her niece's hands. "So much about public life that's especially difficult for a woman. Particularly military matters."

Pulcheria had the look of a very young woman not wanting to show her innocence. "Isn't that why we have generals?" she asked.

"Yes, my dear, but which to choose? Many are treacherous."

"Do you not trust Aetius?" Pulcheria asked hesitantly.

Placidia gave her niece a serious and somber look. "It appears that way only because I wish it to appear that way. I would have you know the tale.

"Bonifacius was my most loyal and trusted general. I asked him to return to Rome from Africa, but Aetius secretly wrote to him and said I was planning some treachery. Bonifacius refused to come. Friends said this wasn't like him and traveled to Africa to find out what was the matter. He showed them the letter from Aetius, and they explained he had been tricked. When Bonifacius returned to Rome, he and Aetius fought for control of Ravenna. Bonifacius won the battle but fell in the fighting. Eventually, I banished Aetius but was forced to bring him back a few years later because we lacked a general who could control the army."

Placidia breathed deeply and looked at the young woman sympathetically. "No, my dear, I do *not* trust Aetius, but we have an understanding. That is the type of thing that you—"

Their conversation was cut short when the young emperor Valentinian burst into the room, greatly startling the two women. "Do you know what your daughter has done?" Valentinian barked angrily.

"I ... well, no," Placidia stammered.

The emperor turned to Pulcheria. "Leave us," he demanded.

As soon as she left the room, the red-faced emperor began to fume again. "She wrote a letter to Atilla. Atilla the Hun. She wrote him a letter, and now he marches against us."

"What? Why would she ... and why would the Huns ...?"

"She wrote the king of the Huns to request his aid in breaking a wedding engagement she didn't wish. Did you know about this?" Valentinian could barely control his rage.

"I knew she was unhappy with the engagement. I never dreamed she'd seek aid from Attila, and why would he care who she marries?"

"She sent him her ring. With the letter, she included her ring."

"Why did she do that?"

"She says to prove the authenticity of the letter. That's not how Attila interpreted it. He saw it as a marriage proposal, a proposal he accepted. He claims half the Western Empire as his dowry. He comes now to claim it."

Placidia's stomach sank, and she placed her face in her hands. She felt responsible for this. Justa had always been difficult, like her father, but how could she have ever imagined such a disaster? Long had she labored to secure peace for the West. She knew what terror the Huns would bring.

Theodoric and Alonia had been fruitful. When news of Attila's advance into Western Europe spread, Theodoric summoned his five sons to the throne room.

When they arrived, the king announced gravely, "The Romans call for our aid. Atilla has crossed the Rhine and turned his march south. He now approaches Orleans. Some say the Alans will open their doors rather than face siege. Aetius assembles a coalition to confront the Huns. They gather now at Arles."

"Will we not march with them?" Thorismund asked.

"I'm afraid we have little choice," the king conceded. "I don't trust Aetius, but he was the only one among the Romans to see this calamity coming and act quickly. He knows the Huns as well as anyone.

"There is much risk in a coalition so varied. Will some find benefit in allying with the Huns? Will Aetius? Still, I fear we must march with them or risk the same fate as our forbearers on the Black Sea. Above all else, I fear the Huns again driving us from our homes."

The next morning, Theodoric stared in the mirror as he strapped on the sword Alaric had bequeathed to him as he lay dying. Alonia could see the self-doubt on his face and walked up behind her husband, put her arms around him, and said, "You should not despair. You will ride to victory."

"I wish I felt so confident," the king replied as he looked at his wife in the mirror. The old couple had lived a long, happy life, but he had always known this day would come.

She knew what troubled him. "My love," Alonia said, "you don't need to be my father. You need only allow yourself to truly be Theodoric, and you will defeat Attila. There is no other I would see protect us in this dark hour."

Her words were more reassuring than he would have thought possible. He wasn't the fabled savior of the Visigoths, but he was their king. Theodoric would not shrink from this moment. He skillfully mustered his troops and rode out with the vanguard at the head of a massive army of Goth warriors.

Attila held court in a large leather pavilion. Animal hides and furs were spread on the ground, and the Hun king sat in an ornate chair pillaged from the Eastern Empire. Fires burned in large caldrons on either side. He had expected the gates of Orleans to be opened before him, but the Alans resisted, and several days of heavy rain delayed his assault. By the time the weather lifted, reports arrived that Aetius had moved north with a huge force. The Hun king decided to abandon the city and retreated north in search of a favorable battle site.

As was his custom on the eve of battle, Attila summoned diviners to foretell his fate. The mystics brought a majestic, pure white ram, which they slaughtered and disemboweled in an elaborate ceremony. They spent much time meticulously studying the beast's entrails.

After a hurried and whispered discussion, the head of their order announced, "These signs foretell a disaster that will befall us in battle, but one of the enemy leaders will be killed."

The Great Hun received these divinations solemnly.

Attila's scouts found a ridge on the Catalaunian plains east of Paris that would be favorable for a defensive stand. He moved his army north to this location. The coalition led by Aetius followed closely. Theodoric split his army into two groups—one he led and the other led by Thorismund.

The night before the battle, Thorismund's group camped around a small village. He and his guard stayed at the inn that night. The men ate bread and drank mead at a crowded table in a stone hall lit by candles and a roaring fire. The mood was somber, the fear of battle palpable, though none would speak of it. Thorismund was distracted. It scarcely attracted his attention when an old woman, hooded and cloaked in black, tried to push through his guard. What could she want? Clearly she wasn't a threat. His mind was only partly focused on the scene before him as he absentmindedly waved her through.

She walked next to his table. "What is it you want, old woman?" he asked gruffly before taking another bite of bread.

"I knew your mother's father," she said in a clear, confident tone.

"*You* knew Alaric?" He smirked sarcastically.

"Yes. I was a servant in Alaric's house." Some of the men nearby began to smirk and whisper.

"You're old but not that old," Thorismund said before taking another swig of mead.

"I did serve Alaric," she replied resolutely. "Your mother would remember me."

Thorismund wiped some mead off his beard. "Fine. You served Alaric. What of it?"

"There is one final task I must perform to fulfill my duty."

"And what might that be?"

"You must not pursue Attila after your victory." The men around them began to scoff.

"After our victory? I like the sound of that. But why would we not pursue Attila after a victory? Why have you such love of the Huns?"

"I have no love for Attila. I speak for the benefit of our people—for your benefit. Pursuing Attila after his defeat will bring only more death and accomplish nothing. There will be no need to clash with Attila or Aetius once the battle is won."

"She looks like a witch," one of Thorismund's officers offered. "Sounds like one too."

"Well, old woman, you're talking to the wrong man. Why don't you tell your tales to my father?"

They locked eyes, and her expression was sorrowful. She didn't respond.

The officer who spoke had heard enough. "Be off, old woman," he barked.

Thorismund maintained eye contact as he took another sip. The woman stood silently until the captain stood, then turned and nimbly disappeared into the crowd.

The next morning, Thorismund was much surprised when his father woke him before dawn. "Why are you here?"

"I have a final command before the battle begins."

Thorismund rose and began to dress. "What command?"

"When the battle begins, you must delay your charge. Stay where you are until you see the result of my charge, then ride where the enemy is weakest."

"You divide our force. Why?"

"I have enough men to force the Huns on this side to turn their full attention toward me. They will not expect heavy cavalry in the center.

The Huns will be hard-pressed on both sides. It will open a gap. That is where you must attack."

"What if the Huns ride around you? They're fabled horsemen."

"We'll take that advantage away by charging straight at them. We will not wait behind rows of spearmen. Our charge will push them back, keep the battle dense, and deprive them freedom of movement."

Thorismund nodded. "Have you slept?" he asked his father.

"No," said Theodoric, stepping forward to hug his son. "I'll sleep well once the battle's won."

At dawn, Attila moved his army to the ridge, but he did so more slowly than expected. Both the Visigoths and the Romans wondered why the Hun leader had waited so late in the day to let the battle begin. Theodoric's company held the eastern flank, with Thorismund safely next to him on the west. The Alans with heavy cavalry held the center, and the Romans defended the western flank. The forces on both sides were enormous, with each army numbering in the hundreds of thousands.

Theodoric agonized over the wait before the battle. Fear gripped his heart, and he clutched his reins low and tight so none could see his hands tremble. The weather was as dreary as his mood. The king's thoughts turned to the advice Alaric had given him as a boy. *Fear is not cowardice. It is the prelude to courage,* he thought. It had taken his whole life, but the time now came for him to stand and fight. He thought of the stories of the heroic deeds of Fritigern and Alaric and the many others who had defended their people. He remembered tales of the disaster that had befallen his ancestors after their defeat at the hands of the Huns and their subjugation by the Romans. He thought of the many women and children whose lives would be ripped apart by the savagery of the Huns. Tragedy wouldn't befall them again.

Not on my watch.

A low mist vanished, and the two armies could see each other across a vast plain. An eerie silence fell as the huge host of Hun riders came into view.

The king's horse walked before an enormous line of Goth cavalry. He turned to face his men, his sword ringing out amid the silence as he held it aloft. The thunder of the enemy's charge could be felt even before it was heard. Theodoric's voice rose above the din of the gathering Hun storm.

"Men! The time now comes to defeat the enemy of our people. The Huns drove our forebearers from their homes, but they will not drive us!" The Goths roared. "Never again will we flee before the Huns!" The barbaric cry of tens of thousands of warriors rang out over the plain as weapons clanged against shields.

Theodoric wheeled his horse, leading his riders into the wave of Hun horsemen flying toward them. Fear now behind him, the king spurred his horse forth, his heart filled with a glorious rage. He drew first blood just before the two cavalries clashed with a deafening force. The righteous wrath of the Goths turned back the great tide of Huns, as the ring of arms roared above the screams of men and horses.

Theodoric claimed no privilege as king to observe the battle from afar, and his courage inspired the men. He spurred his horse to charge wherever the fighting was fiercest, giving the Huns no reprieve from their onslaught. Many Huns fell to the king's spear, and even after it was shattered, he drew his sword and rained furious blows down upon the enemy.

The fighting became so dense his horse couldn't move and was brought down by a Hun spear. The king continued to fight on foot, rallying his troops to reform lines and attack again. The tight press of soldiers prevented Theodoric from swinging his sword freely, and he barely had room to stab at the necks and faces of his foes, but the Huns also had no room to maneuver.

The fiery prince was ill-suited for the patience his father commanded. His captains grew as restless as their horses, waiting for the battle to unfold. Then they began to see it. The Huns didn't expect to find heavy cavalry in the center, and rushed in reinforcements. Theodoric's plan came to fruition as the success of both charges created an opening for Thorismund to drive deep into the Huns' line. His charge found Attila's own guard, and the Hunnic king was forced to seek refuge in his camp, defended by a huge circle of wagons. The battle still raged as the sun set. A red dusk gave way to a cloudy, moonless night. Chaos ensued.

Aetius's force fared poorly and was now divided. The general himself ended up near Thorismund, ignorant as to what fortune had befallen the rest of his army. Fearing the worst, the Roman general stayed in

Thorismund's camp that night. Aetius now believed Attila had delayed the battle to allow his troops to retreat under cover of darkness if the battle went ill. Had that come to pass? Neither side knew the battle's outcome until the next day. Not a man slept through the terror of horrible screams.

Daybreak revealed a battlefield piled high with corpses and mortally wounded men. Screams echoed. Now could be seen legions of men bleeding to death, unable to stand, attempting to slake their intense thirst from puddles and small ponds polluted with blood and gore. The number of dead on both sides was beyond counting.

The Huns had withdrawn into defensive formations away from the ridge. The allies besieged Attila's camp and held him trapped as they plotted their strategy. Attila built a huge bonfire from the saddles of fallen riders. He remained defiant and pledged he would walk into the fire himself to deprive his enemies the honor of taking his life.

With Attila powerless in a besieged wagon fort, Thorismund searched for his father. They found Theodoric's body where the fighting had been most dense. Many corpses had to be moved before the king could be found. Thorismund had to pry the sword of Alaric from his father's dead fingers. The fighting was so intense, even his own men didn't know he had fallen.

Aetius told Thorismund and the other leaders a prolonged siege of Attila's camp wouldn't be worth the cost. The Huns still had substantial forces outside the camp, he argued, and continued conflict would be bloody. Thorismund grew suspicious of Aetius's motives. Did he wish to preserve the Huns as a counterweight to the strength of the rising Visigoth kingdom? Could Aetius really consider an alliance with the enemy the morning after such a great slaughter? Eager also was Thorismund to avenge the death of Theodoric. Why should he bury his father while Attila was allowed to withdraw? He drew breath to lambast the cowardice of allowing Attila to flee, but then thought before he spoke. It was possible further confrontation would bring disaster. They had come to repel the Huns, and that was what they had done. Strange he thought it was how quickly his temper was diminished by the burden of command, and the loss of his father's calm wisdom.

After much deliberation, the coalition leaders all agreed Attila would be allowed to retreat from Gaul with what was left of his army. Thorismund returned home to be crowned king. The Huns never again threatened the Visigoths. Attila himself died a few years later. Following Attila's death, the Hunnic Empire collapsed in a spasm of internal conflict over his successor. The Western Empire itself fell not long after Theodoric's heroic charge.

The Visigoth kingdom would continue to dominate southwestern Gaul and much of Hispania for hundreds of years. It took perseverance, wisdom, and much courage, but the Visigoths successfully completed one of the great migrations in human history. From Fritigern to Alaric, to Athaulf, to Wallia, and to Theodoric, the men all died, but the dream never did. The refugees who appeared on the banks of the Danube in 376 survived starvation, defeated both halves of the Roman Empire, crossed an entire continent, and finally overcame the fearsome Huns. Ragged refugees who refused to accept defeat and subjugation transformed themselves into a mighty nation that changed the course of history.

Maps

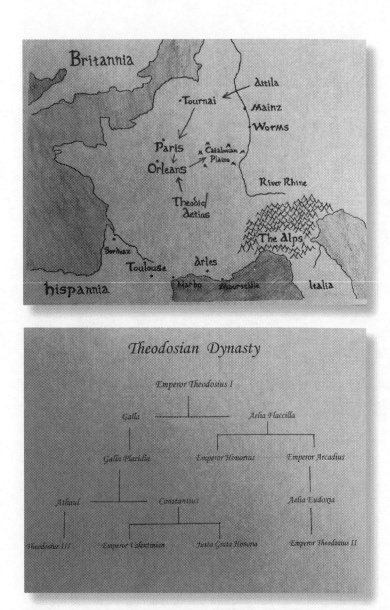

Theodosian Dynasty

Glossary

Aetius—Roman general who led the Western Roman Army against Atilla.

Adrianople—A Roman city west of Constantinople now known as Edirne in northwest Turkey.

Aelia Eudoxia—Wife of emperor Arcadius and mother of emperor Theodosius II.

Alaric—First king of the Visigoths, member of the house of Balt, father of Alonia and father-in-law of Theodoric.

Alatheus—Ostrogothic general who chose to follow Fritigern.

Alavivus—Visigoth general and follower of Fritigern.

Alenia—Mother of Theoric, Alaric, and Daria.

Alonia—Eldest daughter of Alaric and wife of Theodoric.

Athanaric—Visigoth leader who declined to lead his people into Roman territory with Fritigern.

Athaulf—Friend of Alaric, who succeeded him as king of the Visigoths. He married Galla Placidia and fathered Theodosius III, who died in infancy.

Attalus—Roman politician the Senate chose to be western emperor during the siege of Rome.

Arcadius—Son of emperor Theodosius I and his first wife. He succeeded Theodosius I as emperor of the Eastern Empire.

Ariminum—A Roman city on the Adriatic coast, which is now known as Rimini.

Atilla—King of the Huns before the collapse of the Hunnic Empire.

Brechta—Wife of Alaric and mother of Alonia.

Carpathian Mountains—A mountain range stretching from the Czech Republic through Slovakia, Poland, Hungary, Ukraine, Serbia, and Romania.

Cniva—Father of Sarus and Sergeric.

Constantine—Usurper who claimed to be the western emperor during the reign of Honorius before Alaric's siege of Rome. Constantius defeated and executed him.

Constantinople—Capital of the Eastern Roman Empire in modern Istanbul.

Constantius—Roman General who defeated Constantine. Honorius shared power with him as co-Augustus. He married Honorius's sister, Galla Placidia, and was the father of emperor Valentinian and Justa Grata Honoria.

Daria—Sister of Theoric and Alaric and wife of Athaulf.

Dniester—A river in eastern Europe that runs through modern Ukraine and Moldova to the Black Sea.

Durostorum—Roman fortress on the banks of the lower Danube.

Ermenaric—King of the Ostrogoths at the time the invasion of the Huns began. He sacrificed himself in battle after a defeat.

Fritigern—Visigoth leader who chose to enter Roman territory after the defeat by the Huns.

Gainas—Goth general who led the Eastern Roman Army. He was driven out of Roman territory following a revolt, crossed the Danube, and was killed by the Huns. His head was returned to Constantinople.

Galla—Second wife of Theodosius I and mother of Galla Placidia.

Galla Placidia—Half-sister of emperor Honorius. She was married to Athaulf and then remarried Constantius after his death. Her brother Honorius called her Augusta and shared power with her and Constantius. After the death of both Constantius and Honorius, she became "empress regent" for emperor Valentinian until he reached manhood.

Gratian—Western Roman emperor at the beginning of the Hunnic invasion. He was murdered for perceived pro-barbarian policies.

Guntheric—Follower of Fritigern, husband of Alenia, and father of Theoric, Alaric, and Daria.

Hamil—Goth who escaped Hun slavery and marched with Radagaisus.

Honorius—Son of Theodosius I and western emperor after his death.

Jovius—Roman general who befriended Alaric and negotiated with Alaric on behalf of Honorius.

Luca—Widow of Theoric, who subsequently married Thuruar and became Theodoric's mother.

Maximus—Roman soldier who profited from the Visigoth's starvation and later proclaimed himself emperor of the West. Theodosius I defeated and executed him.

Novae—A Roman fortress along the Danube River in modern Bulgaria.

Odothesius—Goth leader who tried and failed to cross the Danube River after the Battle of Adrianople.

Olympius—Roman politician who urged Honorius not to make peace with Alaric. He led a small force, which Athaulf defeated. He also played a major role in the massacre of Goth women and children following Stilicho's execution.

Radagaisus—Goth king who invaded Italia. Stilicho defeated and executed him.

Sarus—Visigoth who lost election as king to Alaric and then betrayed his people by joining the Romans.

Saphrax—Ostrogothic general who chose to follow Fritigern.

Sergeric—Brother of Sarus who briefly proclaimed himself king after the murder of Athaulf.

Stilicho—Roman general whom Theodosius I entrusted to protect Honorius until he came of age. Stilicho claimed Theodosius asked him on his deathbed to also protect Arcadius, but this claim wasn't accepted in the Eastern Court.

Theodoric—Visigoth king who led his people to victory during the Battle of the Catalonian Plains.

Theodosius I—Chosen by western emperor Gratian as emperor of the Eastern Empire after the death of emperor Valens.

Theodosius II—Grandson of Theodosius I, who became Eastern emperor after the death of his father emperor, Arcadius.

Theodosius III—Son of Visigoth king Athaulf and Roman princess Galla Placidia. He died in infancy.

Theoric—Visigoth warrior under Fritigern's command. Son of Guntheric and Alenia, he was the older brother of Alaric and Daria. He was Luca's first husband.

Thessalonica—A major city in northeastern Greece.

Thoris—Goth who escaped Hun slavery after serving as Uldin's translator.

Thuruar—Friend of Alaric and father of Theodoric.

Uldin—Hun king.

Ulff—Visigoth priest and adviser to Alaric.

Valens—Eastern emperor at the beginning of the Hunnic invasion. He fell at Adrianople.

Valentinian I—Western Roman emperor prior to Gratian and the beginning of the Hunnic invasion of Europe.

Valentinian II—Valentinian II was the son of emperor Valentinian I and his second wife, Justina, and younger brother of emperor Gratian. Valentinian II became emperor following the murder of Gratian in 383. Roman General Arbogast, who supported the usurpation of Eugenius, murdered Valentinian II. Eastern emperor Theodosius I led Gothic auxiliaries under Alaric, who defeated Eugenius at the Battle of Frigidus. Theodosius named his young son Honorius as emperor in the West under the protection of General Stilicho.

Valentinian III—Son of Constantius and Galla Placidia, he became the western Roman emperor as a child following the death of his uncle Honorius. Galla Placidia ruled the West as regent until he reached manhood.

Viminacium—A Roman city and fortress along the Danube River in modern Serbia.

Wallia—Cousin of Alaric, he succeeded Athaulf as king of the Visigoths.

Printed in the United States
by Baker & Taylor Publisher Services